The author was born in Wallasey, England, in 1964, and moved to the South of France when she was eleven. She spent her teenage years living in the cosmopolitan city state of Monaco and became immersed in its many languages and cultures. An English girl in a French school, for three hours each week she would sit at the back of the class as her colleagues learnt English. To pass the time, she wrote stories. This led to a lifetime of writing novels, scripts, stories and articles. In her working life, Sally writes marketing communications and manages large international websites.

In 2010, Sally joined the Hogs Back Writers, a club located on the outskirts of Guildford, and she set about turning an old manuscript into this novel: Guy Erma and the Son of Empire. Sally currently lives in Farnham, and she is married with two children.

Guy Erma
and
The Son of Empire

by

Sally Ann Melia

Books may be purchased by contacting the publisher and author at:

Sally Dickson, 39 Alma Way, Farnham GU9 0QN, United Kingdom

Website & Blog: www.sally-ann-melia.com

Facebook: https://www.facebook.com/SallyAnnMelia

Twitter: https://twitter.com/Sally_Ann_Melia

Author email: sallyannmelia@gmail.com

Cover Design: Lazar K., Sugarbricks

Interior Design: Sally Dickson

ISBN: 978-1500951993

Note to readers from beyond the Freyne Empire:
A full list of names, places and things has been placed
in Appendix 1

Contents

Book 1.
Day 1. Morning.

Prologue. Introducing Karl Valvanchi

'Mezzatorra to Control. We are under attack, large attack. Please assist.'

Karl took a sharp breath in, but his reply was steady.

'This is Captain Karl Valvanchi calling Mezzatorra.'

'Karl. It's the SDLA. They're at full strength.'

'We'll be there. Lock yourselves away.'

Thirty-one years old, Karl Valvanchi was a Zaracan warrior. His skin chalk-white, he stood just under two metres tall, with a slim military build. With his ice-white mane cropped to stubble, he appeared almost human, something he was not. He joined his men and they pulled on their flying suits. As one, they leapt skywards and circled up. Karl glanced back. With its high perimeter wall and watchtowers, the centre was easy enough to secure. It was the outlying units that faced the worst attacks.

Mezzatorra should be ok, Karl thought. The scientists had a secure vault the tribes could not penetrate. Some looting, some vandalism, then the tribes would turn and run. If it came to it, the tribes had no weapons of any real threat. Unless they were reinforced by the Dome Elite; unless they had help from the Freyne Empire.

Karl and his men soared towards their destination, arching over the wide grasslands of Sas Darona.

Sas Darona Sas Darona pearl of the galactic sea

Sas Darona Sas Darona where forever my heart will be.

Sas Darona was a giant planet on the disputed border of the Zaracan Democratic Union and the expanding Freyne Empire. The Freyne had tried to claim Sas Darona when vast reserves of monazite were found. The rare metal was essential to the manufacture of light but powerful space magnets. The Freyne hungrily eyed up the easy-to-access monazite reserves on Sas Darona, but too late. The Zaracans had already filed exploration licences with the United Races. Further disputes arose when the Zaracans discovered that Sas Darona was inhabited. Were the human tribes related to the Freyne?

Did it matter?

The Freyne believed Sas Darona should belong to them, and some of the tribes agreed. The attacks on the Zaracan bases had started. The tribes discovered that Freyne traders would pay good money for newly-mined monazite. The attacks on their bases had multiplied.

'Captain. I can see a firewall.'

It was his second, flying at Karl's right shoulder. Karl stretched his sight to look. On the horizon, a white line of fire shot up from the ground. It was coming from the direction of Mezzatorra.

'Is that a shield test?' Karl asked, but the question was rhetorical. Something's not right, Karl thought, then said:

'Karl Valvanchi to Mezzatorra. Report please?'

No reply.

'Captain Karl Valvanchi to Mezzatorra. You requested assistance?'

One of the oldest bases on Sas Darona, Mezzatorra was a crashed shuttle wedged on a rocky outcrop. Too valuable to be abandoned, too remote to be useful, it was perfect for entomological studies.

'Karl Valvanchi to Mezzatorra, requesting clearance to land in one minute eighteen seconds.'

Still no reply.

What was going on in Mezzatorra? All at once there was a loud telepathic reply:

'*Negative, Captain Valvanchi, negative.*' It was a young female voice. '*We have a grade one cy-sect alert. We have initiated the protection shield.*'

'*Cy-sect alert?*' repeated Karl. His heart was in his throat. His next words were a strangled whisper. '*Is it plague?*'

'*For God's sake Karl, just get out of here!*'

Karl and his six men were circling down to the base, the team matching Karl's every move as he led them down to land. All at once Karl heard himself shouting:

'*Abandon formation, fly high, fly fast. Regroup further south. Get out of here.*'

As the squad split, twisted up and away, Karl looked down in horror. The lines of white fire now surrounded the base in its entirety. They reached up, then arched over. At their peak, the lines of fire joined and started to spread like a vast spider's web. The branches and arms multiplied until all you could see was a dome of yellow light encasing Mezzatorra. On all sides, Karl saw his men diving and dipping between the lines of fire before accelerating fast, up into the blue sky above. He himself rolled around a shining beam of fire, banked hard right to avoid another laser-fast connection, and then he was free and flying fast. He sent the new rendezvous co-ordinates to his men as he went.

What was going on? The question filled Karl's thoughts.

The shield had gone up! The final act of desperation of a community faced with Sas Darona plague. With a chill, Karl recalled the briefing by a white-coated entomologist. The plagues on Sas Darona were unparalleled in their ferocity. All animal species on Sas Darona were susceptible and once bitten, sixty per cent died. It had been speculated that the peoples of Sas Darona remained so primitive because the tribes were frequently destroyed by plague. So the Zaracans set themselves to studying the plague. Because of the dangers involved, the research was undertaken at the remote site of Mezzatorra.

What had the SDLA done? That was the real question Karl needed to answer.

Landing on the edge of the savannah, Karl and his men ducked into the forest. They stripped off their flight suits and shape-shifted their appearance as they ran. They started their run as slim, pale aliens, but as they regrouped around the trunk of a vast evergreen, they looked like a small troop of Sas Darona tribesmen, with flat, supple leather lace-up boots, knee-length kilts of roughly woven linen, leather water bottles and meal packs strapped across their chests, and as many as three pairs of matching fighting blades at their waists.

Karl split his men, sending two to Mezzatorra, while he headed off with the rest following the heat signature of their fast-retreating enemy. Speeding through the woodland, the DNA traces of their enemies appeared before Karl's eyes like fading luminescent clues.

'They have a start on us,' one of his men said.

'Not all of them,' Karl replied. One set of traces shone bright. *'They have a laggard!'*

It was not one tribesman, but two. Two young men, one bled heavily from a deep gash to his thigh, the other struggled to carry him through the forest. The Zaracans sprinted up behind them, then leapt out on them from all sides. The two hesitated, fooled by their attackers' outward appearance, and their fighting blades stayed at their belts. Then their hesitation turned to fear, and even as Karl recognised the medallion, the stronger of the two shoved the metal disc into his mouth.

Karl and his men grabbed them. Two of Karl's men disentangled the injured soldier from the other's grasp. From what looked like food pouches they produced bandages, a small hand-held x-ray and morphine capsules. Karl himself grabbed the uninjured rescuer and unceremoniously pulled the metal from between his teeth.

Too late! The young soldier had bitten hard into the dome-shaped poison crystal capsule at the heart of the medallion, and the poison was quick. Karl pulled a syringe from a pocket at his belt and speared it into the broken crystal, taking a sample of the poison. The syringe turned dark red as the intelligent chemicals within did their work finding an antidote. Karl had his arm around the young soldier's shoulder. His index and third finger pressed to his jugular feeling for a pulse. It was fading quickly. Inside the syringe the liquid changed from red to orange, and finally, to green.

The soldier was not more than twenty years old. His skin was paler than those of the Sas Darona tribesmen. His body was heavier. His muscles were

14

toned from a gym and not outdoor living. Karl saw that they had tried to straighten his hair, and at his temples he could clearly see how the skin tint had been hastily applied. As the liquid changed colour to green Karl stabbed the syringe into the soldier's neck and waited, pressing his fingers deeper into the young man's neck, the pulse still fading. Without hesitation he started on a second syringe.

He looked up and saw that his men had tended the other's wound. Under the effect of morphine, the injured boy was weeping and reaching to stroke his companion's hands, pleading with him to live. Karl glanced at the syringe in his hand. Still red, just a hint of orange. He waved to his men:

'You two, follow the trail, but do not engage.'

They raced off along the forest path.

The antidote was ready, the syringe had changed from orange to green in his hand. Again Karl stabbed into the jugular. Again he probed with his fingers around the soldier's neck and the base of his skull. Nothing. He reached for a third syringe. His second placed a hand on his shoulder.

'He's dead, Karl.'

Karl said nothing, just stretched the dead body on the path, carefully pulling the limbs straight into a pose of calm, closing the soldier's eyes and removing the Dome medallion from his neck. It fitted snugly into the palm of his hand, a ring of hard golden metal around a synthetic purple-tinted crystal shaped like a dome. Not just any dome. The large geodesic dome at the centre of the Freyne capital, called the capped Dome, was the training base and military headquarters for the Dome Elite. The crystal had been filled to the brim with poison.

So, the Dome Elite had finally devised a poison that worked faster than the best antidote. If past experience was anything to go by the poison would mutate to acid. He could bag up the body and take it back to camp but within an hour the body would have been dissolved to dust. Karl shuddered. How many times had he seen this now? A dozen, maybe twenty fighters, some had been wounded, most had not. On capture, all had chosen suicide using fast-acting poisons, then acid to dissolve their bodies. No body, no evidence, no proof.

He had one live prisoner, but the injured man was a tribesman. That was different. The United Races paid no heed to primitive tribesmen 'pointing

15

bows and arrows' at Zaracan military units. He would be healed under the United Races charter and returned to his tribe. Again and again the United Races had demanded proof of Dome Elite involvement. Karl looked again as if to check the medallion clasped in his hand. This time they had made a mistake. Or had they? As he watched, he saw the poison was eating into the metal.

'Ow!' Karl dropped the medallion as the acid burnt his palm. It fell from his hand down on top of the corpse. In a matter of moments, like paper on a flame, it had burned to ash and crumbled to dust. No proof.

And yet, something was not right. The tribesman's leg looked as if it had been ripped by gunfire. Karl spoke with sudden fear.

'Can you manage him? I have to get to Mezzatorra.'

Karl sped back through the forest, part sprinting, part flying. Within minutes he was walking along the perimeter of the firewall. Mezzatorra itself was fifty metres away. The firewall was just millimetres thick. It shimmered in the sunlight, but was essentially an invisible yet deadly wall of heat. The same young admin assistant who had radioed the warning, now came towards him. Her name was Sonia, nineteen, newly arrived and lovely. At first glance, she seemed completely unharmed.

'They had explosives, Karl. They blew a hole through the vault walls. And then... Then they were inside. Oh Karl, it was horrible. The lockdown, it's just three rooms. We only had blunted blades. Well, we never thought. Only three of us survived.'

'So they were armed? Guns? Lasers? Grenades?'

'No, just blades, live blades. But they were fast. So fast, Karl. I knew the Dome Elite were the best blades fighters in known space, but...' She started sobbing.

'You saw they were Dome Elite?'

'Yes, I mean no.' She was panicky. Even in these circumstances she hesitated to blame the Dome Elite. Karl knew why. Relations with the nearby Freyne Empire were bad enough without accusing them of terrorism. *'I don't know, Karl.'*

The firewall rippled like a veil on a breeze. In the distance, it disappeared to a haze. Bushes had been incinerated to ash along the line of the firewall. The black scar down the centre of the vegetation was the most obvious sign of the firewall. Still, if Sonia tried to walk through it she would be consumed by the flames.

'*How many died?*' Karl asked.

'*Five of us, and we have found three of theirs too.*'

'*What about the twins?*' Karl asked and immediately wished he hadn't. Gove and Jon were identical twins, brilliant geneticists and fun-loving party-boys who enjoyed their notoriety in the tight circles of entomological research. Sonia released a sob.

"*Gove was badly injured and bitten. Jon ended his brother's suffering...*" she choked, "*and then took his own life.*"

Karl could not think of anything to say as he tried to imagine the laughing brothers so badly injured that fratricide followed by suicide was the only solution.

"*Oh Sonia, I'm sorry... Did you say bitten?*"

'*We've all been bitten... Look!*'

She pushed her sleeve up high above her elbow and showed Karl the many bites down the white flesh of her inner arm. Already they were turning into large pus-filled cocoons.

'*Are those plague bites? Sonia!*'

'*We had to fight Karl. They were stealing poison pills. That's how the main tank was smashed, Karl. It contained a swarm of over a hundred insects. We've all been bitten.*' She nodded to her colleagues who were lining up the bodies in the shade of a great tree. '*But we had to fight. You do understand?*'

'*They took poison pills?*' Karl repeated, aghast.

'*We think the tribesmen stole eight poison pills. That's why we had to fight. If they had just wanted to take the monazite or smash our equipment we would have let them. But when they entered the vault, they only wanted one thing.*'

'*And you are sure the tribes stole eight poison pills?*' Karl repeated, aghast. '*Or was it Dome Elite?*'

Sonia shrugged, shook her head and said lamely '*I saved one.*' It was a brick made of industrial glass and within it was a mini world of plants, soil,

17

water and five or six insects, and mounted on the side was a small explosive.

The insects inside the poison pill were the jewel in the crown of the research undertaken at Mezzatorra. They were not Sas Darona plague insects, they were cy-sects: cybernetic insects. Someone somewhere had decided Sas Darona plague could be used as a weapon. Karl mused. Someone else had speculated that instead of real insects a weapon needed cybernetic insects. So Mezzatorra had delivered. Cy-sects (cybernetic insects) possessed all the attributes of Sas Darona plague but none of the drawbacks. Cy-sects did not require water to spawn. Cy-sect bites were one hundred per cent lethal, one hundred per cent of the time. Cy-sects achieved crystallescence in four hours or less. Cy-sect crystallescence always spawned a further hundred thousand cy-sects.

Next, Mezzatorra had also devised a foolproof delivery method: glass bricks containing miniature ecosystems perfect for cy-sects. In some places the weapons were displayed as decorative ornaments. Each brick was mounted with explosives for remote detonation. Because of their deadly content and the way they cracked open, the scientists called them poison pills. These new plague weapons, these poison pills, were not just deadly. With cy-sects practically un-killable and spawning a hundred thousand offspring every four hours, they went beyond deadly. They were planet-killers.

'Karl Valvanchi to control. They have eight poison pills. We have to lock it down. Nothing takes off. Nothing comes in. They are not getting away with poison pills.'

He turned to speak to Sonia, only to see her crumble. At her back, the two others who had been carrying the dead now lay amongst them. Sonia was still alive though. She moved her arms weakly, swimming against the ground and grass to find a more comfortable position.

Suddenly the full horror of the attack threatened to overwhelm Karl, as he found himself counting again and again the number of the fallen. Eight of his people had died today, more than in all of the previous twelve months. Not only that, but the dead were not soldiers. They were eight leading specialists in a little-known field.

Karl had a choice: head off to chase and find the poison pills, or stay here providing what comfort he could to this beautiful girl as she died. Was it really a choice? Karl sank in the grass across from Sonia. She was within his reach, except the firewall was between them.

"It's not painful," she whispered, and closed her eyes.

As the Sas Darona plague made its deadly progress through the flesh and bones of her body, her face remained recognisable, but she was just the shape of Sonia, not Sonia herself. In the setting sun her body shone, reflecting the light from a thousand different facets of the cy-sect cocoons: the crystallescence. A sight, Karl realised, which was hauntingly beautiful, but also…

Deadly. As the sun set the cocoons split. For one moment, she was a quivering mass. Her body dissolved into a cloud of plague flies. They rose up from her corpse in a cyclone. Nothing was left. The cy-sects seemed to smell Karl and a large group swerved, spun and charged at the shield. Karl Valvanchi leapt back. Unnecessary. The cy-sect swarm fried and burned on the wall of fire.

Sonia had said one last thing to Karl. He felt sure it was the last thing she said when she was still truly human:

'Karl, Karl. Wait. I am starting to forget things. But this is important. We found this, Karl. We found this, and you need to have it.'

She threw the metal disc and chain through the firewall. Karl caught it one-handed.

Karl did not have to look twice to know what it was. He stroked the medallion, polishing its surface with the oils of his palm. It was unmistakeable. The large circular military ID tags were moulded to resemble the Freyne 2 Dome and were worn by the Dome Elite military force who trained there. On one side there was the fighter's name, rank and serial number, and on the other the motto of the Dome Elite. Karl ran his thumb over the circle of letters:

Loyal to Empire, Fear only God.

It's intact, thought Karl. At last, the proof I need. Proof that the Dome Elite were at Mezzatorra.

He relaxed a fraction, enjoying this small moment of success. Then another thought occurred to him:

What did the Freyne want with poison pills?

Chapter 1. The King of Freyne 2

All of a sudden, the prince was afraid. Once again the nightmare flashed before his eyes. It had been cold. It had been dark. He had been alone and afraid. It had all felt so real. Why? He gripped hard onto the metal rail, so hard his knuckles shone white through his skin.

"I don't want to go!"

Nobody heard him. Prince Teodor of Freyne was standing on a small balcony jutting out over the river, looking across to his capital city.

"I do not want to go."

Across the river, amidst the shambolic industry of Domeside, the Dome dipped one rim into the Brant, then rose above the irregular roofs to its capped peak. The Freyne Dome was a geodesic dome made up of identical industrial glass triangles arranged into vast flower-like hexagons. From where he stood, Teodor could easily count the panes facing towards him. But, as always, his eyes were drawn to the cap of the Dome, a ring of rectangular windows topped with a flat roof. The Dome appeared to wear a hat, hence 'capped Dome'.

Teodor thought the nickname in no way captured its vast size. The oldest district of the city fitted inside it. The ancient cathedral, the historic rampart and a maze of old streets, all were inside. Some buildings had, by necessity, been demolished, and in their place had appeared layered skyscraper complexes: sports stadiums, hotels, casinos, gymnasiums, entertainment venues and a space shuttle port. Hidden behind all of these bright lights were the facilities to train and house up to ten thousand Dome Elite soldiers. All encased in the weather-controlled Dome to enable round-the-clock sports and entertainment. It was said that you could set your communicator by the rainfall within the Freyne capped Dome.

Teodor did not remember the grand opening but he had seen the recording. Just four years old, he had worn his uniform of prince of empire alongside his father, King Serge of Freyne. The first thousand Dome Elite had marched out and his father had whispered:

"Salute them Teo, you must salute them!"

How many times had the news channels shown the footage? Every time, Teodor winced to see how, aged four, he had screwed up his face and pulled himself up to his short, podgy height. Clumsily he had aligned his plump fingers to the brim of his cap. When his father saluted, the soldiers had responded as one, fists crossing their bodies to tap their hearts.

"Loyal to Empire," they had cried. "Fear only God."

The sight and sound of it had been too much for his four-year-old self. Unexpectedly, he had fallen onto his backside. And, to Teodor's eternal shame, instead of letting him jump back to his feet, his father had bent down, laughing, to pick him up and hoist him up onto his shoulder. The Dome Elite had cheered.

"Forever Prince Teodor! Forever King Serge!"

Only, his father hadn't… hadn't lived forever... Just seven years later he had been murdered. Two years, one month, twelve days and, Teodor sighed as he made the calculation, twenty hours ago the King had died. The Dome Elite should have protected their King that day. They should have, but they had failed. Now Teo was alone, and last night in his dream, he had been very afraid.

"I am their future King." Teodor set his shoulders square. "I am not afraid of nightmares."

His communicator buzzed him a reminder. He took one last look and turned back towards the goran stables. An outbuilding at the bottom of the Royal Gardens, the stables housed twelve to twenty gorans with apartments, offices and storerooms for their handlers, jockeys, equipment and food. Teodor knew the stables looked like a palace to most people, but he was not most people. He winced. He made his way through the giant arch into the courtyard where Prime Minister Patrick McGuire waited for him.

"It's Princess Simonelle Valvanchi. I think you know who she is, my prince," he added, a little anxiously.

"Yes, the great-granddaughter of the great explorer Nikato Valvanchi."

Teodor had not been able to refuse this meeting. In any case, he wanted to meet Simonelle. She was Zaracan and the aliens were pure telepaths. He wanted to feel for himself what telepathy meant. He also hoped that she might be friendly and maybe reveal herself; for the Zaracans were also shape-shifters. The girl's appearance today was unlikely to be her true self. Now he spoke quickly to reassure his minister that he was ready for this meeting, briefly clicking on his communicator where the outline of a family tree appeared on screen.

Patrick McGuire glanced at it and nodded:

"Her grandfather did not discover the thirteen, but he proved the historical connection. He proved that the thirteen planets of the Freyne Empire had once been one vast human civilisation, about four thousand years ago. He made the discovery when we were still thirteen separate underdeveloped planets with no interplanetary travel, no space colonies, no asteroid wealth."

"That was a hundred years ago," Teodor said. Then, as if reciting a lesson, he added, "The turning point was when Nikato Valvanchi helped us build our first shuttle," Teodor added earnestly: "Nowadays, my uncle the Emperor says our empire is as great as it ever was."

Without thinking, Teodor put special emphasis on the words my uncle the Emperor. He did not mean to, but he still did it. The fact was that since Prince Erederon had died, and his father, the King, had been murdered, Teodor was the only surviving heir to the empire. One day soon Teodor would be King, and after that he would also be Emperor; Emperor of all Freyne.

"Yes my prince," his prime minister replied and continued: "I am sure the Emperor is right. The point is, my prince, the Zaracan Democratic Union is one of the great powers of the United Races. The Valvanchi is one of their most powerful families. Don't be fooled by their democratic credentials! This girl is one of their highest born princesses. I expect you to treat her as such."

"She's thirteen just like me, no?"

"Yes, thirteen. And remember the Zaracans are shape-shifters. They choose their appearance to please people."

"Yes, yes, I know." Teodor did not hide his impatience. Why should he? Was he not tutored in these things?

"Sometimes they want to please just one person." The man nodded ahead of them. The girl waiting outside his office was slim, blonde and slight. As Teodor looked it dawned on him that her long hair was as straw-like and untidy as Lucy's.

So, Teodor thought and scowled, she had read the gossip about him and the stable girl. The politician was still watching him closely, so Teodor quickly rearranged his features to a bland, indifferent look. The man smiled.

"Good luck, my prince. Be careful."

The prime minister stepped back, leaving Teodor to greet the princess alone. Teodor did not hesitate, but reached out to her:

"Princess Simonelle, welcome. I am honoured to greet a guest who has travelled so far."

"Thank you, prince. Please call me Nell, everybody does."

Teodor was taken aback. Such familiarity was unusual. He answered her quickly:

"Then you must call me Teo." She smiled. "Though nearly everyone else calls me Prince Teodor." Her smile faltered, and Teodor wondered why he had said that. Except of course it was true. Very few people called him Teo these days. He sighed.

At least she was pretty, thought Teodor, and then quickly reminded himself: don't be deceived; this is not her true self. He saw the girl's smile falter a little. Was she reading his mind? Or just waiting for him to speak? Teodor panicked, not knowing what to say. In the end he did not have to say anything, as Nell just carried on:

"It's so great to be here. My science tutor said I could choose any subject I wanted. And I had seen the videos and I just fell in love. I mean, it's impossible not to fall in love with the great cats you call gorans, isn't it?"

Teodor looked a little startled. Cats? Who called gorans cats? The girl continued:

"So I have already been to Sas Darona to see gorans in the wild. My uncle Karl Valvanchi took me to see a night camp. The male had such a fine mane. Now I cannot believe I am here."

Teodor mulled over what she had just said. She had travelled from Zarac 1 to Sas Darona and then on to Freyne 2. A journey only a handful of his people might complete in their lifetimes. She spoke as if this was a holiday. Was this what his minister meant when he spoke of the Great Powers? Why did the Valvanchi allow this girl so much freedom, not to think of the expense, to complete what was little more than a school project. She was waiting now, waiting for him to speak. What could he say that might interest or impress this girl?

"Did you travel seventy-five days to get here?"

"Yes." There was a tremor in her reply. What was wrong? Was she lying? About what? Teodor listened a little more closely.

"My father said I could, and my uncle invited me to stay for Magnolia Weekend."

Teodor smiled at her:

"Magnolia Weekend is all about the Magnolia Stakes. Saturday is the greatest goran race of the year. And it all starts right here."

Teodor had led her into the stable courtyard. She gasped. Teodor smiled. He had to admit it was an impressive sight. The Regency Defence in their silver and red uniforms, patrolling: on the lookout for security breaches. The jockeys in their silk shirts and woollen leggings; similarly the stable girls, each one eye-catching in her choice of brightly coloured shirt and slim-fitting leggings. Finally, being led out from their stalls into the dawn sunlight, the great two-metre-high racing gorans of Freyne. Golden, tiger-striped, dark oak, black and golden, the gorans came in every hue of nature. The princess was right about one thing. It was impossible not to fall in love with the great racing gorans.

If there is one place in the empire I love above all other, thought Teodor, it is here, right now, standing in my stables with my gorans.

"Dawn is always the best time to see them. The gorans are semi-nocturnal. They favour hunting at dawn. So we try to fit with their natural pattern of behaviour by training them at this time

Nell said: "Yes, but these gorans no longer hunt."

25

"Oh, they would if they were hungry enough," laughed Teodor. "And they do not mind a bit of mauling if you upset them." He remembered a nasty injury he had witnessed just a month before. An arm ripped from the body of an unwary guard. The princess had stopped in her tracks; she looked terror struck. She's reading my mind again, thought Teodor. She has seen my memory.

"It was only a cyborg," he added hastily. "We try to programme them to be careful, but they have no sense around gorans. The gorans are so dangerous, and the cyborgs are programmed to protect me, so..." He was going to say inevitably they are attacked, but was it inevitable?

"That's terrible. I never thought. All the time I have spent reading and studying, I never thought." She froze again. They were now standing by the half-door of a goran house, and a giant goran was being led from the enclosure at walking pace. She appeared as a wall of fur in front of their faces, so close Nell only had to stretch out her finger to touch her.

"This is Blue Barbrina," Teodor said gently, reaching up to rub the white and blue-grey goran on the shoulder. Nell was talking again. This time Teodor felt sure she was trying to hide her fear, because she was talking fast, reciting even:

"It's... She's an ice cat from Sas Darona. Yes, I know they are the largest of the goran cats. They live around and about the ice flows on the Southern Poles. They breed maybe only once every three or four years, and they only let three cubs survive. Any more cubs – and a mother can bear five – and the two weakest are slaughtered..."

Teodor snorted: "We all live in a harsh world, Nell. Don't feel sorry for baby gorans who are killed by their mother out of kindness when the alternative is to starve then freeze."

Nell nodded. Teodor had a feeling she did not entirely agree. She continued:

"It's her colour that makes her unique. White and blue, they say, though it's really white and grey, just flecks of blue. It acts as camouflage on the ice flows, but to me she is the most beautiful of all."

Teodor interrupted with a smile.

"And Nell, what's more is that the beautiful Blue Barbrina will beat Imperial Rina and win the Magnolia Stakes this weekend... Imperial Rina is the Emperor's goran; she's the only real competition, but Barbie will still win. Come. Stroke her like this."

"I cannot…" Teodor felt sorry her; she was trembling as she spoke.

"Would you like me to help you to tune your telepathy into her frequency? Gorans are low-level telepaths. I only have implants. But you are a pure telepath. They said I would be able to help you. Help you find the frequency. If you would like?"

Teodor asked the question gently, because after all they had just met. Nell nodded resolutely. He hesitated. His people were watching. But there was nothing for it. They all knew what he must do to help the girl. And there was no-one else who had the status to touch her. He reached around her shoulders and, winding his arm up her arm, he pressed the palm of his hand to the palm of her hand. He lifted her arm, and reached out to speak to the goran with his mind.

Teodor waited. Nell was still shaking against his shoulder. Teodor wondered if this experiment was bound to fail. He thought of his mental link to the gorans as a line of light along which he directed his thoughts and commands. All the princess had to do was to align her thoughts along the same line. She was the telepath after all. She should find it easy enough. She only had to see the light. So what was taking so long? He could smell the perfume of her hair, and feel her warmth. She was very pretty.

All at once the line of light in his mind's eye broadened to a wide rope. The princess' telepathy had connected with his, and she now spoke with the goran.

'*I am a friend,*' Teodor heard her thought whisper. He smiled, squeezed her once by way of congratulation, and then released her. He stood at her side, listening in to her telepathic voice as she spoke quiet, calming thoughts to the great cat.

'*You are majestic and brave. You are beautiful and unique.*'

Blue Barbrina turned towards Teodor and Nell. She briefly sniffed Teodor, then nuzzled Nell's belly and chest. Without warning the giant cat licked her face.

Teodor laughed and rubbed the cat behind the ears. Nell looked momentarily stunned but then did the same. Teodor left Nell to enjoy the goran for a moment. He went to take the reins from the stable girl who was waiting and watching.

"She's not even a real princess, you know."

"Lucy. Sssh." Teodor scolded her with good humour. Frizzy, untidy hair, he decided, looked better on Lucy. She looked like she had worked to get that look. And he knew she had been up at five getting his riding gear ready. "She's our guest."

'Are you going to ride Blue Barbrina?' Nell asked.

'Of course,' Teodor replied with disdainful conviction. Then, not trusting his telepathic voice, he spoke the words aloud: "Of course." Nell looked astonished. She too reverted to her voice, and immediately started talking.

"Your best time on any goran is 71k, but this one has exceeded 79k. She has only ever been ridden by three jockeys. In the last year, she has mauled one guard..."

"...cyborg..." interrupted Teodor.

"...and at least three stable dogs."

Nell glanced at Lucy who was still standing nearby. Teodor realised it was meant as a taunt. Lucy looked annoyed.

"Dogs," Teodor repeated. "Only dogs, princess. But I see you know my stats. So, for your sake, princess, I will endeavour to better my best performance. Lucy, you will accompany the princess back to my mother's apartments. She should be there in time to see my fastest lap."

"I look forward to that, my King," Simonelle said with a small bow.

"I am not the King," Teodor corrected her quickly. "My mother rules. My mother is Regent. I am but a prince..." Teodor hesitated, and added as an after-thought: *'In any case, I said you may call me Teo.'*

With a final bow, he lifted his foot into the stirrup and swung up and over, into the saddle set across the goran's shoulders. He took his position crouched atop the goran's shoulders, body angled forward, head down, chin centred on the back of the goran's skull, eyes looking out along the line of the Goran's muzzle to the path ahead. From high above, he glanced back just once to look down on her:

"If I don't see you afterwards..."

"We'll meet at the Magnolia Ball," the princess replied with a bright smile. To which she added a coy farewell: *'Until then, Teo.'*

Teodor tightened the reins and started to move forward.

"Ah yes, parties! All the fun of Magnolia Weekend," he replied flatly.

The goran was already moving at a trot, heading to the courtyard exit. Teodor looked back once. The princess was framed by the buildings of the stables and behind her reared up the vast geometric shape of the Dome. From this angle, it was a black outline in front of the sun, magnified in the bright dawn light and undeniably menacing.

Once again Teodor experienced a wave of fear, as if the Dome was some gigantic beast he could not control. Through telepathy, his goran felt it too, and the giant snow cat reared up and roared in defiance, clawing at the air. All the time rocking in his seat, Teodor sought to comfort the animal:

"Sssh Barbie," Teodor said soothingly. "It's only the Dome."

Teodor rode the goran across the garden and around the palace building, finishing the last ascent at a fast gallop before slowing, then pausing ahead of the long promenade of ancient trees. The straight avenue ran a full two kilometres along the riverbank and was designed for speed.

'Designed to test your nerve, my boy.' That was what his father had said.

'How fast dare you let your goran go, before you rein her in? How fast, hey?'

Teodor grabbed the reins again and focused. He needed speed. More than anything he wanted to be fast. Lowering his chin to brush against the very brows of the goran, he raced to the finish line. Inside his helmet statistics flashed up across his visor. All the numbers were green. It was a new personal best.

Oh Father, if only you could see me now!

Bringing the goran down to a canter, he circled a small lawn where they had set up the blades mat under the balcony of his mother's bedroom suite. Teodor could not see her, and perhaps she was still inside, but whatever her state of dress or make-up she would step out to watch him fight. Teodor checked his communicator.

Yes, he was late. Three minutes late. His mother would be furious.

***

Regent Sayginn stood at the window looking down over the gardens as they stretched out to the stables. She held a small delicate cup between two hands, and at her side Simonelle Valvanchi stood, also looking out.

"That last lap was a record," Nell said with a smile.

The Regent nodded but did not smile:

"Yes, but he's late. He has the best blades instructor in the city and he's late."

Regent Sayginn was nearly always described as petite. Serge – the King and her husband – had sometimes called her fragile, with her slim arms, tiny waist and small feet. As always, at the start of each day she was without make-up and her hair was combed back with a light application of conditioner. She wore a silk gown over her freshly showered body and nothing else. Soon she would submit herself to the hands of her dressers, hairdressers and make-up artist, and after a time she would be deemed ready to step out as Regent.

There had been some consternation at the early morning visit of the Zaracan princess. Some inept assistant had even suggested a five-thirty start, so she might be ready to meet the girl at dawn. In the end the invitation had read: '...the princess is exclusively invited to join the Regent in her boudoir, relaxing before a busy day.'

A good choice of words, Sayginn had thought. At least the princess did not seem fazed to meet her so under-prepared. Well, she was young. Nothing surprises the young.

"Are they from the Dome?" Nell asked, pointing.

Sayginn had been watching her son. Teodor had leapt down to the ground. A stable girl ran up from behind him, and Teodor handed her the reins. Sayginn noticed how the girl smiled at her son with a bright star-struck smile. And Teo, what did he do? He looked embarrassed, and then he sprinted away. So, still somewhat shy of girls, she surmised.

His steward was waiting for him next to the blades mat, a pristine, cream-coloured circle ten metres in diameter, and edged with a thick black line. Across from Teodor and his steward, the men from the Dome Elite were waiting. They looked very impressive in their black uniforms and bulky protection.

"They are so tall..." Nell continued.

Sayginn reflected that the girl was probably thinking how the Dome Elite appeared to be taller than her own race the Zaracans. What she herself noticed was how they towered above the household staff, disdainful of their red and silver uniforms and the multi-coloured silks of the goran jockeys, handlers and stable girls.

"It's the running blades, Nell." Sayginn pointed to the soldiers' feet. The Dome Elite always wore black running blades. "See there, that metal strip, the running blade, slots into the bottom of boots or shoes. It allows the wearer to leap or run up to five times their normal stride."

"And they have fighting blades as well?"

"In combat the running blades are worn with sharp edges so they can be used as weapons, but yes, they also have hand-held daggers which they call fighting blades."

As she spoke, Sayginn checked to see. Yes, the Dome Elite were all fully armed with matching pairs of fighting blades. The black handles of the murderous hand-held daggers protruded above their belts. With blades on their feet for speed and agility, and blades in their hands for cutting and stabbing, the Dome Elite were the deadliest hand-to-hand combatants in known space. Which was just as well, Sayginn reminded herself. The Freyne Empire was a newcomer to the United Races. As such, it still attracted its fair share of smash and grab privateers and profit-seeking raiders. In recent years though, to fly your ship unannounced into Freyne Space was said to mean certain death to all the crew and a change of livery for the ship which would soon be flying under the gold and black of the Dome Elite. Sometimes one or other of their neighbours complained but overall the people of Freyne slept soundly. Who would have thought, Sayginn mused, that in the age of space travel your soldiers had to be experts in the use of blades and flying daggers? Then she added:

"Teo should know better than to keep them waiting."

"He's being quick though…" Nell said, pointing.

Teodor locked on the leaping blades and pulled on the gauntlets, leather sleeves that strapped to his forearms with three small curved blades protruding from the back of his arms.

"Those are the gauntlets," Sayginn said. "They make it easier to slice an opponent as you spin towards him."

"Is that servant kneeling to Teo?"

"Well, he is helping him with his calf greaves," replied Sayginn, "Those are leather lower-leg protection, again with three curved blades poking out from the side of Teo's leg, the better to slice his enemy should he kick out at him."

"And what's that?" Nell gasped. Teodor's steward had offered him a shimmering tunic that shone like crystal in the early morning sunlight.

"It is a diamond protection vest," said Sayginn with pride. "It's a gift from the Emperor. Go on Teo, you must wear it."

Below them Teodor was frowning. He looked like he was going to refuse the shirt. Then Sayginn stepped out onto the balcony and Teodor saw her. She nodded at the diamond protection vest, and then towards a couple of press cameras hovering nearby. She saw her son scowl, but nevertheless he accepted the short tunic.

"It's as light as silk, but when he wears it no blade can penetrate it. It's the ultimate protection," Sayginn explained to Nell.

"And it will look good on the news," Nell said. Sayginn flushed. The girl had clearly read her thought. The diamond shirt would look great on the news. That's why Sayginn wanted Teodor to wear it.

The prince was ready now. Leaping blades on his feet, curved blades protruding from the gauntlets and greaves down the length of his forearms and lower legs, diamond protection shirt and two shining daggers in the palms of his hands, Teodor leapt to the centre of the mat.

"With a blade in each hand," Sayginn told Nell. She frowned as her son spun his blades across the palms of his hands. Since when had he learnt that showy trick?

"With a blade in each hand," Nell repeated with a sigh. The girl already looked totally love-struck, Sayginn decided. "Let's go out onto the balcony, shall we?"

***

Teodor noticed his mother and Nell, but did not allow himself to be distracted. Across from him and with measured consideration, Dome Elite Commander Tilson had stepped onto the blades mat.

"On guard."

The senior instructor span towards Teodor. The prince blocked and repelled the attack with swift ease.

"You were late," accused Tilson, coming at Teodor. His blades spiralled one way and then another.

Teodor deftly pushed back his attack: "Blades is not my only sport."

"There are a thousand boys across the river. Not one ever keeps me waiting."

Teodor felt a pang of guilt. His footing became uncertain. Tilson pressed home his advantage. Teodor was forced into a desperate countermove:

"Goran riding is the sport of Emperors," he said, and with new ferociousness spun into attack, matching his blows and kicks to his words, putting his passion and power behind each blow. He disengaged, stalking the perimeter of the blades mat, flushed and anxious. Was there ever any real prospect he might defeat this man?

"Ready," Tilson called out. This time the attack was unforgiving. Teodor struggled to find a defence.

"Calm, Teodor. Control," Tilson urged. Teodor found a rhythm to respond to the blows. Until the tempo changed; the last attack was fast. The Dome medallion at Tilson's neck swung out and up. It curved towards Teodor's face. The black and gold circular disc was flying fast towards Teodor's eyes. Distracted, he lost his bearings and landed outside the blades ring.

The match stopped. Dejected, Teodor waited for the rebuke.

"To step outside the blades ring is to die, my prince. Instant disqualification…"

"Your medallion," Teodor protested, but stopped. It was a pitiful excuse. Everyone in Freyne knew the rule about the black line. To step outside the blades ring was to be disqualified. It was a mistake that a prince who had trained for years could ill afford to make. Still, the mistake was not entirely his fault.

Just so unfair, to lose like that, just so unfair!

Teodor pulled off his gauntlets, kicked off the calf greaves, and threw all the items down onto the fighting mat.

"Enough, this is only practice! Enough practice to beat some Domeside boy, anyhow."

Teodor looked across the yard to the two yearling golden gorans. He reached up a hand and used his goran telepathy to call them. They raced across the short distance between himself and the stables, and curved their bodies around him. Their heads were already higher than Teodor's. Soon their shoulders would be broad enough for him, at least, to ride them. Still they sniffed his hair and licked his hands, like cubs, and he roughed them behind the ears before calling them to sit on either side of him.

Let the cameras see him like this. A goran on each side and proud to be a prince. If he hoped to impress his people, he had clearly missed his mark with his trainer:

"The Dome fight was cancelled."

"I'm sorry?"

"I met with your mother over a week ago. The fight was cancelled. Did she not tell you?"

All at once, Teodor felt anger bubble up inside him, but with effort he managed to mask the emotions he felt from his face. He did not want Tilson to know he had not known about the fight. He did not want to lose his temper. His efforts at self-control must have been obvious because the man imperceptibly softened.

"Until our next meeting, then. Remember: Calm, Teodor, control."

The Dome Commander always used these words: Calm, Teodor, Control. Yes, Teodor would be calm, and Teodor would be in control, particularly this morning, when Teodor was heading into the Dome.

Teodor nodded a brief goodbye. Leaping blades still attached to his feet and golden gorans racing besides him, he set off into the palace. He bounded up the staircase three steps at a time to arrive in his mother's bedroom suite a few instants later, with the goran cubs right behind him. He made his way to the breakfast table and, without checking whether his mother was present, helped himself. He was hungry; it was only eight and he had already had a full morning. Then there she was, Regent Sayginn Freyne, ruler of Freyne 2.

"My blades. Any day. Any time. Any place," Teodor cried. "Will you yield?"

"Don't say that!" Sayginn scolded him.

"It's what the Dome blades fighters say," Teodor said sulkily.

"Yes, but you're not in the Dome," Sayginn reminded him.

"I like it and they are our people too," Teodor finished, with an angry spin of his blades across the palms of his hands.

"And stop that silly trick with the blades. It's dangerous. Now say good morning properly."

"Good morning, Mother…"

"That was a careless mistake this morning, Teo."

Teodor ignored her criticism and instead asked angrily:

"Why, Mother? Why did you cancel the Domeside fight?"

"The reason I cancelled the fight is because the Domeside boy they chose to fight you will beat you."

"I don't believe you."

"I did not believe it either. But I have spoken to everyone. They all said the same, the security team here, your blades instructor. I've seen the tapes of this boy. The others have been to watch him in training. They all agree: he would beat you, Teodor."

Teodor was still not convinced, so he said spitefully:

"He probably wasn't even thirteen."

"He was thirteen. He was a skinny thing, but he was fast, and he was clever. You would have lost, Teodor."

"Oh, and suddenly I'm not clever enough?" Teodor was shouting now. "Do I not work hard enough, long enough?"

"Teodor!" Sayginn replied sharply.

At that moment, Simonelle appeared from the balcony. Teodor had not known she was there. Now he realised she must have overheard the entire argument, even without her telepathic skills.

"I'd better go…" she said meekly.

35

"No Princess, Prince Teodor…"

"I think Teo wants to spend some time with his mother…" Nell said kindly, giving Teodor's hand a little squeeze. The pair of golden gorans prowled around her, sniffing her; Teodor gently took Nell's hands and pressed them to one of the cub's temples.

'There, now you can talk to these too.'

Sayginn stared at them both, shocked, as she realised Teodor and Nell were speaking with thoughts. Nell saw her and spoke aloud:

"I have to leave about now. I'm meeting my uncle this morning. Thank you both for your hospitality."

"Give my regards to your uncle, the ambassador…"

"It's my uncle Karl Valvanchi I'm meeting this morning, but yes, I will say so to my uncle the ambassador."

As the door shut, Regent Sayginn spoke in a low, angry voice:

"You have to – HAVE TO – control your temper, Teodor. One day maybe you will be a great King. Maybe on paper you are ready, but not if you cannot control these outbursts."

"No Domeside boy will ever beat me… Do you hear me? I don't care who he is. I would not allow it. Do you hear me? And didn't the Emperor want to see me fight at blades?"

"Yes, yes he did. But you can present your exam display, and he'll be impressed by the way you handle gorans."

"Tsk!" Teodor was unconvinced. "You know they'll call me chicken in Domeside if I don't fight."

"Yes, well, the people can say what they want. At least they will not have seen their boy knock you onto your backside."

"Mother!" Teodor was outraged; he knew full well she was referencing his four-year-old self. He picked another sugar roll from the breakfast table and bit into it. He saw his mother frowning. How many rolls had he eaten? Was it two or three? He quickly sought to distract her.

"May I come with you to the space port this morning to see Uncle Freddie?"

"You mean come and greet Emperor Frederon?"

36

"My uncle Freddie, yes." Teodor repeated the words with emphasis. Let's remember who I am, he thought. For an instant, his mother looked confused. She might even have said yes, but then she checked her communicator. She coughed, never a good sign, and said:

"You mean re-organise a rehearsal which involves one hundred children all in costume, twenty adults, including the full crew of technicians, not to mention all the security, the police escort and the drivers. Oh, I am sure everyone would be delighted with any change of plan." His mother paused. "Really, Teo? That's almost two hundred people waiting for your arrival to the Dome."

"Mum, I don't want to go…" Teodor said quietly. Did he have to explain to his mother what he felt about the Dome? The Dome, where his father had been going the day he died. The Dome Elite, who should have protected him. The Dome that overshadowed their everyday lives, and would never go away.

Of course he did not have to explain; his mother replied gently:

"You will have your security." She checked her communicator: "Twelve cyborgs, six cy-wolves and, of course, your bodyguard."

Both looked out to where a cyborg and wolf patrolled the balcony. This one was Andor. Well, he had once been Andor. There had been an explosion. He had been brain dead on arrival at hospital. His family signed the papers for him to become a cyborg. A robot's brain and cortex were wired into his human body. His bones were reinforced with carbon. He was reallocated to the Palace, to live his short cyborg life as part of the Regency Defence.

"Andor's skin is starting to peel," Teodor said quietly. As a cyborg aged, the skin started to blacken and peel away from the body. Cyborgs could survive without skin, but no-one was quite sure for how long. The sight of a half-human, half-robot with cracked, blackened, peeling skin was too gruesome for most to bear. So a cyborg would normally be terminated after two years. That was normally when the skin turned grey. Peeling skin at the wrists was the first outward signs that a cyborg was reaching this final stage.

"That's sad. He was one of the men on duty…"

"…the day father died. Yes, I know. Do I have to go into the Dome?"

"Teodor, what's this about? I thought you wanted to…"

37

"I had a bad dream," Teodor interrupted, and ignored his mother's surprise. "I was in the dark. I was trying to find my way out. It looked a bit like the catacombs we visited last year. A voice kept telling me it was not the catacombs. It was the Dome. I did not know where I was... It was so dark... I was all alone. I was trying to find my way out. Kept trying to find a way out, only... Well, then I woke up."

Sayginn sighed, and shook her head impatiently.

"A dream, Teo. It was just a dream. You have to go, Teo. It's an important weekend: I need to win the Dome Debate. You know that. I plan to take control of the Dome this weekend. You know that too. I will win the Dome Debate, and the Dome will be mine. But Chart Segat has his supporters too. They're noisy, and they will not see reason, but we have to win them over. Your singing with a choir of Domeside children will be – already is – very popular." She reached to run her hand through his hair, but Teodor backed away from her caress, scowling: "It will look good on the news."

"It will look good on the news," Teodor repeated, flatly. "Mum. It was dark. I was cold. I could not find my way out."

"You are their King, Teo," she said. Teodor sighed.

"Prince, Mother. I am Prince Teodor."

"You are the King. Remember the words." Teodor felt his heart sink as his mother continued: "I, Teodor, son of Serge..."

She nudged him, so Teodor reluctantly recited the oath:

"...do claim this planet and its dependencies.

To rule as is my right,

For the benefit of my people,

As guided by our democratic institutions,

And prescribed by our laws.

So help me God.

I do know the words, Mother. I do want to rule this planet. Only..."

"You're a good boy, Teodor. Your heart will tell you when the time is right."

She kissed him one last time, checked her communicator and headed off. She was gone.

Teodor looked at his communicator. Time he was going too. He was expected in the cathedral.

Chapter 2. In the Light and Shadows of the Dome

With a whispered prayer, Guy Erma kissed his Dome medallion and slid it inside his shirt. He stepped up to the edge of the mat. In truth, he knew he did not need God's help today. No, all he needed to win this fight was to be ruthless, and to be quick. The bell had rung. To delay now was to be disqualified. Guy gripped the short fighting blades and somersaulted forward. He landed within easy reach of his opponent.

He twisted into a spinning high kick that caught and whacked the other's shoulder pad. He found his feet while the other was still off-balance, then crouched and sliced his other leg in a circle just off the floor. In so doing, he swept his opponent's feet from under him. The other boy fell. Guy was quick to leap up and on top of him, riding astride his adversary's chest with two blades pressed to his neck.

"Do you yield?" Guy roared into his face. "I yield… I yield…" The other was so fearful he almost wept, and to see this sent a thrill through Guy stronger than any other emotion. His heart beat fast. He rose panting, exhilarated and joyful: He had won!

No-one was watching. Why would they? Across the vast competition space there were over two dozen blades mats. Almost all played host to a fighting duo. As always, his gaze was drawn to where the gym opened onto the vast panes and verticals of the Dome. The light was bright, yet dark geometric shadows fell across the space. Guy loved this gym. He felt he always fought better here, in the light and shadows of the Dome.

In the light and the shadows of the Dome, so help me God.

It was a prayer of the Dome Elite.

One day I will say those words, thought Guy, and wear that uniform.

Now that's a real prayer. He sighed. So help me God.

"Well Done, Guy." Tilson, senior blades instructor, and Commander of the Dome Elite, bent to help him up.

"Thank you, sir. Thank you."

"You do us all proud, you really do…" Unexpectedly, the man drew him over and patted the space on the bench beside him. Guy sat down. For a few moments, they unbuckled Guy's forearm braces, each with a line of three curved blades. Next, off came the calf greaves and the three blades along the back of his lower legs. Finally, they released the latches of the springing blades he wore beneath his feet. Soon Guy had set aside all his fighting equipment together with the two fighting daggers.

"I hope to join the Dome Elite next term, sir."

"Did you submit your forms before the deadline?"

Guy nodded but winced. Meeting the deadline had been the least of his worries. Guy's application to join the Dome Elite was flawed in another, rather more fundamental, way.

"You're not registered, are you?" Both Tilson and Guy knew that without his birth having been registered, Guy would struggle to have his application accepted. "Do you know who your parents are?"

"Well…" Guy hesitated. He rarely spoke of his home life but this was important. He swallowed, then whispered: "Well, one of the models in my house, she always says I…" Guy coughed, hardly daring to say the words: "Lloulou says I am her son…"

Tilson paused, considering.

"Lloulou, huh? I know Lloulou. She's beautiful but she has to think of her career, and if she were to register you… well, the Press…"

"Yes, it's a secret. You can't tell."

"I won't say anything. And you don't know who your father is?"

Guy shook his head.

"No," Tilson said, and sighed: "Thing is Guy, I have boys who are fully registered – both mother and father – both of whom are pleading with me to take their sons. So you see."

41

"But I am the blades champion for my year group. I won the championship, and I was due to fight the prince…" Guy was angry.

"They said he had an injury," Tilson said thoughtfully.

Guy made a clucking sound. "Chicken more like. My maths average is 97.4. Maths and blades. And I was born on Old Mill Lane. You need the best people for the Dome Elite!"

"Calm, Guy. Control!" The man took his hand and patted it gently: "Calm Guy, control. You never know, maybe the fight with the prince will be reinstated."

"Really?"

Guy looked up curiously. At that moment a communicator beeped a reminder and Tilson patted him on the shoulder.

"Keep training. Try to get one of the older boys to prep you. If you did beat the prince, you would be pretty much guaranteed a place in the Dome Elite."

Tilson stood up but before he left, said again.

"Be ready, Guy. Be ready."

Be ready for what? wondered Guy. Be ready to beat Prince Teodor at blades, when the fight had been cancelled?

With practice over, Guy headed out of the Dome and down the elegant tree-lined Old Mill Lane. House Jewel was the first and the most ancient of the seven-storey town houses, with a spacious fashion boutique on the ground floor, and an imposing colonnaded entrance leading up to the VIP salons for private clients on the floor above. House Jewel was the oldest of the Freyne 2 fashion houses and it was Guy's home, but he never used the front entrance. He headed up a narrow alley to the back of the house.

Guy now met up with the crowds of factory workers heading into the tall, dark manufacturing units. They were the men and women of the daytime shift starting at eight. They were replacing the night shift who had been working since eight the evening before. The night workers were recognisable by the weariness of their walk and the dark shadows under their eyes, but the day workers did not look any healthier, even though they had had a full night's sleep. Factory work was hard and unchanging, but it was the engine behind the empire-wide sales of fashion coming out of Old Mill Lane.

Guy wound his way swiftly between the workers, making his way to a fire exit door onto the back stairs. Racing up the narrow, dark steps, he noticed the doors were open into the main house, and on the lower floors he saw the cleaners in action. He tiptoed through the third and fourth floors where the models would still be sleeping, and at last he arrived in the bright attic workshops, perfect natural light being deemed essential to fine fashion.

The attics of the main house were where the true craftsmen worked. Embroiderers, finishers and designers had been working through the night. Now they were calling for fresh coffee and breakfast rolls. Guy smiled. He let himself through the small cupboard door to a vertical ladder to the highest loft in the house.

This was where he had been born. This is where he had lived his entire life. Guy was an unregistered Domeside orphan living in the attics of the fashion house, House Jewel, on Old Mill Lane. And he was not the only one. In House Jewel alone, he counted forty-three half-brothers and sisters. Whether he was really related to any of these children, he could not know. They were, however, the closest thing to family he had. They all shared one giant attic fitted with a rudimentary communal bathroom, but only thirty bunks. So a variety of cushions and mattresses were also strewn across the floor. Most of these children would end up working in the factory across the back alley, but not all of them. Old Mill Lane offered some opportunities for them as designers, artists, models, but for Guy there was only one future: the black and gold uniform of the Dome Elite.

Guy crept up into the attic. Since it was early he expected to find the children sleeping, and instead he found pandemonium.

"Sara, what's happening?"

"Well, all the kids have to go to the cathedral, but they've decided to do a press thing so we have to wear the new coats, and there are ten photographers outside."

Guy nodded. The orphans of Old Mill Lane were famous for their beautiful coats and the neat lines they formed to and from school headed up by an exquisite model or handsome designer. Though excited, the children were well-drilled. Soon they marched down the main stairs. Some were singing.

"Sara?" Guy queried. He hardly ever trod the plush carpets of the main house.

"It's all right. We have permission. We get to see the new salon, too."

Guy peered down at the new designer salon. It was a minimalist black and white combination with one perfect black goran fur before a white geometric fireplace.

"Where's the fireplace?" Guy asked. The main salon in House Jewel dated back three hundred years. It had been famous for a huge antique fireplace.

"They moved it."

"They moved the fireplace?"

"Yes, the design team said it had to go, so they moved it to the Pink Salon on the second floor. But that new chimney is causing problems. Marline told me the fireplace was smoking last night. Let's hope they fix it."

From below, a designer called out.

"Guy, if you're going out the front door, you need to wear a coat. If not, we'll throw you to the borgs."

Guy shook his head. He snapped his running blades to his feet.

"No thanks. I'll take the back stairs. It will be quicker anyhow. I have to be somewhere. I'm going to the cathedral later."

"How much later?" Sara was incredulous. "Guy, you can't be late! They will definitely throw you to the borgs!"

She was speaking to thin air. With his blades on his feet, Guy was already speeding down the back stairs and away.

Guy Erma left House Jewel and made his way across the Dome to the bistro. If House Jewel was the beating heart of Freyne's legendary tailoring industry, the bistro in the Dome was its showcase. The walls displayed the latest fashions. The waiting staff were young models. Established 'faces' within the fashion business would often be found lingering over coffee and chatting with customers and fans.

He was crossing the square when the Battle Borgs charged out from the military gym. All around, Guy heard quickly-quietened shouts and a few squeals. Women hastily drew scarves over their heads, or grabbed their infants to them, concealing young faces against their bodies. Children leapt back as they approached. Boys sprinted away to hide behind street furniture or alongside other Dome Elite.

The Battle Borgs of the Freyne Dome were cyborgs, half-human, half-robot, but they were old. Some might have a head of hair like a wig stuck to a robotic face. Others had no hair, but had faces where the skin was mottled grey and black, with large cracks revealing the robotic mechanisms below. They had been so frequently modified, so extensively improved, that they retained very little of their humanity. The Battle Borgs were known to be unpredictable, especially around women and children. Often it was deemed to be affection gone wrong when they killed an infant or molested a girl. Whatever the cause, the authorities never accepted any fault in these terrible warrior robots. It was up to civilians to take the necessary precautions and avoid their attentions.

Guy did not want to run, he crouched down into a ball and covered his face with his hands. "Throw him to the borgs!" It was a frequent threat made by his blades instructors to slow or inattentive students. Guy had always thought it was a joke, although he had also heard dark rumours about boys being thrown into fighting cages, given blunt blades to fight against hardened Battle Borgs for their very lives.

Fanning his fingers, Guy peered out as the last of the borgs passed. He steeled himself to look directly at their fearsome faces. He forced himself to assess the strength of their metal hips and shoulders. What moves would he use if he had to fight a borg? Would he be one of the few who allegedly fought and survived?

As the Battle Borgs moved on, the square returned to normal. A sigh of relief passed over the crowd. Guy straightened up, shook back his hair and headed into Bistro Jewel. The place was extremely crowded, he thought, and not with the usual crowd. These were off-planets visitors, strangers come from afar for Magnolia Weekend. He passed close to a table of Zaracans loudly ordering a frisebury breakfast.

"Valvanski…" Guy hissed under his breath. One of the aliens glanced up at him. Guy glared back, concentrating on thinking up crude images and hoping they might use their powers to see them. *Serves her right,* he thought, seeing the startled look on the visitor's face. *Telepathic weirdo.*

A few minutes later, Guy found them. Lloulou and Marline were sitting together in a corner booth, one of the private ones with curtains, drawn back just now. Lloulou was beautiful as always, even this early, and with hardly any make-up. For over ten years, her slim, tall elegance, her dark geometric cut, her pale skin and eyes so brown they were black, had made her the undisputed face of House Jewel. She offered him a cheek as he arrived, and he kissed her gently.

"Mother," he whispered.

"Sssh!" she replied nervously. Nevertheless, she patted the chair next to her.

Guy shrugged.

"Hi, Guy!"

Guy smiled at Marline. She had grown up as Guy had in the attics of Old Mill Lane. Like him, she did not have a father and could only guess at her mother, but she had the jet black curls, bright blue eyes and smooth cream skin characteristic of the all-important Domeside look. So no longer did she sleep on lumpy, overcrowded bunk beds. She was one of the lucky ones. She had been offered a chance to escape a future in the dismal clothes factories. At just fourteen, she was the youngest and newest House Jewel model and Guy could not believe the transformation. He reached over to kiss her on the cheek, but she turned, and with more enthusiasm than he expected, she kissed him on the lips.

Guy pulled back and frowned. Then a moment later, he said:

"Did you see the Valvanski? When I passed their tables I made sure I was thinking of my bum, you know, just in case they were reading my mind."

"Oh Guy, you shouldn't. Lloulou says we must always think of our favourite dress when we see a Valvanski. The little princess was shopping on Old Mill Lane yesterday, but she didn't come into House Jewel." Marline sighed: "Apparently her father gives her whatever she wants."

"Marline," warned Lloulou.

"I know. I know. We're not supposed to talk about clients, but it's only Guy!" She held up her finger and thumb pressed together tight in a mime that meant 'keep your mouth shut!' He held up his own hand, index and thumb pressed together, and nodded to both Lloulou and Marline. This time the finger mime meant 'I can keep a secret.' Both girls smiled. Lloulou looked relieved.

"You're late," Lloulou scolded him, but she was smiling as she said it.

"I had blades training. It's for my exams. I want to join the Dome Elite."

"You mean you want me to ask Chartsie to let you in the Dome Elite."

"Please Lloulou, I will run all your errands for a year."

"Not if you're in the Elite you won't!" Lloulou smiled at him.

"You'll be on Sas Darona living with the tribes, fighting Valvanski..." Marline hissed with mock terror. Guy just smiled. He certainly hoped to see the tribes of Sas Darona for himself one day.

"Marline, Guy's too young for that." She paused. "Oh, here he comes."

Sure enough, Guy had turned to see Chart Segat arrive with the press in tow. He was the Administrator of the Dome and Mayor of Domeside. He had once been a military commander, but in recent years had gained a lot of bulk. Guy knew he was reasonably fit. He still trained every morning with his Elite. With his thick black hair worn in shaggy curls around his wide, plump jowls, he was the face of Domeside, the leader of the Dome Elite. Guy noticed how he had stopped alongside a banner that read:

The Dome Debate

YES

Five More Years

He stood and pointed, grinned and postured, groaned and laughed, all the time the photographers and their flying droids were taking pictures. Finally, with what seemed like an almost comic about face, Chart Segat noticed Lloulou. He shambled across the café towards her. The sheer size of the man made his progress through the crowded café a series of collisions and squeezes.

Chart Segat laughed this off with his usual loud bonhomie and self-ridiculing charm. Journalists loved him, and kept sending in small camera droids to capture his every grin and grimace. When Chart kissed Lloulou, it was a photo frenzy. With the shouted encouragement of the newsmen, Chart kissed Lloulou three times. Lloulou, Guy noticed, did not seem to mind and then the Dome Elite closed in. Chart Segat laughed to see one journalist struggling to get a last photo, while being blocked by a Dome guard twice his size.

"The only story this weekend is the Dome Debate."

He roared at the young man: "Five more years! Five more years of investment and progress. I don't care what Regent Sayginn says. Investment. That's what the Dome needs."

It was only after the photographers had their shots that Chart Segat stepped up to the table. He took great care closing the curtains and batting any last camera droids away. Finally, the guards, the press, and everyone else was outside. Just Guy, Marline and Lloulou were all alone with Chart Segat. A tray overflowing with fresh food and drinks arrived.

"Give us a hot cup, Lloulou darling. I'm parched. I really am."

Lloulou gave a small smile, picked up the pot to pour and said archly:

"Chart, I need to talk to you."

Chart Segat gave a theatrical groan: "Please!"

Lloulou handed him a full cup with a smile. Chart Segat first sipped, then gulped the hot drink.

"So, Lloulou talk about what?"

"This is Guy Erma, Chart. I told you about him."

Guy looked gratefully at Lloulou. So she had already spoken to Chart Segat. This was more than he had expected. However, the reply was also unexpected:

"Funny to think he is the only one," said Chart Segat. Guy saw a strange look on Chart Segat's face, and wondered what he was talking about. "We can't throw this one to the borgs," he added with a laugh.

Lloulou continued: "He wishes to join the Dome Elite."

Chart Segat let out a sharp laugh: "Have you not got a place for him at House Jewel?"

"Chart, well of course, we're all working this weekend." Guy sighed. Why did Lloulou have to say that? She knew he hated all the fuss around the clothes, the sheer boredom of the modelling. No wonder the only thing Marline ever talked about was the money.

"I'm not interested in fashion," Guy said firmly. "I want to join the Dome Elite."

Chart Segat cackled in a way that was anything but a laugh.

Lloulou silenced Guy with a look and the index to thumb mime, and continued:

"Chartsie, House Jewel would love to have Guy Erma, of course we would. But you need him more... He won the Dome blades competition, and he's good at maths. He is perfect for the Dome Elite."

"I'd like to help, but you know I can't influence Elite admissions. Not this year, not with the Dome Debate. It's exactly the kind of thing Sayginn is looking out for, you know that."

The man reached for a breakfast roll. With his eyes, he had dismissed Guy and was already thinking of other things.

Asking Chart Segat was my last hope, Guy thought with dismay. He tried to hide his disappointment. Chart Segat was looking at him once more. With a sly smile, he continued:

"Anyway, with those looks..." He winked at Guy. "He has the look of Erederon, don't you think, Lloulou?"

"Hush, Chartsie!"

"Either way, he should make a good living."

Guy was angry. Why did grown-ups always assume he would become a model? As for Erederon, that was the name of the Great Emperor Erederon Roderick Marcus Andreus, ERMA for short. It was said that the great Emperor had been brought up in Domeside by a milliner and his wife. In his childhood he had modelled some clothes. This was before the hundred year war killed all the direct heirs, and put him, the last surviving bastard, on the throne of Freyne. It was in his honour that all bastard boys in Domeside were called ERMA.

It was Erederon's looks: dark curls, pale skin, bright eyes, that were deemed the Domeside ideal. The children on Domeside were brought up with the fairy tale that they would start life as models and end up as princes, when in reality most would end up on the twelve-hour shifts making clothes and living in the dark alleys of old Domeside. Only a handful like Marline might be chosen for the catwalk. And yes, like Marline, Guy had the Domeside look. As children growing up Guy and Marline had been as alike as twins, but Guy Erma could not stomach the idea of a life wearing skin-tight trousers and smiling on cue. Angry now, he repeated:

"But I'm good at maths, as well as blades. I want to join the Dome Elite."

Chart Segat looked put out, he said to Lloulou, "He has pride, this one." Then, sneering at Guy: "Too good to be a fashion model, hey?"

"Chart, no. Guy's a champion at blades."

Chart Segat just snorted in derision.

"Good at blades, did you say? How good?"

"He won the Domeside-wide competition," Lloulou repeated. "He was going to beat Prince Teodor."

"That was you, was it? And you're not registered are you? No mother, no father?" Guy looked quickly at Lloulou. She shook her head. He looked at Chart Segat. He, too, was looking at Lloulou. They both know, he thought. Both Lloulou and Chart Segat know who his mother was, so why were they persisting with this 'no mother, no father' line? Guy had thought that at last Lloulou might claim him, and that might just be enough.

The irony was, if he had been born to a factory worker, his birth would have been registered, and in all likelihood his place in the Dome Elite Junior would have been guaranteed. Instead, Guy was the son of a fashion model, his father unknown, his birth unregistered. This put the Dome Elite beyond his grasp and left him only a small number of career choices. Unless he could convince Chart Segat to make an exception. He had helped other boys get into the Dome Elite, Guy knew that. He looked straight at Chart Segat. The man nodded and reached to stoke his cheek:

"Guy Erma, Domeside unregistered orphan, I might have a job for you after all." He smiled enigmatically and reached into his pocket to pull out a huge roll of money. He peeled off a large number of notes and gave them to Lloulou, who checked them with a glance and relaxed a fraction.

"Have you got everything you need?" Chart asked quickly. Lloulou nodded, and they kissed once more.

"As for you…"

Guy had never seen so much money before in his life. He looked up, startled. Too late – Chart Segat had seen him staring.

"Ah-ha! This interests you, don't it?" He rocked the hand with the money-roll, before hiding it away. Chart Segat just smiled: "I thought so. I have something in mind for you. Do as you're told and it's the Dome Elite and no questions asked."

Guy sat up a little straighter: "My blades are sharp, and yours to command, sir."

Chart Segat patted Guy on the head: "Just you remember. Be good, or else I'll throw you to my borgs." Then he paused, as if remembering: "No, actually, I won't throw you to the borgs."

Guy started to laugh. Of course, they would not throw him to the borgs, it was a Domeside joke. Wasn't it? He stopped when he saw Lloulou was not laughing. Nor was Chart Segat, but as he left Chart Segat patted him on the head:

"You're a good boy, Guy Erma."

Guy stood a moment stunned. Was that it? Had he done it? Was he in the Dome Elite? He turned to see Lloulou. She gave no clue as to what she was thinking. Was she smiling, or was she sad? He could not tell. He nodded once at her. It was a thank you of sorts.

"I have to go. They are expecting me at the cathedral..."

Chapter 3. A Roar of Fire and Light

So finally, it comes to it... Teodor thought. I have been dreading this all week. Now there is no turning back.

He paused to look up at St Joseph's Cathedral, said to be the beating heart of the Dome. At the top of the entrance stairs, there was a massive door where a bishop and head teacher waited for him.

A good sign, Teodor told himself. There was no cathedral in my nightmare. Tunnels yes, cathedral no.

Pull yourself together. You only have to sing.

All at once, he remembered the alternative. Oh, why had his mother cancelled the blades fight? How would it feel to be making his way to fight in the Dome Elite gyms?

Would he be afraid if he had a blade in each hand?

***

Waiting, always waiting, Guy thought impatiently, how long did it take for a prince to get dressed?

All the other kids had their costumes on – admittedly they had arrived in the cathedral over an hour before the prince – but there was a buzz of excitement that the teachers were finding hard to contain. Guy was not in the choir of Domeside children. Guy was the prince's understudy and stand-in. Over the past month he had taken part in a dozen singing rehearsals where the prince himself had not been present. He had enjoyed being the stand-in prince. He had even enjoyed the singing, well, maybe not exactly singing, but certainly the praise and attention he had received from being centre stage.

Supposedly all this made up for not having to fight the prince at blades. But it didn't really. Guy only had to close his eyes to feel the weight of his fighting blades in the palms of his hands and imagine stepping up across a fighting mat from the prince. Still, it was not to be now.

As an understudy, he did not have his own costume. In fact, his only role today was 'to be introduced'. Guy was due to meet Prince Teodor before handing over the role to him. This was considered a great honour. Only, right now he had been waiting twenty minutes for this so-called 'great honour'.

If only they would let me fight the prince. Yes! That would be great. Meet him with a blade in each hand.

Guy kicked the skirting board.

***

Inside, the cathedral was vast and beautiful, Teodor reflected. He was glad they had built the Dome around this sacred place. It was said to have been a church for over three thousand years. As with all truly ancient cathedrals the altar was shielded from popular view by a large single tapestry curtain. On Sunday, the curtain would be drawn. The population would lean in to glimpse the priests and their rituals and instead they would see Prince Teodor leading a choir of Domeside children.

"It will be spectacular," the art director had assured Teodor's mother. "It will also be emotional. You will see. They will call it genius."

Teodor was unconvinced.

It was a trick which involved drawing a curtain, a vast curtain for sure, but still a curtain. Nevertheless, the artistic team had their way. What had started as a small performance of a children's choir had grown into a no expense spared production, complete with lights, special effects, abstract art installation as a set, costumes created by a top designer from Old Mill Lane and high-definition surround sound.

Just a trick involving the curtain, let's just get this show over and done with.

Peeking through the half-open door, Guy saw that the prince was wearing the angel costume now, sandals, tunic and shorts. The designers had said it was supposed to look like a blades fighting outfit, but Guy could not see it. Also, Guy would have liked to have seen some evidence of the so-called injury that had precluded the prince from entering the blades' fight. He expected to see a bandage on one of his knees at the very least. The prince's legs were bare. He was wearing stupid looking lace-up sandals. Complicated to put on – flimsy too – and were they painted with real gold? There was no sign of a bandage, none at all. Maybe the prince was chicken after all. Guy kicked the skirting board again.

I am going to be late for Maths.

***

The costume does not help, Teodor thought. Bad enough that he had to stand up and sing in public, but that they also decked him out in gold shorts and shimmering chiffon. No wonder he was having nightmares!

It was years since Teodor had given up trying to have a say on his clothes. He was forever told how hundreds if not thousands of jobs depended on his wearing Old Mill Lane Fashion. He had to live his life as a walking-talking advert for the craftsmen and women of Domeside. He sighed inwardly and tried not to give the clothes a second glance.

Oh no. Now the press had arrived for the inevitable photos. He forced himself to smile and pose. When would this be over?

***

Guy saw one of the teachers look sharply in his direction. Guy put his foot down where he was going to kick the wall again, and focused instead on the neat pile of clothes on a nearby chair. Guy found himself looking at the labels. The prince had been wearing a handmade designer shirt and suit by the looks of it, the very best Old Mill Lane had to offer. His shoes were handmade too. As Guy peered down, he saw the prince's name carefully painted inside the heel; he felt a little sick. He could not imagine spending so much money on shoes, yet it looked like he and the prince might be the same size. He moved his own boot-clad foot a little closer.

Yes, he and the prince wore the same shoe size. What must it be like to wear shoes like that?

He peeped through the door again. Photos, they were taking photos. Guy looked at the time and made a decision. Calmly he bent down, picked up the shoes, put them in his bag and started walking towards the exit. The choir master called to him.

"Guy, Guy boy…"

Guy froze. Had he been caught?

"Guy, we want to do the solo one more time, just while we wait?"

"Sir, I've got double maths."

"C'mon Guy, be a good lad. All the kids…"

It was true, the crowd of costumed children was becoming ever more boisterous, with hysterical laughter breaking out here and there.

"Always singing," muttered Guy. "I thought the first time I met Prince Teodor I would have a blade in each hand."

"Life's not fair. Hey? Still, we've not thrown you to the borgs, not yet, anyhow." Guy looked up and saw his teacher laughing. "C'mon, just one last time, then you can go."

As Guy took his place centre-stage looking out over the innumerable rows of empty seating, he knew he should have felt elated. Instead disappointment overwhelmed him.

Life, his life, was just plain unfair.

***

Teodor stood to one side of the altar watching his understudy sing. The boy has a pretty good voice, Teodor thought, a little shaky on the top notes. This boy had been playing his part during all the previous rehearsals. Teodor hoped he would have a chance to compare notes, because while he knew his songs, he was not sure on the moves or the cues.

"Thanks Guy," the choir master said, "that was great."

As soon as the music stopped, Teodor watched astonished as Guy started moving. The boy was fast. He had grabbed his bag, and his coat, snapped his running blades to his feet and bounded off. He skirted round where he knew the choir master would be. He paused a moment. Teodor saw him looking directly at him, neither fear nor reverence in his eyes, from the far side of the altar. Teodor had been that close to meeting him. The prince watched the boy hesitate, check the time once more and run.

"Guy…" the choir master called.

Too slow, thought Teodor. That one moves like the wind. The Domeside boy was already at the door, there he paused and shouted: "Double maths!"

"Guy, don't you want to meet…" the choir master shouted.

You're wasting your breath, thought Teodor, indeed the boy was already headed out the door at a trot.

"…the prince?" The choir master finished apologetically and shrugged.

"Double maths," repeated Teodor. "Impressive, now I do want to meet him. What was his name again?"

"Guy Erma, my prince. Everyone knows Guy Erma," the man added with a smile.

"Guy Erma? Really? Everyone knows Guy Erma?" Teodor repeated, "Tell him I was sorry not to meet him."

"I will, my prince. Are we all set?" Then he was distracted: "What is it?"

One of the men, who had been smirking a few minutes before, was now standing and blocking the altar.

"The prince's communicator is interfering with the sound system. He has nice kit but the equipment here is not that sophisticated, and well…"

The man was speaking very fast, and if Teodor did not understand the detail, it was clear by the way he pointed and gestured, what he meant. Teodor unclipped his communicator, and paused to glance round.

There were two cyborgs he could almost touch, on this side of the altar. Another two were patrolling with cy-wolves inside the curtain. There was his bodyguard sitting just three metres away in the audience. The communicator did look strange with his costume. He went and placed it with his clothes.

Funny, my shoes are missing. Tsk. I do not have time to look for them now.

***

Guy laughed, delighted to be free. He bounded down the stairs to the square. In front of the cathedral the market was in full swing. Guy ran between the stalls where he could more easily disappear, all the while taking in the bustle, colours and movement of the early morning trading.

The market was different today. After all, it was Magnolia Friday, the first day of Magnolia Weekend. The bakers were displaying special magnolia cakes, the florists hung bouquets of fresh magnolia blooms, and the veg stalls great bowls of the season's friseburys, red, plump, and shining with juice. Guy felt a thrill just to see them. Friseburys meant it was the end of winter. Everyone loved Magnolia weekend.

"Hey, Guy boy. Over here Guy!"

***

"Prince Teodor, this way. Here my prince!"

Irritated, Teodor walked back. He glanced down the tight spiral stair to the catacombs and glimpsed a Regency Defence Guard and cy-wolf hiding just out of sight. He took his place at the centre of the altar. Ignoring both the cheeky wink of one of the girls and an older boy cuffing a youngster, Teodor paused to take in the vast space of the cathedral.

Why does my bodyguard suddenly seem so far away? Where is the Regency Defence? Where were his cy-wolves? Teodor moved uncomfortably, he was well aware that the Regency Defence, in their designer red and silver uniform, was not a fighting force like the Dome Elite. It was a small security troop which had been selected for their loyalty and family connections. No, the real muscle today was the giant cy-wolves, the largest and strongest of their kind taken from the wild, and fitted with cyborg brains that made them easy to control, and metal fangs and teeth that made them impossible to withstand. Teodor wished for a moment that he had a cy-wolf at his side. Of course, they would never allow it, cy-wolves were dangerous. He sighed:

Oh, I wish this was over.

He nodded to the pianist, counted out his introduction in his head and started to sing.

The sound was perfect: just his voice and a piano ringing out across the cathedral. Teodor stepped forward one step, moving with the song, then remembered to keep his place. He rocked back. His sandal caught on the trap door. What was under there? He wondered. Where were the children? He took a moment to glance over his shoulder. The choir was still not moving. Unless he was mistaken the older boys were holding back the youngsters, but why? Teodor turned quickly back and led the chorus.

***

Guy stopped as he heard his name called a third time and turned back to see a small plump market stall-holder. The man was running after him. He had only run a few steps, but he was flushed and out of breath. Guy knew what he wanted. Delighted, he ran back.

"Juke! Hi Jukona!"

"You are still ready to help me tomorrow? At the Magnolia Stakes. I'll pay you."

"Yes, yes of course." It was the highlight of the weekend for Guy, to see the greatest racing gorans of the empire running in the Magnolia Stakes.

"Ok. Now, you have to be ready at five. Five, do you hear me?"

***

Five, Six, Seven, Eight. Teodor took a last breath as he counted the intro in his head. At least this was the third verse. It was nearly over…

The main lights went out, and in the gloom, Teodor heard a young boy gasp. The curtain fell closed in a rush of wind, and another child shouted. The main spotlights went out, all at once Teodor could not see. He heard a little girl start to cry. In the gloom, Teodor saw the curtain rocking on its hooks.

Where was his bodyguard?

An explosion at his feet engulfed him in smoke and light, and sent him tumbling onto his backside.

Where were his cy-wolves?

The flash had left him blinded. Dazed and disorientated, he tried to stand. Shots rang out above his head. He crouched down low, in a running position. He looked round for a chance to escape.

Who were his bodyguards shooting?

The barrage of fire continued. There was a huge crash and the altar shook.

***

If Juke was still talking, Guy was no longer listening. He had heard something. A shout! He looked towards the cathedral. A shot? Now the entire market was falling silent. Automatic gunfire. Traders and customers turned. Screams, children's screams. Guy looked at Juke and then looked at the cathedral.

"I'd better go back," Guy said.

A great creaking crash sent birds flying round the square, and a cloud of wind and dust billowed out from the cathedral doors.

***

Teodor realised the giant curtain had fallen from its hooks to the ground. The resulting wind dispelled the smoke. He looked around, seeking safety. Instead, he saw men in black uniforms leaping towards him. Only they were not men; they were not even cyborgs. Teodor's attackers were the Battle Borgs of the Dome Elite.

59

Teodor raised his leg to kick the first borg's arm as he reached to grab him. Even in the gloom, he saw in horror that this Battle Borg's skin was fully grey. A deep black crack ran from the base of his thumb up his arm, gaping wide at the wrist to show dead rotten flesh and beneath, his robotic core. Then another black mottled face was looming down on him. Teodor slapped the face in a spinning blades turn, grimly satisfied to feel the paper-like cheek rip under the palm of his hand. The third Battle Borg, however, just grabbed him by the waist and threw him over his shoulder. The stench of drying and decaying flesh filled Teodor's nostrils. There was a jolt as Teodor realised they had carried him in a jump down through the trap door. They were taking him.

***

Guy started to move past Juke, only to find the trader had caught him by the elbow, and held him tight.

The bang of the explosion echoed round the square.

"No, Guy, no. Don't go there."

"But…" The bang was echoing around inside his head.

"No Guy. There's nothing you can do."

***

"I am your prince, let me go!" cried Teodor.

He kicked and beat his captor with his hands and feet. The Battle Borg paused, threw him to the wall, letting him fall to the ground. There, the borg kicked Teodor in the legs and belly, and slapped him hard around the head. Teodor could do nothing but cower; he tried again.

"In the name of the King, I command you…"

They pressed a cloth over Teodor's face. Dazed, breathless and with blood in his mouth, Teodor recognised the smell and desperately tried not to breathe. So they slapped him again, and he gasped.

"I am Prince Teodor…"

The fumes immediately overwhelmed his senses. When the borg threw him over his shoulder once again, Teodor was limp. He could not move, could not hear, could not smell, but he could see and he could feel, and he knew they were running.

***

Guy and Juke watched them running. Dome Elite, soldiers, some stall holders, all running across the square towards the cathedral. In the distance sirens were sounding. Guy still hesitated.

"The kids," he said at last, he meant his half-brothers and sisters of House Jewel.

Juke held his arm in a vice-like grip:

"Go to school, Guy. Go to school. There's nothing you can do here."

Book 2.
Day 1. Midday.

Interlude. Diplomatic Exchange

From: Ambassador Nikato Valvanchi II, Freyne 2
To: Captain Karl Valvanchi, Sas Darona

My dear Karl,

Just dropping you a line, I am experiencing a few difficulties organising a display of tribal dancing for an important forthcoming event here on Freyne 2. Any intervention on your part would be much appreciated.

Your dear brother,

Nikki

From: Captain Karl Valvanchi, Sas Darona
To: Ambassador Nikato Valvanchi II, Freyne 2

Dear Nikki,

No can do. Sas Darona is in lock down following Mezzatorra.

Sincerely,

Karl

From: Ambassador Nikato Valvanchi II, Freyne 2
To: Captain Karl Valvanchi, Sas Darona

My dear Karl, my dearest boy,

I do not think I explained myself fully in my last communiqué. I am organising what you might call an elegant evening at the Embassy as part of the Freyne Festival of Fashion and Sport, often referred to as: Magnolia Weekend.

Unwisely, you may think, we settled on a Sas Darona theme many months ago, and we had already put in place all the necessary arrangements to have some speciality foods – Sas Darona Sand Lizards no less – and displays of tribal dancing.

The council has decreed: It would preferable if the Dome was closed, as a precursor to Dome Elite activity being ended on Sas Darona. This entertainment is an important part of our plan to influence the Freyne. Regent Sayginn has promised to attend, even the Emperor himself ...

From: Captain Karl Valvanchi, Sas Darona
To: Ambassador Nikato Valvanchi II, Freyne 2

Dear Nikki,

Please do not 'my dear brother' me. You and I were never that close. You know that as well as I do.

As for your entertainment, are you suggesting we break quarantine just so your guests can eat chilli lizards? Perhaps, for a truly authentic Sas Darona experience, we should send you a nest of cy-sects as well? How about Sas Darona plague as a life or death experience? Would your guests find that amusing, I wonder?

Of course, I agree: The Dome must close. However, under the circumstances, I recommend you make alternative plans.

Cordially, Karl

From: Ambassador Nikato Valvanchi II, Freyne 2
To: Captain Karl Valvanchi, Sas Darona
Cc: Ex-Ambassador Nikato Valvanchi I, Zarac 1

Dear Karl,

I don't know what you are suggesting. Sas Darona plague on Freyne 2? All I am asking for is a consignment of Sand Lizards.

Are you threatening me?

Nikki

From: Ex-Ambassador Nikato Valvanchi I, Zarac 1
To: Captain Karl Valvanchi, Sas Darona

Karl,

Your brother copied me your last communications. I am appalled that you threatened him with plague and certain death. Your brother, as you well know, is doing a good job in difficult circumstances.

As your father and head of the Valvanchi house, I command you to do everything in your power to help him.

It is a Council Decree: The Dome must close.

I have written to your commanding officer and made it abundantly clear. Your brother's requests are supported at the highest levels from within the Zaracan Council.

Your family expects,

Your father.

From: Captain Karl Valvanchi, Sas Darona

To: Ambassador Nikato Valvanchi II, Freyne 2

Dear Nikki,

The Dome must close.

I am on my way, together with the tribal dancers and sand lizards. We expect to arrive Friday. Please make all necessary arrangements.

Karl

Chapter 4. The Valvanchi Diplomatic Corps

Karl Valvanchi had taken a simple personnel carrier to travel from Sas Darona. From its cockpit he admired the simple elegance of the spaceport, which looked like a vast space snowflake. Six broad tunnels made the spokes of the snowflake and lead to a central transit hub, from where shuttles sped down to the surface. Along each of the six branches ships were parked, nose first, clustered by size, class and origin. But as Karl approached the spaceport high in orbit above Freyne 2, he started to wish he had chosen a different craft.

Of course, Nikato would have lent him the family yacht, if Karl had allowed it. The yacht, at least, would have been ostentatious enough to stand out among the array of visiting dignitaries and celebrities. Freyne 2's Magnolia Weekend was a must-see festival among some of the United Races Elites who liked the fact that money alone could not buy you access to some events, you had to be famous, you had to have influence not just across known space, but even as far as this primitive back water. And if you were not 'known on Freyne 2', then 'how splendid' to be 'totally anonymous' for two days, while all the time spending vast sums of money on fashion and entertainment in the hope of being noticed.

Not that Karl was interested in impressing the United Races jet set. He was born Valvanchi. In a nutshell, he had nothing more to prove. No family in all the United Races had more influence, no individual had more access to such seemingly unlimited finds. And yet Karl had also turned down this birthright when he had joined the Zaracan Space Rangers. Not for Karl, the life of a gilded prince working his way from one prestigious diplomatic posting to the next. Neither had he wished to join the financial units with their vast fortunes, he had no interest in the mysterious blacks arts they used to grow this wealth.

No, it was when he saw the rank of parked Dome Elite carriers, that Karl wished he had a more impressive craft. His small military ship with its proud Zaracan colours and Valvanchi flag of white and turquoise seemed to shrink to insignificance as it passed under the bows of the great black Dome Elite troop carriers. The Dome insignia, the outline of the geodesic dome, thirty-three triangles joined into great flower-like hexagons, was emblazed in gold on their prows.

"Room for eight ships," he said aloud to the captain as he stood on the flight deck watching their approach. "Probable capacity eight fifty to one thousand men… and another four empty bays over there…" he pointed. The captain nodded, but was not really listening.

"My guess is those four, or maybe just three, have been trapped on Sas Darona by the lock-down."

"How many men do you think the Dome Elite have in training on Sas Darona?"

"I had thought just under a thousand, but now I wonder." They were passing a huge cargo ship, again painted in Dome Elite colours: "That's one of their supply ships, so you have to wonder."

"Maybe the Dome Elite have bases elsewhere in the Freyne Empire?" The captain said mildly.

"No, the Emperor forbade it. In theory, the Dome Elite is a training scheme for the poor boys of the city. It was supposed to prepare them for the regular army. Only the Emperor reneged on that promise as well. Those boys that do transfer to the normal Imperial Army find they are little more than servants to the main troops and deprived of any form of advancement – however skilled they are."

"So King Serge got himself his own personal army."

"So King Serge got himself his own army, and all at once he was a real threat, a true power. So they killed him."

"Who?" the captain asked, curiously.

"Who knows? There's a very short list of possible suspects… However, they did not count on Chart Segat. He has kept the Dome Elite running in Serge's absence. Oh they cut his funding, so in turn Chart Segat set to whole-scale mining of monazite on Sas Darona. To do so he needed the co-operation of the tribes. Those tribes who were most eager to help were those with a grudge against us. So we got ourselves a war to manage on Sas Darona, and the Dome Elite goes from strength to strength."

"They say he will be voted out at the Dome Debate."

"Yes, let's hope so. Regent Sayginn should retake control as her husband did before her."

"What difference will it make?" the captain asked.

"Well…" Karl smiled as he thought about it. "The big difference is that the Regent has signed a whole host of treaties with the United Races. She has to curb and clamp down on the illegal activities. And if she does not know about them, well, Nikki and I have a list."

The Captain laughed. Karl watched as he smoothly pulled the ship into its docking bay.

"No-one to meet us?" Karl asked, looking out a side window into the empty reception lounge.

"We haven't got all of our paperwork yet, so we stay on board until it arrives…" The captain said, all businesslike. Karl ignored him.

"There's nobody out there."

"It's still safer to stay on board, sir."

"I'll let the boys off. We've all been cooped up for too long."

"Yes, but…"

Their ship had been allowed to dock on an isolated gangway, distant from most other ships, and now Karl walked out into a utilitarian reception lounge. There was little to see, just a row of folding seats, a pile of forgotten crates, a drinks machine and a bin. The lounge being on the outer edge of the station, the gravity was a little heavier than Karl expected. He walked stiffly over to the large window and looked down onto the planet below.

The Sas Darona dancers had quickly followed him off the shuttle. Out of the confined space, they sprang into life, turning somersaults and spinning. Distracted by their youthful athleticism, Karl did not notice the heavy tread of boots until they were just beyond the door. As they came through the door, the eight Sas Darona tribesmen drew themselves into a line along the far wall. Karl sensed they were both in awe and in fear of the Dome Elite. For his part,

Karl was just curious. This was the Dome Elite on their home turf, so to speak. He was impressed by the pristine cut of their uniforms, the shine of the gold and yellow trims and details, the smooth faces, clean hands and polished boots. They were men of whom any commander would be proud.

He heard a low whistle and saw his ship's captain urging him to return on-board. It was too late for that; the Dome Elite had already seen him. Their commander called to his lieutenant for a checklist, having glanced at the crate of Sand Lizards and then at the tribesmen. Unexpectedly, he strode across the space, lifted the chin of one of the tribesmen and stared into his face. The tribesman blinked just once in acknowledgement, and quickly now, the Dome Elite commander turned on the spot and walked back.

He knows him, Karl thought. But I thought these dancers were from friendly tribes. He caught himself glancing at the eight slim youths at his side; had his careful checks been in vain?

"Fine looking warriors," the Dome Elite man said.

Maybe it was not the tribesmen who were at fault. Maybe this man had himself been on Sas Darona? Now the Dome Elite Commander was looking at Karl. He made a play of checking the paperwork twice before looking again at Karl.

"And you are?"

"My name is Captain Karl Valvanchi."

The Dome Elite commander paused; clearly, the name was known to him. Karl could see the flutter amidst his men. He was quietly pleased his name alone had drawn their attention.

"May I ask your name?"

"I don't have to tell you. But you may call me Commander Tilson." Tilson tapped the clipboard in his hand. "We have no details of passengers on the manifest, so what are you doing here?"

Karl wondered whether he had to reply, but in the end he decided he had little to hide:

"I am travelling to see my brother, Nikato Valvanchi. He is the Ambassador on Freyne 2."

"Well, in that case, we need identification papers, a visa, a letter of introduction and are you claiming diplomatic status?"

Karl half-shrugged, as he did not really know.

"Then you will also need a letter of invitation signed by Regent Sayginn – do you have that?"

Karl was momentarily distracted by how apprehensive the captain of his shuttle now looked. Had he known this would happen?

"I have my United Races identification card," Karl said mildly, with a smile. If he had meant it as a joke, he was taken aback by its reception. The Dome Elite Commander just barked back at him:

"That is not a valid identification on Freyne 2 or anywhere in the Freyne Empire."

"Of course not, it's only valid in all of known space, except for this backwater empire," Karl replied sharply. His brother Nikato had hypothesised that the Freyne liked to have their own identification procedures so they could keep close tabs on all visitors from outside the empire, but whatever the reason, Karl was annoyed now. Out of the corner of his eye he saw his Captain vigorously shaking his head in a warning.

The Dome Elite Commander smiled and said with some relish:

"Under our laws you are an illegal alien and I will therefore be taking you into custody."

Karl was speechless. Were the Dome Elite serious? Did they not realise who he was? He had not anticipated that this might be a possible outcome. That he should be a prisoner of the Dome Elite was unthinkable. Would they really go through with this charade?

"Let me just call my brother," Karl said quickly, aware that the Sas Darona tribal dancers were riveted by this exchange.

"Hold him!" ordered the Dome Elite Commander. In an instant, four Dome Elite soldiers had Karl immobilised. The commander reached to remove the communicator from Karl's forearm.

"I'll take that."

"I don't need that device to speak with my brother," Karl said fiercely.

"Well you can try of course," smirked the Dome Elite Commander: "But you'll find this lined with mixed alloys, to protect our equipment from unwanted telepathic interference."

"Commander," the captain protested. "Karl Valvanchi is a senior member of the Valvanchi family; if you continue like this you will face a serious diplomatic incident."

"Shut him up."

One of the larger Dome Elite soldiers stepped forward, blades in both hands. When he went to strike the Captain, he did not use the cutting edge but the blunt handle of his dagger, grasped within his fist. With one blow across his temples, the Captain was knocked unconscious to the ground.

"Strip search, I think."

Karl wrestled against his captors. He knew of many simple strategies to prevent his clothes from being removed, but before he could employ any of them, he saw the blades flash in their hands, and then with lightening moves they sliced the cloth from his body.

"Leave his shorts," called the Commander." I'm off to lunch after this, and I don't want to ruin my appetite."

Now Karl was spread-eagled against the vast window looking out over Freyne 2, wearing only his underpants and his boots. His clothes were sliced to ribbons around his feet, and he was bleeding from numerous small cuts where the soldiers had not been too careful with their razor sharp blades.

'Nikki, where are you?' Karl sent a desperate telepathic cry, even though in all likelihood, his brother would not hear him.

'I'm here, I'm here.'

On cue, Nikato Valvanchi, Prince of the House Valvanchi and Ambassador from the Zaracan Democratic Union to Freyne 2, with four guards and an admin assistant, crashed through the double doors. Running alongside her uncle wearing her house colours of turquoise and white was the thirteen-year-old Nell Valvanchi, now shape-shifted to her slim self, pale skinned, black-eyed and with a mane of turquoise and white hair tied in loose bunches down her back.

Nikato's assistant was panting but he quickly handed the necessary paperwork to the Dome Elite commander.

"Karl Valvanchi Identification, Karl Valvanchi Visa, Karl Valvanchi letter of introduction and a letter of invitation signed by Regent Sayginn herself."

Nikato drew himself up to his full height and shouted down at the Dome Elite Commander:

75

"You will release MY Brother, at once. And don't think the Regent won't hear of this."

The Dome Elite Commander seemed entirely unfazed. He took the paperwork and spent several long minutes checking every page. Finally, he nodded to his men.

"Lunch!" he said quietly. With a sharp salute, he and his troop disappeared as quickly as they had arrived.

Nell skipped across the space and took her uncle's hand, heedless of his near nudity. Karl bent to kiss her on the hair before turning angrily to Nikato:

"Nikki – how could you be late? How could you not have the correct paperwork?

"You gave me two days' notice. If you want to know, it's a miracle I have any of the paperwork – only because the Regent knows of you."

"The Regent knows me?"

"Yes, Regent Sayginn is very interested in Sas Darona."

"But look at me. You were late, and look at me. Look at him." He pointed to the captain who was being helped to his feet. Another ship member had brought Karl his luggage, and he was now rummaging for more clothes.

"Look, I'm sorry. What can I say? The traffic planet-side was awful."

"The traffic planet-side was awful," Karl repeated in utter disbelief. He had found a shirt and pulled it on.

"Uncle Karl, uncle Karl. It's not uncle Nikki's fault," interrupted Nell. "It's really not his fault. Really. The traffic was awful. You see, Prince Teodor has been kidnapped. There was an attack on the cathedral. There has been a security lock down. But they have taken him. He's gone."

Karl hesitated; he needed to take his boots off to put on his trousers.

"Prince Teodor, you mean the heir? The heir to Freyne 2?"

"And the heir to the empire," Nell said seriously.

"But how? Where is this cathedral? What was he doing there?"

"He was singing with a choir of Domeside children," Nell said earnestly. "His poorest subjects."

"And this cathedral?"

"St Joseph's Cathedral," Nikato replied. "They call it the beating heart of the Dome."

Chapter 5. The Emperor of all Freyne

The one-year-old goran cubs had had their white teeth stained black, and though already sharp, they had been further shaped into pointed fangs so that they exactly matched the black-varnished, pointed fingernails of Emperor Frederon.

It was not unusual for an Emperor or prince of Freyne to travel with goran cubs at their side. Imperial transports were long and wide, the passenger cabin was shaped like a basin, which allowed yearling gorans to curl up calmly at their owner's feet. However, these tiger gorans were not calm. One hissed and spat at Sayginn, then reached up to claw her hemline and snarled. Sayginn flinched.

From behind, a claw-like hand with black nails grabbed the cub by the scruff of its neck and pulled it back. The cub hissed and spat, but then cowered as it turned to see its tormentor. Emperor Frederon growled at the cub, revealing his own teeth – which were also stained black and filed to sharp points. The cub beat a hasty retreat.

Black varnished nails, black filed teeth, black beady eyes, long black curls framing a narrow, cruel face, this was Frederon, the Emperor of all Freyne.

And my future husband... thought Sayginn bleakly. Did he really think he could ever replace Serge?

Sayginn only had to close her eyes to see her dead husband, King Serge. She only had to pause for one instant, and the memory was still fresh. It was over two years earlier that he had left the palace for the last time.

"Chart is coming to dinner tonight, he's just back from Sas Darona, so make sure you wear something suitable. You know what he's like."

Yes. That was the last thing he ever said to her. She remembered it well and as always, it reminded her. Chart Segat had once been an ally and a friend.

Serge had laughed as he spoke, and he had kissed her. He had taken the seven-year-old Deodran by the hand, and headed out the door.

Yes. That laughing smile had been the last time she had ever seen him.

And Deodran, her youngest... The young boy bounced into the car as the butler held the door open, pulling his father behind him, shouting mock commands to the driver and giggling. That was her baby, her Deodran: small, slight and golden, with dark, soulful eyes. He had died that day as well.

After they had gone, she had headed back into the palace and up the sweeping stairs. Her eldest son's bedroom was on the second floor. Outside the palace was ancient, over five hundred years old. Inside it was modern, with vast open spaces, all white marble, stark and geometric, all trimmed with blood red rubies and lines of silver. Red and silver – the colours of the King.

Serge had been the King of Freyne 2 and five other planets, including the monazite-producing Serge 1. His had been – still was, some said – a prosperous and well run domain, the industrial heart of the Freyne Empire. Sayginn was his wife and Queen. She walked on, past the full length screen of herself in her wedding clothes with Serge on her arm.

"I was lucky he chose me."

Sayginn had been just nineteen; Serge had been thirty-one. He had been in need of an heir, and Sayginn had quickly obliged. Now she had two sons. Deodran was seven and her eldest, Teodor, was aged eleven. Oh, there had been a couple of miscarriages, as well. The Freyne Imperial line was notorious for its lack of fertility. Maybe that was why he picked her. Hers was such a lowly family, a Barony to be sure, but long since out of favour and impoverished. Serge instinctively knew he should choose from outside the normal circle to ensure himself an heir. So Sayginn became his Queen.

She had tapped lightly on the door before heading into his bedroom. Teodor had been propped up on pillows; a comic book abandoned on the covers. He had looked flushed and tired out. He had smiled hopefully as she entered and had reached one hand out to her, so that she sat on the bed.

"Well, Deodran went with your father in the end."

79

Teodor had nodded once. Sayginn had looked where he looked to his dress uniform hung ready, as if waiting. Waiting for nothing now, since Teodor was staying in bed. It was eleven-year-old Teodor who should have been in the car, but unexpectedly he had been sick at breakfast. And when the nurse had diagnosed a slight temperature he had been sent straight to bed.

"Never mind Teodor, never mind."

She had squeezed his hand and bent to kiss him, and that was when they had heard the first explosion. In shock, both had turned towards the open window, the sounds of shouts, of running boots, an alarm. They had sat listening and waiting, watching how the net curtain billowed inward with the blast, then settled back in place. Sayginn had managed to stand up, shaking her fingers free from Teodor's grip, when the second explosion came.

This time the blast was accompanied by a bright white light. The blast was so strong that Sayginn saw the windows shatter. The nurse was thrown from the chair where she sat reading. A mother's instinct caused her to throw herself across the bed to protect her eldest son. They lay clasped together, clinging to each other as debris from the windows settled around them. Only this time they heard nothing. An infinite silence seemed to follow the blast. Sayginn lay listening, willing herself to hear something: rescuers running, ambulances howling, shouted instructions – anything. But all she could hear was her son sobbing underneath her, sobbing and shaking as he moaned again and again:

"I want my father. Please, where's my father. I want my father. I want him."

Twenty-six people had died in the blast: the King, Prince Deodran, his five immediate household staff, ten members of his Dome Elite security and nine onlookers. The doctors had said the King would have survived the first blast. They even speculated that he had had enough strength and mobility to gather the injured seven-year-old Prince Deodran into his arms. It was the second blast that had killed them. Their remains were so indistinguishable Regent Sayginn had begged for the bodies to be left entwined. So it was she had buried her husband and her younger son in one coffin, in one grave. Two years on, there was proof that one of the two bombs was manufactured in the Dome. Chart Segat himself was under investigation for the murder of King Serge. No longer an ally. No longer a friend.

Serge's crown had passed to his son Teodor, but Sayginn was to be Regent until he came of age.

I should be glad, thought Sayginn. I had thought I was the lucky one when I married Serge.

Now the girl from the impoverished, overlooked, ancient Barony house was being considered as a possible wife for an Emperor. What did it matter that the Emperor was sixty-two years older than her in these days of rejuvenation treatment?

She turned to where Emperor Frederon was finishing an interview. Frederon could not be called good-looking. His nose was angular. His much discussed hawkish look was a practised mannerism. The Emperor would narrow his eyes, stick his chin out and peer at you with unfriendly eyes. His tall, slim body was the result of a careful diet and repeated surgery, not exercise. His hands were strong. He had a habit of clenching and squeezing his fingers around small stone balls. Occasionally, this frequent use would lead to the stone exploding between his fingers. And then, of course, were his famous black nails, shaped into points, which the Emperor himself referred to as his claws.

Chalky stones exploding between strong fingers tipped with black claws, a piercing look, and the power of life or death over all he met. Was it any wonder most of the court was nervous around him? And yet, they told Sayginn she had nothing to fear. He was to be her husband. Sayginn wondered if they had said the same to Frederon's eight previous wives, who were all abandoned – even those who had borne him daughters. Frederon wanted – no, needed – a son. He also wanted to seize the six planets that rightly belonged to Teodor.

Sayginn looked across at Frederon once more; he was chatting with a press droid which was hovering between them. He was good at press. And a weekend of entertainment at Magnolia Stakes was very newsworthy. He would make the most of it. So should Sayginn, so she smiled when the droid camera pointed towards her and squeezed the Emperor's hand when this seemed to be required. Finished at last, and without ceremony, Frederon pinched the droid between finger and thumb and tossed it from the car window. Only now that they were alone, in the small cocoon of their transport, did the Emperor relax. He dropped his false publicity-hungry grin, and eased his shoulders into the leather of the seats. Sayginn relaxed a fraction as well.

"Sayginn, it is good to see you. You look well."

She looked at him. This close it was hard to ignore his aging skin and jowls. Were those cataracts in his eyes? I do not want to marry him, Emperor or no Emperor. If I marry him I lose my independence, my planets, my power, even my son, thought Sayginn. I owe it to Serge to stand alone and run his planets and educate his son as he would see fit.

"Thank you, my Emperor... I must get this message." Sayginn looked nervously at the alarm flashing in her communicator.

"Freddie – call me Freddie. Switch that off!"

"Yes, of course, I will take the message later at the palace," said Sayginn, rebuked. She quickly switched off the flashing light.

"Have you thought any more about my proposal, Sayginn? You must marry me. We two must stick together; me, an old widower, and you, my nephew's widow. Apart we wither, our houses wither; together, oh Sayginn, we would be so strong! Have you read the contract my people sent you?"

"Four sons, Freddie?"

Sayginn had thought it was a misprint, and had had the clause queried. The answer had not pleased her. The Emperor expected her to bear four sons.

"You will not mind? I know you will not, Sayginn. You understand, don't you? Our marriage means power and influence. You give me these sons, and we will both be more secure."

"Yes, but what about Teodor? He is also your blood."

"My brother's grandson. So yes, my blood, but not my direct line. Teodor is already King of Freyne. I predict in that role he will be greater than his father. But he is not suited to be Emperor. By his character, he is not suited. Give me a son, Sayginn – no, give me sons – so we might choose which boy should be Emperor. Now kiss me."

Sayginn looked around for inspiration and instead saw a newsreel running on a small screen with the sound muted. She saw shots of destruction and darkness in the cathedral, weeping children, a teacher shot dead...

Where was Teodor?

On the screen, the news reporter was talking while a droid showed shots of the destroyed curtains, the blasted artefacts, trampled, blood-stained headdress and torn, scattered sheets of choral music.

"You see this?"

A ticker tape across the screen was summarising: At least ten die in cathedral explosion. Frederon snorted in disgust. He does not seem surprised, thought Sayginn panicking; she looked again at the Emperor's face and then at the screen. He knew about this!

"We would be stronger if we were married. This kind of nonsense would stop if I had sons."

Another headline flashed red and white: Prince Teodor missing, feared dead.

"What?" She could barely take in what the Emperor was saying. Teodor dead? Could it be true? No, a single word was a scream inside her head. Her breath came out in pants: "No, no, no..."

"Sayginn, just sign the contract. I will place all my power and influence to retrieving your boy."

Sayginn pulled her gaze away from the screen to look at the Emperor in disbelief.

"What?"

"He's alive, he's been taken – that's all."

"You did this?"

All at once Frederon stretched across the car and pinned Sayginn up against the window with a claw-like hand around her neck.

"You forget, Sayginn. Without your son, you are nothing. A wealthy widow somewhat past her prime – you should be grateful I considered you at all."

Chapter 6. The Cy-wolves of Empire

"One day you will be their commander in chief," his father had said. "Whenever you enter the Dome to view the Dome Elite, you must remember that one day you will command them."

Teodor had gone with his father, King Serge, to inspect the new intake of Dome Elite Junior. One of the boys was said to be a superb blades fighter and there was to be a display match.

After Teodor stepped out of the car, they were greeted by Commander Tilson and then he took the salute. No falling on his backside this time, Teodor must have taken the salute over five hundred times, but still the Press replayed the image of his four-year-old self falling down. As he walked along the line of Dome Elite Junior, he wondered if they expected to see him or a baby. The youthful soldiers were not much older than himself, Teodor reflected. Just fourteen and he was nearly twelve. He noticed a smudge of white dust on the cuff of one the soldier's jackets.

His father had told him to inspect the troops and not to hesitate if he saw anything amiss. Well, a white mark on a black uniform was certainly something wrong. Teodor realised he had stopped in front of the young soldier and his father was looking back at him curiously.

Teodor looked up into the smooth face of the boy who was looking at him.

"You have something on your cuff..." He saw the boy glance at his commander, and only when the commander nodded did he move, holding up his arm to look.

"I'm very sorry sir." He sounded embarrassed and quickly dusted it off. "It won't happen again."

"What's wrong with your eye?" Teodor asked him. Under the brim of his cap, the boy had a nasty black eye.

"Oh!" he hesitated. "I got it in training. Eyes take the longest time to heal."

"I see. Well, that's talc on your sleeve," Teodor said correctly. "I use talc on my hands when fighting blades myself."

"It stops the blades slipping," the boy admitted. "I was practising just before your arrival."

"Oh well, that explains it. This soldier was practising blades right up to the last minute. That's good, isn't it, father?"

"Yes, it certainly is."

As it turned out, the boy with the talc on his hands was the blades fighting star they had come to see. When he took out his blades and stepped onto the mat, he was breath-taking in his gymnastic training and accuracy of his spinning blades.

"An unregistered boy from Old Mill Lane?" his father had asked.

"But it does not matter who his parents are, we had to let him in," Chart Segat replied.

"His blood should be tested and his parents prosecuted," King Serge had said bluntly.

"What good would that do?" Chart had asked, a little sharply.

King Serge had sighed: "It's illegal, that's all I know, but you're in charge of the Dome. So I'll let you decide."

Later that night, Serge had come upstairs to wish Teodor goodnight. They read a few pages of his book together and then Teodor said:

"I want to fight blades as well as those Domeside boys do."

"Those boys eat, sleep, fight. They live for blades. You know that, don't you?"

"Yes, but if I'm the Commander in Chief…"

"You might have to give up some of the time you spend in the goran stables."

"Oh," Teodor had sounded disappointed. "Well, I suppose…"

"No, seriously, every time I ask: where's Teo? Oh, he's goran racing. Where's Teo? Oh he's nursing goran cubs. Where's Teo? Oh, he's cleaning out the stables. Where's Teo? He's grooming gorans. With you it's eat, sleep, gorans. You live with your gorans."

Teodor laughed; his father added slyly:

"Where's Teo? He's hanging out with the stable girls."

"Dad! Stable girls are not really girls."

"No?"

"No. Well, for instance, they ride gorans as well as jockeys and they don't mind getting messy cleaning up and stuff."

"I was madly in love with a stable girl when I was young."

"Dad! I'm only twelve?"

"I guess I must have been fourteen or fifteen, but she was my first love and I'll never forget her."

Teodor crossed his arms and shook his head in serious disapproval. His father just smiled: "You're sure you want to give up goran time to learn blades?"

Teodor sighed: "Well, I have to really, don't I? But if you can get me a good teacher I'll work twice as hard, so I don't have to spend that much time away."

"Good plan – I'll find you the best coach in the city. I'd do anything for you, Teo."

His father always had a solution, Teodor thought woozily. He always knew what to do. What would he have done today? What would he have...

I have to get a grip!

Teodor had given up trying to remember the name of the drug they had made him inhale, but he recognised the symptoms from his kidnap training. Loose, uncontrolled limbs, foggy, distorted vision, hearing so muffled he might be deaf and no sense of smell at all. His head had been jolted to one side during the running. He was somehow holding it in place: one ear against his attacker's back, one eye on what happened behind.

All he knew for sure was that they were Battle Borgs.

He had thought they would be running through catacombs and long forgotten tombs, since they were underneath the cathedral, but in fact these were long, narrow maintenance tunnels. So long and so straight, he saw the Regency Defence coming up behind them in pursuit. They were after him. They had let loose the cy-wolves, and they were getting closer. He wondered what they would do. They were programmed so they could not hurt him, but they would attack the borg that carried him. Mentally he braced himself. He imagined the huge wolf leaping at his captor's head. He was going to fall; he had better be ready.

Instead, what happened was that the borg stopped, crouched and turned. With his gun, he shot the nearest cy-wolf through the head and machine-gunned his companion. Then he sent a volley of fire towards the Regency Defence before sprinting away. Teodor plainly saw the two cy-wolves, one dead, his head twisted back. The other whimpering in pain but despite his injuries he was still crawling after the prince.

Teodor looked and remembered his two gorans. If he had brought them with him this morning as he had hoped, they would be dead now. Instead, these two brave, so brave, animals had given their all to save him and now lay dead and dying in this dark, damp corridor.

He was glad when they turned a sharp bend, and the fallen beasts were beyond his sight. Glad but horrified when he saw his captors throwing a 'snake' behind them as they ran on. A snake was a coiled rope of bullets. Rising like its namesake predator, the gun spiralled upwards and unleashed a circle of fire, starting high and spinning low. Teodor glimpsed the machine as it spit its indiscriminate cyclone of death. He thought of the Regency Defence trapped in that narrow corridor. Nowhere to hide except backwards. Could they even get out of range fast enough? No, they had to dive to the floor, and get ready to sprint away from the head.

Silence. The bullets were spent, only the snake-head remained.

"Ten, nine," Teodor counted down the seconds, "eight, seven, six…"

Bang. The explosive sound surging along the tunnels was all but deafening.

"Damn them," Teodor cursed, "a five-second fuse. Why did they set a five-second fuse? Damn them." The reverberation of the explosion shook Teodor and his captors. What about Teodor's guards, his rescuers? Teodor looked back at the clouds of dust. Had they survived? Then his heart leapt. Bounding over the bodies of fallen colleagues, the Regency Defence were still coming. Fast as athletes, and strong too, surely they must succeed. Weaving through their legs to lead the charge were two more cy-wolves, surely this new wave would free him.

Teodor felt himself falling: his captors had opened a drain in the floor. There was a ladder and the cyborg rapidly climbed perhaps ten meters downwards. Too far down for the cy-wolves to leap, thought Teodor. He was tumbling helplessly against his captor's back. His hands flew out on each side, uncontrolled and uncontrollable. His right hand knuckles ripping against the rough concrete, his left wrist banged and twisted back against the metal ladder. He could see these injuries, but he could not feel them. Now one cy-wolf sniffed down the drain, then leapt back as shots were fired upwards. The other sat and howled. A clear signal to the rest as to where Teodor had gone.

The last thing Teodor had seen were grenades being lobbed up through the drain hole, as the ladder was blasted from the wall. Now they were sprinting by torchlight, through a dark sloping tunnel. He was wondering how much further they might go. They came to a corner, stopped, and Teodor heard them unlocking a door. Then on down a further two narrow flights of stairs, a corridor, another shaft and a ladder.

Behind and above him Teodor could hear the deadly crackle of another machine snake. This time the explosion was so loud that the ceiling seemed to shake, and his captors passed instructions amongst themselves. They eased themselves carefully down the next ladder and Teodor immediately saw why. Below was a narrow ledge along the side of what he guessed was a city sewer, a deep turgid river of filth running slowly.

As his eyes started to burn and weep, Teodor was grateful he had lost his sense of smell. He saw them pushing one last snake gun up onto the hatch and locking it behind them. Wearily, Teodor closed his eyes, whether to try to reduce the stinging or simply because by now he could no longer bear to helplessly witness the slaughter of those who were trying to help him.

In the darkness of his closed eyes, he felt the borgs running again, agile as gymnasts, running along the narrow ledge. This capture, Teodor realised, had been carefully rehearsed as well as ruthlessly planned. They arched around a corner, Teodor swinging out over the steaming brown liquid, then they stopped.

Teodor thought they might be shouting. He wearily opened one eye and saw across the tunnel three more borgs standing and waiting. Were they going to jump? It was a two metre distance that was wide even for these machines.

The borg who was carrying him lifted him from his shoulder, and as if he were a ragdoll, he tossed Teodor from one side of the tunnel to another. He was free for a few moments as he flew through the air over the river of sewage. The cyborgs on the far side grabbed him by his body and tried to get him to stand. His legs buckled under him. He sat crumpled like a broken doll on the sewer ledge. Across from him, the first team of captors was heading off at a run. Now this new team took him by the hands and unceremoniously swung him out from the wall and dunked him in the sewage waters.

Teodor's mouth would not respond as he tried to close it. He did close his eyes and for an instant he thought they would drown him as his head became fully submerged. Then, with relief, he felt them yanking him back up, wrapping him in a sleeping foil. Teodor managed to open his mouth but not to spit or gag. He had a feeling his mouth was full of sewage, only he could not taste it.

Unsurprisingly, his new captors headed off in a different direction to the original team. Teodor guessed the sewage dunking was to prevent any remaining cy-wolves from tracking his scent. Just before they rounded the corner, Teodor glimpsed his pursuing rescuers: cy-wolves and Regency Defence. Of course, they would keep coming, only this time they headed in the wrong direction.

Teodor tried once again to cough or spit his mouth clean. He was at least partially successful. His new captors noticed and by way of reward, covered his face with a fresh drug drenched cloth. So, finally, Teodor's world turned to blackness, and he saw and felt no more.

Chapter 7. Regent Sayginn of Freyne 2

Guy Erma came out of maths and started hearing the stories. There had been a terrorist attack in the cathedral. Prince Teodor was feared dead. Guy switched on his communicator and found three urgent messages.

"Hi Lloulou, I'm alright."

"Oh God, Guy. I put you on the list of the missing, but thank God you're alright. I thought you would have been injured at the very least. Were you not at the front?

"I was the understudy, remember? I did not perform because the prince was there. I had double maths."

"Can you come down to the clinic? I just want to see you with my own eyes."

"I'm on my way. I'm nearly there – were any of our kids hurt?"

"I'll tell you when you get here."

Going to my maths class saved me, Guy thought. Maybe it was a sign.

***

"So the curtain fell closed and we lost sight of the prince."

Regent Sayginn was walking through the blood-stained confusion of the cathedral. The captain briefed her robotically on the morning's events.

"We then shot the curtain down from its hooks and caught these images of the kidnappers."

Sayginn had seen the stills and short video on her way to the cathedral. She watched, as great Battle Borgs seemingly from the Dome Elite grabbed then dragged her son Teodor off down into some tunnels.

Oh! Teo had tried to fight them off.

Her heart ached to see his brave kick, his spinning turn. But they were three, he was just a boy. Now it was her turn, she must fight to get him back.

"Why did the curtains close?"

"We don't know. We are checking the control panel."

"And the children who were killed? Was it from the grenades?"

Sayginn had asked the same question three times now. Each time the answer was the same, and even less palatable.

"The kidnappers used smoke canisters, not grenades. It was one of our men who used the grenade to open the hatch. Also, we fired to bring down the curtain and then at the men we saw attacking Prince Teodor. We destroyed two of the borgs."

"You're saying that most of the Domeside children who were killed or injured were hit by the Regency Defence?"

"The prince was under attack."

"You might have shot the prince himself."

"No, we could all see him. The trace in his blood makes him visible to us. He is well trained. He threw himself to the floor the instant the shooting started. He was never in any danger from our shots. We were shooting directly at the kidnappers."

"And indirectly into the choir of children standing behind him."

"They were not our target. With the smoke canisters, there was limited visibility…"

"You know there will be an enquiry. The men involved will be lucky if they are not prosecuted for murder. They mutilated and murdered innocent children."

"But Prince Teodor was under attack."

Sayginn looked around the cathedral. The altar drapes, the hangings and the wooden pews had been set ablaze by gunfire. The altar itself was slick with blood and she had been told some of the children had been treated there before being transferred to hospital. Everywhere there were blackened shoes and bloodied clothing. As she watched, two medics raced to where the cyborgs had found another body part, a small hand. They picked it up and froze it, probably hoping to reunite it with its owner.

Amidst the chaos, there was a small chair near one of the side doors with a neat pile of clothes. Sayginn walked over and realised that they were Teodor's clothes. She picked them up and nervously stroked them. What had he been wearing? She sought the answer, then remembered: the Angel costume, tunic, shorts and sandals. She had thought he looked gorgeous, now she realised in fact he had been vulnerable.

This kidnapping had been devilishly clever. They had known that Teodor's security would be light. They had found a way to separate him from both his communicator and his clothes. Both would have made it easier to find Teodor, with his communicator it was practically impossible for him to hide. Even his clothes had hidden tracking devices sewn into the thread; while unsophisticated and relatively easy to block, they might have been helpful.

His shoes too, she looked around, where were Teo's shoes? Maybe he had them on. It was a small crumb of comfort, but it was something. Teodor still had his shoes when all else had been stripped away.

"Are the choir children being treated in the Dome?"

"Yes, many are in the St Joseph's clinic across the way."

"Take me there."

***

Guy Erma found them on the second floor of the St Joseph's clinic. Both Lloulou and Marline were wearing professional make-up and silk wraps that were characteristic of fashion models between shoots. At his approach Lloulou reached to give him a squeeze and then looking into his eyes, stroked his cheek. Guy felt like he was melting, she was so beautiful, then he jumped. Marline had come up from behind and given him a bear hug and a kiss on the neck. Guy struggled a moment, then froze, and she took the hint and released him. Quickly Guy put some distance between them, but seeing the hurt look on her face, said gruffly:

"You alright, Marline?"

"I only get paid fifteen an hour for rehearsals," she said at once, and she was complaining: "And there's four hours of rehearsals, so that's…"

"Sixty pounds, or…" he paused a minute then came up with the calculation: "Twenty five pence a minute. I know because I worked out that I earn twenty pence a minute working for Juke. Last week, I worked five hours and he gave me sixty pounds."

"Yes, but that's market work," Marline sniffed. "Oh, you'll never guess what. The Valvanski princess – she had booked an appointment at House Jewel." Guy felt himself flushing…

"What?"

"Well, I did what you said. Thought of a dress and how hot you were. I know she was reading my mind."

"Well, good. Her account is worth a lot of money."

"Marline…" Lloulou rebuked her. "We don't talk about clients."

"Sssh…" Marline shushed him.

Guy quickly held up his thumb and index in the mime that said: "I can keep a secret," he whispered:

"What do you want with all that money?"

There was a sudden doubt in Marline's eyes.

"Go away," she said at last, sulkily. "You always get me into trouble."

***

The St Joseph's clinic was worse than Sayginn could have imagined and still she knew it was the right thing to do. The children who had been chosen to perform with Prince Teodor were all from Old Mill Lane. There were also some who were thought to be unregistered. Technically not even orphans, they were non-persons. This had thrown the healing process into some confusion, since these children could not be formally identified. Lists of the

93

wounded, missing and dead contained names, nick names, clothing details and even Fashion House brand names, this being the only identity a child might have.

'I think she is from the Riffaut.'

'I know him, he's House Jewel.'

There were even a number of unidentified children too ill or injured to speak. The youngest were often mute with shock. Around these children was a growing host of hysterical young models and fashion crafts people trying to identify them. As well as gangs of children rushing through the wards chanting lists of names as they created a grim tally of their friends, living, injured or dead.

The models from Old Mill Lane had been in rehearsal in the Dome Atrium in advance of that evening's fashion show. They had heard the explosions from the cathedral, and had sprinted to the scene, the press in hot pursuit. From what Sayginn could see, each girl was trying to outdo the other with an outpouring of emotional hysteria. Most of the models, Sayginn reflected grimly, were too young to be parents to these children, while she herself already knew her son was not here. Would that he was!

Amid the chaos, Sayginn realised she was, herself, part of the problem. She had arrived with four bodyguards and a host of press, so despite her best intentions her presence was now blocking the entire reception area of the clinic. A senior surgeon had not seen her. He came charging up, yelling at the press:

"I thought we told you to get out of here. Security... Security... Oh, your highness, I apologise."

Now Sayginn saw there was something she could do.

"Men, help the hospital security to round up and get the press out of here."

"Get those children out of the corridors!" the surgeon was shouting. A gaggle of red-faced youngsters were dragged protesting from the wards back to reception. The surgeon was about to address Sayginn, when a young girl walked straight up to them and started talking:

"You see, we can't find Timmy and Ollie, Nats was in that bed there a minute ago, but she's disappeared, some say she's having an operation, but she was not really hurt that bad. She did not need an operation, what are they doing to her?"

"Can we look at the lists?" another, younger, girl demanded.

Sayginn looked again at the confusion of papers on the reception desk. Someone had obviously tried to set up three lists, but in the confusion, three sheets had become half a dozen. It was unclear what the muddle of names and crossings-out really meant.

"I can sort this out," Sayginn told the surgeon. "I'll sit there. Send all the children to me. I'll get their names and the names of the missing and I'll send them back to school."

"Would you?" The surgeon sounded relieved. 'Thank you, my Regent,' he added hastily.

Sayginn was surprised how effective this simple plan proved to be. The novelty of talking to the Regent attracted the children like bees to honey. At first, they crowded round her shouting, but soon enough she had them marshalled in a neat line. As each child stepped to the front they had her full attention:

"Your name please. Your age. Your house. Are you registered? Ok, that's you. Now for the missing, give me the names and ages of any children you think might be missing. Ok, now off you go, back to school."

It did not take long. With her deft kindness, Sayginn processed the ten children, and then passed the task to two hospital PAs. Now the surgeon led Sayginn to where some of the unidentified children lay.

"I am afraid there are no boys... Your highness," he said. "No boys of the right age, I mean."

"You mean among the injured," replied Sayginn, she understood he was referring obliquely to Teodor.

"No, nor among the dead," he added gently.

Sayginn said nothing. She already knew this, but it was a relief to hear someone say it. Around them the news screens were broadcasting a cacophony of news with the story changing every fifteen minutes and the fate of Teodor got worse with each headline.

"We are pretty sure the prince was taken. We have images of him being snatched alive."

The surgeon stopped, he was shocked: "Then, why are you here?"

"These are my people too."

"And your highness, if you don't mind me asking. Any clues as to who it was?"

"They were wearing Dome Elite uniforms."

"Well, obviously," the surgeon replied with a sigh. "But second-hand Dome uniforms are two a penny in the flea market."

"I'm not saying it means the Dome Elite were involved."

They had arrived in a small private room with a single bed just off the main children's ward. Inside, it was warm with just a whiff of fresh blood in the air.

"This boy is about six, unidentified. We think he was standing next to another child who was killed by a shot though the head. That's what he told us. He turned to look at his friend, and saw the shot. He was blinded by fragments from the other child's skull."

Sayginn was so shocked her mouth dropped open and she rocked helplessly trying to find her balance. The child looked tiny in the oversized bed. It was as the surgeon had described, worse really, because except for the bandage across his eyes, he was perfect. They were already calling the surgeon away, so Sayginn was left alone. Slim and dark-haired like many of the Domeside boys, his lips were moving, seemingly silently, but as Sayginn leant over him, she started to hear his words.

"Is anyone there?" the child whispered, "Is anyone there?"

Sayginn's heart ached, for his words were interspersed with breathless sobs. She sat down on the side of his bed and took his hand:

"I'm here."

"Please don't go. Please don't leave me." Sayginn stroked his hair back from his face, but then she froze as the boy said: "It's too dark, I'm so afraid." Tears now ran freely down her face, as she remembered Teo's words that morning: It was so dark, and I was all alone.

***

Chart Segat had arrived, he had been downstairs in reception giving interviews, now he was posing at the bedside of injured children, constantly haranguing the doctors, the bystanders, the press droids. Guy sighed. What was Chart Segat talking about, anyway?

"The Regency Defence opened fire with live ammunition..." Chart Segat was saying. "A quite unnecessary use of deadly force... another example of Imperial ineptitude and cruelty against the poorest people in the city..."

The Regency Defence are not proper soldiers, Guy thought. The Regent would be better protected by the Dome Elite.

Then, to Guy's surprise, Guy heard Chart Segat say:

"The Regency Defence are not proper soldiers. The Regent would be better protected by the Dome Elite."

Of course, if King Serge had not died that day, if somehow the Dome Elite could have saved him, Guy sighed. Like all Domesiders he felt it deeply, the day the Dome Elite had failed. Never again. A nurse poked him. She was trying to draw the curtains around the bed. Guy slipped inside as Lloulou beckoned him forward. Marline batted some of the cameras outside. And Chart Segat pushed his way in.

"How many from House Jewel?" he said abruptly.

"Well, I think we have four injured and possibly another four dead..." She whispered: "Did you know about this?"

Chart Segat shook his head and muttered: "Why did the Regency use live ammunition? Why?"

"Well, the prince..." Lloulou started to explain, but she gave up after a few words.

"I would have laughed if they had shot him as well. You need to get back to rehearsals, Lloulou, you and this young thing." He pinched Marline's cheek. She giggled, but he was serious: "You need to lead by example for the other girls. Oh, and bring this chap to the drinks party tonight." He put a hand on Guy's head.

"You mean the Emperor's reception? It's a bit late..."

"I'm sure he won't say no to earning a few notes at the after party." Then, to Guy: "Will you?" Guy glanced at Marline. She gave him a bright, excited smiled.

"How much?" Guy asked. He was speaking to Marline, but Chart Segat just laughed.

"How much indeed?" He patted Guy on the head. "You'll be serving drinks," he said seriously. "Don't worry! Those boys get good tips too." He chuckled. "How much indeed? You're a good boy, Guy Erma. You're one of us now."

He held open the curtain and the three passed outside, they left the ward and were walking towards the exit when Marline gasped.

"Is that the Regent?"

***

Regent Sayginn had finally stopped sobbing and was grateful for the small basin in the boy's room to wash her face. Sobbing would not get Teodor back. What was she doing in the hospital, anyway? What could she possibly learn here? She checked her communicator. She noticed something else. The communicator always flagged up details of people she knew in her locality. Could it be? Just outside?

She stepped out of the private room, and coming down the corridor was Chart Segat with his inevitable retinue of courtesans and a young boy. All paused and the women curtseyed. Chart Segat pressed his right fist to his heart in the salute of the Dome Elite. The boy, who had appeared to freeze, now did the same.

One of the women spoke. Sayginn recognised the face:

"It's Lloulou, isn't it? I always enjoy my clothes from House Jewel."

"We're so sorry about Prince Teodor," Lloulou replied.

"We'll get him back. I'm sure he's not gone far." She glanced at Guy, "Is this your boy?"

Lloulou looked a little embarrassed but finally, after some hesitation she said: "Well, he's House Jewel."

"I see…" Sayginn noticed the disappointment flash across the boy's face. So, she thought, the boy is Lloulou's son and he knows it. And Lloulou is lying to me to protect who? Herself? Him? "Cheer up, young man." Why had she said that? The boy's skin was paler than most. His eyes were piercing blue. But the black curls were pure Domeside – Sayginn would have them trimmed. Still, she liked his slight, slim, tall frame. Destined for the Dome Elite I bet, thought Sayginn. Well, he will have a better future with me at the helm than he would have had if the Dome was under the control of Chart Segat.

"You are so familiar, do I know you?"

"No, Ma'am"

Lloulou cut in with a note of pride:

"It was he who was going to fight Prince Teodor at blades."

"Aha, so that's why I recognise him. The little blades champion, yes, well done young man. I have to tell you Teo was very disappointed to cancel the fight."

Why had she said that? It was she who had cancelled the match. She could still hear Teo's aggrieved complaints from that morning. Why do I have to sing? A good question, why did Teodor have to sing? She remembered her reply. "It's about the Dome. I'm taking it over this weekend. It's not a popular move, so you must sing." So, to protect herself, she had sent her unprotected son into the Dome alone. Only he had not been unprotected, there had been twelve Regency Defence soldiers. Twelve and it was not enough. The boy had said something.

"Sorry, I didn't catch that."

"My blades. Any day. Any time. Any place. Will you yield?"

"Don't say that," Sayginn said in a whisper, only she wasn't talking to Guy.

"My blades. Any day. Any time. Any place. Will you yield?" Teodor had cried, as he bowed to her at the end of his blades practice.

"Don't say that!" Sayginn had scolded him.

"It's what all the blades fighters in Domeside say," Teodor had said sulkily.

"Yes, but you're not from Domeside," Sayginn had reminded him.

"I like it and they are our people too." Teodor finished with an angry spin of his blades across the palms of his hands.

Contrary, opinionated Teodor, he was right, as always. Sayginn focused on the boy in front of her. He looked startled.

"Sorry, I didn't mean you." Tears, no, not tears, Sayginn pleaded with herself. Fortunately Lloulou spoke.

"Guy!" scolded Lloulou. "My lady, you must excuse Guy his manners."

"My blades are yours to command, Regent," he repeated more soberly, but Sayginn heard another voice:

"My blades are yours to command, Mother. I still like any time, any day, any place, better…" Oh, Teodor!

Resolutely, Sayginn turned to Chart Segat: "A word in private."

She batted away a droid camera from in front of her face. She nodded to her security who started to pinch and throw the cameras away. Sayginn pushed open the door to the private room and Chart Segat stepped through. The door was closed behind them. The small boy was sleeping now. Sayginn smoothed a curl back from his face. Chart Segat stared down at the boy from the foot of the bed, the blood on the eye bandage was worse than Sayginn remembered. As they stood there on opposite sides of the bed, Sayginn reflected they must look like the child's parents. She noticed the helpless anger on Chart Segat's face, Sayginn realised it was now or never:

"Have you got him, Chart?"

Chart Segat did not move. Sayginn asked again.

"Just tell me Chart, do you have my son?"

Chart Segat replied with anger.

"Oh, that's right, the men were wearing Dome Elite uniforms, so of course you think…"

Sayginn let loose her impatience:

"It's not what I think. I know you control everything that happens in this damn Dome of yours, or do you deny it? You have done this. I don't know why you even deny it."

"Stop it! If anyone has done this, it is you. You, Sayginn. With your Dome Debate. You, Sayginn. Closing the Dome. You. Calling me a murderer. Threatening everyone and everything here. As if I would murder Serge, murder Prince Deodran. No. Sayginn, you brought this on yourself."

Sayginn had heard it all before, she brushed the accusations aside:

"You know I don't mean to close the Dome…"

Chart Segat looked at her, shaking his head in disbelief.

"Finally," he said. His voice was deep and satisfied.

100

Sayginn did not reply. She knew that though she had kept her plans secret many speculated that if the Dome shut at all it would only be for a matter of days, because what else could you do with all the men, women and trainees in the Dome except keep them going? It was the outcome that Sayginn needed to change. So that the Dome was no longer a training camp for mercenaries, but a military force to protect and defend the Freyne.

"You just want to get rid of me," Chart Segat said quietly. "Have you forgotten that we were once friends?" He sounded sad, as if in mourning for having been so set aside.

They were standing close now. Sayginn could smell Chart Segat's raw energy and passion. She remembered him well as the sexy, flamboyant guest at Magnolia Palace. As mayor of Domeside he was an inevitable part of most of public appearances. Always with a compliment for her, flirting, occasionally hugging her, and if he saw Serge looking, he would make a joke of kissing her hand. 'The most beautiful girl in the empire', he would shout. Serge would laugh; flattered that another man should admire his wife. After all, how could Chart be serious when he always had impossibly young girls on each of his arms?

"Not friends, Chart," Sayginn realised that this might not be the best approach: "Maybe we were political allies. We shared the goal of revitalising Domeside and we succeeded. So, yes, we worked together. But he was my husband, Chart. We don't know who killed him. And today it's my son. Someone has taken my Teo and he's all I have left. He's everything, Chart."

"Sayginn… Let me stay on at the Dome. You want overall control, you can have it; just give me something. I did not kill Serge."

"I don't want to hear about that." Sayginn turned away towards the door, and pressed her forehead to the cool wood. "Where is my son, Chart?"

He paused for a moment looking at her, then said:

"Give me back my power. You know the evidence against me is inconclusive. Say something. Then I will have my authority back. Then, yes. Maybe I will be able to help…"

Inside Sayginn jumped, outside she did not move: had he said he knew where Teodor was?

"My son? Chart? Do you have Teo?"

"Help you find…" repeated Chart with a smile: "whatever mad firebrands have pulled off this stunt."

Sayginn shook her head. So it was not him. Could that possibly be true? She could not speak. Firebrands, Chart Segat had said. There were rumours of ultra-militant Dome Elite. If they did exist it would mean Chart Segat had actually lost control. Maybe he was right. Maybe it was her fault. She had wounded him and as a direct result she had brought this attack on herself.

"They come back from Sas Darona…" Chart Segat said quietly. "…changed."

"What are they even doing on Sas Darona? Their presence there is illegal."

"Sayginn, how high is the ivory tower you live in? You and your Barons own everything, have everything, and want more. What kind of democracy is this, where your people have nothing? A Dome guard earns one thousand four hundred a month. Your shirt costs more than that, your handbag ten times that amount. Your shoes, palace, gorans, more than the entire budget of the Dome. Through your greed – yours, the Emperors and the Barons – nothing is left, or almost nothing. What crumbs you do leave on the table, like the Dome Elite, there is such intense competition…"

"Save me the lecture on poverty and inequality," Sayginn sneered. "My government has done more to increase routes to prosperity than any other legislature in the Freyne Empire. More even than Serge, but if the Barons do not get their just rewards, they will not take the necessary risks. The risks that are needed to expand the empire. "

"Expand the empire, why? To have more poor people? Ever expanding desperation? You should be praying I do have your boy, because my boys, at least I look after them."

"Chart Segat, I am giving you one last chance – give me back my son and I will speak for you in the future."

"What, when I face charges for murdering Serge? I did not do it, Sayginn – will you not hear me? I did not do it. Listen to me, just let me keep the Dome, any job title will do. We could work together, like the old days, building Domeside together. What do you think?"

"You disgust me: your politics, your whores and the blood of my husband on your hands. Give me back my son. Or you will never have a part in the future of the Dome. Do you hear me? Never."

Book 3.
Day 1. Evening.

Chapter 8. The Battle Borgs of Dome

"Teo, Teo, wake-up Teo." He had woken in his room, it was still dark and his father was leaning over his bed: "Cream Carolina is having her cubs. If you want to choose one, you need to be there."

Teodor had quickly got out of bed and pulled on the clothes he had ready at his bedside. Moments later he'd run down the stairs; his father had a small cart waiting for them at the back door. Teodor felt his heart beating within his chest at the effort, but also in anticipation. Entering the stall of a birthing mother goran was perhaps the most perilous of all activities one undertook when breeding the great beasts. However, for a jockey to bond with his ride, the telepathic connection had to be made early, it had to be made from the very first.

"You will come with me, won't you father? You'll stay with me?"

"Of course, I have to stand behind you, if you want to make the connection."

"Yes, I know, but promise me you will be there."

"Teo, my boy, I am always there for you…"

Teodor remembered standing beside the great female goran, calming her with his thoughts while watching for the newborns. He had a fresh towel hung over his shoulder and was wearing rubber gloves. He would pick the cub up, clean and cuddle it and then make the connection.

He looked over his shoulder, his father was two steps away. With a nod his father directed him forward.

The cub is coming, thought Teo. It is almost time.

He bent to take the newborn, but instead of the baby goran, he was suddenly reaching into the roaring, snarling face of the mother goran, with her claws out. She slashed at him.

Teodor woke. It was dark. It was cold. He was shivering all over from the last vision of his dream.

"That didn't happen," his rational brain told him. "Nothing like that happened. The cubs came close together, you picked each one up, and with one in each arm, you made the connection. Cream Carolina was a sweet goran, she would never attack you." He remembered the day well. His father patted him on the shoulder:

"See, you didn't need your old Dad after all."

"Yes, I did," Teodor remembered saying. "I always need you Dad."

I really need you now, he thought bleakly, and as the dream faded he felt the pain grow. His body crumpled around him, his knees under his chin, his feet twisted up at odd angles, one arm behind his back, one curled in his lap. He wanted to free his body, but quickly realised he had been dropped into a narrow tube. He moaned. His head ached, and he was thirsty. He tried to cough, managed to spit a foul taste from his mouth; and then he gagged at the smell. His clothes, his body, his hair, all caked in the filth from the sewer.

"I have to get out," he thought urgently, and in a blind panic, he placed his feet on the floor. Ignoring the pins and needles that cut into his calf and thighs, he pushed himself upwards, impatiently pulling his right arm from behind him and shaking it back to some sensitivity. Only he could not stand, his head crashed against a flat surface. He reached up with his hands and realised the tube had a lid. At his feet, he kicked to make sure the base was also sealed.

He could not stand up straight; the best he could achieve was a three quarters crouch, with his feet flat on the floor, the top of his head pushed up flat against the top. He drew his hands up and turned on the spot, feeling the smooth curved walls. The diameter of the tube was so narrow he only just managed to turn around. At the top of the tube, there was a narrow grille just under the lid. He pushed his fingers through and pulled himself upwards. Try as he might, he could not see through the narrow gap.

He started to shout:

"Help me. Is there anyone out there? Help me. I'm in this tube." He beat and thumped the walls of the tube. Made of metal, it made a vibrating echo.

He heard footsteps, the heavy tread of a soldier. Teodor redoubled the amount of noise he was making, while craning his neck to put his eye up to the grille.

"My name is Prince Teodor, let me out of here!"

Surely, they would know he was missing by now. Surely they would be looking for him? If he could just make himself known.

All at once he heard metal on metal snap together. The top of the tube lifted up. Quickly Teodor followed it, standing up to his full height and looking up, he saw it was not a man, it was a Battle Borg. If this cyborg had once been a man, it was a long time ago. The man must have been dismembered in battle. It had robotic arms and hands. Its legs had been amputated at the hips and replaced with robotic legs and wheels. The eyes were mechanical; the neck reinforced; its only last remnants of humanity were its face, body skin and hair. Only his hair was balding, mottled black and grey, his skin cracked and cratered, a large scab having fallen away from his face to reveal its mechanical inners. This Battle Borg would be used in the vanguard, sent forward to die a heroic death. He was perhaps the most frightening thing Teodor had ever seen, but at his core he was also a machine.

All Battle Borgs were programmed to follow orders, and at the top of the chain of command was the King. This machine had to do what he said:

"Thank goodness. It's you."

Teodor pushed his weight upon his hands to rise out of the tube, and so he did not see the blow that struck him hard across the temples, and sent him tumbling back down.

"No, please, you must help me get out. My name is Prince Teodor. I am your commander in chief. You must obey me."

The Battle Borg had pulled a cloth from a sachet, and now pressed it across Teodor's face, pinching his ears hard when he saw Teodor was trying not to breathe.

"Sleep, Prince Teodor, sleep," he hissed down at him. Teodor tried one last time to lash out, but his strength was too slight, his captor too strong, the drugs too potent. He felt his legs crumbling and slipped back down into the tube.

"No, please, no. I am your prince. Please, no. You have to help me."

"Calm, Teodor, sleep now." The borg threw the cloth into the tube so Teodor could not escape its vapours and the lid closed on top of him again.

Teodor heard the metal clicking into place. He clawed at the tube one last time, hoping to the very last to climb out, but the footsteps were fading away, and in the distance a light went out. Teodor valiantly held his breath, as he reached the lid, using his fingers to look for any weakness, punching it with his knuckles to push it upwards. His legs had turned to jelly, so he slipped as if broken to the floor of the tube. His eyes were still open, looking up at the grille, but all his movement had stopped. His hearing gone, as well as his sense of smell, but he still had time to think. Not long, he guessed, but a few seconds.

Here he was alone and in the dark, captive somewhere. Was he still in the Dome? And he could not get out. Exactly as he had dreamt. Well, not exactly, but clearly his dream had been some dark premonition. He thought how he had woken in a cold sweat that morning, how scared he had been in his comfortable bed. That fear had passed in a couple of seconds. How afraid was he now? He felt so dozy, part of his brain was chronicling his sensations. He was wet and cold. His limbs were twisted and bruised. There were untended cuts and grazes. What worried him most was the lack of voluntary motion, and the darkness. He knew he would soon lose the ability to blink.

Wearily, he closed his eyes. Now he was alone inside his head. Why had the borg not obeyed his command? Most cyborgs could not be reprogrammed. Were Battle Borgs different? Teodor thought wearily, Battle Borgs of Empire.

"War is a terrible thing," his father had once said. "When you are at war, you have to accept that dreadful things will happen, and in turn you have to fight with all your might to survive. The Battle Borgs are our greatest weapons."

Teodor had been accompanying his father on yet another inspection of the military facilities within the Dome. Chart Segat had been there and had been demonstrating some new huge weapons that could only be hoisted aloft by a small number of Battle Borgs with the right kind of reinforced mechanical arms.

"But are they still human?" Teodor had asked. His father had not replied as Chart Segat had spoken:

"We have over a dozen volunteers for this upgrade."

"I don't want men who have working arms to sacrifice their humanity simply to use these weapons," Serge had replied curtly.

"No. I know that. But losing their arms does not reduce their capacity for humanity. If they have over sixty per cent brain function, they remain human."

"How can you be so sure?" Serge had responded quietly. "I don't believe your humanity resides only in your brain."

"You mean how can a man be human if he has super human powers?" Segat had said with a smile and Teodor recognised a familiar debate.

"Precisely," Serge replied.

"Are they human, Dad?" Teodor had repeated.

Chart Segat had smiled down at him.

"The point is, they are dead and we control them. Human or not, in battle they are under our control."

Under whose control? Teodor wondered. Who controlled these Battle Borgs? Chart Segat?

"This weekend is all about the Dome Debate," his mother had said, "I plan to take control, and it's not a popular move."

The Dome Debate? Teodor thought. Is that what this is about? What had his mother said? Something about the Dome Elite becoming her army, after the Dome Debate... His brain was becoming fuzzy now. Vaguely he had visions of himself riding a white snow goran, the Dome Elite running with blades ready, riding across the plains of Sas Darona to fight who?

Who was he fighting?

He heard his mother's voice.

'He was thirteen. He was a skinny thing, but he was fast, and he was clever. He would have beaten you Teodor.'

No, no! Teodor thought, not when I have my gorans and my army. He will not beat me.

Chapter 9. Whatever Chartsie says

Thud. The blade had embedded itself deep into the wood. Guy Erma, who was standing at the furthest point from the target, now span and threw a second blade. This one embedded itself exactly at the twelve o'clock position on the target.

Maximum points, he thought to himself, a twelve and a bull's eye, maximum points. The target accelerated towards him on a wire. Guy retrieved his blades with a smile. He polished them briefly on his sleeve and then stepped aside for the next boy. He put his blades back in his holster, snug up against his sides and kidneys. He then walked back through the gym. The Dome Elite were coming in at the end of their duties and the training mats were filling up. Training robots were being set aside, and an instructor was calling a vast crowd of soldiers into formation for a warm-up routine.

Guy rolled his shoulders as he walked, easing the stiffness he had built up over training. He and the other boys had the run of the gym between school's out and six. Then the boys had to clear out, but it was these minutes of handover that Guy lived for. Dallying on the edge of a blades mat, shyly watching some champion or battle hardened veteran spinning blades with breath-taking precision, or counting the ranks of Dome Elite chanting their way through a hard-learnt battle routine.

Guy heard a cheer.

Des had appeared across the gym, he was being greeted and congratulated every step he took, but eventually he made his way to join the large group of training men. Des Parks was coming to the end of his third year in the Dome Elite. This was also the third consecutive year he was blades champion. He was dark haired, slim and fit, but he was also deeply tanned. And that is why they applauded.

"…back from Sas Darona…" Guy heard a boy mutter.

"How the heck did he get back?" said another.

"Sas Darona has been locked down for three months."

As Des reached the central training area the ranked men stopped in their routine. Then they parted, falling back to the edge of the blades mat and applauded. This was something of a tradition among the Dome Elite. A returning hero was given a moment to shine and Des did not disappoint.

Without hesitation, he performed three consecutive back somersaults before taking off into a corkscrew spiral kick, landing in a high backwards kick that would surely smash the face of any opponent. The crowd roared their approval and pushed in to congratulate him.

Guy grinned and set off at a sprint around the perimeter of the gym, pausing at a water fountain before squeezing and squirming his way through the crowd with a cup of water in his hand.

"Hi Des, here – take this!"

Des grinned down at him, took the cup of water, downed the contents in one gulp, threw the cup aside and embraced Guy in a bear hug:

"Hi kiddo! You still training?"

Guy nodded, speechless with delight. His hero had remembered him. Someone else was talking to Des now. Yet, Des turned back and caught Guy by the chin, and lifted his face up:

"Hey Guy, you still live in the House?"

Guy nodded. Guy, like Des, had been brought up in House Jewel.

"And you see Lloulou?"

"Every day," Guy smiled.

"Ok. Ok. I might have a job for you."

"Oy, Guy Erma, you should not be here. Get out." It was an angry shout from a Dome Elite Junior, the same one Guy had beaten that morning in training.

Des whispered: "Get going. I'll catch you later."

"Not so fast, you can fill up my water bottle first."

111

The junior held out his flask. Guy took it and in light leaps, headed back to the water fountain. Unknown to him, Des' eyes were following him. Once Guy had his back turned, fixed on the water and the tap, they jumped him. There were four or five juniors, including the boy Guy had beaten at blades that very morning. Oh, Guy reached for his blades, but they grabbed his arms and pushed him through a double door. Guy tried to kick out but another boy threw himself bodily across his legs, pinning him to the floor by his blades. But as the doors shut, they were no longer visible to either the instructors or trainers. Then the punishment really started: a hard volley of punches to his belly and chest, and last of all, a hard slap around his face.

"Do you yield?" the boy sneered. "Do you yield?"

He lifted a fist closed around the handle of his blade. Guy winced in anticipation when a familiar voice rang out.

"Stop that this minute…" It was Des, of course, and with him two other seniors. They made quick work of pulling the juniors off Guy and confiscating their weapons.

"What do you think you're doing?"

"He had it coming. What with the girls like 'Ooh Guy Erma', and he's Chartsie's pet and Lloulou's too and 'Oh I don't want to be a fashion model.' Who does he think he is?"

Des pushed the boy against the wall and pushed his arm painfully up his back:

"So that justifies you going at him six against one? Does it? I have a good mind to tell your commanding officer; your prospects won't look so good with a report of cowardice on your file."

"Just leave off will you, he's not badly hurt."

"Get out of here!"

The six juniors raced back into the gym. Des nodded to the two other seniors and they left as well. He bent to help Guy up.

"You ok, kiddo?"

"I guess. My ribs really hurt."

"Ok. C'mon."

Des put an arm around him and, using his pass, led him into a private elevator.

"Where are you taking me?"

"We'll get them to check you at the Elite clinic."

"No, don't do that. I'm not yet Dome Elite…"

"No, but I'm with you, and you were injured in training."

The doors of the elevator had opened into a severely narrow metal corridor. There was an officer waiting at the door of the elevator. Des saluted him, fist across his chest to his heart, and when he looked questioningly at Guy, Des just pointed to the blood running from his nose. The officer nodded. Along the narrow corridor, there was just one admin assistant moving quickly, carrying a box of silver Dome medallion awards. Des quickly led Guy through the double doors and into the spacious military clinic. The receptionist took their names, an orderly took one look at Guy and found a hover chair, and they were taken straight through to the treatment room, a wide room with over twenty beds and clustered monitors. A young doctor came over, checking his screen as he came:

"Des Parks? This boy is not Dome Elite."

"He got these injuries in a Dome Elite gym."

"How's that?"

"Six Dome Elite juniors decided they did not like the look of him."

"Is that true?" the doctor turned to Guy.

"Yes, sir," Guy said.

"Did you do anything to upset them?"

"No, sir."

"Well, we're not busy, so I'll take a look, but in future you should stay away from bullies. Do you hear me?"

Guy nodded, all the time thinking this was particularly useless advice.

The doctor continued: "Take your boots off, and your shirt."

Guy tried to oblige but in both cases his ribs were too painful. Des helped him sit on the edge of the bed, then bent to undo his boots.

"Here, let me get that."

The young doctor brought a scanner over to check Guy. Des gingerly helped Guy out of his shirt. There was a nasty red mark on his pale skin."

"Six of them, hey?" the doctor remarked. "You're Guy Erma, aren't you? You were due to fight Prince Teodor, weren't you?"

Guy nodded, but said nothing. Everyone knew Guy Erma.

Later Des helped Guy back into his clothes. His skin had returned to its healthy state, and the doctor had given him a sheet of physio exercises to be completed each hour.

"So, did you want to see Lloulou?" Guy asked tentatively.

"Well no. And yes. Tell her I love her, as always." Guy nodded. "But actually I need her to talk to Chartsie, tell him I'm back from…" he hesitated and pointed to his tanned forearms. "Well, you know where. I really need to speak privately with him."

"Oh?"

"What with Magnolia Weekend and the Dome Debate, his office says I can't see him until next Thursday, so…"

"Next Thursday?"

"I need to speak to him urgently. It's important. Look, if she says 'no', then say Mezzatorra. Tell her it's about Mezzatorra."

"Mezzatorra? Wasn't that a battle on Sas Darona?"

"Yes. Sort of."

"Please tell me."

"You know I can't. But I have to get an urgent message to Chartsie. Tell Lloulou. Tell her. No, beg her."

"I will. I'm sure Lloulou will help. She spoke to Chartsie about the Dome Elite for me."

"She asked Chartsie? And?"

"He said no. Not with the Dome Debate, but he said there would be a fight…" Guy trailed off, he was confused by the whole thing.

"Did Chartsie say he would get you into the Dome Elite or not?"

"Lloulou said I should be in the Dome Elite, and Chartsie said there might be a fight, and if I won, I would be in. Then Lloulou said I had to do what he said. Exactly what he said."

Des sat very still for a moment, then finally, nodded.

114

"That's what she said to me too."

Guy sat very still, his hands and face were suddenly freezing cold. He had known Des all his life. And he remembered the ambulance, Lloulou screaming, the blood dripping from the black boots. The adults had shooed him and the other boys up to the attic, out of the way. In the dismal surroundings of the shared space, they did not know what injuries Des had sustained, so what they had imagined was worse. Guy swallowed hard.

"Chartsie won't do that to me."

Des sighed, he hugged Guy a moment:

"Let's hope so, kiddo." He sighed, then said again: "Don't forget to talk to Lloulou for me. Mezzatorra. Urgent and important. Got that?"

***

"Oy, Guy! Hey there Guy Erma!"

Emerging from the military complex, Guy looked over and smiled. Running on blades he covered the distance between them in a few instants.

"Hi Sebastian, you ok?"

Sebastian was perched on the corner of an ornamental pot plant. As Guy approached, Sebastian concealed the smoke inhaler within his sleeve, then behind his back. Guy knew if Sebastian was hiding it, he should not be smoking it. As he wondered whether he should say something, suddenly Guy was roughly pushed aside by two men. Guy had an instant to recognise the uniform, then he bit back a laugh. Casually, Sebastian showed the men his ID; they nevertheless insisted on a blood sample as well. A few minutes later they hurried away.

"That's the fifth time today," Sebastian said, mournfully holding up his index finger, and showing the multiple pin-pricks where blood samples had been taken. "You would think they had never heard of me."

Sebastian was not just a model, he was a celebrity. He was a lookalike for Prince Teodor, identical to the young Prince in his hair, his face, his height. Guy knew he was one of the best paid models on Old Mill Lane, yet today he was being made to pay for his success in a completely different way. Guy shrugged; all at once he felt a tightness in his stomach as he remembered the sound of the explosion, the sight of the dust cloud materialising at the cathedral door, the blood on the pillows of the children in the clinic.

"You should just be glad you're not him," Guy said hoarsely.

Sebastian looked at him.

"Sorry, I forgot – you were there, weren't you?"

Guy looked away. He had cleared his head during training, and he had no intention of going back over it now. So he said curtly:

"Not really, I left early – I had double maths." Sebastian did not seem to believe him, so Guy added: "Dome Elite entrance exam?"

Sebastian did not reply, just looked a little bored.

"Well, don't just stand there, take a pew. I'll look less like him if I have a Dome Elite guard at my side."

Guy smiled. Sebastian was cool. He tried to perch alongside him, hoping his face could look calm and aloof as well. Before them was a scene of chaos. The central square of the Dome was being remade in advance of one of Magnolia Stakes' great set pieces: the annual Festival of Fashion. For three days, the great fashion houses of Old Mill Lane would present new collections, throw open the doors of their secret studios and workshops and unveil new talent, be it models or designers. The whole event started on the Friday of Magnolia Weekend, with a dinner which featured displays and catwalks from the eight main houses and up to a dozen smaller concerns.

Today was Friday afternoon, the last technical rehearsal was in full swing and they were running late. Guy watched as another array of lights was hoisted upwards. In the rafters above, black suited lighting technicians scrambled to secure and manually adjust the great lights. Finally the head designer of the Riffaut walked along the catwalk, pausing at intervals and shouting out colours.

"This is the cold white, it has to be here."

The circle of light moved.

"And I need the warm white here. No, I said here…"

"Oh, there you are Guy!" Guy looked around. It was Marline. Guy frowned. He knew what she wanted. Guy checked his communicator and said:

"It's not time yet."

Marline replied: "No, but soon. Lloulou said I was to look out for you, make sure you weren't late." She turned back to Sebastian.

"Hi Sebastian." She nodded towards the stage. "I thought we'd have time to rehearse – a proper rehearsal."

"Nah, we'll get five minutes at the end, if we're lucky." He sucked on the smoke tube. "Hey, don't look so worried, you'll do fine. You're a Domeside beauty – you know that, don't you?"

Guy smiled to hear the compliment, and looked up at Marline; she only shrugged.

"They say I have to get a big order, at least one big one. I don't know what that means."

"It means you just need to be your own beautiful self and make some rich customer want to buy your look."

"They say that if I don't make a sale, they may demote me or even fire me…"

This is fashion model talk, thought Guy. He had nothing to say, but Sebastian spoke.

"Cheer up. Have faith in your old friend Sebastian. Even though you are House Jewel and I am the Riffaut, I'll give you a tip. First, don't listen to those who say they won't serve a Valvanchi. She's coming to House Jewel, isn't she?"

"Yes, the other girls say they won't talk to her because she is the niece of Killer Valvanski. They say if you model for her it's like you're helping the enemy."

"Ok, the situation on Sas Darona is messy, but technically they are our allies. So listen, she's an only child, her mother is dead and her father never says no to her. Money is no object, and I mean: money is no object. So remember, the Valvanchi always like to know the history of a piece, the name of the designer, the origin of the fibres, the story of the seamstress…"

Marline still hesitated.

"Valvanski, really?"

"Valvanchi," corrected Sebastian. "Ask Guy here. What would you say Guy if Marline sold a wardrobe of clothes to Nell Valvanchi?"

Guy looked up, first at Marline, then at Sebastian.

"Well, better House Jewel," Guy said at once, then as an after-thought: "Marline is, after all, the most beautiful girl in Domeside."

117

"See?" Sebastian said. "Even the Dome Elite agree. So don't be an idiot, but if that does not work, remember the name Baristella: very new money and lots of it. The son came into the salon this morning and I showed him the gold and platinum hand carved communicator, told him there were only three in existence and that Prince Teodor had one, and he bought it. Eighty-five thousand, just like that, and he bought the belt and cufflinks to match. Then we started on shoes – four handmade pairs, one brown, one grey, two shades of black, and after that the clothes... You have no idea, over three hundred thousand in two hours."

"Yes, but I can't model for boys, like you."

"There's a sister. Amber Baristella, and I could tell they had plans for her."

"Plans?"

"Like, Prince Teodor-type plans."

"Really?"

"Prince Teodor is only thirteen," Guy interrupted, but Sebastian ignored him.

"What with those pictures of him and the stable girl, the Riffaut was saying the young girls of the court have suddenly become a lot more interested in him."

"Poor Prince Teodor..."

"Yeah, well, if he's still alive. I don't know what I'm going to do if they've killed him."

Guy looked sharply at Sebastian. He was so close in looks to the young prince – the most perfect of all the lookalikes – that his presence at many events had fooled or misled many who claimed to know the prince well.

"At least I could stop taking the height inhibitors, and, I don't know, grow a beard. Do you think I would suit a goatee?" Sebastian was still talking to Marline.

"Surely they're going to find him?"

"Are they even looking? Hey, Guy, you've been inside. What says the Elite?"

"Well, I was training there. Lloulou said I could go."

"What she actually said," Marline said wickedly, "was that she could not bear you fidgeting anymore and would you please go and burn off some excess energy."

"Well, I have to train to make the Elite."

"Yeah, yeah…" Sebastian silenced them both. "Listen, what's going on back there? Did you hear anything?"

"Not really, some of the guys are saying there's bound to be a general recall, but right now everyone is still on leave. It's Magnolia Weekend."

"So the Dome Elite are not looking for the prince?" Marline said surprised.

"Some of them are saying why should the Dome Elite help when the Regency Defence killed and injured all of those Domeside children."

"That's rubbish, that's not the reason…" Sebastian shook his head impatiently then nodded across the space to where a large banner was being removed. "That's the reason, I tell you. That over there."

Marline and Guy both looked where Sebastian was looking.

"Oh," Marline said quietly.

Five more years.

Chart Segat for the Dome.

Five more years.

"They're going to kill him. I know, I just know it," said Sebastian.

"Oh, Sebastian, and you're topping and tailing the display tonight," Marline said. She was referring to the fact that Sebastian had both the first and the last outfit of the Riffaut's catwalk. As Teodor's lookalike, he was the star of the show.

"A last – hurrah!"

"Not necessarily…" They all turned at the familiar voice. "Hi Sebastian, long time no see."

"Des!" Sebastian hugged him. When they were standing side by side it was easier to spot that Sebastian and Des were similar in age. Not an innocent, not an ingénue, Sebastian was a seventeen year-old model who

119

knew his craft. Through hard work and determination he always appeared identical to thirteen-year-old Prince Teodor.

"Let's go and grab a beer…" Sebastian said. "I need one, or maybe three."

"No way! As Marline said, it's your show tonight. I'll buy you a bite and a coffee if you like? And put that away." Sebastian took the smoke stick off him. "You need a clear head tonight."

"No, Des. You don't need to buy me anything," Sebastian looked embarrassed. "I had a good client…"

"I don't care about that. I'm your mate, and before you get any ideas, I'm not taking you for three courses at Bistro Jewel. C'mon."

Marline and Guy were left standing, watching them leave. Simultaneously their communicators beeped.

"That's us," Marline said.

"You go, I've got these." Guy showed her his running blades. She shook her head.

"No way. You'll only get me into trouble if you're late!"

Guy shrugged. He was watching Sebastian and Des. Des had taken him to Juke's food van and now he had purchased a large coffee and a ham roll. A combination Guy knew was the cheapest meal in all Domeside. Des was sharing the cup with Sebastian and had ripped the roll in two. They perched themselves across from each other on high stools. Guy could tell Des was already deep in a tale from the savannah of Sas Darona.

"Guy, c'mon." Marline was pleading now. Guy nodded once and followed her. Yet again he wished he was older, that he and Des might be true friends. Then he felt a deeper pang, he would have liked to have just one friend really. Just one other boy with whom he could pass the time of day and share everything. With a sigh, Guy set off after Marline.

It was not far. A large gym had been converted into a green room. There were racks of clothes at the centre, surrounded by clusters of mirrors, one for each of the houses of Old Mill Lane. Within their area, hairdressers, stylists, and make-up artists worked up a frenzy preparing their models. Guy and Marline slipped through the crush until they found themselves standing at Lloulou's shoulder as the make-up artist finished her work. She smiled to see them reflected in her mirror.

"Thanks for making sure he got here, Marline." Marline nodded and headed off. Lloulou reached up to stroke Guy's cheek.

"Good boy, you remembered to wash your hair. Dana here will dry it. She's the only one I let touch my hair."

The make-up artist, Dana, smiled and gave Guy a wink.

"Hey gorgeous, you make my life too easy."

A golden haired boy passed by their section wearing a tweed jacket.

"Who's that?" said Guy. "Is that..?"

"No!" said Lloulou. "It's another one of those lookalikes from the Riffaut. They won a contract to dress Prince Teodor this season, so they have all these boys made up to look like him."

"But..."

"Fake the hair, adjust the skin tone, and insert false lenses. I think two had surgery to shape their noses and cheekbones."

"I thought Sebastian was the only one," said Guy.

"No, it was too much work for one. And Sebastian is a bit too old really. The new boys are younger. There's eight lookalikes now. Remember, if they are good, they could make an entire career imitating the prince."

"I guess..." Guy said, vaguely remembering Sebastian's assertion that the prince was most likely dead.

"Oh, look..." Dana said. Lloulou and Guy looked up on the screen above them. The news showed Regent Sayginn talking to camera.

"Put the sound up," Lloulou said.

"To you, my people, I do declare my first duty..."

"She doesn't mean that!" said Dana petulantly. "What about our kids?"

There were shouts of agreement from around the green room.

"Sssh," said Lloulou. They all listened in silence, until finally, the Regent concluded:

"...to Teodor, my Teodor, I love you very much. You know of my love for you. I am thinking and working towards your freedom from now until the next time I hold you in my arms. I love you, Teodor. We all do." The screen snapped to a photograph of Prince Teodor grinning and hugging a young goran cub.

Guy leant in close to Lloulou and whispered:

"Will they kill him, really?"

Lloulou shrugged her shoulders and kissed him.

"Poor Sayginn, I know I could not bear it."

Guy nodded and blushed, he knew she was talking of losing him, her only son.

"Lloulou," Guy whispered urgently, now he had her to himself. "I saw Des today. Do you remember Des Parks?"

"Has there been a shuttle from…? I thought it was locked down?" Lloulou whispered. Guy noticed how she did not say Sas Darona out loud, though that was what she meant. Sas Darona had been in lock-down for three months. No Dome Elite had got in or out. What was Des doing here?

"He says he urgently needs to speak to Chartsie, but the office won't get him an appointment until Thursday. He asked me to say: will you talk to Chartsie?" Guy whispered.

"Hush!" Lloulou said severely, she held up a hand, index and thumb firmly closed together.

"Please Lloulou. He said I was to tell you it was about Mezzatorra."

"Mezza-what? Ok, tell him I'll let Chartsie know he's back. Mezza-what?"

"Mezzatorra."

"Mezzatorra. Got it. Now hush. Let's have a look at you." Lloulou pulled Guy onto her chair in her place, and, kissing the top of his head, she said: "What do you think, Dana?" she said, as the hairdresser came back. "This one could never pass as Prince Teodor."

"No, but he could easily pass as a young Prince Erederon," Dana said unexpectedly. "He so totally has the look."

"Oh, Dana! You're right. Blow-dry his hair in Erederon's style. I'll look for that black eyeliner he preferred."

"No, no! Well, ok, but no eyeliner…" protested Guy.

"Oh, c'mon, Guy. Do you want the Riffaut to take all the Imperial glory?"

Guy smiled up at the beautiful face. There was nothing he could refuse her. So it was that a short while later he admired his reflection, black skintight trousers, a white silk shirt and a sparkling red waistcoat. Then the stylist offered him a black jacket. He pulled it on, turned the collar up at the neck and flicked back his hair.

"Nice," he said quietly to himself. As soon as the word escaped him, he was embarrassed. All round there was a chorus of remarks from the women and girls. He knew he was a success.

Chapter 10: 3D Models and Avatars

"So who is Erederon?" Karl asked languidly. He was lounging on a low sofa in Nikato's study at the Zaracan Embassy. Nell sat on a stool across from him. She had a pen and paper and was drawing a family tree of the Freyne Imperial House.

"You need to be neater than that, Nell," Karl said, imitating the voice of a tutor-droid. Nell just laughed, she knew who the real teacher was here.

"There's two," Nell replied sternly. "First, Old Erederon, or Erederon the Great. He was the Emperor before Frederon. He was the only one to survive the hundred year war. He was the last bastard son. He was raised and lived in Domeside before they called him to the Imperial throne."

"Ok. Old Erederon, Frederon's father. And Frederon is the current Emperor."

"Yes. The second Erederon is Prince Erederon who was the first and only son of Emperor Frederon so far. He's dead."

"Died in a terrorist bomb?"

"No, Prince Erederon crashed his flyer, died instantly."

"Ok, Erederon the Great (dead), father to Frederon (Emperor – alive), father to Prince Erederon (dead)."

"And how is Teodor related to them?"

"Well, Frederon had a brother Sergeron. He had a son Sergeron also, normally abbreviated to Serge, hence King Serge. King Serge had two sons Teodor and…"

"Don't tell me! Sergeron?"

"No, Deodran. He was the baby prince who was killed by a terrorist bomb in the car along with King Serge."

"Ok. So, Frederon (Emperor) is brother to Sergeron (dead?)."

"Yes."

"Sergeron is dead. He was father to Serge (dead.) Father to baby Prince Deodran (dead) and finally, Teodor, the only surviving male heir."

"That's right. He's the Emperor's great nephew."

"Will you two be quiet? The Regent is about to speak."

They all looked expectantly at the newsreader, who said:

"Good evening. The six o'clock news will be broadcast after a message from Her Highness the Regent Sayginn."

The information screen went blank. The chords of the Regency anthem started up, and the screen displayed the Regent's coat of arms.

Karl whispered hurriedly: "And how does the Regent Sayginn fit in, is she related?"

"No. Regent Sayginn married King Serge, but she was born of one of the lesser families. There are twelve Baronial families in the empire: five major Baronies, the Imperials and six lesser families. But what lesser actually means is that there have been no marriages between them and the Imperial for several hundreds of years."

"So, Sayginn – lesser Baronial family – was she lucky then, to marry Serge?"

"Yes, very lucky. Except of course…"

The head and shoulders of Sayginn appeared. Behind her on a stand was a painting: King Serge, Sayginn, Teodor and Deodran, with Prince Teodor standing to the fore.

"Hush, you two," Nikato said.

"…Serge is dead," Nell whispered.

Karl nodded and stretched out the full length of the small sofa, taking care to keep his boots hanging over the armrest. Nikato raised a disapproving eyebrow, but Karl ignored him. Nell snuggled up against Karl. She pushed up herself onto the sofa and wrapped her arm around Karl's neck. Karl stroked her hair, and kissed her brows. All three concentrated on the screen.

"Citizens of Freyne 2, my people," Regent Sayginn stared sternly into the cameras. "This evening's news broadcasts and your evening papers give details of the violent kidnapping of my son Teodor, as he was undertaking charity work in Domeside. My son was taken, but another dozen children are dead, and more are injured. This was a terrible crime that was inflicted on both myself and my people. It is to you, my people," her voice now a note more serious and sincere. "I do declare my first duty." She paused, then continued, "You can be sure that while my son is in captivity, I will not compromise the economic prosperity or safety of this planet." Sayginn clarified her meaning by adding:

"Any decision taken now, and during this period, will be reviewed by Prime Minister Patrick McGuire and the planetary committee. He will continue to do so until Prince Teodor is returned to his rightful place, here in Magnolia Palace." Another pause, then the Regent adopted a new and angry tone:

"To the kidnappers! I remain the head of the Regency Defence. I will employ all it takes to find my son. Release my son, unharmed. For you will be caught, I promise. So help me God."

In a deliberate break, Sayginn took a sip from a glass of water. The camera zoomed in to her face as she became more persuasive:

"To the people of Domeside, some of you know a great deal about the horrendous act that took place today. The video files are being carefully scrutinised for evidence. There will be prosecutions after the terrible actions in the cathedral. No man is above the law. Also, if you" (the word 'you' was accented, so it sounded like pleading) "come forward with information that leads to the release of my son," the camera switched to the portrait, "I will ensure you will avoid prosecution for kidnapping, and you will receive a reward that reflects my gratitude to see my son returned here, alive and well." Another slight pause. Sayginn, who had dropped her eyes, returned her gaze to the camera. Her voice was soft:

"Finally, to Teodor. My Teodor, I love you very much. You know of my love for you." Her emotions were now strong.

"Everything I do is working towards your freedom. From now until the next time I hold you in my arms, I love you, Teodor. We all do." The screen snapped to a photograph of the Prince Teodor grinning and hugging a young goran cub, and a repetition of the final bars of the anthem.

"Not a dry eye in the house," Nikato said wryly. He picked up the control and switched off the screen.

"How old is she?" asked Karl.

"Thirty-three, so older than you, little brother."

"I'm thirty-one. Is it true she will be forced to marry the Emperor?"

Nikato frowned, then said in the mild tone he always used for rebukes:

"Not forced, but many of the Barons think it would be desirable."

"She can say no?"

"Yes, but she will also try to gain some advantage for her son."

"What advantage?" Karl asked. "Prince Teodor is heir to two crowns, both the Kingdom of Freyne 2 and the Empire of Freyne."

"Yes, but he is not the Son of Empire," said Nikato.

"Son of Empire?" Karl asked.

"Deep down, the Emperor still wants his own son to succeed him. Even if it was an illegitimate son, an Imperial bastard. If Frederon had his way, he would be the next Emperor."

"So Teodor might not become Emperor?"

"If the Emperor died tomorrow," Nell said firmly, "Teodor is the only heir."

"But long term," Nikato explained, "only the title Son of Empire will secure the Imperial throne for Teodor. So far, the Emperor has refused to give it to him. Anyhow, we are leaving for the Dome in thirty minutes, are you ready to go, Karl?"

"Yes. Do I need to change?"

"You have read the schedule for this weekend?" Nikato asked and Karl thought he sounded a little waspish, so in reply he lied.

"Of course, it all looks great Nikki," Karl hesitated. "But I'm ok dressed like this?" Karl was wearing combats and a t-shirt. "I have this jacket." He held up a light, leather flying jacket that Zaracan troops wore when off duty. Karl thought he saw a flicker of amusement pass behind Nikato's eyes, but all he said was:

"You are who you are, Karl."

"Great!" Karl was relieved.

"Uncle?" Nell said, looking uncertainly from Nikato to Karl.

"Your uncle is who he is," Nikato said to her, "Whereas you…" He pointed to the door.

"I have to get changed," Nell smiled and left gracefully.

Karl watched her go, bemused, then said:

"Nikki, would you mind…" Karl pointed to the library next door. Nikato nodded once. Karl went into the next room, and tried to remember what he had been doing.

Since he had arrived a couple of hours before, Karl had spread himself over most of the Ambassador's once tidy library. His intentions were clear. All across the space were plans and screens of information, as he pieced together the detailed structure of the Dome. And the Dome was huge.

It was called a mini-city, and after several hours Karl was only just starting to get his head round the scale of it. There was a one hundred thousand-seat stadium for ball games, six swimming pools of different sizes, from small training pools to massive competition pools, and seating for a further ten thousand, plus three further arenas with seating of seven to fifteen thousand. There was a vast entertainment complex, shopping over three levels and restaurants; then on the upper levels there were apartments, two hotels and an entire floor given over to conference suites and meeting rooms.

Finally, there was the quasi-military sports complex with barracks for ten thousand men, and a transport hub, including all types of land and hover transport and an extended runway to allow the small fleet of military shuttles to transfer to the space stations. Underground there were further gyms. Room after room was given over to weapons, as well as a vast military kitchen, storage, cellars and refrigerated units.

Karl had started to compile 3D graphics of specific military areas, and some 3D models of the more complicated corridors and tunnel systems. In addition to the main speedways and side corridors, the Dome had a network of large maintenance tunnels, and narrow passageways at the centre of the pillars of the Dome. The massive steel structure needed its strength, so access was restricted. Karl experimented with avatars to see how large you could be to climb up, down and along the verticals and horizontals of the Dome. He was too large, but smaller robots or boys would slip through easily enough.

What about a boy who was the size of Teodor? He reconfigured the avatar and watched.

Hearing someone behind him, Karl quickly blanked the graphics with its avatar. Nell stood in the doorway wearing a gown.

"Oh, it's you." Karl restarted the image and Nell crept in and stood alongside Karl at the centre of the 3D graphic of the Dome.

"Are you looking for him, Uncle Karl?"

"Well, not really, but it's a puzzle isn't it?"

"It's not fair," Nell said. "I keep thinking how it's not fair. He was doing charity work and they kidnapped him. They will get him back, won't they Uncle Karl?"

"Well, Nell, I'm not sure."

"What would you do if it were me kidnapped in there?"

"I think I would be dismantling their Dome even as we speak," Karl said with a growl.

"Really?" Nell looked shocked and delighted.

"Fortunately, there are also other methods. More than ninety-five per cent of the Dome's infrastructure is covered by cameras. I expect there are video streams, audio streams, comms. Everything will be being checked; should they find anything suspicious, pretty soon someone will have a Regency Defence guard knock on their door.

Of course, whoever kidnapped Prince Teodor is probably aware of the methods that will be deployed to get him back, so that leaves the black zones and the quiet zones."

"Black zones? Those are the areas without camera coverage, aren't they?"

"Yes, and in the Dome, we're talking about Chart Segat's admin suite, here in the cap of the Dome, and a variety of areas here linked to the military training facility, likely to be heavily guarded. I expect these will include prisons and a weapons and munitions store."

"A prison block. Well, if there's a prison block, won't they be keeping him there?"

"You would think so and it is a black zone, so it could be. But it was searched by the Regency Defence this afternoon, and they did not find him."

129

"Tsk."

"Probably they are moving him around. To keep ahead of the searches – but then every time they move him they could end up in the visible zone. See those screens there?" Karl pointed at more video feeds on large screens. "Those are video feeds for the corridors here, here and here."

"The corridors just outside the black zones."

"Yes, that's where we are likely to have first sight of him unless you can think of anything else?"

"Me?"

"Yes, you have a young brain – where do you think they might hide him?"

"In a cupboard."

"Droids can check those, they should be finished soon. They'll start over just in case."

"Nothing?"

"No."

"They could be hiding him in a box or something. I mean, look at those deliveries."

Karl looked at one of the access points; they could see large boxes being delivered and moved around the Dome."

"It's a fashion show. They have been moving stuff in and out all day. I could run an algorithm. What we need is something that would show us where something is hollow and large enough to hide the prince."

All at once, a large stack of crates lit up orange on the display.

"Ooh orange, so why are those boxes orange?"

"Because they meet the criteria of the algorithm: they are large and hollow, and the prince might be inside."

"Really?"

"No," said Karl. "Look at the signs on the boxes, its a delivery of melons," he said, reading the exterior. "Send a mini-droid to check them." Another room was flashing on the map.

"Where's that?" asked Nell.

"It's one of the rooms in the cap of the Dome. There's a party there, but it's a black zone, as well. I don't have the installation plans for that black zone, obviously, but I found this layout. It's the catering plan for tonight's cocktail party."

"Everybody is having parties tonight," Nell said. "It's Magnolia Weekend!"

Karl nodded absentmindedly, then explained. "The algorithm is saying that those cocktail tables are hollow, and the space inside is... oh, that cannot be right!"

"It must mean the bases, the columns. But they look narrow."

"Well, Prince Teodor is not much bigger than you. Algorithm, give him space to breathe at least."

"Oh!" Nell exclaimed. At once, all of the tables on the layout turned from orange to black.

"Ok, so not the cocktail tables. Phew, there are at least a hundred of them."

"Can you not send roaches to check? Just in case."

"The cocktail party is in the black zone. I'll put it on the list for when they move them. It will be under a heading: Nell's idea."

They laughed, though Nell stopped first.

"I hate the thought of him being locked up somewhere, all alone."

"Yes, but he'll know they're looking for him."

"He's only thirteen, the same age as me. What if they hurt him?"

"Nell, Prince Teodor rides two-metre-high gorans. Anyone who does that has got to be pretty brave. He knows they're looking for him. Most likely, he's curled up fast asleep somewhere."

"Ok, we're ready."

Karl turned to where Nikato was standing in the doorway.

"You look very nice, Nell."

Karl looked at his niece properly, and realised she was wearing an exquisite handmade gown. It was like one piece of material falling from her shoulders to her knees. It was colours of flames. Similarly, her hair had changed colour to be all over orange and red, like fires in the deep.

Nikato, too, was wearing a full dress suit, entirely lilac in colour. On top, he wore an outlandish swirling coat that did not close. The coat was made of purple brocade and trimmed in crystal-specked fur.

"Don't forget your jacket, Karl."

Karl frowned. "Where are we going?"

"You remember Karl," Nikato purred. "The Festival of Fashion. The reception party? I have organised a Sas Darona-themed party with tribal dancers and fried-chilli sand lizards. We have to promote House Duet – you know, the Zaracan fashion industry?"

Karl felt sick at this rebuke. After all his protests and the sheer effort of bringing the tribal dancers and sand lizards, he had forgotten. Or maybe he had never realised. The party was tonight, his first night. And it was a fashion party at that. A fashion party on Freyne 2, the capital of fashion for the entire empire. And Karl was wearing combats?

"I'd better get changed," Karl said quickly.

Nikato took a look at his communicator, and with a hint of victory, said "I'm afraid we haven't got time for that."

"Why do I think you have been waiting all day to say that to me?" Karl asked quietly.

"You can't change who you are, Karl."

Karl picked up his jacket. His casual uniform suddenly felt scruffy and unappreciated.

"You know Nikki, you're right. I don't need any fancy clothing. I do know who I am. I will wash my face though." Karl nodded to the attendant mini-bathroom off the library. Anger flashed in Nikki's eyes.

"The cars are downstairs. Don't take too long."

As Nikato and Nell left, Karl reran the algorithm error message. The cocktail tables were all orange again. In amongst the error messages, the word 'grille' was highlighted in orange.

"Right," said Karl thoughtfully. "Right."

***

The Embassy had sent a large contingent to represent the Zaracan Democratic Union, including many of the young female staff who were all dressed up for the occasion.

"Also, you'll have your fitting appointment. It was the only time they could fit you in before the Magnolia Stakes Ball," Nikato told Karl.

"Magnolia Stakes Ball?" Karl asked Nikato, as they climbed out of their hover car into the Dome atrium. "Oh my, oh my."

"Take a good look," whispered Nikato. "It's a whole other world."

"Oh, is that Regent Sayginn? I must offer my respects."

"Karl, no, the Emperor."

"Just give me a minute, Nikki."

"What's he's doing?" Nell asked in stunned silence. "Does he not realise the protocol?"

"Sssh, Nell! I'm listening. Oh, for goodness sake, Karl." Nikato fell silent. Nell could see he was concentrating on maintaining a telepathic link to Karl.

A few moments later, Karl was walking back. He looked a bit crestfallen. He did pause once to look over his shoulder, but then he re-joined Nikato.

"Well, that went well," Nikato said archly. "I'm so glad you never even attempted a career in diplomacy."

Karl, Nikato and Nell, together with the others, walked through the fashion show, admiring the floral displays, the catwalks, the women, the clothes. They were an intimidating clan, Karl realised. These ten tall Zaracans, all with long, sweeping multi-coloured manes, entering the party dressed in the finest Old Mill Lane fashion. Ten tall Zaracans and him, the tallest and most impressive of them all. His casual combats were gaining him more stares than all his colleagues, and as he passed, his name – sometimes mispronounced as Killer Valvanski – echoed at his back.

Killer Valvanski indeed! They had not seen him cradling a dying Dome Elite, willing him to live, applying the best antidotes the Zaracan Union could devise. Did the Freyne even know how most of their losses on Sas Darona came about? Did they know that their young men had orders to commit suicide rather than surrender? That the Dome they loved, the medallions they so admired, when worn by their soldiers on Sas Darona were instruments of instantaneous death?

"Chart Segat," Karl whispered. He nodded a short distance away, where the Mayor of the Dome stood at the centre of a group of admirers. Immediately Karl started walking. Nikato pinched Karl by the upper arm to stop him.

"What are you doing?"

"I want to get a look at that man. Get his scent, you know what I mean? In military speak, it means sizing him up."

"Ok, but not too close. He'll freak out."

"Look, I need to get his scent. I just need to."

As he came up behind him, Karl heard Chart Segat cackling at some joke, loudly, with drink:

"…And each of those boys is being paid three times the normal price."

'What was so funny?' Karl thought. He looked where Chart Segat was looking. At first he thought it was a display of mannequins, like a window of fashion. Then he realised that what he had thought were mannequins were actually human models. In this case, mostly young men and some boys; all wearing fashion. The sign above said the Riffaut. It meant nothing to Karl, not at first. As the realisation dawned, his jaw dropped open. There were eight boys in the tableau; all eight were identical to Prince Teodor.

"DNA check," Karl said in a low voice.

"Nell, you have a telepathic link to the boy?" Nikato asked. Nell nodded.

"Use it!" Karl urged.

Karl watched as his niece looked from one boy to another. Each time, she was reaching to the boy with a telepathic link. Teodor, with his low-level goran telepathy, should immediately react as he felt it. None of the boys even noticed her, and a tear rolled down Nell's face.

"No. He's not there."

Nikato sighed: "That was a long shot."

"Karl Valvanski." The booming voice was unmistakable. The intended insult in the mispronunciation, even more so. Chart Segat had seen Karl and Nikato and pushed his way through the crowd to greet them. "And another 'ski. Is this another of your brothers? And oh, look! A mini 'ski. Are you enjoying the party, 'skis?"

134

Nikato did not reply, just bowed his head. Nell shrank to Karl's side and Karl put a protective arm around her. Karl just stared at Chart Segat, wishing he had a telepathic link to this man. He could see the strength in his vast body. He could read the cruelty in his eyes. He could smell excitement and fear. Fear? What was Chart Segat afraid of? The forthcoming trial? On his lapel was a stone-encrusted badge: Five more years, it read. Was it simply that Chart Segat feared losing control of the Dome?

Chart Segat was still talking, entertaining his entourage with his insults:

"Well, I'm sure any of our girls would be happy to entertain you. They will just charge you double and expect to be paid in Zaracan currency." Chart Segat roared with laughter once more.

'*Have you got his scent yet?*' Nikato spoke in urgent thoughts.

'*He stinks of beer. And something else,*' thought Karl. '*A fearsome appetite for power.*'

'*That's what makes him so dangerous,*' was Nikato's thought reply. '*C'mon, let's go.*'

Nikato led Karl through the crowds towards the Zaracan fashion house Duet, with its modest display close to the exit. The fitting did not take long. Karl thought he would hate it, but he found himself admiring the quality of the materials and the detailed stitching. There were no outlandish colours, either. Karl thanked the tailor and stepped back into the party. In front of the House Duet stand, a crush of people had grown. Karl saw a procession of people coming towards them, with the crowds falling back and applauding as they passed. Hemmed in on all sides, he stretched up to see over the heads of the people in front of him.

Chart Segat was leading Emperor Frederon out. The two leaders were escorted by a group of impossibly beautiful models wearing sparkling red and jet black outfits, including, Karl noticed, a couple of youngsters. Wasn't it a bit late?

"Now the private parties will be starting," said Nikato. "Oh look, they are taking the disk jet to Chart Segat's office." The Emperor Frederon, Chart Segat and eight others had stepped onto a small circular disk. Seemingly without any other support or guidance the disk jetted up to the summit of the Dome. A further group crowded onto a second disk. The crowd was cheering wildly. Karl could understand why. Standing atop the disk with no visible support, these chosen few looked like gods, flying upwards on their own silver meteors of speed.

"Whoa," said Karl. "Disk transport – I did not know the Dome had that. It's not on the plans."

"Must be new!" Nikato replied, "because clearly they do."

"So that goes up to Chart Segat's private rooms?"

"Yes, in the cap of the Dome."

"What goes on up there?"

"Trust me! You do not want to know."

"But would it be normal for the Emperor and Chart Segat to be together?" Karl hesitated. "Nikki, did you know there was a connection between Emperor Frederon and Chart Segat?"

"It's hardly suspicious, Karl. Chart Segat is the leader of the Dome and was a friend to King Serge. Emperor Frederon is a supporter of the Dome and King Serge's uncle. Of course they know each other. What's more, over three thousand people saw them."

"I see." Karl didn't see. There were so many connections. So many relations of trust, family, betrayal and power. There were secrets and lies, ambitions and personal frailties. Who, if anyone in this complex web of Freyne power plays, was innocent?

Karl paused a moment longer, looking up at the Dome's cap. He grasped Nikato's arm and said with passion:

"Nikki, I need to know everything. If… well, the prince, that boy prince. He might still be alive."

"Can you feel him here, in the Dome?"

"No. Well, yes," Karl paused. "He is here, I know it. And I think I might be the only one who can get him out."

"Sssh," Nikki's rebuke was abrupt. Karl turned quickly. Standing a short distance from the stage, Regent Sayginn was watching the Sas Darona tribal dancers.

Chapter 11. A Festival of Fashion and Flowers

Sayginn sipped a glass of fizz and moved closer to the performance space. She was hoping no-one would talk to her, wondering once again why she was here. How could she possibly be helping Teo? She remembered her words from a couple of hours before…

"So, what now?" Sayginn was restless. "I have cleared my entire diary. So for God's sake, give me something to do."

Regent Sayginn and her Prime Minister, Patrick, were watching the viewing statistics for the broadcast earlier that evening. Over seventy-eight per cent of the Domeside population had seen the broadcast. Now it was being repeated on every channel. It would not be long before they achieved saturation coverage.

"We need to look again at your diary, but you're not going to like it."

"Patrick, no. I'm not going to any party. What about the press? How can I attend a party when my son has been kidnapped?"

"I'll manage the press. You need to go back to the Dome."

"I've already spoken to Chart Segat."

"His inner circle, Sayginn. You need to get to each of them and, eyeball to eyeball, ask them directly."

"And how can I do that?"

"At the Festival of Fashion? I can guarantee they will all be there."

"Oh no, Patrick! I can't possibly…"

Sayginn was momentarily distracted. One of the screens was showing footage from the viewpoint of a cy-wolf as he raced along a narrow maintenance corridor after Teodor. The animal had come so close, so very close, to freeing the prince in those first vital moments after the capture. All in vain the Battle Borg had been fast, accurate and unafraid. The cy-wolf had been destroyed.

Sayginn watched the film playing on a loop. These were the last and best pictures of Teodor from that morning. Alive, yes, but drugged. His limbs hung loose, his eyes glazed, and yet, and yet. His fingers were twitching as he tried to reach the cy-wolf. He was trying to escape. He had been well-trained. He knew he had to fight – whatever horror might come his way. Here he was fighting, trying to escape until the faint overcame him.

"Oh, sweet Teo!" she muttered. "Hang on, my darling, Mummy is coming to get you."

Her car pulled into the entrance of the Dome atrium and she was presented with a long garland of flowers. The Festival of Fashion was this year themed to celebrate flowers and fruit. The displays and decorations were made of over two million individual blooms and fruits, so the press said. Sayginn was prepared to believe them. As she entered, the perfume was overwhelming. Garlands, columns, gardens and wall displays were all made of flowers and the dinner was already underway.

The Festival of Fashion dinner was a lavish affair with three thousand places set at circular tables throughout the Dome atrium. This was a vast open space at the entrance to the Dome. As with the cathedral, the architects had rebuilt the entire ancient village square within the space, though not without improvements. The faux antique buildings had been built of panels and modules, which meant that on occasions like this the facades were detached and raised high into the space. The opened buildings doubled the available space. This evening, caterers had set up tables of food and drink in a variety of these extensions, while magicians and other entertainment took place elsewhere. Sayginn made her way to the Emperor's table set on a raised podium near the entrance of the Dome. From there she had a fine view over the atrium, but also out through the panes of the Dome onto the city.

"You're late," the Emperor said flatly. "We waited, but in the end... you have missed the first course. Sit. Wine! So, still no news about Teodor?"

Sayginn shook her head. She had thought she was hungry, now she knew she was not. She did take a glass of fizz and drank it quickly. Unexpectedly, she saw someone coming towards her:

"My blades are yours to command, Regent." It was the one phrase of Freyne Karl knew fluently. He was confident that he had said the words without any trace of an accent. "Let me help you find your son."

Karl had seen the Regent as he entered the Dome. Leaving his brother, niece and diplomatic delegation behind he went to kneel at her side and kissed Sayginn's rings, as he knew her followers and Barons did. Besides the Regent, the Emperor had turned to look at Karl Valvanchi. He laughed aloud to hear what Karl had said.

"Is this your only ally, Sayginn? Your own people have turned against you, so you align yourself with the alien Valvanski?" He mispronounced the name with a hiss and leered up at Karl. "I trust you enjoyed the Dome Elite stretch, very good for the spine, they say."

"Freddie, Karl is here on a diplomatic visa," Sayginn protested mildly. "Please let me handle this."

"Yes, I might just carve his jugular from his neck." Frederon curved his black-pointed nails towards Karl in a menace. Around the table, the other guests laughed at this.

Only Sayginn was appalled, but she noticed how the press droids were spiralling around taking pictures and videos of the encounter. So she smiled politely at the Emperor and turned back to Karl. Though he was almost two meters tall, with broad, strong shoulders, all she could see was an earnest young man at her feet. She knew he was the same age as her. Right now, he looked so much younger. So much passion, she thought, does he not realise what I must now do?

"Your offer is generous, Captain Valvanchi. But I can assure you, with all the forces of the Regency deployed to find him, my son will surely be returned to his rightful place by nightfall."

Sayginn smiled at Frederon, seeking his approval. He said nothing, just sneered again at Karl. Karl ignored the Emperor and persevered.

"Let me advise you. I have great experience of fighting the Dome Elite, fighting and killing them on Sas Darona."

On the words Sas Darona, Regent Sayginn closed her eyes a moment, as if in prayer. How could someone so talented in one field be so ignorant elsewhere?

"Captain Valvanchi, that is a lie. There are no Dome Elite on Sas Darona, why would there be? The Freyne Empire recognises Zaracan sovereignty on Sas Darona." Sayginn glanced at the Emperor to check he had heard what she said. He was grinning at her. "Your offer is very generous, Captain Valvanchi, but alas I cannot accept your help. This is an internal matter of the Freyne Empire. Thank you, but no. This is a matter we must resolve for ourselves."

Karl bowed and backed away slowly. Sayginn could see he was a little confused, and maybe a bit distracted. Finally, he turned back to his brother. Her gaze followed him, lingering on the strength of his legs, and the narrowness of his waist. She didn't notice Frederon, until he grabbed her by the upper arm, and yanked her back. He hissed in her ear:

"That's what you like, hey Sayginn?"

"Freddie!" replied Sayginn faking surprise, as she quickly tried to cover her tracks. "The Valvanchi Captain, well you heard him, brave and impetuous. But I said no, we hardly need Zaracan interference in our affairs."

"I could not agree more," the Emperor replied smoothly. "And when we are married, you will break every one of the agreements, promises or understanding you have with those long-haired telepathic weirdoes. I will sit beside you and watch you do it." Frederon bent forward and with some theatricality, kissed her on the nose. Frederon was talking of multiple layers of trade agreements. Reciprocal arrangements Serge had carefully built up to the great prosperity of Freyne 2. Sayginn knew they could not survive without them. What could Frederon be thinking? He wanted her to be completely dependent on the empire, and tied to its fate. He smiled at her, as if he, too, could read her thoughts, then finished with vicious glee: "What's more, you'll enjoy it. When we are joined as one, you will love me as a true wife. Because together we will be powerful enough to do without those Valvanski. We could push their pale, slim faces into the dust."

He mispronounced the name again, and Sayginn shivered at the insult.

'Oh dear god, help me, Karl Valvanchi,' thought Sayginn, closing her eyes, struggling to stay calm. She was nodding in agreement as the Emperor spoke, yet hiding her eyes lest the press droids catch a picture of her looking tearful. Only then she noticed. A short distance away, Karl Valvanchi had stopped. He was looking directly at her. Sayginn heard him.

'I am ever at your service, sweet lady.'

He had not spoken, of that Sayginn was sure. Maybe she had imagined it? She forced herself not to look. Had she imagined the words that his straight, strong gaze seemed to convey? All at once she was captivated. Karl had offered to help rescue her son? Just to think of this unexpected offer, from a man known to be a great warrior and leader of men, brought tears to her eyes. For a moment, she could not breathe. She allowed herself one look. Karl was now speaking to the Zaracan Ambassador. Strange to think those two were brothers.

Nikato was a shallow man, all her advisors agreed. He enjoyed fine fashion and fine food and liked to think of himself as a patron of the arts. Sayginn had once caught him sneering when she spoke of the Dome Debate. Did he not appreciate the months of negotiations which had gone into gaining the votes for this milestone election? Also, his reported passion for the arts also extended to some of the younger dancers who performed in them. One young star had reported being terrified after an incident at an embassy party.

In contrast, Karl Valvanchi was a life-long soldier and warrior. She had read his reports on his encounters with the tribes on Sas Darona. She was touched by the details he provided of the lengths he took to save and heal the tribes' wounded. How he adhered exactly to the United Races rules of engagement when fighting the tribes. His repeated demands for new research into poisons and their antidotes.

(Which she knew was actually for use with the Dome Elite, only she pretended not to know. Just as she always denied their bases on Sas Darona. Oh Serge, why did you start all that?)

Last year, Karl had even written a paper setting out the case for why the Freyne should be given limited mining rights for the monazite that Sas Darona had in such great quantities.

(This would have been a useful start, though not all that Sayginn, and Serge before her, had wanted.)

Sayginn remembered how Chart Segat had dismissed the paper, saying the Zaracan were offering a cherry, while they kept the cake for themselves. But Sayginn saw in his writings an ally and a man of character. He was also a hero and victor of many battles, and now he had offered to rescue her son. If ever she had seen a white knight, Karl Valvanchi was it. Long estranged from the Valvanchi clan, enemy of the Dome Elite, was he the one person she could trust?

'Yes, I think I possibly am.'

141

Again, that clear, strong voice, was he speaking to her by telepathy? He was so far away she could just see the top of his head, yet here he was using his telepathy again. Could the Valvanchi do that?

As dessert was served, the tempo of the music changed. Sayginn knew what was coming, but still she looked up. From above, eight catwalks came down on chains, like the opening of some great flower. Beneath them, the other tables – like insects – were moving swiftly aside on wheels. Around the atrium, the newly mobile guests were reaching for fresh glasses of fizz. As the catwalks fell slowly into place, and even as they touched the ground, the impossibly beautiful models of House Jewel and the Riffaut paraded into view. This was the Festival of Fashion, the opening party of Magnolia Weekend.

The great, the good, the famous and infamous were all present at the party, enjoying the fountains of wine and the extensive buffets of food. Along the walls in alcoves, when not parading the catwalk, the houses displayed their collections in living tableaux. So many beautiful people admiring each other, and keeping an eye out for the latest model, male or female, who would become the face of the season.

Sayginn was about to say something to Emperor Frederon when she saw the boy on the catwalk. She immediately stood up from the table. Her chair crashed to the floor. She made her way down, off the podium. Her pace quickened to a run...

"Was this a joke?"

The boy turned and looked at her. Sayginn stopped. Now she heard the footsteps and voices.

"It's not him," said Sayginn aloud.

"It's the Riffaut," one of the organisers was saying, "They have styled their models to look like—" he stopped talking when he saw the look on Sayginn's face. "I'll get them to stop the show."

"No, no," Sayginn said, and as if to prove she could do it, she turned and watched the boy as he twirled and span at the end of the catwalk. "It's a good likeness. There's no harm done, no harm at all."

Having had a good look, she nevertheless turned her back on the catwalk and walked back. The Emperor handed her a glass of fizz with a sad smile.

Sayginn said nothing.

The Emperor took her head between two hands and pulled her close: "Poor Sayginn. Poor, poor Sayginn. Let me protect you." He bent down and started to kiss her. Sayginn groaned inside but dutifully stood still for the kiss. All around the people were applauding and the news people were jostling to get their shots. As he released her, Sayginn stepped back with a bright smile and tried to look delighted. She knew that if she must marry Frederon then in the eyes of the press the marriage must be a success. She would have more power if people thought the Emperor loved her. So she yielded to a third kiss, aware all the same of the angry glint in Frederon's eyes. He, for one, knew she was play-acting. Sayginn tried to defuse the situation with some small talk.

"Which house is this, then?" Sayginn nodded to a human tableau across from them.

"House Jewel. The beautiful Lloulou?"

"Of course, Lloulou."

"Yes, and rumour has it that one of those two youngsters, or maybe both, are her love children?"

"Lloulou had another child?" Sayginn said, and wished she hadn't. As Regent she was not supposed to know models by name, let alone be aware of their illegitimate children.

Lloulou sat at the centre of the piece in a red glimmering gown, stretched back on a small sofa. To her right on a cushioned stool sat a younger girl in a white lace gown with a red ribbon detail. There were three other male and female models. Finally, at Lloulou's elbow, stood a young boy in black and white, with just a splash of red at his waist. He was offering a bowl of red friseburys.

"How old are they?" Sayginn asked.

"Both Guy and Marline are both working, so they are both fourteen." The reply was quick. Chart Segat had taken an empty seat besides the Emperor. Sayginn wondered, had he been invited? By whom? Frederon? Sayginn also knew at once by the quickness of his reply that he was lying. What is he lying about? She wondered. What else is he hiding? Unbidden tears filled her eyes, and she stared straight ahead hoping both men would think she was enthralled by the tableau.

Breath by breath, her emotion subsided, and she was able to see the models from House Jewel as they acted out a short sketch. The boy offered fruit to Lloulou, who refused, but the girl accepted, only to have it snatched from her by another. There was an element of juggling and tomfoolery, and then it started over. The girl did not look fourteen, she looked older, the boy... well, Sayginn was not sure, either way both these children were fourteen, so no concern of hers. Her eye was drawn to the boy again, he was so fresh looking, and the shine on his hair. She turned away, not wishing to stare, and saw something strange: Chart Segat was pointing out the boy to Frederon. Only there was something secretive in his gesture, and no words were exchanged between them.

Sayginn looked again, wondering what was going on. Just then the spotlight fell on House Jewel. On cue, two young men led the parade along their catwalk, a dozen models followed. Sayginn noticed Lloulou prepping the two youngsters, the girl stepped onto the catwalk, spinning and skipping, but the boy still hung back. Stage-fright, realised Sayginn, she could see Lloulou with her hand to his shoulder, pulling him forward.

He's not fourteen, thought Sayginn, he's younger! And they are forcing him to work!

All at once the boy exploded onto the stage in a dazzling display of somersaults and hand springs. He reached the end of the catwalk and span on the spot in a high-kicking display of youthful blade fighting. Sayginn just stood with her mouth open. *Astonishing.* Teo was learning those moves, but this boy was better than Teo. Was it disloyal of her to think so? She looked again. It was the same boy. He had been at the clinic that morning with Lloulou. Of course. She had seen him with Chart Segat. She had wanted to protect him, then. Protect him? What about Teo?

Teodor! Thought Sayginn, he reminds me of Teo. All at once the glass slipped through her fingers; she quickly closed her hand before it fell, but the drink had poured all over the floor. Her head was spinning, she was leaning against whom? Oh, ok, Frederon. Frederon checked that she had her balance then released her carefully. He looked genuinely worried.

"Are you ok, Sayginn?" Frederon asked quickly, "You're not are you?" Frederon hugged her and for once held her, stroking her hair as he pressed her face into his neck. "If we were one, then when they attack you, they attack me too! Let me help you get him back!"

Sayginn nodded, her mouth failed her. She could not speak. The Emperor continued.

"We must get your boy back. Even if it means keeping the Dome open. I mean it, Sayginn. He's my heir, and I refuse to countenance any possible harm to him."

Sayginn was stunned. There had been a slight lull in the music, and almost half the room had heard the Emperor. Frederon, ever the performer, took this as a cue, and repeated with greater emphasis:

"He is my heir, and let it be known I will have no harm done to him. Let it be known!"

Sayginn's eyes turned to Chart Segat, who had heard everything the Emperor had said. Chart Segat was smirking. Sayginn's eyes darted left. Frederon was smiling too. The two were sharing some joke she was not privy to. What had the Emperor just said? Why was Chart Segat smiling?

"He is my heir, and let it be known I will have no harm done to him. Let it be known!"

Sayginn looked over the words, in her head. Was there some second meaning she had missed?

Chart Segat was standing up as the catwalk finished, applauding and calling out 'bravo'. He now turned to them:

"Emperor, Regent! Come! Time to join a private party. I have something very special in mind," he added with a smile to the Emperor, and mimed a clash of spinning blades. "Regent, you should come too."

No, thought Sayginn, no more parties. She had seen and heard enough. Her place was not here, she must head home and give leadership to the men fighting to save her son. And when she took over the Dome... Sayginn hesitated, if she took over the Dome. It was the first time she had experienced real doubt. The Dome Debate was less than twenty-four hours away. What if Teodor was not found?

Sayginn needed to get away. She ignored Chart Segat. She needed help. Real help. She could think of only one person. And for the first time she realised clearly how useful it was to be a non-telepathic race. For neither Chart Segat nor Frederon must know what she was thinking.

"You know what, Freddie? I think I might go and have a look at the Sas Darona tribal dancers," Sayginn said. Then to soften what she had said, she added: "I want to stretch my legs."

145

Chapter 12. Cy-wolves, Cy-rats and Cy-roaches

House Duet was the Zaracan fashion house which had set up on Old Mill Lane to try and compete against the established houses, and possibly to learn from them. Sayginn felt more relaxed now that Frederon had gone up to the cap of the Dome and allowed herself to mingle with the guests in a private area of their exhibit, and taste the obligatory fried chilli lizards. She spoke with Nikato, and noticed how young Nell persistently stalked her, looking for a chance to speak. This evening the girl was wearing an orange dress and had changed her hair colour to match. It was a common tele-skill amongst the Zaracans, which she had seen in news programmes and documentaries, but she had not realised how startling it was in real life.

"Please excuse me," Nell apologised. "I do not mean to be a bother when… Only, it's Karl's fifth birthday, we always celebrate fifth birthdays as important milestones."

"Karl?" Sayginn glanced around her. Karl Valvanchi was keeping his distance. Sayginn saw he was watching the tribal dancers. Sayginn took this as a cue to walk over and look too. Nell followed. She was still laying out her plan.

"My cousin, Karl Valvanchi the third, it's his fifth birthday next month, and I wanted to invite Prince Teodor to come to Zarac 1 to join the celebration."

"Regent Sayginn." Karl bowed, but his eyes were drawn back to the stage.

"Authentic Sas Darona tribal dancers?" Sayginn asked, wondering why he was so interested. Surely he had seen them before?

"How many are there?"

Sayginn looked at the fast moving troupe. They wore identical costumes, and as they danced intricate, bedazzling moves, it was difficult to tell them apart.

"Seven, I think," Nell said quickly.

"Seven," repeated Karl thoughtfully.

"If it is a battle dance, is it a training dance or a victory dance?" Sayginn asked.

At that moment one dancer span across the stage in a fast display of spins and jumps.

"Eight!" cried Nell. "There are eight of them."

"Eight!" Karl repeated. All at once he seemed more relaxed. "Eight dancers all the way from Sas Darona." Karl concluded. "I feel responsible for them, that's all." They watched the dancers for a few beats more. "I interrupted you."

"Nell wants to invite Prince Teodor to your party."

"My son's party. My son, Karl Valvanchi the third, is five years old, an important milestone."

"I see. I do not think I have met your wife, is she here?"

Was Karl Valvanchi married? Sayginn wondered. Karl must have read her thoughts, because he said bluntly:

"It was a five year contract. My family insisted. You know how these things are?"

Sayginn did. The Valvanchis were similar to the princes and Barons of Freyne; marriage was rarely about love.

"The marriage contract was not renewed." He paused, "We split on good terms. My sons are in school on Zarac 1."

Sayginn listened carefully. The Zaracan approach to marriage was so pragmatic, so practical. Yes, they made political marriages, but as per business deals, they had set objectives and time frames. Was her contract with Emperor Frederon, the request for four sons, so different? Yes it was, she concluded.

She looked at the tall, slim Captain. He was about thirty, so a little younger than herself. He was the third son of a great house, admittedly a

Zaracan house. He had access to unlimited wealth, by anyone's standard; he was a fine prince and a fearsome fighter. But he was also a Valvanchi. He had mentioned the end of one marriage contract. What he was in effect saying, was that he was newly single. Was he telling her he was available?

She hunted around for something to say, and remembered her purpose. With one last check that both Chart Segat and Emperor Frederon had gone, she framed the thought as if it were spoken words.

"Karl, I need your help to free Teo."

"My lady, it would be my pleasure."

"Please, my car is outside. If you come back to Magnolia Palace, I can brief you."

Within fifteen minutes they were back in Magnolia Palace, and Sayginn led the way to a large room off the main ballroom.

"This is our theatre of operations."

Karl Valvanchi stood beside Regent Sayginn on a high balcony looking down on the antique ballroom at the heart of the old palace. Wire-net scaffolding had been raised alongside each wall, and now dozens of wide screens had been hooked in place. Across them flowed fast displays of images and data, often with split screens responding to several feeds from below. This was a hastily pulled together command centre. They were still erecting screens along the bottom wall. As the number of screens increased, so the feeds separated and migrated to one feed per screen.

Below them, islands of four to six desks were already in place, with analysts working on small screens and tablets, taking places at desks, and transferring data feeds to the larger screens, meeting in tense ad-hoc stand-up groupings before dispersing into quick, meaningful action.

Sayginn knew all this purposeful activity should fill her with hope, but she was still thinking about Chart Segat and Frederon. The way they exchanged secret glances. The insincere invitation to the party in the cap of the Dome.

'*He is not as powerful as he thinks.*' Sayginn heard the words in her mind, and glanced up at Karl.

'*Who?*' She mouthed.

'*Neither of them is as powerful as they would like.*'

Sayginn hid a smile, but with more confidence led Karl down the stairs: "We have trained for so many years, though not for this exact scenario."

At the bottom of the stairs, thirty large dog cages were stacked in uneven pyramids; alongside was a small cluster of desks and a veterinary-style operating table. As Karl and Sayginn approached, a large wolf leapt onto the table and rolled over obediently onto his back. Two white-coated vets immediately pressed memory chips into the centre of his rib cage. On command, the wolf leapt to his feet and down. The next wolf quickly followed suit.

"Cy-wolves," Karl nodded, impressed. Sayginn patted the nearest animal with a small smile. These animals had proved so brave in the tunnels under the cathedral. Not one had survived, but the cy-wolves alone had been within millimetres of freeing the prince.

"What else do you have?"

"Cy-rats and cy-roaches."

On a smaller table, an assembly line of rats were being passed down from cages, and having new circuit cards inserted into their necks.

"And the roaches?"

Another analyst brought out a large plastic crate, within which were hundreds of cockroaches, each fitted with a third metal antenna and glittering 360° camera.

"We just give them a pulse," said the analyst.

The white-coated technician took one of the cy-wolves' chips and slipped it into the side of a black box with a hose-like extension. He tapped a few commands and then pushed the hose nozzle deep into the pile of roaches.

"Stand back," he said and pressed the final key. An electric pulse ran over the roaches, then rippled across and between them, until each had been electrified. "There!"

"How many do you have?" Karl asked. Sayginn smiled, she was thinking about how she would carpet the Dome with roaches, if she could. Once programmed, these insect cy-roaches, just like the cy-wolves, would not, could not be stopped in their single-minded mission to find her son.

"Within the Dome, there are almost fifteen klicks of corridors and tunnels. We already have two thousand roaches. This is the next wave of two thousand. It should be enough. Maybe. We're not just relying on physical

149

contact. We are pulling in all the surveillance videos from throughout the Dome and all Domeside. We'll be using large-scale analysis. Within the next hour we will have plotted the whereabouts and activity of every known resident in Domeside. Next, we start on exception analysis."

Sayginn was talking about the intelligence effort. Karl looked up. Now the information on the high screens started to make sense, it was video streams from within the Dome.

"We have all communications on tap and are using intelligent image matching to look for Teodor in any of the data streams. Finally…" She walked over to the eight desks that seemed to have been set up first, where around twelve analysts used stools and jostled for small amounts of desk space. "This is individual analysis; we have three key suspects at this time. We are on them like proverbial electronic glue. Once we have them fully tagged, we work outwards through their network of family, contacts, connections, colleagues and friends."

"What are the Dome Elite doing?"

"As yet," Sayginn hesitated, then finished: "we have not specifically requested their assistance."

"But it is every citizen's duty to aid their prince," Patrick said quietly.

"Karl Valvanchi, may I introduce Patrick McGuire, he's my prime minister."

Sayginn caught herself thinking that there could not be two more different people. Patrick, who knew everyone in Freyne high society; he was affable and unimposing; he also knew everyone's secrets, their weaknesses, and who was a genius when it came to organising votes and gaining political compromises. Then there was Karl, the tall hero, who needed neither friend nor family, and was known for going into battle alone.

"Pleased to meet you, sir."

"Karl Valvanchi, the honour is all mine."

Patrick looked at Sayginn. "So, any news from the festival?"

Sayginn shook her head.

"Regent Sayginn, what is this?"

Nikato Valvanchi had arrived. Sayginn did not remember inviting him, but she could hardly say anything. Still wearing his purple brocade robes, he wandered around looking at everything. He was pointing at an organisational chart pinned up above one of the monitors.

Sayginn looked and was immediately embarrassed. The drawing was an organisation chart, its title was clear: 'New Management for the Dome'.

"I thought the Dome was going to be closed? Closed down completely."

Patrick and Sayginn exchanged glances, then Sayginn said:

"Let's go somewhere private."

She led Patrick, Karl and Nikato to the small study off the main ballroom and shut the door. After the bustle and noise of the ballroom the office was quiet – serene even. Sayginn picked up a screen from the desk, and motioned her guests towards a large boardroom table. They sat down, with Patrick and Sayginn on one side, and Karl and Nikato opposite them.

"Let's talk about who has taken my son," Sayginn said.

"In all likelihood, Chart Segat has pulled this stunt to try and change the result of the Dome Debate," Patrick replied.

"I think the Emperor is involved. He said that if I signed the marriage contract as proposed, Teodor would walk free," Sayginn said.

"He's bluffing. Maybe he does know something. Maybe he does want to put the heat under you to force you to marry him on his terms," Patrick said. "But Frederon would not endanger Teodor, he is still the only heir. No, this kidnapping is about the obvious. It's about the Dome Debate."

"Yes, but look…"

Sayginn pointed to one of the screens where Chart Segat led the Emperor from the fashion show.

"He should be in jail," Nikato said sharply.

"Once he is deselected as administrator of the Dome, then we can start legal proceedings," Patrick McGuire replied mildly.

"You mean after the Dome Debate. We have to have Teodor back before then," Karl said firmly. "So, what are we doing to investigate Chart Segat?"

Patrick hesitated.

"Well, Chart Segat is a democratically elected official of the Freyne government. His offices are in the cap of the Dome. We're not even sure what the layout is up there. No comms, no video, no audio, a perfect black spot. No-one can access it without the permission of Chart Segat."

"We'll see about that," Karl said quietly.

Patrick turned to Sayginn:

"Actually, if you think Chart Segat is being used by Frederon, I say that gives us hope."

"How's that?" Sayginn said quickly.

"Chart Segat was devoted to Serge. I can't believe he would harm his son. He knows Teodor, has known him all his life. He will not forget what he owes to Serge," Patrick said and added: "No, this kidnapping is about the obvious. It's about the Dome Debate."

"Maybe we could delay the Dome Debate," suggested Karl. "then they would have no reason to hold him."

"Or they may hold him longer, until the debate is over," Sayginn replied. Then, after a hesitation, "Maybe we should share our plans for the future of the Dome?"

"You said the Dome would close," Nikato said.

"The Dome must close," Karl added.

Sayginn shrugged, trying to appear indifferent.

"Yes, it will close. It will close for at least twenty-four hours. But with all the employment, all the men, all the boys, all their families, all the money it generates, I can't see how we can close the Dome for good."

"We had been led to understand that a Yes vote in the Dome Debate meant the Dome was to close Sayginn, may I call you Sayginn? The Zaracan Council would prefer the Dome was closed, and the Dome Elite disbanded, in its entirety."

Sayginn stared at Nikato Valvanchi. To give herself time to think, she went to take a drink of water. Patrick moved in and he said, pointedly:

"That will be decided democratically on Saturday by the Parliamentary Committee at the Dome Debate."

"Of course it will," Nikato Valvanchi replied and added in a quiet voice, "but unless the terror movement on Sas Darona is curbed soon, we may have to consider sanctions against the planet from where the terror originates."

Sayginn glanced at Patrick to see if he had heard. Nikato's emphasis was clearly on the word 'originates'. That was not an insignificant threat. If the Valvanchi decided to impose sanctions, it would mean the end of all the trade deals that Freyne 2 depended on for its prosperity. It did not bear thinking about – the loss of jobs, the reduction in trade and the resultant economic decline that would follow. Sayginn forced herself to remain calm. Patrick said:

"The Freyne 2 government recognises the Zaracan ownership of Sas Darona."

Sayginn nodded and added:

"We have already provided support against the terrorists in every way we can, short of direct military involvement."

"Yes, indeed you have. We now have proof that the men are trained and equipped from the Dome." He paused for effect and Sayginn's thoughts raced; until now, no-one had proved the link, though it almost certainly existed.

"Proof?" Sayginn allowed one eyebrow to rise to underline her scepticism. Nikato emptied a white envelope into the palm of Sayginn's hand. She caught the chain between finger and thumb and glanced down: of course, a Dome medallion "found on the body of a Sas Darona terrorist. That is the root of the problem, Sayginn. The Dome must close."

Karl interrupted Nikato with some passion: "The Regent cannot be expected to sacrifice her son in the name of the Dome." Karl Valvanchi looked directly at Nikato. "He is her only remaining son."

"She is young, if she marries again…"

Sayginn let out a squeak of despair.

"You must be kidding," Patrick added quickly.

"Please, Lord Valvanchi – not Teo – my son, Teodor, is so well suited, so well prepared for his role in the empire."

"He cannot be abandoned," Karl said firmly.

"It is your men, Karl who must suffer and die if the Dome Debate does not go ahead, if the Dome is not closed."

"My men are well equipped. My men are well trained. Teodor is a thirteen-year-old boy, who took off his communicator to dress as an angel. You cannot expect that boy to fight our war for us."

There was silence at the table. On a screen a newsreader was showing images of Teodor from that morning, wearing the gold and chiffon costume of an angel.

Karl said quietly:

"Send me in – I search throughout the Dome, find the prince and bring him home. If I can do so before 5pm tomorrow, then by all means, the Dome Debate can go ahead."

"I'm sure we can manage…" Patrick said, a little alarmed, showing the preparations all around.

"Such action would go against diplomatic protocols," Nikato barked.

Sayginn said nothing, she glanced up at Karl.

'I think you are the only one who could get him out.'

Karl smiled at her and said aloud:

"If you want the Dome Debate to go ahead, who else would you send? The Regency Defence? The Dome Elite? Do you think Chart Segat will actually give him back?"

They all sat in silence as they considered what he had said.

"I should utterly forbid it, utterly forbid it," Nikato said fiercely, but then he paused and added quietly, "Just keep it out of the press."

"I could not agree more," Patrick said unexpectedly.

"Do you really think you will find him?" Sayginn said, and her voice trembled with unexpected hope.

"I may be the best chance that boy has."

***

Later Sayginn strode aimlessly across the Magnolia Palace gardens, until she reached the stables. She knew the combination, the stable door slipped open. Inside, the beast stretched out its full length across the stall. The first successful Gen. Eng. cross-breed using the genes of the ice cats of Sas Darona (where else?). Blue Barbrina had inherited their ice-white colouring and tufted ears and brows that Sayginn refused to have barbered to improve the goran's aerodynamics. She also retained their innate ferociousness. The ice cats of Sas Darona instinctively attacked all other males, including its own grown-up offspring, to defend territory. This was a true match for the only competitor at the Magnolia Stakes: Frederon's Tiger. Despite its incredible strength, the tiger was a breed of almost impotent domesticity. It would be cruelly whip-provoked to a pre-race fury.

Blue Barbrina lazily opened one eye to gaze at her. Sayginn knew Blue Barbrina would have already identified her smell and sound. She knelt down in the synthetic hygiene fibres and gently stroked the goran's head. "You would stand no nonsense, would you my beauty? You'd just go in there and kill 'em." The purring stopped abruptly. The goran growled. A jockey was standing in the doorway with a torch.

"Hi Paulio, you should be sleeping, big day tomorrow."

"Oh, it's you, your highness; I always sleep above the stable on the night before. Yes, you're right, a big day. She'll win, you know."

"The pair of you will win," said Sayginn with conviction. The man looked uncertain.

"Ma'am, I wanted to speak before but they wouldn't let me. I'm your best jockey for sure, yet Barbrina never runs at one seventy for me." Paulio sounded tense and unhappy. "We know she can do it. Why, she's done it three times under you! With me, never! Not even one six eight, I don't think tomorrow will be a first either." Sayginn stared in dismay at her principal jockey, why hadn't she been told? The Jockey continued quickly and persuasively: "She knows you and loves you. If you rode her then victory would be sure. Ma'am, I really believe it. I'd put my life savings on it. I've heard it said that the Emperor's Tiger Imperial Rina's highest speed to date is one seven one." He looked up and shook his head. "I can't match that."

Sayginn ran her hands through the beast's mane. It was lush and silky. The huge goran rolled over for her to scratch her belly.

"Look how she loves you, Ma'am."

"So you think I should ride her," said Sayginn thoughtfully. "You're so sure you'll lose, Paulio."

"I've lain awake now every night for a week and despite all the training. She's in perfect shape, but under me she just does not perform. Yes, I think I'll lose."

155

"Well, we can't have that," said Sayginn. "I'll ride her in the stakes tomorrow."

Chapter 13. Canapés in the Cap of the Dome

The disk rose swiftly from the Dome atrium towards Chart Segat's private offices. From the tableau and catwalk in the atrium, to the private drinks reception in the cap of the Dome, Guy had never felt so weary. Nevertheless, he perked up when he saw the Dome Elite in full dress uniforms. They were wearing fine wool military jackets with golden buttons and braid. Designed on Old Mill Lane, by House Jewel, no less. How fine they looked. Even as he was admiring them, Guy remembered with horror his own appearance. Yes, he was wearing House Jewel, but... He looked down at the sparkling waistcoat. Red shiny boots too, the trousers were tight – more like leggings, and the jacket was cut as short as a girl's. With his make-up and hair, which he had been instructed to keep long for Magnolia weekend, what did he look like?

"I look like a fashion model," Guy thought bleakly. "When what I want is to look like them." Next, with a note of panic: "What if they see me?"

Guy fell back as they left the disk and walked behind Lloulou and some of the other models. Here he would be unnoticed behind their beauty and style. Here he could hide or try to hide. He hung his head, and looking down at his feet he immediately got vertigo.

The uppermost sanctum of the Dome, the highest point of the Dome, had the most extraordinary view in the entire city, a three-sixty panorama. The architects had made every surface transparent: the floor, walls and ceiling. Through the floor all the sports facilities, all the entertainments, restaurants and shops, all the board tunnel avenues and small interconnections, all were spread out like a giant model.

Giddy with tiredness, and hungry, for a few moments Guy had the impression he was floating in space, then he felt a finger lift his chin.

"Don't look down. You'll make yourself sick." Lloulou had come back to where he was glued to the spot. She smiled kindly into his pale face.

"Chart Segat particularly asked for you," Lloulou said encouragingly. "I'll make sure he notices you, and then you can go. You look dead on your feet. Here take this, and go and offer it to the Emperor."

Guy sighed. Now he was to serve food. He was wearing fashion and taking orders. All in full view of the best soldiers of the Dome Elite. He couldn't think of anything more humiliating. Still, Lloulou wanted him to do this. She was smiling at him with that beautiful smile.

So it was that Guy held a silver tray of nibbles high on one hand, with his other hand was on his hip to balance, and walked towards the Emperor. The Dome Elite was holding the crowd a little way back. Guy noticed Des arriving late, hastily straightening his jacket. Des saw Guy and let him pass. If some of the other Dome Elite were smirking, Des just nodded. Guy felt that Des at least understood; after all, he too had once been in House Jewel. Three years before, Des would have done anything to get a place in the Dome Elite.

The party was not bad, thought Guy. A large conference space was transformed with silver palm trees, lights and chrome furnishings, including fancy cocktail tables, with large bright columns mounted with circular tops.

As Guy approached the Emperor, he noticed something odd. A Dome Elite cyborg, one of the big Battle Borgs, had removed the top of one of the tables. Chart Segat and the Emperor Frederon looked inside. It was a clever design, thought Guy. Was it a storage unit as well as a table? He heard the Emperor say:

"You will have a full pardon for Serge's death, and you will have the Dome, but for God's sake clean him up. I'm pretty sure she'll cave in, if not tonight, then..."

Guy was close now, so without even trying he could see. He let out a little gasp. The Emperor span round and stared at him.

"How long have you been standing there?" Beside him, the borg was snapping the table top back into place. The borg glared at Guy, who stepped back, afraid. The skin on his face was grey and black. It was riven with deep cracks from under the eyes to its chin lines. Guy had never been this close to one of these Battle Borgs before. They were known to be unpredictable around children, even boys. They were housed and trained away from the

158

general population. Guy was so mesmerised by the borg that he did not hear the Emperor until he poked him and repeated sharply:

"What did you see?" the Emperor barked. He was glaring down at Guy, a finger ending with one of his famous black claw-like nails, pointing into Guy's eyes.

"Nothing." The lie was effortless. His fear so intense that he had, in fact, forgotten what it was that had startled him. "I saw nothing."

"Don't worry about this one," Chart Segat laughed. "He's a good boy." With one hand, he was miming for Guy to keep his mouth shut. Guy nodded, a little panicked. Then he was reassured because, in effect, he could not remember what it was he had done that had triggered these angry outbursts. He started to back away.

"Wait!" said the Emperor. Guy looked up, a little startled. The Emperor was staring at him, Guy was transfixed.

"That face? Is this the one you told me about?"

The Emperor was staring at him. Guy was transfixed.

"Guy's House Jewel, my Emperor. Some say Lloulou is his mother."

Frederon stood a moment, completely still. Guy had never known such scrutiny. He could not help himself, just glanced down his body. No, he was not naked. Neither was the Emperor impressed.

"Working is he? Fashion model?" Frederon added with distaste. He reached to lift Guy's chin with the point of his blackened index finger. He was looking closely at his features. "Fourteen is too old probably. Where has he been? Could be surgery, Chartsie? Expensive surgery, but still... Has he been tested?"

"The tests are illegal on Freyne 2," Chart Segat said with a shrug. "The Regent said Prince Teodor was the rightful Son of Empire."

Frederon snorted.

"He could be too, if she would only let me have a hand in his education. But this one looks like a fashion model, and if he has been working... well then." Frederon was looking at Guy disdainfully, perhaps a little sadly. Guy had had enough. He took a deep breath and found his courage.

"I'm not a fashion model. I'm only thirteen. I want to join the Dome Elite."

159

The Emperor seemed surprised. He relaxed a fraction, then said:

"The Dome Elite, better and better." The Emperor laughed bitterly, before saying: "Thirteen?"

"Yes sir, my birthday is not for three months."

"You have an honest face, at least." The Emperor sighed: "Thirteen? Dome Elite? He is still too old really." Finally, Frederon said to Chart Segat: "Oh, you may as well bring him to my yacht to test him. And his birthday is in July, so too young as well. But Chart…"

What were they talking about? To enter the Dome Elite, Guy had to pass tests in maths and blades. Anxiety assailed Guy like a wave, and he rocked unsteadily on his feet. A heavy hand landed on his shoulder, and Guy looked at Chart Segat for a clue. Nothing.

"He's not too old. He's not too young either." Chart Segat and Frederon exchanged glances. Guy had no idea what this meant. "He's a good boy. He'll do as he's told. You know me, Freddie. He'll do as he's told, if not, I'll throw him to my borgs," Chart Segat replied smoothly, running a hand through Guy's hair. Guy could not help squirming a little. He glanced around to see if any of the Dome Elite had noticed. Des was watching. He made a 'calm-down' movement with his hand. Guy stood still again.

All at once Frederon had a hand around Chart Segat's jugular. His black nails spearing his arteries. "I want him back, do you hear me? And don't you dare touch him. I want him back unharmed. I am paying you to hold him. Keep him until the time is right. Then you will get your reward."

The two men stood face-to-face, glowering at each other, and with a theatrical flourish Chart released Guy. The boy quickly backed off. He was glad to look up and see Des taking the tray off him and leading him away.

Guy did not look back. He followed Des out of the bright lights into Chart Segat's bedroom suite. There were several interconnected spaces, and then at the centre of the room was a single enormous bed, wide enough to sleep four or five adults. It rose up on an ornate carved platform and was set in a vast carved bed frame.

Des tugged him forward, but Guy stared up at the three vast statues stretching five metres up at the head of the bed, two women and a man, their three bodies touching and arms and legs crossed and intertwined. Then he blushed, for he realised that while the man was clothed, the women were naked. He quickly looked away. Along the far wall, there was a vast

160

bathroom. There was a large Jacuzzi, a wall of showers, and another two parallel baths, all on view through the glass wall. Guy saw that some of the younger girls were giggling on the edge of the Jacuzzi, goading each other to strip off and enter the whirling bubbles. He recognised Marline. She was still wearing her white dress, but she was perched on the edge of the Jacuzzi with her feet and ankles in the bubbles. It looked like her hem was already soaked through. She saw him looking, smiled and blew him a kiss, and with a wink stretched one of her legs down into the water, squealing as the bubbles rose around her knees. Guy looked away.

What was Marline thinking?

Alongside the bathroom were the only dark triangular recesses in the entire Dome. On one side, the walls were the glass plates of the geodesic Dome, on the other, the walls of the bathing area. There was no light, but Guy knew where they were headed. Des was leading Guy to a junction point of the Dome, where pentagons joined triangles. Guy nodded with understanding, as Des pulled away one of the panels. He reached into one of his pockets and pulled out a head torch.

"You're not too exhausted to climb?"

Guy shook his head.

"It's a closed party, what with the Emperor. No-one gets in. No-one gets out." Des explained. "Except you. Lloulou's orders. Chartsie will throw me to the borgs if he finds out it was me, though."

"He won't do that," Guy said, a little too quickly.

"Oh, won't he? It's Magnolia Stakes weekend. They like their fights bloody this weekend."

"Chartsie won't do that to me," Guy said firmly.

"C'mon Guy, it was not that long ago. You remember don't you?"

Des lifted up his left foot and untied his lace to reveal the injury he found so easy to hide, for while Des had a human foot and ankle, beyond the heel the foot had gone and was replaced by a hideous claw-like prosthetic.

"I always think that Chart Segat took my foot two days after my fourteenth birthday."

"But he gave you the Dome Elite."

"But he gave me the Dome Elite. Remember, Guy – you have to do whatever he says."

"I know, Des. I know."

Des nodded. He took his hat off, turned it over, then put it back again. Guy realised something was wrong.

"What are you doing here, Des? How did you get back?"

"Tribal Dancing." Des sighed, and then said: "Valvanski ordered dancers for his party."

"Killer Valvanski?"

"No, his brother. Nikki Valvanski. He's Ambassador to Freyne."

Guy nodded. He had thought all Zaracans were Valvanski, but maybe not. Maybe only if they were brothers. Had Killer Valvanski a brother? Des had said something, Guy listened:

"... so I was the only one who was fit enough to learn the moves. Someone had to get back here."

"Serious, hey?" asked Guy.

"I was at Mezzatorra," Des hesitated. Guy waited, but Des said: "I should not be talking to you."

"Please Des. Please tell me. Who would I tell?"

Des sighed and shook his head.

"Chart Segat has still not made time yet."

"I told Lloulou."

"I know you did. I should have realised with the Magnolia Stakes."

Guy said nothing for a few moments, just looked back at the party. He glanced up at Des:

"Will you be..." Guy nodded towards the girls, "partying?"

"No. I'm on duty."

"Oh, ok. Will you keep an eye on Marline? Make sure she's ok?"

"Marline? She's here?"

"Over there. She's only just fourteen."

"I know, but Magnolia Stakes should be a good weekend for her. Marline knows what she wants, but yes, I'll keep an eye on her. And I'll see you tomorrow. We need to train."

"I'm working tomorrow at the Magnolia Stakes."

"Well, that's good. I'm there too. Look, you need to climb down two sides from here, but then at the junction take the bottom maintenance horizontal heading west. You should count six or seven grilles, and you get to the changing room on the seventeenth level. The grille is loose. Just be careful you jump clear of the benches, it's a bit of a drop."

"I know where you mean. I've done it before."

"Not at this time of night, you haven't. So just be careful. It's late; you're tired, be careful."

"I'll be fine. Thanks, Des."

***

Teodor woke as he tumbled within the rolling tube. At first his instincts were all wrong. He put his hands up and, tumbling, felt his fingers pushed back. He tried to find his feet only to fall hard on his knees and feel them scuff. He was continuously turning and tumbling, rolling over and over. He put his arms over his head and tucked his knees under his chin. Rolled up in a tight ball, he felt a bit better; he felt a fraction in control. Even the stench of the sewer seemed to have dispersed.

He realised his tube was being pushed along, and beyond there was a huge amount of noise from a loud music system. He heard the sound of tables crashing and banging, and much yelling. Then they started to accelerate; whoever was pushing the tube was running now. The tube turned faster and faster.

Bang! The tube bounced up a steep incline and stopped. As Teodor relaxed a fraction, he felt the wetness spreading over his thighs. He had peed his pants. He sighed in exasperation, then remembered. It was hours since he had last visited a bathroom. It had been back at Magnolia Palace, a small suite off his bedroom. His bedroom. Home!

Hours, he had been captive for hours. That meant it would have been on the news. People would be looking for him. No, now was not the time to

163

think of home and even less the time for self-pity. He could still hear voices. There were men out there. Maybe these men were already looking for him. Time for me to get out, he thought. He started kicking and banging on the sides of the tube. The top of the tube made a very useful echo, and when he kicked it hard the metal even moved slightly. He heard footsteps coming closer. He kicked faster and harder. Click. Click. Click. Above his head, the clips were being undone. The end of the tube was pulled away. Teodor propelled himself after it, falling in a heap onto a metal floor.

"My God, what happened to you?"

A man, a workman by his overalls, was standing over him. Teodor tried to find his feet, and reached up to grab and steady himself.

"My God, what's that smell?"

Teodor heard shouts and saw three huge Dome Elite Battle Borgs hurtling towards him:

"I need your communicator. I have to call my mother."

The man just stared. Teodor looked around: the borgs were getting closer.

"Please, I must call my mother."

"Sorry son, but it won't work here. We're six stories under the Dome."

The Dome Elite was upon them. Teodor leapt from the platform in a spinning kick, but there was no strength in him. The nearest borg just ducked away. Teodor ran, but his legs were still rubbery from the drugs and the hours of confinement. He had managed five steps before he stumbled. They were upon him.

"Let me go," Teodor cried, surely one of these machines must obey him: "Let me go, I am your prince."

"Wait..." the workman said, he grabbed at the arm of a borg. "Isn't that..."

The borg span round and took the man by the neck. There was a crack, and the workman fell down dead. The borg turned back and ran after his colleagues. Teodor looked back once at the fallen, crumpled body and froze. The workman had recognised him, had been on the point of helping him, and now he was dead. These borgs were the deadliest of kidnappers; how could he even begin to think he might escape?

***

Guy Erma was tired. The climb down through the pillars of the Dome had been long and hard. Coming out of the dressing room at last, he used the walkways to speed out of the Dome. Finally, he made his way to the back alley behind Old Mill Lane and climbed up to the attic rooms under the eaves. In the shadows, he made out the muddle of bunks and mattresses of the bedroom he shared with over forty others. He found his spot, peeled off his trousers, shirt and shoes, and shimmied in, pushing Jonny to the left, and letting Pal roll over and hug up against him.

Jonny had his thumb in his mouth, yet without waking, he snuggled up to Guy's shoulder. With a younger child on each side, Guy felt the warmth spreading over him, it was easy to relax. Images of the day flashed before his eyes: the Emperor, Chart Segat, Lloulou, Marline, the cathedral, his choirmaster, the prince. All at once he heard the explosion and saw the doors of the cathedral forced open by a cloud of dust. Suddenly he was lying awake and staring at the ceiling. He remembered now. What had the Emperor said? *You will have a full pardon for Serge's death.* Who? King Serge? So, Chart Segat would be pardoned for killing King Serge. Had he actually done that? *...and you will have the Dome.* How could the Emperor say that? What about the Dome Debate? And then there was something else.

It was not a full person he had seen at the bottom of the cocktail table. He had not been close enough for that. He had just seen the feet. He had not even been sure they were human. Only now he remembered. The sandals, he knew where he had seen those gold lace-up sandals before. They had been part of the angel costume that Prince Teodor wore that morning in the cathedral.

Guy lay considering his options. Chart Segat knew. The Emperor knew. Did Lloulou? Well, she was Chart Segat's girl. What about Marline? Marline knows what she wants, Des had said. What was that exactly? Money? Why did she want so much money? Tilson, he had been there too. And Des, did he know?

Was there no-one he could tell? If there was, then what would they say?

He remembered the mime. The one that told him to keep quiet. Finger and thumb pressed together telling him to be quiet. Obviously it was a secret, but what had he seen? A dirty golden sandal, a body crushed inside a cocktail table. Chart Segat had seen it too. Guy remembered the money roll in Chart Segat's hand at breakfast. Lloulou's face all smiles, when he paid her.

165

You're a good boy, Guy Erma. Chart Segat had said, you're one of us. That was what he had said. Then suddenly Guy was asleep.

Book 4.
Day 2. Morning

Chapter 14. Dream of Mezzatorra

Karl's dream was a patchwork of memories and he dreamt he was flying. Fast and low above the Sas Darona savannah. Where was he going? What was he doing, flying so fast? Then he saw it. A line of white fire shot high into the sky.

Was that the shield?

Where was he? In his dream, Karl accelerated fast and then braked fast. Mezzatorra was a crashed shuttle wedged on a rocky outcrop. Too valuable to be abandoned, it was ideal for a remote centre of cybernetic entomology.

"Mezzatorra. Permission to land?"

No reply, just a babble of panicked voices and shouts.

What was going on in Mezzatorra?

"Negative, Karl, negative. For God's sake Karl, just get out of here!"

Karl looked down, he was holding a Dome medallion. He ran his thumb over the circle of letters:

Loyal to Empire, Fear only God.

The Dome Elite, mused Karl. The medallion exploded into a cloud of insects that swarmed towards his face and poured like water into his eyes, the passages of his nose and attacked the gums of his mouth and the soft tissue of his ear. His whole head was encased in flames. Karl was screaming.

Karl woke in the dark; his shirt soaked with sweat. The room was dark at first; he turned to the crack of the curtains and saw a line of light on the horizon. It was dawn on Freyne. He was a long way from Sas Darona. He was many miles from Mezzatorra, and the insects – the cybernetic plague flies – had all burned and died on the shield of fire.

What was the Dome Elite of Freyne doing attacking Mezzatorra?

He walked to the window and pushed the curtain aside. The light was reflected over the multi-faceted panes of the Dome. Karl held up a hand to protect his eyes.

"Another Dome," he thought grimly. He thought back over the previous night, the fashion show in the Dome, Chart Segat and Frederon on a disk of fire.

Can you feel him? Nikato had asked repeatedly the night before.

No, Karl could not feel him. He had the frequency of Teodor's telepathy, but he could not hear him. Why not? Was he…? Karl ignored the obvious. Could the boy be sleeping? No, not sleeping, Karl would have heard him breathing, seen his dreams. The Dome was big, with layers of structures and buildings, would that have blocked him? Karl did not think so. Drugged then? Yes, maybe that was it.

Karl looked once more at the Dome, then, turning away from the light, he saw Magnolia Palace on the far side of the river. Even if he was drugged, there was one person who might be able to feel the boy. As he had helped her to her car she had said: "Anytime, anywhere". For a moment, she had laughed.

Karl thought of the golden hair spilling over her face. Those fine features, a long slim neck. She was a Queen, and the rulers of Freyne chose their consorts carefully. Karl doubted there was a more beautiful woman in the empire. He checked her calendar and smiled. He knew where she was.

Chapter 15. Chart Segat's Sea Gods and Mermaids

Teodor heard footsteps. He could not see who or what, but Teodor cried out anyway:

"Good morning, can you help?" The sound stopped in his throat as two Dome Elite Battle Borgs came into view. One he recognised from last night, the other was new. Bitter hatred sparked momentarily, but it was washed away, in the wake of self-imposed control. He had to escape. If he was in the Dome, he could not be more than fifty yards from some public space. Just fifty yards to freedom. He had to escape. He flopped down, as if in despair, but he was, in fact, calm and relaxed. Hastily rearranging the chains behind his back, he pressed the palms of his hands to the wall on either side of the metal ring.

"Give me your hands boy, so that I can unlock you," the borg said. Teodor did not move. 'Come closer, come closer,' he urged silently.

"What's wrong with you then, didn't you hear us?" He bent forward. That was what he was waiting for! In the blink of an eye, he threw his legs up and out, catching the borg under the chin and throwing him backwards. The full impact had not hit the machine on the jaw, or it would have surely killed him, shards of bone shooting up into his brain. It had been strong enough to send him spinning, though. Teodor now looked at the other borg. Younger, less machine, he retained a human's cunning. He was out of Teodor's chain's limited range. He eyed the prince calmly. This one was wiser than the rest, Teodor thought grimly, only not in a good way.

"Prince Teodor, it's shower time. Surely you'd like clean clothes." Teodor straightened slightly; suspicious but listening. He turned as the other tottered

171

to his feet and lunged towards the boy. He punched Teodor just once. He raised his fist again. The other borg cried:

"Stop!" It was an order. "I think Teodor will be reasonable now. Won't you, Teodor?"

He unlocked the chains. His companion held Teodor to the floor by holding one enormous metal fist pushed into the small of the boy's back. They smothered him in a rough blanket, twisting it into a bundled sack, and throwing him over a shoulder.

One of Teodor's hands slipped out through a crease. He heard the cyborg curse and push it inside none too gently. He understood and pulled it back, but the cloth remained partially open. He saw that they were running through narrow maintenance columns, before briefly appearing in the main public avenue, and then... Teodor's heart leapt even as his stomach churned. They were flying. They were soaring up, seemingly with no visible support, through the Dome.

Desperately and painfully twisting his neck, Teodor saw that they were standing on a plate of metal. Disk transport, thought Teodor in awe. He had seen clips of the discs flying up through the Dome. Now he was travelling aboard one. The small disk continued to cling to the shadows and corners of the vast edifice, moving up through wide gaps in the levels. Teodor caught tantalising glimpses of the three synthetic sports fields, stacked like uneven playing cards, the arenas themselves perched precariously, or so it seemed, on stilts above a vast, sectioned, circular swimming pool.

Teodor had seen films and videos of the breath-taking multi-layered sports fields, designed to hang above and around each other at seemingly impossible angles. He could see facilities that looked clean and welcoming. In amongst them, the people moved in purposeful ant-like harmony; in amongst them the Dome Elite jogged in tight formations with clarity and determination. This was the Dome exactly as his father, Serge, had envisaged it. Teodor had had to be kidnapped to see it!

The disk carried on up past the light and mirror systems, up near the cavernous roof of the huge level three playing fields. Teodor looked out with interest at the mezzanines and terraces. He could see blades mats, ball courts, gyms, shooting galleries, casinos, climbing walls, amphitheatres, flight simulators and bars. The entertainment units gave the place an innocent commercial aura, but this was a facility to train an army.

The platform bobbed and hovered as it followed the line of the ceiling towards the Well of Light. It was the central feature of the Dome where sunlight was reflected from the large windows under the Dome's cap and flashed down a series of mirrors to provide the very heart of the Dome with reflected natural light. The mirrors were very high and spotlessly clean. Teodor instinctively closed his eyes as they swung into the column of magnified sunshine. At least it was easy to guess his destination. He was en route to the cap of the Dome.

The disk moved as smoothly as any lift. It arrived at its destination and then moved up smoothly and accurately though a circular opening. Teodor glimpsed the amazing panorama that he had only previously heard tell of, and then they were moving again. This time though, they didn't go far; he felt them swinging him down and braced, but the blow was still unexpectedly sudden. As he kicked his way free of the blanket, they had already turned and left, and he was alone.

After a few moments Teodor's eyes adjusted to the light and the first things he saw were the bright taps of a triple shower and beside it a deep, exotic bath. He stood up and moved towards the bath, touched the delicate multi-coloured mosaic on the surrounding walls and half-smiled at the images of sea-creatures and mythical sea folk.

Teodor walked his fingers across the controls for water, oils, perfumes, steam and other; this was all very nice. He leant back against the bath and examined the room; the floor was thickly carpeted and adorned with fluffy rugs. Everything was colour coordinated, bath, basins, towels and carpet: gold and bright magenta, the Emperor's colours. It made his mother's best silver bathroom seem plain and drearily functional in comparison. Across from the bath, the wall above and around the basins was a wall of gleaming mirrors.

Teodor shyly looked at his reflection; those stupid sandals were now tattered and dirt-caked; filth-streaked limbs, the ridiculous short white angel tunic, sodden and blackened, blood spotted at the neck under his bleeding face. A dusty, sleepy face, shaggy hair, large scared eyes, but no tears, no tears yet.

He turned his glance away from his reflection and saw between the basins a pile of clothes on a low stool. He walked over and looked down. All the clothes were black. All bore the outline of the geodesic Dome in bright yellow-gold.

Of course, he thought. With a purpose now, he stepped into the shower.

"So, what do you think?"

Sayginn did not know what she thought. Karl Valvanchi sat across from Sayginn at her breakfast table, having arrived just fifteen minutes before. Sayginn wondered what would happen if the Emperor walked in and found the Zaracan here.

Had the Emperor always disliked the Valvanchis? Sayginn could not remember.

For many years now, he called them alien enemies and was openly critical of their interference in the affairs of the Freyne Empire. Sayginn wondered if she should send Karl away, or ring and invite some other person to join them. If the Emperor did discover them alone together, he would be furious. She did not want to alienate him when likely as not she would be forced to marry him very soon. So, when Karl first arrived, Sayginn tried to keep their conversation businesslike; she quizzed him about Mezzatorra.

"Last night someone left this newspaper article in my car, it concerned Mezzatorra, and it mentioned your name. What happened exactly there?"

Sayginn sat in silence after Karl had told her everything. Finally, she said:

"I thought the Sas Darona lock-down was just to try and stop the SDLA. The press here have made no mention of poison pills, of cy-sects. Is that the research they were doing at Mezzatorra? Those are terribly dangerous weapons."

"What interested our scientists was their ability to reproduce."

"You mean the crystallescence when a human turns into a colony of cy-sects?"

Sayginn had taken time to research cy-sects the night before. She had watched with mounting horror the images of animals being attacked and crystallising into colonies of cy-sects. She had not taken the next step to look at the images of similar human suffering, but Karl, she knew, had witnessed just that. He sat on one side of the fire shield while a few feet away colleagues and friends died of plague.

"It's horrific, yes, but it's also amazing from a scientific point of view. A small amount of energy multiplies one hundred thousand times. This conversion is something we would like to replicate in our own miniature robots, our nanites... The gains to our industry..."

"But the risks? Did you not think about the possibility of an attack by the SDLA?"

Sayginn found it hard to imagine any part of life which did not include a concern for security and the possibility of terror.

Karl shook his head: "The SDLA is made up of primitives. Our base had a secure vault. They should never have penetrated. No, someone gave the SDLA advanced explosives. And Dome medallions were found..."

Sayginn hated the word primitives. The SDLA had a tribal culture with interesting arts and crafts. On Freyne, it was widely considered a pre-cursor to, and perhaps a more preferable, human existence; a romantic view, admittedly, given the high infant mortality and short life span. Nevertheless, these primitives were still human. As for his talk of Dome medallions: "But now that you have been on Freyne a few days, you can see how commonplace Dome medallions are – all the boys, all the young men. There is a hierarchy. Apparently some have special engravings and some metal colours are particularly rare, but a Dome medallion is as much a fashion icon as a symbol of armed conflict."

"Indeed, I can see that, but on Sas Darona, and outside this system, a Dome medallion only means one thing: Dome Terror. The Dome Elite is becoming infamous on the trade routes, and of late they have been more brazen in their illegal mining on Sas Darona. The Dome must close, Sayginn."

Sayginn wanted to say Sas Darona should be part of the Freyne Empire, but she held her tongue. Sas Darona had large stocks of monazite and was on the edge the Freyne empire. For close to a decade, historian archaeologists had sought to find evidence of earlier human colonisation. Traces had been found on all the planets of the thirteen, but not so on Sas Darona. Maybe Sas Darona had once been part of the ancient empire, but there was no way of proving it. It still rankled amongst the Barons and princes of Freyne, that the Zaracans, with their long experience of the arcane procedures of the United Races, had been quick to pull the levers of power and lay claim to Sas Darona. Now the Freyne could only watch as monazite remained in the ground despite their well-publicised, widespread shortages. She drank some tea, then said quietly:

"How would you feel if the Dome stayed open, but I was in charge?"

This time it was Karl's turn to play for time, taking a bite from his breakfast roll, stirring his drink thoughtfully. Sayginn watched and took a quick inventory of her feelings. It was a long time since she had felt so attracted to any man. Here she was drinking her tea, and she was wondering whether he liked the pose she had taken with her cup hanging loosely on one finger. Had he noticed how her hair was loose – not pulled back, as was her habit? Did he mind that she was wearing goran jockey silks and fine wool leggings? Did he find the casual attire attractive? Did he even know that the princes and Barons of Freyne deemed the scent of a goran's fur deeply erotic, and there was no finer ornament to a love chamber than a deep goran fur spread out on the bed? If the Emperor had been in Karl's place, he would have thought her attire flirtatious, perhaps even a tease. But what of Karl? Did he even like her?

"Unfortunately, it's not me you have to convince."

Sayginn's heart leapt. What Karl appeared to be saying was that she had convinced him? He might well support her in running the Dome. He might like that, so he must like her. Did he like her? She looked at him, and knew her eyes had given her away. She smiled, he smiled, they both laughed through mutual embarrassment and enchantment:

"So, what do you think?"

Sayginn looked at him properly; something had changed. Karl no longer looked like himself. He had been changing ever since he arrived, but now the difference was quite marked:

"You have adjusted your skin tone, as well."

"Yes, that's easy enough to adjust."

"Contacts on your eyes."

"Shields. I have to disguise my powers."

"And your hair…" Sayginn could not resist reaching where his cropped white hair had been replaced by thick long curls. She caught one ringlet on her fingertips and watched thoughtfully as it curled around her finger. "I think they call it the 'Domeside look'".

"Yes, but do I look authentic? I mean, I'm never sure our people get it entirely right. Do I look like the Freyne to you?"

Sayginn said nothing. Whether it was because he looked like one of her people now, she could not tell. All she knew was that she could not bear to be so distant from him. She stood up from the table.

"Come closer. Let me see you in the light."

Karl followed her and stood a moment with the morning light shining on his face. Slowly Sayginn lent in towards him and kissed him lightly on the forehead. Karl looked a little taken aback. It was a kiss, a kiss on the forehead, but still a kiss. Then Sayginn said:

"Go with my blessing, Karl Valvanchi. Go and save my son. Do whatever it takes."

This time she kissed him on the lips. Karl stared down at her, then quickly checked the room. He had glanced furtively at the servants. Only the servants were robots. Sayginn watched as he checked the door. Yes, it was closed. Sayginn thought once again of the Emperor coming through that door and discovering them together, then she felt his arm around her waist, and he pulled her closer.

"I thought you were supposed to marry the Emperor?"

"Marry him, give up my planets and my rule, and become mother to four new sons." Sayginn had not meant to sound so bitter. She looked up at Karl: "Is that what you want too, power, marriage and sons?"

"The five contract will not be renewed. My sons are on Zarac 1."

Sayginn was confused by this answer. Karl sounded like he was talking to himself.

"You did not answer my question," her voice was little more than a sigh. "What is it you want?"

He looked down at her one last time and said:

"I want what I cannot have."

***

177

Teodor paused to examine his reflection. As he straightened the yellow collar he realised that of all the strange fashion outfits he had been obliged to wear over the years, this was by far the most extraordinary. They had provided him with a complete uniform of a Dome Elite Junior. If the press caught a photo of him dressed like this, it would be guaranteed to make both the tea-time news and the front page.

Funny really, he thought, the outfit was mostly black with yellow-gold details. The undershirt and laces were yellow; there was a luminescent edge to the neckline and cuffs – a striking but not such an unusual combination. No, it was the geodesic Dome embroidered on his breast and back pocket that was what looked so strange. He said the motto once more to himself:

Loyal to Empire. Fear only God.

It meant that the Dome Elite's first loyalty was to the Emperor and the thirteen planets. It also meant the only thing they feared was God, neither man nor machine, certainly not any man-made laws of justice. What made them think they were justified in kidnapping their prince?

He sighed and since he could think of nothing else, he picked up the stained and ripped angel costume and dropped it in a small bin. He heard an automatic door open and looked back to where he had come in. No, it was still locked shut. The movement had come from another direction. A section of the mirror had slipped away. He strolled over, glancing once more at his reflection. No, he decided, he did not look like himself, but at least he did not look like the broken, filthy boy he had seen in the mirror just a short time before.

"Calm, Teodor. Control." Unbidden, the encouragement came to mind. He straightened his shoulders and stepped into the light.

Through the open door, Teodor saw that Chart Segat was in conversation with a young Dome Elite. Teodor paused, was this right? Was he free to go? Quietly he stepped forward. Neither turned, so Teodor listened, Chart Segat was saying:

"But this is all the evidence you have?"

They were looking at a fuzzy image on the screen. Teodor thought it looked like one frame, a still taken from a film. It was out of focus, either that or it was a ghost.

"I was right behind him, Chartsie. I saw him change. The explosion, it had injured two men. No, not men: brothers, twin brothers. I heard him gasp,

178

swear, something. When I looked, he was right there, a Zaracan soldier. Then he switched back to being Dome Elite."

"… A Zaracan infiltrator led the attack on Mezzatorra…"

"His idea, his plan, his leadership…"

Zaracan? Mezzatorra? Wondered Teodor. It was the name of a base on Sas Darona. It had been much in the news; he could not remember why. But was not Sas Darona in lock-down? Teodor looked at the Dome Elite youth with interest. He was tanned. Had he just returned from Sas Darona? But how?

"Mezzatorra?" Teodor repeated aloud.

Both turned towards him.

"What?" gasped the tanned young Elite.

Chart Segat just laughed. "He's from the Riffaut, Des. Forgot to go home after last night's party."

Teodor did not understand what Chart Segat meant, so he said crossly:

"I am Prince Teodor of Freyne, and this season I am wearing House Riffaut."

"He's good, isn't he?" joked Chart Segat.

The young Dome Elite had fallen silent. Teodor pressed on:

"Chart Segat, may I have your communicator? I need to call my mother and tell her I am ok."

For a moment, Teodor thought Chart Segat might say 'yes'. He would pass him a communicator, and he would be on his way home. Holding his elation at bay, Teodor picked up a sugar roll from the breakfast trolley, ripped off a corner and ate it. Teodor sensed rather than saw the young soldier's disapproval but ignored him. He glanced away. He had thought the bathroom had a mirrored wall. In fact, it was a transparent glass wall. They had watched him as he had showered. This revelation shocked him. He had been naked in the shower and they had seen him? Had there been cameras as well?

He found he was coughing with indignation, choking on the sugared bread in his mouth. With fresh anger, he turned back to Chart Segat. The man was watching him closely. Their eyes met. Teodor saw he was laughing at him.

"I do not think so, Teo."

Teodor squared his shoulders:

"I am Prince Teodor of Freyne. You owe me your obedience."

Chart Segat snorted in contempt.

"I owe you nothing."

"You there!" Now Teodor addressed the young Dome Elite standing across from him. "Pass me your communicator, I must call my mother."

"Ignore him, Des."

The Elite Guard looked at Chart Segat, but did not move. Teodor pressed on:

"Des, is it? Des Parks?" Teodor knew by the look of horror on the young man's face that he was right. But was it really him? Teodor had picture posters of Dome blades champions in his bedroom. Only Des no longer looked like his picture.

It's the tan, he thought, and the hair. Sas Darona! Oh, I must call my mother!

"Remind me, Des. What is the oath you swore when you joined the Dome Elite? I'll tell you. You swore to serve your Regent and protect the empire. So, Des Parks, give me your communicator."

Teodor held out his hand. His fingers almost touched the converted communication device. He had used the name three times on purpose. Across from him the young guard was so startled, the jug slipped from his hand and milk spilled over the plates and tray.

Des turned to Chart Segat.

"He's not from the Riffaut, is he?"

"You may go, Des," Chart Segat said quietly. Teodor saw the young man hesitating. His mouth opened and closed several times, and finally, he said:

"This is not right, Chartsie."

"YOU MAY GO, DES."

The youth snapped to attention, blood had drained from his face. One moment Teodor had been elated. *This is not right.* A Dome Elite, a Sas Darona Dome Elite had said that. *This is not right.* Now he saw and felt the other's fear. As the footsteps receded, Teodor realised he would be alone. Chart Segat called out:

"Make sure Guy is ready. Tell him to have his blades ready." Des was perplexed. He followed Chart Segat's gaze. In turn, he scrutinised Teodor again. This time Teodor realised he had no idea what the soldier was thinking.

"Oh, and Des?"

Chart Segat held up his index and thumb in a mime that said: "Keep it quiet."

The door closed. If Teodor had hoped for some last minute change, some chance of rescue, it had been in vain. Of course these men were loyal to Chart Segat, and why not? Chart Segat ruled supreme within the Dome. As the door closed, Teodor remembered: *This is not right*. There was hope in those four words. Teodor turned back to Chart Segat. He would not give up. Not yet.

"This is about the Dome Debate, isn't it? Even if you force a change, it will only be overturned once I am free." Teodor stepped a little closer, and tried persuasion: "My mother would be grateful if you were to free me now."

"Yes, your mother must be worried. But don't you see, Teodor? Your mother only has one son to worry about. I have ten thousand boys and men for whom I am responsible. What will happen to them when the Dome is closed?"

Teodor paused to consider:

"I don't think my mother intends to close the Dome." He wondered if this was a terrible secret to have revealed, so he added: "Not forever, anyway."

Chart Segat sneered: "And she really thinks she can run the Dome without me?"

Teodor considered: 'So that was his grievance.'

"I will speak to my mother if you like, but ultimately you must face trial for the murder of my father." Teodor paused, "and my brother."

Too late, Teodor realised this last remark had been a mistake.

"I did not kill the baby boy," yelled Chart Segat. He was referencing the terrible headlines denouncing him as a baby killer as well as King's assassin: "I did not kill either of them. Nor did my men set that bomb. Ten of my men were killed in that explosion. Do you think I would murder my own blood? For that's what they are. These men, these boys, they are my blood."

181

Teodor knew Chart Segat had always denied any involvement in his father's death. To hear him speak so eloquently, to see his distress, for a few moments Teodor was inclined to believe him. He tried a more gentle reply:

"In that case, you have nothing to fear. The courts will prove you innocent."

"Innocent. No, it is you who are innocent, if you believe that the truth comes out in a court of law."

"Chart Segat, I am your prince and I am your future King. Let me go and I swear I will speak with my mother."

"Future King! Just look at you. Without the Regency Defence, you are nothing."

"Chart Segat, this is outrageous. The Dome Elite belonged to my father."

Out of nowhere, the hand sprang out and pulled Teodor forward by the nape of his neck. Now Teodor's face was just inches from Chart Segat's, as he whispered:

"And now the Dome Elite belongs to me. If I were you, I would not be so sure I was going to survive this. After all, if I killed your father and brother, why not you? No. If the vote goes against me at this afternoon's Dome Debate, you will die. I will throw you to my borgs. They like fresh meat, and they like to play with their meat too. So your only questions should be: How long will they toy with you, my borgs, hey? How long before they finally kill you? An hour, six hours, a day?"

Teodor opened his mouth to speak but no words came. He went to move but found he was frozen to the spot. He stared at Chart Segat and all he could feel was horror. The mask of jovial eccentricity had fallen from Chart Segat's features and for the first time Teodor saw the ruthless ambition of the man. At the very last, he looked away, only to hear Chart Segat say: "Take him away."

Two giant borgs had stepped out from the shadows. Teodor had a moment to consider their mechanically enhanced limbs, their blackened flaky skin and hair, and the lightless eyes, before the first borg stepped forward and pushed Teodor forward:

"Head between your knees."

Teodor could do nothing but comply, as another cyborg appeared and tightly tied Teodor's elbows together behind his knees so tightly his head was locked in position, before roughly turning him over. Teodor was now tied up like a sack with his bottom as the base, and they grabbed him by the ankles and hauled him up.

Teodor's legs stretched and he felt his head being clamped between his knees. Pain immediately cut into his arms from the tie: pain from the weight of his hanging body. Teodor tensed, pulling up on his arms and legs. The pain receded for a few moments, but as he released it came back with two-fold intensity. He had little time to think about it because he found himself being dropped into a military backpack. A capsule of sleeping salts was thrown in with him and he saw the light disappear. Above his head the bag was closed and he felt himself being hoisted onto someone's back.

Teodor struggled. He discovered the bag had a vertical stripe of netting down one side, and when he pressed his face against the laces he found he could breathe clean air. The guards were moving at a rapid jog. He wrestled to find a more comfortable position, managing to free his head, but he was rewarded by a random punch into the side that whacked his shoulder and back, and was only inches from his neck and head.

"Ow!" He cried out, but the only reply was another punch, this time striking his thighs. The blow also caught his hand, cruelly twisting one of his fingers. His yell was desperate:

"In God's name, will nobody help me?"

Even as Teodor fretted and struggled against his confinement, he heard his mother, her voice was inside his head:

'Teodor, where are you?'

Teodor stopped moving. Was that really his mother? Through the netting on the side of the backpack, he could see he was on a cyborg's back. They stood atop the flying disk, but he could also see further. Looking out, he glimpsed Magnolia Palace through the panes of the Dome on the far side of the river. He had heard the voice coming from the palace. Goran thought-control was a form of low-level telepathy. Teodor had never appreciated it might range this far.

'I'm in the Dome, in a backpack, I'm upside down. They kicked me.'

'Where are you?' The voice was like a whisper.

'Mother?'

Teodor saw they had descended behind the massive sports stadium and he no longer had direct sight of Magnolia Palace. He closed his eyes and

183

concentrated, but the contact was gone. Had she heard him? What had he said? Why had he been so stupid? He had told her about the kicking. He should have told her Chart Segat was involved. Frustrated, he moved around desperately to find a comfortable position. The sleeping capsules had fallen close to his face. The smell made him feel sick. Another slap and a threatening growl:

"Just shut up and sleep. If you know what's good for you, you'll shut up and sleep." Teodor was impossibly uncomfortable. His back, arms and legs were all at awkward angles. Yet, despite everything, the sleeping drugs were powerful. He started to drift off.

***

Karl Valvanchi snapped his fingers and all at once he was himself again. Short, white, cropped hair; pale, cream skin and eyes alight with his special powers. Across from him, Sayginn did a double take and stepped back. The change had been instantaneous, and it was shocking. One moment she had been looking into the face of a Domeside man, the next she faced an alien. Karl did not know whether he should be relieved or insulted by this more honest reaction. Clearly, his disguise was effective and convincing, but if Sayginn did like him – and he was beginning to think she might – she was less enamoured of his race as a whole.

"We should try to tune in your telepathic senses," he said, trying to return to business as usual.

"Yes, will it take long? They are expecting me downstairs."

Karl was more hurt than he expected by this businesslike response. Had she not just kissed him? Seemingly that meant nothing. And why would it? They were both aware of familiar restraints: the disapproval of family and the outrage of the press. For them to be close friends was dangerous, anything else was almost unthinkable. Allies, that was safe. An ally provided assistance when one's son was taken. An ally did not expect to be kissed when he morphed into a Freyne citizen. By her reply, Sayginn had shown she had understood. She was making a reference to the operations team in her ballroom searching high and low, using every conceivable method to retrieve her son.

"If you just…"

He reached out to her, and cautiously she let him take her hand.

'There, can you hear me?'

"You're not speaking to me are you?"

'I'm not using my voice box to speak with you.'

"I did not know I could…"

'Goran thought-control is fairly primitive, but the networks are similar to my telepathy. I can boost what you broadcast or receive, and I can let you in on a secret.'

Karl moved over to the drinks cabinet which was close to the dining table. He took out a bottle of fiery Freyne sweet liqueur. He poured a small quantity into the bottom of two glasses.

'Alcohol will boost your powers. It has the effect of relaxing the synapses and makes communications easier. Drink up.'

They clinked glasses. In that instant, they were close again, another shared smile. Karl placed both hands on Sayginn shoulders and pointed her at the Dome.

'You're his mother, if anyone can hear him, you can. So listen.'

Sayginn stood quietly. Karl saw her puzzling about what he had said. He reached with his thoughts inside her head, and probed her powers:

'Reach out.'

She was still now. Her body was still, her mind calm. Karl breathed in the perfume of her hair and felt the smooth warmth of her skin through the palms of his hands.

'*Concentrate!*' she said.

So she had seen his thoughts; Karl should be pleased; he glanced down at her and caught her looking up at him with a teasing smile. Their eyes met, and this time she did not flinch, she looked plainly into the spots of light glinting out from his irises. Warmth spread out from Karl's heart across his chest into his arms, forearms and hands. Without even thinking, he had grasped and turned Sayginn, and then he kissed her. Her mouth was soft and slightly open in welcome. She responded by reaching up, not to curl her fingers through fake curls, but to run her hand over his shorn head and gently caress the rim of his right ear. One kiss gave way to a succession of kisses as their bodies moulded together.

185

'IN GOD'S NAME, WILL NOBODY HELP ME?'

Teodor's voice rang out clearly. It was like a bolt of lightning through Sayginn, who fell back from Karl's arms, and span round to look at the Dome. Karl followed, and wrapping his arms around her waist pressed his face into her hair.

'Hold the connection,' he urged. *'So I can see him.'*

All at once, Karl felt himself giddy from blood pumping in his head. There was a sharp pain in the fingers of one hand. His senses were overwhelmed by the smell of sick, and...

'Sleeping gas!' Sayginn said. Her breath came out in gasps as she saw what Teodor saw, felt what he felt.

'Speak to him,' urged Karl.

'Teodor, where are you?'

'I'M IN THE DOME. IN A BACKPACK. I'M UPSIDE DOWN. THEY KICKED ME.'

The words were clear enough but were jumbled together with a quick succession of images, then nothing.

'Try again,' urged Karl. He listened as Sayginn called to Teodor. Words of love, words of loss and emotion. Each time, there came no reply, and her despair grew. At last they both stood quietly, listening and feeling.

'He's gone,' Karl said quietly.

'What do you mean he's gone?'

Sayginn was panicking. Karl saw that she thought he meant Teodor was dead. He did not. He tried to explain:

'No, not that. I think he's fine; he was in range, and then he disappeared out of range. I thought I saw an image of disk transport in his thoughts, and a military bag.'

Karl had seen a lot in Teodor's thoughts that he did not want to tell Sayginn, not until he made sense of it. He had made a mental recording of the few instants they had been in contact and already he had rerun the memory three times. There were faces and places, but also harsh words and rough treatment. The insights made him truly afraid for the boy. Now, more than ever, he knew he could not leave that boy to face the might and menace of the Dome alone.

'Yes, I saw the bag, and it felt like I was flying.'

Karl looked across the river to the Dome; he already had a theory as to why and how the brief encounter had come about. From where they stood they could look out through the window, across the gardens and the river, and through the panes of the Dome to the cap of the Dome. He had not seen it because he had been kissing Sayginn when Teodor had shouted out, but if he had been looking he would have seen the disk floating down; Teodor would have been there. And no, he had not seen the boy, but even if he had, he would not have known what he was seeing.

It was the kiss that had triggered strong emotions in Sayginn and boosted her basic telepathy, helping her hear her son over such a vast distance. He pointed as he tried to explain:

'See where we have an unblocked view of the cap of the Dome? The disks fly up there to the cap.'

"He was flying down..." She interrupted, she was speaking now. Karl stroked her hair and kissed the parting of her golden hair.

'Yes, I thought so too... But the disk passed behind one of the buildings, at this range it would block the contact. At least we had contact.'

"That was him. In real time." Again her spoken voice; she sounded sad and tired.

"In real time. Now tell me everything you remember. Everything."

"His hair was wet. I felt that, and I thought he was wearing a Dome Elite uniform. What did you see?"

"I caught glimpses of all sorts of things in his mind. But wet hair means he probably had had a shower. Clothes too, it means they are taking care of him."

"But the disks only travel to and from the cap of the Dome. Chart Segat has his bedroom up there. And his bathroom..." She paused, panic was swelling inside her. Karl stroked her hair again and tried to soothe her with comforting thoughts, but she brushed them aside, and replied in quiet despair: "Oh Karl, we have to get him out."

"Sssh. I scanned him for injuries. There was some bruising, and he was hungry, but I think he was mostly unharmed."

She did not ask how or why, simply sobbed one heart-felt sob, then, pulling herself together, she coughed and said with determination:

187

"We should go downstairs. They are tracking all movements. They will have tracked the disk."

At that moment, and seeing the turmoil inside her head, Karl wanted to kiss her, only he knew it was not the time. He simply nodded, and they headed off.

Soon Sayginn and Karl were standing by the desk of a young analyst; he had pulled up a file, and they saw three Dome Elite Battle Borgs standing on a disk floating down from the cap of the Dome.

"Can we zoom in on that backpack?"

'Oh, look – it's moving!' Sayginn used thought speech, not wishing for anyone to know what she thought until her fears were confirmed.

'Ouch!' thought Karl in reply. *'That's when they hit him, I think; that's when he cried out.'*

"Can you get in closer?" urged Sayginn. "Is that netting down the side? Keep focusing in, there."

'If they ask, don't mention telepathy,' Karl urged.

'I know,' replied Sayginn.

Above their heads, as the camera zoomed in, they saw part of a face pressed up against the netting of the backpack. The head was upside down, and the skin distorted where the lace bit into it, but the eye was wide open, and it was clear blue.

"Iris identification," the analyst said calmly. Then after a moment: "It's a match." Standing up, he shouted: "We have first contact! We have seen him."

Every head in the room turned towards them. Chairs creaked as analyst stood up, and there was the clatter of staff running forward to look. Within an instant, a crowd of soldiers and analysts looked at the screens, now showing several views of the floating disk, its passengers, the backpack and the face and eye peering from the side netting. A huge cheer rang out.

Patrick McGuire called them to attention.

"Ok, everybody! Heads up."

He pointed up, they all turned to look. At the centre of the main wall was a clock; it read twenty-three hours, fifteen minutes. It was the amount of time Teodor had been missing. Briefly another statistic flashed across the screen in amber letters: sixty-four per cent. It was the probability of finding Teodor alive. It was a life statistic. All the historical data was clear, the longer the prince was gone, the less likely it was that he would return without injury, or even at all. Karl could see the emotion building up inside of Sayginn as she looked at the numbers on the wall; then she gasped. Patrick McGuire tapped his communicator, and the timing changed. Now Teodor had been missing for only thirteen minutes, and his chance of survival shot back up beyond eighty per cent.

Patrick nodded with satisfaction and addressed the crowd:

"Ok everyone, set to work. This is a hot lead; we have to get on top of it." Then to Sayginn and Karl: "C'mon. I'll bring you up-to-date."

Karl walked with Sayginn around the ballroom, listening and watching. All the time he was waiting for the information on the flying disk, where had it come from, where had it gone. It turned out the disks were outside of the monitoring of the main Dome systems, and only visual files were available. Analysts were now scrambling to rectify that. For now, the only information they had was that the disk had returned into the Dome Elite Military complex, from where there were no audio or video feeds. None of the three Battle Borgs on the disk had been seen since. None had been identified.

"Those borgs are so old, I am surprised they are still in service," Patrick remarked.

Sayginn looked at the close up photos. They were unmistakeably Battle Borgs of Dome, and with their massive metallic structure, their mottled, cracked skin and mechanical eyes, she could think of no more terrifying jailors for her son.

"Surely they are still cyborgs and cyborgs are programmed to obey a direct order from Teodor, do you think he has forgotten that?" She asked.

"Again, until we can identify those borgs, we cannot know what modifications have been made. The iris scan showed signs of drugs. Maybe Teodor is not fully conscious."

"He would know they should obey a direct order. He would know," Sayginn repeated. "We should send our men to check the military prison bank again," Sayginn said thoughtfully.

"We did that yesterday, but there were long delays in getting access. If he was there, they had plenty of time to move him."

"We need to catch them unawares. The prison is the obvious place," Karl said.

"We should also send a forensics team into the cap of the Dome. If he was up there we should find a trace of him, particularly if he used the bathroom. If we find that, we can pin this kidnap on Chart Segat," Patrick said. "We are still waiting for permission to gain access to the cap of the Dome, we sent a request yesterday. Freddie went there for a party, but they won't let our people anywhere near."

"Why not?" Sayginn sounded petulant. Karl was surprised that she seemed to believe Chart Segat would or should co-operate, when it was staring her in the face that he was the one who had orchestrated the kidnapping. Ultimately, he realised she thought herself a force for good and expected her people to think the same.

"See no evil, hear no evil, know no evil. They do not want us to know what goes on up there."

Sayginn let out an exasperated sigh. Karl reached out to her with his thought voice:

'I can do that. I can gain access to the cap of the Dome, and I can check the military prison.'

Patrick was explaining the different legal procedures employed to force Chart Segat to comply, but Karl continued.

'I can go in under cover, and quietly look for the boy, or traces of the boy.'

'And you won't get caught?'

'I am a telepathic shape-shifter from an advanced technological society, Sayginn.'

Her eyes widened in alarm, and she glanced up at him with sudden wonder.

'They won't know what's hit them.'

He smiled.

'Nevertheless my Regent, do I have your permission?'

'My permission... I'm begging you. Please. ' Her thoughts were brimming with delighted laughter. Karl smiled and bowed. He said his farewells and

took his leave. He looked back at the door, and saw Sayginn looking after him.

'Don't give the game away', he urged.

'I won't say anything; you're my secret weapon.'

'I meant don't give the game away; you're my secret love.'

There was a pause, and even at this distance, he thought she might be blushing. Eventually, she found her voice.

'I'll be careful,' she hesitated. *'You're my secret love.'*

Book 5.
Day 2. Midday

Chapter 16. The Magnolia Stakes

Guy Erma wiped his face on a small ragged towel. It had been a mad rush closing the store on Dome Market Square after the morning crowds, then dashing three miles south to set up another stall at the racecourse. Like last year, they had done it, and (thought Guy with a smile) they would probably do it again next year. The stand was perfect too; the old trellises covered by brand new boards, the awning decked with artificial greenery, carefully washed and spruced up by Juke's hard-working wife, whom Guy nicknamed in mock reverence: Mrs. Juke. There was only one item for sale, in little plastic boxes and served with a napkin: the season's first friseburys.

Guy sniffed and licked the skin of the red fruit, but he did not eat it just yet. It was one of his free friseburys and a bribe from Juke who, time and time again, reminded him: "You've got yours, now keep your hands off the rest of the stock." Guy chuckled and put the fruit back into a hidden container. He adjusted two of the plastic boxes to slip a third into the back row and wiped a small spot of juice from the edge of the stand. Everything would be perfect today. He lightly snatched up his frisebury again, caught the torn skin with the sharp edge of his teeth and pulled it away. With a strong circular move, he pressed the fruit whole into his mouth. As he bit down, it exploded inside his cheeks, what pleasure! Juice ran down his chin to be licked up later as a tasty reminder of the earlier delicacy. Roguishly, he beamed.

Juke was calling him. Guy tried to hide his exasperation as the man repeated for the third time:

"Yes sir, the stall looks beautiful." He spoke slowly and deliberately. "Fit for Chart Segat, fit for an Emperor, and the Emperor is going to see her, too.

Prime, prime site this, right next to the staircase, where all their fine, fine lordships will pass on their way to the Imperial balconies. No other site like it on the course! Golden Magnolia Weekend!" On the final words, he stretched the vowels into a fervent chant: Gooolden, Maaagnooolia, Weeeeiik'n.

Guy looked up speculatively at the empty, overlapping balconies, and eyed the magenta-carpeted stairway. The stairs led up to the VIP suites. The Emperor had one, of course. Did Chart Segat have one too? Would they see him? Would he serve them?

Des arrived and made a play of looking around the quiet racecourse and idly chatting to stallholders. The Magnolia Stakes was due to open to the public at 11am – there were thirty minutes to go and the market traders who had arrived at six were long since ready.

"I'm working, Des."

"Not now, you're not. Ask Juke."

"Juke, can I take a break?"

"What for?" It was a gruff reply.

"It's me, Juke. I have to prep Guy for a blades demonstration later today." It was the first Guy had heard of any blades demonstrations; he looked up, interested. Des just shook his head; Guy knew not to ask. Des added hurriedly, "I'll have him back by eleven."

"Ok, go on then, but no later than eleven fifteen, mind you. I know what you boys and your blades are like."

"Good," said Des in an undertone. "We've got to get you something to eat."

"I have eaten, Des," Guy replied, not quite believing his luck.

"Half-a-dozen stolen friseburys does not make a meal, Guy. A fighter must start his day with breakfast. And you have a busy day ahead of you." Guy grinned. "Did you hear what happened to Seb last night?"

"Sebastian? From the Riffaut? No, what?"

"There was you, worried about Marline, and Seb started drinking heavily and he so annoyed Chartsie. He had him locked up."

"What?"

"Safest place for him really. He was really drunk. He's really upset by this kidnapping of Prince Teodor, him being a lookalike and all."

"Poor Sebastian, and the Elite have still not been mobilised."

"Nope. Oh, here we are. What do you want to eat?"

A short while later they were munching on breakfast rolls of meats and eggs with steaming hot drinks alongside. Guy was also unlacing the pack of blades he always had stowed in his backpack. He knelt to help Des with his cuffs and calf shields first as he was the junior fighter.

"I looked up Mezzatorra on the system," Guy said. "What is exponential entomological investigation?"

"You don't want to know." Des changed the subject. "I need you to look at this. There's not very much footage of this young chap, surprisingly enough, but this is from yesterday. I think it is a level five display."

"It is the study of insects, I know. But why are insects exponential? It does not make sense."

Guy moved his hand in the shape of an exponential curve.

"Calf greaves, Guy."

Guy offered his legs to Des for foot blades and calves.

"Did you get a chance to look around? The system said Mezzatorra was a United Race beacon science institute. That means it was unique, doing unique experiments."

"The study of Sas Darona plague," Des said. "That's what the scientists did at Mezzatorra."

"Did?"

"They are all dead, Guy. That's what the Dome Elite did, ok? That's all the Dome Elite ever does. Now, will you look at the chap on the screen?"

Guy said nothing. If the Dome Elite had killed the scientists, they must have had a good reason. He looked at the small screen Des had unfolded onto the table. 'The chap on the screen' was a boy wearing a diamond protective shirt and performing a display within a pristine blades mat laid out on a small lawn at the entrance of goran stables.

"That's Prince Teodor," said Guy. He bit his tongue. Genius, he thought, why not say something stupid? Of course it was Prince Teodor. Who else would wear a diamond shirt?

"Training, yesterday morning," Des added unnecessarily. "There were snippets on the news, but I downloaded the whole sequence. I do not know why they always criticise him. He's at least a level 5, I would say."

"Blades is not about display. It's the fight that matters," Guy replied automatically. Nevertheless, he reran the demo sequence with interest.

"Is he fast, do you think?" Guy was having trouble concentrating because of the questions racing around his head. Why was Des training him? Why today? Why this video of Prince Teodor? Did this mean the fight might be reinstated? Was the prince not taken?

"Hard to tell, the camera distorts the action. But he's strong, and he's super fit."

Guy nodded and tried to think of something else.

"He looks a bit heavy to me."

"Maybe, but see this." Des paused the film at the first clash between the prince and the blades master. Guy watched carefully.

"Is that Tilson? Is he his instructor too?"

Des shook his head dismissively. He rewound the film.

"There. Tilson is hitting him there. But look, he just takes it and bounces back – then Bang! He hits back. Ouch! I would not like to be on the receiving end of that."

"Show me again," Guy rewound the film and slowed it down. Subconsciously he was mimicking with his hands the move of the prince's punch: "Oh, I see. I think Tilson could have turned a little faster."

"Well, certainly. You'd have to do so. You could not take many hits like that."

"What, me?" Guy started to protest: "Des, the fight with Teodor was cancelled. And after yesterday… Maybe he's…" Guy wanted to say dead, but all he could think of was the golden sandals.

"Taken, he's alive." Guy looked up at Des. All at once he realised Des knew something. Maybe Guy should confide in him, tell him what he had seen?

"It's not right," Guy said softly. "He's our prince."

Guy's heart leapt, for though Des did not reply, he knew from his eyes that he agreed. It was wrong of Chart Segat to have kidnapped the prince. This certainty was followed by the ever-present Dome mime for silence: finger pressed to thumb and a quick shake of the head. *Don't talk about it.*

Des was pointing at the screen: "The display. Concentrate. We do not have much time. Do you know that display?"

Guy shrugged. He did know it, but what was the point of saying so?

"Didn't I see you practising it once? Or twice? Did Lloulou not give you the money for the test?"

Guy shrugged. Of course he had wanted to ask. But Lloulou always seemed short of money.

"I did not ask. Blades are about fighting, not display."

"Go on, show me." Des pointed the screen at the wall. A small image expanded to fill the white space. "Just as a warm-up. If you do not know it, or can't remember it, you can copy him."

Guy hid his contempt. Of course he could remember the examination display. But did he know it as well as the prince, with his diamond shirt and hand-picked tutors? That was the real challenge. He leapt down from his stool and bounced to the centre of the available space. They did not have a blades mat, just four random items of clothing placed in a square. The room was not a gym, just a dilapidated meeting room in the basement of the grand stand. It was now mostly used for storing tables and chairs, all of which were deployed for the Magnolia Stakes event. Only a few broken items and the scratches across the walls remained to bear witness to its previous use.

Guy started slowly. He was watching the prince and shadowing his moves just a fraction out of sync. Within three or four steps, he had matched his rhythm and needed no further cue to continue the intricate display of turns, kicks and balances. He saw Des walking along the line of an imaginary blades mat, watching: the prince's film reel on the wall above; Guy in real life on the floor before him. Suddenly, Guy stopped thinking and let his body do the talking. With each stretch, he reached higher and further than the prince. His long, slim limbs gave his kicks greater precision and distance. His fast spins let him slip a triple spin into a routine where the prince only managed a double. As they came to the end, Guy held the final pose just a moment long enough to prove the point, then said:

"I'm better than him."

"You're better than him at blades, for sure."

The two paused a moment to watch the boy in the diamond shirt dismiss his blades instructor. He dismissed Commander Tilson, no less. Then called two great gorans to his side. The final image on the tape was a frozen image of Prince Teodor with two yearling gorans licking and sniffing his hands.

"Life's not fair," Guy said quietly.

"Life's NOT fair," agreed Des. "On guard?"

Guy laughed and spun out of the way as Des bore down in a fast, hard attack. Their blades clashed, and they parried. Careful to stay within an imaginary circle, they duelled back and forth. Des sometimes pressed home a hard attack. Sometimes he relented, allowing Guy to make his own attack before defending himself against Guy with elegant ease. They were both laughing as Guy's communicator rang out. Momentarily distracted, Des used a jab to knock the blade from his left hand and put his dagger to his neck:

"Do you yield?"

Even though he was beaten, Guy was grinning from ear to ear. He felt such a dizzying sense of elation. He was in a blades fight with his hero, Des. Even to have lost the fight, it was still a dream he had long imagined. Now it had been a brief reality, only it was over all too soon.

Juke's voice was shouting from Guy's communicator.

"I need you back right now, Guy. I said quarter past, not half past, not quarter to twelve. Get a move on."

Guy smiled grimly.

"I yield."

Des nodded.

"You're in good shape. Oh, yes, and a message from Chartsie. You're to join the party again tonight."

"Lloulou said she did not want me to work tonight."

"Chart Segat said 8pm."

"Yes, but…"

"C'mon Guy! If you want to get into the Dome Elite, you'll do whatever Chart Segat asks, hey? Whatever he says. You hear me, whatever Chart Segat says. Or he'll throw you to his borgs."

"No, he won't"

"Won't what?"

"He won't throw me to the borgs. He said so. I think he knows who my father is."

"Well, maybe. He and Lloulou go way back."

"I think Chart Segat is my father."

"He told you that?"

"No, but…"

Juke was shouting again.

"Whatever Chartsie says, Guy. Whatever he says. You have to do it."

***

"We are calling the suspects A, B, C. We cannot identify them yet. But they belong to Chart Segat, of that we have little doubt," Patrick told Sayginn. Karl Valvanchi had left an hour ago. Sayginn had only left the operations room for a brief change of clothes, now she was ready for the Magnolia Stakes. But before she left she undertook one last turn around the monitoring stations. After the initial excitement of the disk there had been no further sightings of Prince Teodor. Most likely he was securely locked away inside the Dome military complex. Somewhere they still could not access.

On the screen, the computer showed possible matches between the masked captors and the Dome Elite. When a match was found, a dizzying array of photos followed. The photos showed further images of the same man in different places, and as often as not, as part of Chart Segat's entourage. Sayginn felt fear growing within her as she looked at the photos. All night they had been talking about the Dome Elite, as if it was some giant anonymous beast. But now she was looking at the faces of the men who had taken her son.

"Which brings us back to the question of motive." Patrick was thoughtful. "Chart Segat said he wanted a seat at the table on the future of the Dome. But did they just do this to catch our attention, to make us listen?"

"He also said he did not kill Serge."

"He has said that all along," Patrick said bluntly. "Maybe we should have listened."

Another image popped onto the screen.

"This is Des Parks, Dome Elite. He was seen leaving Chart Segat's apartment about six minutes earlier." Patrick sounded pleased with himself.

"Do you think he might have seen something? Can we bring him in for questioning?"

"Not with this evidence. Only if we bump into him. These three men are Battle Borgs of Freyne. If we see them, we will grab them and run a diagnostic on their key programming. But him? He's human. Ok, he's only seventeen. But if he shows up at the Magnolia Stakes racecourse, we intend to grab him and persuade them to help us with our enquiries."

"Persuade?"

"There is, of course, a radio station at the racecourse. There are also a couple of sound-proof rooms where we will start inviting individuals to help us with our enquiries."

"No!" Sayginn said quickly. She knew what Patrick meant by this euphemism. He was talking about torture. Otherwise, why bother with a sound-proofed room?

"Regent, there is always a little bit of horse play. The occasional fight when the Regency Defence meets the Dome Elite."

Sayginn's head was spinning. They would try and cover up the questioning and beatings as some inter-military unit skirmish. Should she protest? She glanced over and reminded herself of the images in the maintenance corridors. The Elite had used snake droids in narrow corridors. Regency Defence and cy-wolves had been cut to shreds.

"I need results. I do not need to know the details. But he is only seventeen."

"Yes, and I will give him every chance to help us with our enquiries." Patrick McGuire replied smoothly. Something had caught Sayginn's eye.

"What's that?"

She pointed to a small screen, perched on another cluster of desks. Newsfeeds were starting to appear.

"That is the surveillance around the Magnolia Stakes Racecourse. It will help us track the key individuals. We hope to record all meetings and all conversations. These droids are scanning all the different areas and sending back these live feeds.

Sayginn glanced at the screen. There were multiple views of the racecourse, which was still largely deserted ahead of the opening, together with its restaurants, bars and kitchens.

"Yes, but what's that?" Sayginn insisted.

"Oh, it looks like a couple of Dome Elite. They're boys. I'd say."

"What are they doing?" Sayginn could see what they were doing. She just wanted someone to confirm what she was seeing.

"Well, it looks like they are copying Prince Teodor's blades display."

"Why today?" Sayginn wondered then quickly: "I recognise that boy. What's his name?" Sayginn felt her pulse race. She did recognise that boy, and she knew when she had seen him.

"Hold on. He's unregistered. Domeside orphan…"

"Wait!" Sayginn was shouting as she remembered: "He was with Lloulou at the Clinic. He's the one who was due to fight Teodor at blades! And the other one…"

"The other one is Des Parks," Patrick said quickly. "Again."

Both Sayginn and Patrick had moved closer to the small screen.

"The kid, is he any good?" asked Sayginn.

"Well…" Patrick hesitated, then said, "Teodor is strong."

Sayginn had a sudden insight. Sayginn had seen Lloulou at the Clinic with Chart Segat. It was well documented in the popular press that she was Chart Segat's mistress, but the boy had been there. Sayginn had seen Lloulou at the Festival of Fashion, and fleetingly, Sayginn remembered the dazzling display of blades along the length of the catwalk. This boy had been there too. And what had the Emperor said? One or both of those children is said to be Lloulou's love child. She had seen the boy with Chart Segat as well. So this boy was close to Lloulou, or even Lloulou's son. He was also known to Chart Segat:

"Rewind it. They were talking beforehand," Sayginn said. She was looking at the boy. This film was black and white, but still there was no ignoring the shine on his hair, the life in his eyes. There was also something familiar about him. "There. While they are eating. Is there any audio?"

"No, this feed came from a mini-droid. We can use lip-synchronisation," the analyst said.

"Of course, speaking with their mouths full," muttered Patrick, peering at the black and white image, then: "That bit there. Where they are pointing at Teodor on the screen."

"Why this sudden interest in Prince Teodor?" Sayginn said aloud, and Patrick shrugged. Sayginn had a doubt. What if this boy was just interested in watching Prince Teodor because once he had thought he might fight him? Maybe.

"His disappearance is all over the news," Patrick said glumly. Clearly he had doubts, as well. They both stood and watched. After a few moments, the audio transcript of their speech started to appear on the screen.

I would not like to be on the receiver end and that.

"That doesn't make any sense."

"The lip synchroniser does not always match exactly what was said."

"Oh, what did the other boy say there?"

"We do not know. His head is turned away. We cannot see his face or lips."

Well, certainly. You have to – you cannot take hits and that.

"What does it mean?"

Sayginn began to think this was folly on her behalf. Lloulou had always denied she had had a child, so this boy could be anyone. She was about to turn away when three words appeared:

Taken. He's alive

"What was that? Rewind that? Can you clean up the Audio?"

Tolkien, He's a liar

"Hold on, the translation changed, rewind it again."

Taken. He's alive

Sayginn was staring at the words.

"I cannot believe he said that. He knows something. He must have seen Teodor. Bring him in. Bring them both in."

"This feed is fifteen minutes old. Are they still at the racecourse? Someone check. Our guys will be there in five minutes," Patrick added. "Find those boys. We need to have a chat."

***

Guy was adjusting the display when he heard the beeping. He ignored it at first, then looked up and saw a droid pointing in his face. It sounded an alarm and a red light flashed on its casing. He looked at the droid and turned to look around. Behind him there was a stock of friseburys in small presentation tubs, and nothing else. Guy reached up to switch off the droid, but it dodged away. Guy then saw the emblem on its casing: Regency Defence. Across the plaza, they were coming.

Panicked, Guy ducked under the stall tables. He materialised about five metres away from the droid and ran. Obviously he could not outrun a flying droid, but he did want to get away from the Regency Defence. Only, where to go? He looked up and realised. There was one place. He raced up the carpeted stair to the VIP suite where Chart Segat was entertaining his guests. As he reached the door. He saw with relief that Chart Segat was still welcoming his guests. Guy tried to slip through the door, but he was caught and pushed back by a Dome Elite guard:

"Hey, Guy... Where are you going?"

"The droid, the droid. It's after me?" Guy shouted, panicked. He made so much noise he had attracted the attention of Chart Segat who looked up indulgently. His smile faltered as half a dozen Regency Defence arrived in the reception area. One guard marched boldly forward to grab Guy, and pulled him away from the Dome Elite.

"Chartsie!" shouted Guy in despair.

"What's going on?" Chart Segat said.

"This boy needs to answer some questions. It's by order of the Regent."

"Ok, but this boy is Dome Elite. And he's underage."

"Well, you can accompany him, but we have executive orders. This boy is to be questioned."

Chart Segat nodded grimly and waved forward four more Dome Elite. In tight formation the Dome Elite, Chart Segat and Guy were escorted from the VIP suite to a small meeting room in the racecourse business centre. The first and second floors were guest suites for the races, but the ground floor had been taken over by the Regency Defence. They had installed a further monitoring station with screens and terminals. Analysts and communications experts all worked under large images of Prince Teodor in a variety of guises, including a photo of him in the angel costume the day before.

***

Sayginn had only arrived at the Magnolia Stakes twenty minutes ago. Already she wished she could leave. She quickly found even the goran races could not distract her. The result of the first race was a foregone conclusion and Sayginn felt little satisfaction as her colours were again hoisted high on the winning posts. From her box she had a view over the entire course, the stands and the people. She could even look into the other VIP boxes, but for all that, all she could see was Chart Segat.

She knew he was here, she had seen him promenading with Lloulou on his arm. That beastly man had walked through the crowds, basking in his status as celebrity leader of the Dome. Women swooned. Men fawned. Boys ran errands. Lloulou, the most beautiful woman on all Freyne, had her hand twisted around his arm. Sayginn watched him now mingling with his guests, lots of Dome Elite uniforms, and sports celebrities. He was listening to one, joking with another, always a quip, a comic look or a laugh. Did the man never stop? Then there were the girls. Sayginn watched the younger, more raucous, scantily clad girls crowding around Chart Segat. Who was that? Simon Ssochen, that sleazy octogenarian owner of three Domeside nightclubs. Still, he was younger than the Emperor, she reminded herself grimly. At her elbow, she heard one of her stewards cough.

206

"Security say they have found the other boy."

"Good, I will come at once."

***

Chart Segat did not once let go of Guy's hand. Both he and Guy were looking right and left as they assessed and understood the effort the Regency Defence had deployed to find the prince.

"Is this him?" The man in the suit asked. "Chart."

"Patrick." Chart Segat greeted the minister. "This is Guy Erma. He's Dome Elite, so he's under my protection."

"Are you his father?"

"No Patrick, I am his fairy godmother. I am Chart Segat, Mayor of Domeside, Commander-in-chief of the Dome Elite. Since this boy has no father, he is my responsibility. What do you want with him?"

"I am Patrick McGuire, prime minster to Regent Sayginn, head of her government and commander of the Regency Defence. This boy needs to answer some questions."

"Not without me, he doesn't."

"Very well, you can sit in."

Guy, Chart Segat and the three others were led into a small meeting room with a blacked out, mirrored wall. Even as Guy wondered if the room was being monitored through the mirror, he saw Des, shirtless and chained to a chair. His shoulders were red with lash marks. There were cuts under his eyes and across the bridge of his nose.

"Des!" cried Guy and ran to stand at his side.

"So you two know each other?"

Guy looked up at Patrick McGuire and panicked. Chart Segat and the Dome Elite were standing in the entrance looking wary. None of them acknowledged Des or even seemed to recognise him. By their defensive stance and the way their hands cradled their blades, he could sense their anger.

207

"What's going on here?" Segat said, trying to sound cheerful but somehow not quite managing it.

"This boy is withholding information about the kidnapping and whereabouts of Prince Teodor."

"Are you quite mad?"

"Watch."

On the screen they showed Des and Guy in conversation, watching a video of Teodor. From the beginning when they were eating rolls and joking, through to Guy's blades display in sync with Prince Teodor. Finally, to the fast blades combat and ultimately Des's victory.

"So the boys were training at blades this morning. I don't see how that is relevant," said Chart Segat.

"Here." Patrick rewound the tape and showed a small segment of conversation where only one side of the conversation could be heard:

Tolkien, he's a liar.

The audio transcript offered helpfully. They rewound the tape once again:

Taken, he's alive.

"Taken, he's alive," Patrick repeated with satisfaction.

Suddenly Guy was afraid. Somehow, his conversation with Des from that morning had been overheard. He was normally careful about his surroundings. Had he not seen the camera?

"That audio transcript changed," said Chart Segat at once. "It's unclear, and we cannot hear what Guy says at all."

Guy looked again. It must have been a flying miniature camera, tiny too. Or else Des would have seen it, surely?

"Because he is facing away from the camera. But we would like to know what he did say. Can you remember, young man?"

Guy looked at the screen. He knew perfectly well what Des had said. The way he mimed for Guy to stay silent. They had been talking about the prince, no, not exactly talking. Guy had realised Des knew something. He had wanted to tell him about the gold sandals, but what had he said exactly? Had they said Teodor's name? Guy watched the short clip of the film again. It was not clear what he and Des were talking about except for the last phrase. He looked at the screen again:

Lip sync accuracy check:

Taken he's alive   55% accuracy score

Tolkien, he's a liar   45% accuracy score

The two percentages jumped out at Guy. Suddenly he knew what to say next.

  · "Des said Tolkien, he's a liar."

"Of course he did," said Patrick McGuire looking down on Guy with a wry smile. "But can you remember what you said before that? I mean, who is Tolkien?"

Guy hesitated. He had not thought this through. He glanced around for inspiration. Chart Segat was just behind him, in front of him was Des. Someone was missing. Tilson. Where was Commander Tilson?

"Tilson," Guy said slowly. "What Des said was: Tilson is a liar."

Both Des and Chart Segat looked over at Guy, waiting.

"Tilson, he's a liar," Guy repeated with more conviction. None of the Regency men looked like they were going to refute this. The lip synchronisation was clearly not very accurate.

"Right, and who is Tilson?" Patrick asked.

"Commander Tilson is a senior blades instructor in the Dome. He's my teacher, and he's Des's teacher." Guy was much more certain of this. He was pleased with himself. This might work, he thought.

This hope did not last long. There was a sudden harshness in Patrick McGuire's eyes. He looked totally unforgiving. Guy wondered what he had said to anger him. Once again, the Regency Defence looked at Guy and then at Des and replayed the tape.

Tolkien, He's a liar

"Ok, that's plausible, but what were you saying here? What did you say before Des said: Tilson he is a liar."

Guy looked at Des. He tried to think of something he might have said. He tried not to think about the conversation of that morning, nor the cocktail table with the foot in the golden sandal. He tried not to think of Des. Des had nodded in agreement when he said 'Teodor is our prince'. Guy tried only to think of the ever present mime, the one that told him to shut up. He had to keep quiet. He had to think of something, he had to. Unbidden, he remembered Marline sitting on the edge of the jacuzzi.

"Well?"

Suddenly the words rushed out of Guy in a clutter.

"I said Tilson_was_telling_me… no_TilsonwasBraggin' 'cos hehadkissedMarlinelastnight."

"Sorry, I didn't catch that?"

Guy found he was blushing. At his side, Des was looking up at him with growing incredulity.

"It's a bit embarrassing because Tilson is our teacher, and we should not have been talking about him really."

This lie seemed to work, but still Patrick was unrelenting.

"Ok, but I'd still like to know what you said."

"I'm sorry and all…" Guy started apologising to Chart Segat. He did not know why. In turn, Chart Segat looked startled and nodded towards the interrogator. Patrick said:

"Yes, so you have apologised. So now tell us, in a nice clear voice, what you said."

"I said," Guy paused and swallowed, not quite believing what he was about to say, "I said: Tilson was bragging he had kissed Marline last night, and Des said: Tilson, he's a liar."

The Regency Defence men paused. Even Chart Segat seemed a little taken aback. Finally, Patrick said:

"Who is Marline?"

"She's my half-sister. She's a model from House Jewel."

"Of course she is. And the party?"

"Chart Segat's party in the cap of the Dome last night."

Guy was emphatic, of this he was sure. No-one could contradict this simple fact. Tilson was a blades instructor. Both had been at the party.

Whatever he had said was irrelevant. The whole lie was a careful construct of several truths, and as such it was undeniable.

"Convenient," Patrick said. The interrogators seemed to know when they were beaten. They looked between themselves and shrugged. Chart Segat quickly stepped forward and pointed to where Des was still bound to the chair:

"I don't think you'll object if I get this boy to a doctor. You know he's only seventeen?"

The Regency Defence untied Des and helped him up. They handed him his shirt and jacket.

"Nice tan," sneered one of the men.

"Des has been training in the southern mountains," Chart Segat shouted angrily.

The Regency Defence men just snorted. Chart Segat was quick to escort both boys outside.

"Quick thinking, kiddo," Chart Segat said in an undertone.

"Thank you Guy. That was clever of you," Des added shakily.

Guy's elation at this praise was short-lived. As they stepped into the corridor, the door of an adjacent room opened and in the doorway was Regent Sayginn. As Guy glanced over to her, he saw behind her that she had been watching him and Des through the mirrored wall.

"I know you," she said simply. "You're Lloulou's boy."

Guy paused, but with Chart Segat's hand heavy on his shoulder, he knew better than to reply.

"Guy has no mother or father," Chart Segat replied.

Sayginn ignored Chart Segat. Stepping closer, she gently stroked Guy's cheek.

"Teo is thirteen too," she said so softly. Guy wondered if anyone else had heard. He looked up at her. She was not like either Lloulou or Marline. There was a soft openness to her face, which was quite unlike the hard grimaces and glamour smiles of the Domeside models.

"Have you seen Prince Teodor, Guy?"

211

Guy's heart accelerated to a fast sprint. He felt sure that Chart Segat could feel it too. He swallowed and nervously glanced up at the man, but the Regent gently took his chin and turned his face back towards her.

"Well?"

Guy could not lie. So once again he fell back on the truth.

"I saw him in St Joseph's Cathedral yesterday morning. I was his understudy, playing the part of the angel in rehearsals. So I saw him in costume, but then I left. I had to go to school."

"I see. I did not realise you were there as well," Sayginn said thoughtfully.

"I wasn't," Guy said quietly. "I left just before… Before the explosion."

"We don't know what happened to Teodor, you see?"

Guy nodded. His heart was still beating fast and hard. The only thing he could think of was the dirty golden sandal and the crumpled shadowy form in the base of the cocktail table. The only thing he could feel was Chart Segat's hand heavy on his shoulder. He looked left and glimpsed the band of gold on Chart Segat's finger. It was etched with words in bold capitals like teeth, both inside and out. Inside it read: Fear only God. Outside it read: Loyal to Empire. Guy swallowed nervously: Loyal to Empire, Fearful of God: the motto of the Dome Elite.

"Have you seen him?" Sayginn insisted gently.

It was all Guy could do to shake his head briefly. He wondered if she could see how he was trembling from this effort. Guy knew he had seen Prince Teodor. Now he remembered that boy who was the same age as him and he was going to be the next Emperor of Freyne. Sayginn was carefully looking at him. Her hand once again gently stroking his cheek. This woman was Prince Teodor's mother, why would Chart Segat want to hurt them? Loyal to Empire, all at once, Guy made a decision.

"I am Dome Elite, Ma'am."

"Yes, I can see that."

Guy looked up at her. He wanted to tell her he would help if he could. He would save the prince given a chance. Rescue him, whatever it took. Only Chart Segat was standing so close, Guy could feel the warmth of his body at his back. All he could think of was the simple oath of loyalty that all Dome Elite swore.

"I swear. I am Loyal to Empire. I Fear only God."

He looked expectantly up at the Regent. Surely she would understand that he was loyal to her, that he loved the empire. For another long minute, he looked into her face. Then Chart Segat said:

"So help me God."

Sayginn turned away from Guy to glare at Chart Segat. He stepped back from her barely concealed anger.

"What about you, are you loyal to empire? Do you fear only God?"

"I am, I am loyal to empire."

"Then perhaps you can update me on what the Dome Elite have done to find my son."

"Is this a formal request for the Dome Elite to help in the search and rescue of Prince Teodor of Freyne 2?"

"Does there need to be a formal request?" Sayginn was shouting now. "He is your prince. He is your future King. He is your future Commander-in-Chief."

Chart Segat looked a little scornful but still he said: "Then I will, of course, mobilise the Dome Elite at once." He glanced around a little disparagingly at the amount of tech the Regent had at her disposal. "You know you only had to ask, Sayginn."

"Let them go," she snapped.

Sayginn and Patrick stood and watched as Chart Segat, with his hand on a shoulder of both Guy and Des made a quick retreat.

"Guy Erma," Patrick said. "At least now we know his name."

"The boy was lying. That's as plain as the nose on his face. But also it is clear he belongs to Chart Segat. The other one, Sas Darona you think?"

"Not sure how he got back. Sas Darona is in lock down," Patrick muttered.

"I don't want to know," Sayginn replied curtly. "Sorry, I did not mean that. Pick him up again after this weekend. For now, just keep close tabs on all of them. One or all of them should lead us to Teodor."

Her steward had come alongside:

"They are waiting for you in the changing rooms, my lady. The three o'clock race."

Sayginn checked the time. Karl had said he would free her son, what had happened to him? How much longer before Teodor was free?

Her steward coughed by way of reminder. Patrick came up to her. He glanced at the time.

"Are you sure about this? Are you sure people will understand why you're racing?"

"I will try and make them understand," Sayginn hesitated, "And if nothing else it will give us more publicity. More headlines."

"What, Regent races while son in captivity?"

"Regent races in the name of her captive son."

Patrick sighed.

"Ok, I'll go and sit with the press team and make sure they get it right."

Sayginn nodded to her steward and bodyguards. It was not far to go.

"Oh, Sayginn," Patrick called after her. "You had better win."

***

Sayginn stood tall before the mirror in the jockeys' changing room. The sound of the crowd was a muted hum from the dressing room. She breathed deeply, willing the anxiety of the day away, then stretched so high she could almost see her pulsing heart below her rib-cage. Pushing her palms vertically upwards she reached higher, lifted onto her toes, then released, her body falling forward into the crouched position she would take on the goran's neck. She let her head hang loosely down and her vision framed her lower body, then she clenched her legs, felt the electricity ripple and saw the muscles move under the flesh. Slowly she stood up again to her full height.

Deep breath, slow whistling release. *I have to win,* she told herself. *I have to win, for Teodor's sake.*

Her eyes turned to her riding gear. She leant over, picked up the leggings, lifted one foot and rolled them up. Black leather boots, snow-white woollen riding half-pants, wide black leather belt, generous red and white silk shirt

214

and the silver crown proudly emblazoned on the back. Checking the straps on her helmet one last time, Sayginn pulled it on and adjusted it, lifting the visor so the crowds would recognize her face. She turned to find her butler and jockey waiting. They nodded their approval.

"The press are outside?"

"As always…"

Sayginn stepped out and went down the steps onto the turf of the display area, to where Blue Barbrina stood. There was a rumour in the crowd as people noted the Regency colours; startled glances at the silver embroidery, then shocked stares into the well-known face: the Regent was to ride Blue Barbrina. The rumour became a murmur, as the words were repeated from one to another: the Regent is to ride Blue Barbrina! The Regent Sayginn… Blue Barbrina. The murmur was interrupted by an excited yell: ride her, win with her! The crowd moved, closing in to the barrier to see for themselves. A news presenter stepped up to talk to her.

"I am dedicating this race to my son, Teodor. He is not here today. He was taken yesterday. We have not got him back. I don't know where he is. But I do know that he loves these gorans and he would want Blue Barbrina to win. So, Teo, if you are watching this, I am racing for you, my love. I want to win for you."

The crowd cheered once more, and Sayginn noticed with wry satisfaction that the odds in favour of Blue Barbrina winning had markedly improved. Reassured and energised, Sayginn led Blue Barbrina briskly into the starting gates. Only then, as the runners lined up, did the crowd's roar start to fade. Sayginn remembered her pledge to win. She wondered if that had been reckless. She checked the competition: they all seemed so young. For the most part, these jockeys were in their twenties. Paulio, one of the oldest and most experienced, was only thirty-two. Each goran was different in size and colouring, and vaguely the same weight, although the parameters were very broad. There was only one strict rule: all gorans had been born within the same two weeks in April, exactly two years ago. All the runners in the Magnolia Stakes celebrated their second birthday within one week of the race. Sayginn thought of Dark Daniella; her cubs were due in the next few days. There would be six goran-cubs, the vets had said, one of whom, thought Sayginn, will race this race in two years' time.

Blue Barbrina growled in a low voice, as if reminding Sayginn to keep her mind on the race in hand or maybe it was antipathy to Imperial Rina who was being forced forward into the neighbouring box. Sayginn noted how the Emperor's goran was foaming at the mouth, her yellow eyes watering, and looking back, Sayginn saw the cause: the red lash marks on the goran's back and haunches. Lowering her visor, Sayginn now leant over Blue Barbrina and started an insistent and persuasive monologue: "See Rina, Barbrina, we must beat her, to survive. She is the enemy above all enemies. See Rina, and beat Rina, my beauty." Blue Barbrina let a sharp, angry growl escape. Sayginn looked around; they were under starters orders now. She crouched forward, tensing up her thighs, knees and ankles. Then she whispered to Barbrina the familiar words she used to start a race.

"Time to start Barbie, ready? Time to start, Barbie. Ready. Time to start. Go!" The gates shot up, thick hind legs propelled sleek bodies in a dive up and forward. Blue Barbrina bounded from the start. They were away!

In the first straight, Sayginn concentrated on increasing Blue Barbrina's speed. She paid no heed to Imperial Rina's initial head-start. Red luminous speedometer figures shone inside her helmet, Blue Barbrina accelerated to 55km/h after five bounds, 65km/h after seven. The winner would be the goran who reached its fastest speed first, then maintained it for the three circuits of the course. Blue Barbrina was coming up fast on the first pointed bend. This would be the most dangerous, with the gorans still on top of each other in a densely pulsing pack. Some lesser felines reached out claws to injure the stronger players. Blue Barbrina fended off one such blow with a swooping paw push within her coursing movement. But on the inside, Imperial Rina caught Blue Barbrina's left jowl with a subtle flick of her hind limb. Blue Barbrina pulled back, somewhat miffed at the taste of her own blood.

With urgent words, Sayginn tried to mould her pain into anger. Barbrina needed little encouragement, as they came out of the curve; the red digits flashed 70k, then 71k, then 74k, 78... 76... 79... 74. In rhythmical pounding movements, Blue Barbrina caught up with Imperial Rina and matched her speed for one circuit, at last inching past her rival as they entered the third circuit.

Sayginn felt panic fringe her surge of excitement. Blue Barbrina was stretching her advantage with every stride, and she was a body's length ahead of Rina and two lengths ahead of the rest of the field. Coming into the bend Imperial Rina closed in on the inside. Even as Sayginn urged Blue Barbrina on, she heard her screech and she threw her head back in such a way that Sayginn nearly fell. With a lightening glance over her shoulder, Sayginn saw that with a vicious claw Imperial Rina had opened the soft fleshy paw-pads of

Blue Barbrina's right rear leg. Then Imperial Rina was upon them, pouncing from the right, rising onto her rear legs and lunging forward with strong front paws, as if to push Blue Barbrina out of her path. By chance, the smallest of her talons locked into Sayginn's tensed thigh. As Imperial Rina pulled back, she ripped away a fragment of muscle; Sayginn's scream could be heard in the Imperial boxes. Spectators stared helplessly at the images of the conflict at the bend.

Blue Barbrina reacted to Sayginn's pain, lashing up and out at Imperial Rina. Sayginn shouted quick encouragement and Blue Barbrina leapt forward into the race again, even as a third goran went to pass them. Blue Barbrina streaked ahead at 75km/h. Imperial Rina, her bottom jowl now ripped in four regular cuts and hanging away from her toothy jaw, chased Blue Barbrina with evil growls and hisses.

There was no catching Blue Barbrina as she bore her wounded rider to the safety of the arrival post. She raced past the screaming masses from Domeside, ever-stretching the distance between her and Imperial Rina. Her gait was a shadow lop-sided, blood spotted the front rows on each excruciating impact, but the red digits never dipped below 74km/h as she took the final bend to cross the finishing line five lengths ahead of Imperial Rina.

It was a victory the like of which had not been seen at the Magnolia Stakes for many years, and the crowd loved it. Two equally matched gorans, a bloody fight, a severe injury and a victory for the underdog. The cheering and screaming continued unabated even as Sayginn cantered to a stop. She smiled and waved in her triumph. Beneath the bravado, she was concerned to feel Blue Barbrina's limp become more marked. At her call, a vet tended the paw even as Blue Barbrina stopped. Sayginn's sodden riding pants were almost black with his seeping blood and had left a dark stain on Blue Barbrina's snow-grey coat. Blue Barbrina turned and dropped her head to sniff the wound, and then before Sayginn could move, her thick tongue swished out and licked the length of the fifteen centimetre incision. Her saliva was warm and seemed healing. Sayginn fondled the beast, roughly scratching her behind the ears and gazed with love into her dark eyes.

As they announced her name, Sayginn stepped onto the podium unaided and stood straight as the Emperor placed the gold medal around her neck. Then both turned to watch the Regent's colours being hoisted to the sound of the Freyne anthem. As the last fanfare sounded, Sayginn could feel the throbbing of the leg wound like a drum in her head. The music ended and she

217

smiled, but it was a feeble effort. She pinched her thigh to hold the burning at bay just a little longer.

As they filled her arms with a huge bouquet it was like they had given her a heavy sack. She first sighed then sank to the ground, seemingly overwhelmed by the weight of the flowers. Her last thought was bleak: the time was 3.24 and still no news from Karl Valvanchi.

Chapter 17. An Adventure on One Summer's Day

It had been a sunny day in early spring, and Teodor was coming back from the goran stables when they jumped him. A handkerchief was pressed to his face, his legs were kicked from under him and a sack was pulled over his head. Later, when he woke up in a cave, he was sick for a full five minutes, throwing up all the food from the previous twelve hours. The mock kidnap was meant to be as real as possible, but on that occasion, he had escaped.

"What you have to understand," his father had said, "is that in the case of kidnap it is the last two minutes that are the most dangerous. I can get within two minutes of rescuing you. Just as I come within shouting distance, they will kill you out of hand. It won't be fair. It probably won't be particularly clean. It will be quick. Whether with a double shot to the head, or a knife to your throat, you'll be dying as I cover the last fifty yards to free you."

Loosely bound in a cave, Teodor had known he was beside a lake. He had waited, waited until his captors had become more relaxed. One was taking a call. The other was taking a leak. Quiet as a shadow he had crawled away from his prison. Before he had got ten yards away, the King was running in to pick him up and carry him away.

"Inevitably, I will know where you are being held. We will have all communications monitored. Anything said – even on short wave radio, even by semaphore – we'll hear, we'll see." Teodor remembered how his eyes had been blue and full of laughter. His father had been merry that day, though what he had discussed was deadly serious.

"The city will be locked down. The planet will be locked down. Unless they are very quick, their only option will be to sit tight and hope. And what hope will they have, when I deploy hundreds of cy-rats, and thousands of cy-roaches?"

"Cy-roaches!" Teodor had said in disgust.

"Military issue, top secret, very fast, very dangerous." And he ran his hand up Teodor's leg and across his chest to his neck like a rapid insect. Teodor squealed and his father laughed, and they wrestled a few moments. Teodor remembered how his father had lifted a finger for silence.

"Thing is, cy-roaches will be programmed to your scent, your DNA, your fingerprints. Whatever it takes. We will find you."

"So I just wait?"

"Have you not been listening?"

"Oh yes, you said the last two minutes were the most dangerous."

"You have to escape but you don't have to go far. You just have to be clever. Chances are, my men and I will be camped just outside, waiting to liberate you."

Teodor nodded quietly and pressed his cheek to the King.

"I will escape father, I will escape and you will be waiting."

The fleeting memory was a welcome change from the nightmares, Teodor thought, as he started to wake. As his head started to clear he became more aware of the aching in his shoulders and legs. He was still trussed up, with his elbows behind his knees. The floor was cold and hard. His sight was blurred at first, then he heard a voice saying:

"Are you awake?"

***

The west entrance of the Dome was often nicknamed the 'Glass Palace', with its two transparent walls shedding bright sunshine in rippling rays onto the complex, and the magnifying glass wall opening onto the swimming complex. Karl came out of the lift and stared at a three-metre-high scantily clad Freyne woman walking across the east wall. The image rippled and disappeared into distortion. Karl was left straining to see the small figure

220

continuing to stroll round the edge of the leisure pool. He breathed again as he understood the illusion. Next, he looked around the lobby at the many information computers, three dimensional representations and maps of the Dome. High on his right was a huge and ever-changing information board of events, on-going and future, underneath a row of ticket booths.

"Seven Levels of Sport and Pleasure" read the welcome sign.

Karl was not interested in the public areas. They were covered by cameras. Nor was he interested in the military levels whose security could also be accessed. He wanted to check the black areas. Those areas designed so no cameras or microphones could access them. There was no location more secret than where Karl proposed to go today.

Nikki had given Karl the four men he requested but they were young security guards, very green, Karl had surmised. He had spoken to each of the soldiers: none had combat experience. Karl was tempted to leave them behind but they were desperately anxious to please, eager to help the great Karl Valvanchi.

"Try not to do too much damage," Nikki had said. "And no casualties."

He had even furnished Karl with blunted blades, but Karl had refused, saying simply:

"Battle Borgs of Dome?"

"Human casualties zero," Nikato had said.

Karl and his four young companions had been given Dome Elite uniforms and had shape-shifted into Freyne men at the embassy. They then had to wait for two senior embassy guards who were to accompany them. They had waited until they were in the car before shape-shifting effortlessly into elderly Freyne maintenance engineers. They were now wearing worker's dungarees, adorned with a badge that said air-conditioning. It was standard procedure for Zaracan diplomatic missions to assure their own services. Nikato had a small team who owned and ran a number of small businesses, including an air-conditioning team. Now they were using one of their companies' trucks and some of their uniforms to gain access to the Dome. They were dropped in a narrow alley a short walk from the Dome and entered the complex on foot.

"Where are you going?" Karl asked the fake air-conditioning engineers.

"We do have a job to do," he replied. "Unless you require our services as well."

Karl shook his head. He reran the briefing from earlier that morning. Nikato had not mentioned that his men would be working on the air-conditioning. Had he? The plan had been for the air-conditioning team to show Karl and his men the entrance to the prison, since they were familiar with the layout of the military block within the Dome.

"I thought the bill of works was a fake?" Karl said at last. Something was out of place. Karl could sense it. Why was this not mentioned at the morning's briefing?

"It's a cover, allows us to wait until you need to leave. You know where you are? It's that door there." The man seemed to be implying he was wasting time. Karl nodded.

"Very well. And thank you."

"I'm Alton. Just give me a call. We will be ready whenever you need to leave."

"Thanks Alton. Right then."

For the plan to succeed, Karl Valvanchi had to access the prison unannounced. He also had to secure all exits so the guards had no chance to move Prince Teodor. Karl had studied the layout of the prison block. He had few details as it was part of the black zone. Nevertheless he had to try. Karl was confident in his own Freyne appearance. His companions were wearing the black woollen caps the Dome Elite sometimes favoured, so their transformations were less obvious. Even he could see that the youngsters' shape-shifted Freyne appearance was not perfect. Still, he needed back-up for this part of the mission. Or did he?

Karl hesitated once again. Should he take these four boy soldiers with him? The uniforms were ok, the first security guard had barely looked at them. Karl had no idea if the badges they wore were correct. The best approach was a fast approach. To his relief, his security pass worked seamlessly and he led his men towards the prison block.

There was a small reception desk, but it was empty. Above, on the wall, a screen was relaying images from the Magnolia Stakes, with crowds now queuing eight deep near the entrances.

"Can one of you check the desk?" Karl said. "See if you can switch off the security alarms from here."

"I'm tech-trained, Karl. I'll do that."

222

"Thanks?"

"My name is Zeb."

"Thanks, Zeb."

The young man scanned the interfaces with his communicator. A few moments later, Zeb started to type in some codes. Karl led the other three to where a spiral stair opened down onto the floor below. Karl paused on the top step to catch his breath, the descent was to be completely blind, and those below would see and hear him long before he reached the bottom. Karl knew this first approach would not be won with force; only the disguises would buy them time, and the fact they knew the password would give them credibility. With this thought, he leapt down the stairs.

They arrived at a small office with three men on duty. One of them probably should have been on reception, now it was he who came forward to greet them. Karl gave him the fake instructions, to give himself time to look around. It was a small square room and beyond was Chart Segat's private prison. The three guards looked alert, nervous even. Karl saw that they had been watching his approach on screens. He had rehearsed several excuses and scenarios, his men were briefed to act on a code word. But as he assessed the small room, he decided there was no point delaying. He took a breath and reached with his mind to the cells beyond the office.

If need be, he would stun these guards then search the cells until such time as the Dome Elite fought back. Any fight in this confined area would be deadly. He should expect to lose at least one of his companions. There was a high probability of injury to himself.

'No casualties," Nikki had said.

The guard behind the desk had said something. He was scrutinising the orders.

"So you have orders from Chartsie to take Prince Teodor to the Magnolia Stakes. You are joking, right?"

***

Teodor woke in pain. He was lying on his side. His elbows were still tied behind his knees. His head was twisted at a cruel angle on a concrete floor. He struggled a little, then peered around. He was in an old-fashioned cell,

223

concrete on two sides, metal bars on two sides. He could see into neighbouring cells. There was someone there. That someone had said something, now he spoke again:

"So, are you awake now?"

Teodor saw feet. A face bent down to his level looking through the bars. For a moment, Teodor thought he was dreaming again, for the face looking at him was his own face.

"If you scoot over here I might be able to help. I have this." He held up a small knife. Teodor could not decide whether he looked more like a worm or a bug. Still, he crawled using his elbows and knees until he was pressed up against the bars. The boy with his face reached through, slipped his knife inside the tie, and started to cut:

"Well, it's cutting. But it's tough plastic. It might take a while. Can you bear it?"

Teodor gasped, but managed to rasp "Yes. Please carry on…"

The boy nodded and set to it with renewed concentration. In the end, it only took a few minutes. Teodor was sitting up rubbing his elbows where the binding had cut into him and shaking the circulation back into his legs.

"Take it easy," the other boy said.

"Who are you?"

"Well, I'm Teo. Prince Teodor to you," the boy said with a laugh. "No, my real name is Sebastian. I said something Chartsie didn't like, so they had me locked up here all night. I hope they have not forgotten me. I'm dying for a hot bath and a proper sleep – in a comfortable bed, you know."

"Chartsie?"

"I told Chart Segat he should free Prince Teodor. I was quite drunk, but you see I'm a lookalike for Prince Teodor. That's how I make my living. People pay us for all sorts." He hesitated. "You'll find out soon enough."

Teodor was dumbstruck. His head swam. He felt a bit sick. He tried to remember when he had last eaten. He tried to think where he could be sick in this tiny cell. Most of all, he tried not to think of what a prince's lookalike might be called on to do.

"Do you mean…?" he said at last.

"Waiting on tables, serving drinks, being decorative at parties. That's what I meant," Sebastian hesitated, then changed his mind and joked instead: "It's surprisingly well-paid."

Sebastian looked at him closely, then said: "I don't know you, do I? You're not the Riffaut, are you?"

"I wear House Riffaut," Teodor replied softly, "And you do know me. We've just never met before."

The boy looked at him a few minutes longer, then he said slowly:

"You haven't had surgery, have you?"

Teodor shook his head.

"You have?"

"Cheekbones," the boy replied and pointed. After a moment he sat down close to the grille and took Teodor's hand. He whispered: "You're him, aren't you?"

If Teodor was shocked at the familiarity of his touch, the warmth of the boy's hand seemed like electricity spreading right to his heart. He closed his own hand around Sebastian's.

"I'm Teodor, Prince of Freyne. Yes."

"I model your clothes, you know…"

"I figured you might. Do you enjoy it?"

"I think so. It depends. Earlier in the season they had in mind for you to wear a lot of pink. We did this whole photo shoot. At the same time, they were talking about you fighting Guy Erma. I just said: 'A boy who is a blades fighter would never wear pink'. And when they saw the photographs, they were angry because I looked so sulky, but ultimately they redid the collection. You only had the one pink outfit in the end."

"One pink outfit," Teodor was laughing, outraged. "Yes, I saw it. I told them to put it back in the wardrobe."

"Did you? I wish I had seen that. I knew I was right."

"Pink! Really…" Teodor was disdainful. He laughed. Sebastian joined in, side by side in neighbouring cells, fingers intertwined through the bars.

"I was due to fight Guy Erma, you know? Do you know him?"

"Yes, everyone knows Guy Erma!"

"Everyone knows Guy Erma? Is he any good?"

"Who?"

"Guy Erma, is he any good at blades?"

"My God, yes. He spins like the wind and bites like a goran. None of the juniors can stand against him."

"I'd like to meet him."

"I'll tell him."

"Tell him. I want to meet him with a blade in each hand."

"Go, Prince Teodor," Sebastian laughed and added: "Look, if I do get out of here, I'll tell them I saw you."

A glimmer of an idea occurred to Teodor.

"Maybe we could swap places?"

"We have to get you out," Sebastian agreed. "But for you to wait tables for Chart Segat? No, I think not." Sebastian thought a moment, and then said: "I tell you what. You could pretend you are one of us. Most of the Elite don't know you've been taken by their lot. Just find one who doesn't look too bright and then tell him you are from the Riffaut. There are eight of us with your face. Tell him you have a photo shoot, and if they don't let you go, you won't get paid. And if that doesn't work, say: I'll give you a cut. Can you remember all of that?"

Teodor paused, then said:

"But please sir, I'm not him. I'm House Riffaut, and there is a camera crew waiting. If I get paid, I can give you a cut."

"Good accent. But you must say: the Riffaut, no-one calls it House Riffaut anymore."

"Ok. How much is a cut?"

"Well, this weekend you're likely to get seven to eight thousand, so a cut is at least five hundred. That's good money for the Elite."

"Ok. Thanks. I'll remember," Teodor hesitated. A thought occurred to him: "If I get out of here."

"You'll get out. The Dome is loyal to empire, Teodor. I don't know what Chart Segat thinks he's doing. You're our prince. You're our own blood."

"It was a Dome bomb that killed my father," Teodor said bleakly. In his mind, he could clearly picture the two explosions. He remembered the one coffin, how his mother had buried the two bodies together.

"They were hugging – they were in a hug when they died. I can't separate them." She had been weeping as she tried to explain.

"Actually," Teodor said slowly, "it was the second blast that killed them. The first bomb – the Dome bomb – injured them but did not kill them. The shield on the car kept them alive. It was the second blast…"

"The second bomb was not Dome Elite," Sebastian said quickly.

"No, it wasn't even from the Freyne Empire. No-one knows where it came from. My mother thinks the Dome Elite brought it in from somewhere."

"Dome Elite spacecraft only operate within the twelve. They have not got the range. The United Races will not give them passes," Sebastian said.

"Well, we won't know anything until there is a trial. Chart Segat has to be brought to account."

Sebastian moved uncomfortably.

"What happens to the Dome and the Dome Elite if Chartsie is locked up? Can you wait until I get paid, at least?"

"I don't know. I honestly don't, but I'll think of something."

"Sssh. Did you hear that?" Sebastian did not need to say anything more. Tense now, they both sat listening. They could hear doors opening and maybe footsteps, until they heard something else, much closer.

"Someone is coming," Teodor whispered. And in that moment, he had never felt so hopeful.

***

"An order from Chart Segat to take Prince Teodor? You must be joking, right?"

Karl did not reply. It was a long shot. He was about to say something when all three Dome Elite turned to stare at one of his companions. The young man had lost control of his appearance. He was now himself, a young Zaracan man, with a long white mane, wearing a Dome Elite uniform and standing at the heart of the Dome Elite military prison. Awkwardly, the young man shape-shifted back to being a Freyne, but like a faulty light-bulb the disguise slipped a second time. The three Dome Elite guards watched with open mouths.

As Karl considered his options, all at once he heard Teodor:

...It was the second blast that killed them. The first bomb – the Dome bomb – injured them but did not kill them...

The voice was loud. The boy was close. He had found him. He looked down the corridor with new interest.

Attack. Karl gave the order by telepathy. From his hand, Karl dropped a number of gas pellets. They whizzed and spun around the small space, exploding into the faces of the startled guards and causing them to keel over, fast asleep. The three young soldiers leapt forward and bound and gagged them.

"Gently," Karl said, as he walked round each one, taking their weapons from their hands, lowering them to the floor and checking for a pulse.

"Three Dome Elite down – no casualties."

Karl leapt over the console and plugged in a memory handle. His eyes shone white as with his mind he checked the databanks. On his command, the doors of all the cells sprang open. He nodded to his men, all had now resumed their Zaracan identities. Karl would have rebuked them but he knew how exhausting continuous shape-shifting was to youngsters. He glanced up at the security cameras. Yes, the place was covered with cameras, they were in trouble if anyone was watching. He sighed and nodded wearily for them to carry on. Someone was bound to see them. Their best chance of escape was speed. The young soldiers bounded ahead like puppies, looking into each of the open cells. Karl strode along the corridor and double-checked each cell in turn. They were black steel, lightless cells. Clearly some of the inmates had not seen daylight or even light for a while. You could tell by the way they sat or lay stunned at the sudden opening of the doors. Teodor was not there. Karl strode back the way he had come, counting the cells as he went:

"Two, four, six... But I felt him, how can I have missed him? Twenty, twenty-two, twenty-four. There's a door here, cover me."

But Karl could still hear Teodor talking. It was if he was in the next room.

It was the second blast that killed them.

What was the boy talking about? Where was he? Karl concentrated. He saw the cells. They were made of stone with iron bars. Teodor was looking at himself, in a mirror? No, not a mirror, a lookalike. Riffaut! Karl had a memory of the human tableau from the night before. He brushed it aside. The cells. He realised. The cells were connected. The cells were made of stone. It was not these cells.

He snapped back to the present and looked hard at the black metal cubicles. The prince was not here. But he was close. The voice was so loud in his head.

Where was the prince? He started to run, opening all the doors on each side as he looked. He had to be close.

"Sir?"

"He is here. He is close," he told his men. "We have to find him."

"Sir, look."

The young man was banging on a panel in the wall. It was hollow. Karl looked over the wall and found a hand hold. There was a door on the back wall. Karl tried the handle, then kicked it open.

Beyond was a narrow spiral stairway. Karl could not see the bottom. The soldier at his side released two small flying droids that had been folded away in his armour. They zipped down into the darkness. Karl checked his communicator to see what the droids saw. One droid was blasted on arrival, but the second starting relaying images.

A table, some half-drunk coffees and a newspaper, three chairs, and a Battle Borg pacing, weapon in his hand. Behind the borg, Karl saw another row of cells. These were older cells, almost a dungeon. They had locking doors, and a key hooked up on the wall alongside each one. Karl glanced again at Teodor's thoughts:

Yes. These were the cells where Teodor was being held.

Karl felt a thrill, he looked again at the droid image. Just one Battle Borg. Just one. He looked at the three young soldiers.

"Ok. I'll take the borg. You stay up here and protect our retreat with Zeb." Karl nodded back towards the tech soldier. "Two come with me. Covering fire. Remember, the borgs we can kill. Ok?"

Karl had let slip his disguise for a moment. Now he shape-shifted back to become a Dome Elite soldier. He pulled his Dome medallion out of his shirt onto his chest. He set off at speed down the stairs. He was swiftly through the door, comforted to hear the young soldiers following close on his heels. He kicked the door open.

Not one Battle Borg. Six Battle Borgs of the Freyne Dome Elite. He saw at once they had used a magnet to turn the droid, and keep it pointed away from them. Karl brought his blades up. He threw both blades in different directions simultaneously. One borg staggered as the blade was buried deep into its skull. The other had just reached up and caught the blade after it had bounced off his head plate. Now he span it back towards Karl. Karl avoided the flying blade, but the borgs were closing in. At that moment, his two young companions leapt out from behind him. Blast gun at the ready, the first soldier disembowelled the nearest Borg with a lethal blast of fire at no range. The borg keeled over. At his side, another borg picked the young soldier up by the back of his neck. He pulled the weapon from his hands and swung him up and into the ceiling. Karl leapt forward. His fist now encased in metal he went to punch the borg in the eyes. But a third borg had grabbed Karl from behind.

Karl could only watch helpless. His companion was swung up and whacked into the ceiling. He was then allowed to drop two meters to the floor. The borg stepped onto the small of his spine. The soldier screamed as his spine was crunched to pulp.

The second soldier came screaming through the door now. With a large laser knife, he attacked the borg that held Karl. Karl felt one of the claws open a fraction. He span out of the borg's grasp. He caught a glimpse of a weapon being brought to bear on his companion. Karl span back. With a blade tight in his fist. He embedded it deep in the borg's brain. The borg fell forward and as he was dying, he grabbed the other Zaracan by the neck. The young soldier was thrown to the ground and tumbled beneath the borg as it fell. As Karl looked down in dismay at his wounded but not yet dead companions, he was thrown aside, and momentarily blacked out. He was aware of two Battle Borgs racing off behind him towards the cells.

No, thought Karl. That was where Teodor was being held.

***

"What is it?" Sebastian asked. Teodor had leapt to his feet, and was frantically pacing around his cell.

"I think they're coming. They're coming for me."

Sebastian stood up. They both looked to where the noise of a fight, crashing metal, and a scream could be heard through the door.

"They are only fifty meters away," Teodor said and hesitated. What was it his father had said? *It won't be fair. It will be quick. Whether a double shot to your head or a knife to your throat, you'll be dying as I cover the last fifty yards to release you.*

"I have to get out."

"There is no way out," replied Sebastian.

All at once, the door to the cell flew open and the Battle Borgs were there. They looked first where they had left Teodor, then where he was stood close to Sebastian. They leapt towards him.

"No!" Teodor yelled and dodged. "Let me go!"

He ran forward, ducking under the arms of the first borg, making for the open door. Instead he ran straight into the second borg. It grabbed him. He was tossed over the shoulder of the largest borg and then they were off, running at breakneck speed. Teodor was screaming and kicking as they went, but they only stopped when they reached the lift. Teodor felt the sharp bite of an injection into his neck, and then saw the black rucksack being opened. This time, the drugs were quick.

He thought he heard someone shouting his name.

"No," he whispered. "I don't want to die."

His eyes went dark. It felt like he was falling.

***

Karl had two injured men at his feet, and two live Battle Borgs to fight.

'Only two,' he told himself backing up a fraction. 'I can take two.' He hesitated. 'These two, then the other two, then Prince Teodor."

231

With new urgency, he swung both arms out. His limbs encased themselves in metal and blades. He ducked to avoid the blades the borgs threw at him. He sent four of his own blades flying. The borgs avoided two of them, but one blade planted itself in a single human eye, while the other lodged itself deep in an upper arm.

The borg with the blade in his eye was now completely blind. His robotic arms reached up frantically to pull it out. With even flinching, the other borg yanked Karl's blade from where it was buried in his forearm and leapt forward onto Karl. Karl span and brought up a bladed foot, slicing at his abdomen. He barely scratched the protection the machine wore. The other borg had regained some control. Blood spurting from its gaping eye socket, it ran forward blindly.

Karl span away from the blind borg almost into the embrace of the other borg.

"Over here!" he shouted.

The blind borg charged towards Karl. Karl ducked out of his way, and flattened himself to the wall as borg and blind borg grabbed at each other. The more one borg tried to defend himself, the more his blind companion attacked.

"Just two more," he thought. He came round the corner, and saw them coming out of the cell. They were carrying something. That something was screaming and kicking.

'That's him. That's the prince,' Karl thought, with some desperation.

Karl leapt into the path of the lead borg, blades up and ready. The machine lifted his metal fist like a battering ram. He sprinted towards Karl with Teodor over his shoulder. Karl loosed two fighting blades. The borg ducked. With the other hand the borg lifted Teodor by the scruff of his neck, dangling him in front of his face like a shield. His other fist was still pointed forward, ready to ram Karl aside. The Zaracan reached up to grab Teodor, only to feel the Borg's metal fist ram into his chest. Karl was thrown back, flat against the wall. The borg carrying Teodor had forced his way through. Karl went to chase him.

Only, he found himself pinned to the wall with two blades across his neck, thrown by the last borg. Out of the corner of his eye, he saw that the borg carrying Teodor was running through the door and up the spiral staircase. For an instant, Karl thought of his two companions at the top of the stair. He felt the blades cutting into his skin. He could think of only one thing. Pressing his hands hard against the wall, he leveraged his feet up and kicked out into the borg's abdomen. As the borg staggered backwards, Karl grabbed a blade from his hand and spun around in a deadly spin, cutting the borg's head from its body.

He looked along the corridor to where Teodor had gone. Then he saw something move in the cell beyond. Hope leapt up in his heart. Karl stepped into the cell. It was exactly how he had seen it through Teodor's eyes: four connecting cells all with grilles in the place of walls. There was a boy in the third cell, and he looked like...

"What's your name?"

"Hi, I'm Prince Teodor of Freyne."

"No, you're not," Karl replied.

"He's still alive," the boy said.

Karl swallowed, and reached out to feel. After a moment, he opened his eyes once more.

"Yes," he agreed quietly. "He's still alive. Just."

That was something at least, that despite everything the borgs had kept the prince alive.

He turned back to the lookalike boy and pointed into the next cell. The plastic tie lay cut and abandoned on the floor:

"He was there, wasn't he?"

The boy was peering round Karl to the carnage in the corridor beyond. His mouth fell open but he said nothing. More gently, Karl Valvanchi said: "Do you want to get out of here?"

"Yes, please."

"Ok, then tell me everything."

Karl walked back through the prison, checking his men as he went. Of the two soldiers who had fought with him against the six cyborgs, one was unconscious, Karl suspected a broken spine, and the other crawled out bruised but with serious injuries from beneath the cyborg Karl had killed. Karl lifted the unconscious soldier, noticing once again how young he was, and they went upstairs to the prison bank. Another of his soldiers was unconscious with a cruel injury to his face and neck. The last soldier, Zeb, looked stunned but relatively unscathed.

"They went that way."

Karl called Alton for his transport, and wondered how they would get out. He was in the heart of the Dome Military unit with four Zaracan soldiers, all of whom were themselves (the two injured could not shape-shift back to Freyne). He pulled his flying cloak from his rucksack; the other soldiers did the same. They wrapped the injured men in their cloaks, switched their cells to invisible, shape-shifted back to Freyne and headed up out of the prison to meet up with the two air-conditioning engineers who were also their drivers.

"No casualties?" Alton asked with a sneer.

"Tell Nikato, there were no Freyne casualties," Karl replied. "Take these boys back to the Embassy, they have had enough for today."

"Not me, Karl," It was Zeb talking. "I can carry on."

Karl looked at the young technical soldier.

"After this, you want to carry on?"

The soldier nodded. He looked determined.

"Our next target is the cap of the Dome – you have a flying suit?"

A short while later, Karl and Zeb were outside in the main Dome atrium. In amongst a stack of tables and clusters of plants from the Festival of Fashion the night before, Karl and Zeb pulled on their flight suits. They set them to invisible. Then they waited. Soon enough a circular opening appeared in the floor of the cap of the Dome. They saw the disk taking off from the atrium and on-board were four Battle Borgs.

"We have to fly faster than that disk," Karl said quietly.

As one, they leapt into the air and spiralled up through the buildings of the Dome before accelerating ahead of the borgs on their disk into the very cap of the Dome.

Chapter 18. Of Sandals and Shorts

"This is Karl Valvanchi. I have accessed the cap of the Dome, and I am currently searching for forensic evidence of Prince Teodor in Chart Segat's bathroom..."

Cleaning. No entrance.

Karl had hung the neat sign on the door of Chart Segat's bathroom. It was clear. It worked. No-one entered. Just as well. Karl had released ten thousand nanites across the floor. Smaller than cy-roaches with a hive-like intelligence, they worked like an intelligent tide. Karl sat back and watched. The nanites released across the bathroom tiles communicated amongst each other by practically inaudible clicks. Go forward. Go backward. Turn around. Stop. The mini-machines barely larger than ants constantly communicated their position to their colleagues as they jostled to cover as much ground as possible, as quickly as possible.

With their silver casings, they looked like a wave of ball bearings rolling autonomously across the floor. As they had no on-board processing capability, they were constantly broadcasting their findings back to a central processor. Karl sat on the side of the bath holding the processor aloft to allow for clear reception. He watched as the display created maps of the bathroom. The traces of Prince Teodor were numerous. His footprints had been identified on the floor, his blood found on the tiles and in the shower, his hair was in the plug and on the towels. The nanites were overheating with excitement at the contents of a small bin.

Karl stood up and walked over. He bent to pick up a piece of clothing or cloth; gently shaking the nanites to the floor he discovered a pair of short shorts. At first, he could not identify them as the colour was wrong, and there was a terrible smell. He picked up a handful of nanites and placed them on the material, then read their reports:

Sewage

Silk

Sweat >>> Positive ID: Prince Teodor.

"Sewage?" Karl wondered aloud, and then voiced the command: "Sample sewage."

At once, the number of links to Prince Teodor doubled as the nanites identified all the traces from before Teodor had washed. Karl wondered whether the evidence he was gathering could be used in any investigation. He guessed they would call it an illegal search. Yet how else could they get the evidence when the Dome Elite barred both the Regency Defence and the Police from the cap of the Dome. Karl meticulously saved the data and checked the camera droids were filming the scene in an orderly and methodical way. He started to dictate into his communicator:

"I have found the clothes that Teodor was wearing on capture. There is no doubt these are his clothes. They exactly match the description of the angel costume. Also there is an exact match DNA sample on the clothes. This places Prince Teodor in Chart Segat's bathroom in the last twenty-four hours."

Karl hesitated. He remembered Sayginn that morning. How she had wept when she realised that Teodor might be alone with Chart Segat. 'He fought to escape the borgs,' Karl reminded himself. 'The boy is alive and he's still fighting. I have to keep on fighting too!'

Once again Karl reached out with his telepathy. He could feel Teodor, but he was deeply drugged or maybe unconscious. But he was alive.

Karl continued dictating his findings for several minutes. He combined all the data and sent a back-up to the embassy. At his command the nanites returned to their carryall, Karl briefly checked the number was correct, zipped up the small bag and replaced it in his backpack. It was not the cleaning the Dome Elite had in mind.

Not that anyone seemed to notice or care what this Dome Elite soldier was doing. The large space was a hive of activity as decorators, artists and special effects men – and more – transformed the space from a sparkling silver beach paradox to a dark dungeon, complete with human robots acting out terrible tortures and suffering. Karl stopped staring and walked into the small office. Zeb briefly glanced up. Zeb had deactivated the security camera and was working calmly.

'I did not think I needed a tech specialist,' thought Karl, 'but Zeb is clearly enjoying getting direct access to the Dome systems.'

"How's it going?"

"I cracked the overall security about five minutes ago. Now I'm trawling through individual accounts. You want all of Chart Segat?"

"Everything."

Karl was instructing Zeb to pull every file Chart Segat had ever created. Every image he had captured. Every communication he had ever made. A person's entire life could be constructed from this data.

"He has an interesting private email that is heavily blacked out, but otherwise I think I have it covered."

"Keyword search: Sas Darona, Magnolia Stakes," Karl prompted. The machine could also analyse vast amounts of data, and Karl needed answers fast.

"Magnolia Stakes throws up ten thousand results. Not huge but what specifically are you looking for?"

"Taken? Combine with St Joseph's Cathedral."

"Yes, that works. I have just one hundred communications."

"Recent?"

"Yes. Ok, buzz me the highlights."

Karl leant against the wall as comms flashed before his eyes. He quickly scanned the dates and messages. What exactly was he looking for?

Suddenly, he saw it:

Prep the men. Prince's arrival delayed by fifteen minutes.

Karl showed it to Zeb:

"This communicator: is there anything more of this conversation?"

"Ah, interesting, he forgot his encryption for one message only, the rest of the conversation is black."

Karl nodded.

"The private email you spoke of. You get that. If you hack it here, then download the entire file to one of the guys at the embassy. Well done." Karl thought a moment, then said:

"I'm going to need the code to control those Battle Borgs."

"Dead right," Zeb said grimly and smiled: *"Deciphering it right now."*

"Good. Hurry up. We're going to need it."

***

The girl was wearing an evening gown of blue silk patterned with blue roses, it had a tight, fitted corset waist, and wide full skirt that was ruched and lifted at the back into a bustle. The blue perfectly matched the blue of her eyes, and her skin looked pearly white next to it. When she had not moved or said anything for almost a minute, Marline approached. The other model and sales assistant were huddled in the far corner, whispering. Marline had been a bit shocked by their casual rudeness towards the young alien princess. It would not surprise Marline if the girl hated this dress.

As she looked into the girl's face for a clue, she saw a single tear was running down her face.

"Princess?"

Marline sought around and found a box of tissues nearby. She quickly handed one to the girl, who nodded gratefully and blotted the tear away.

The girl nodded her thanks but did not say anything. Marline could not help but feel sorry for her. She had come to House Jewel alone, if you discounted the two huge Zaracan guards who never let her out of their sight. She had been treated, if nothing else, disdainfully by the other girls, and now she was standing alone looking at her reflection in the glass.

'This is not right,' thought Marline. 'A girl should have a mother when she's choosing a ball gown.'

'My mother is dead,' came the reply. Marline looked into the sad face. She had not seen the girls mouth move, but she was sure she had heard her speak.

'Telepathy,' The girl replied with one word. Marline was at first shocked, then, with more practical insight:

238

'Useful.'

'Why useful?' Nell asked, still talking with her mind.

'The other girls say it's treason to speak to a Valvanski, I mean Val-van-chi.'

Marline was careful to pronounce the name correctly inside her mind.

The girl smiled gratefully.

'So do you really hate this dress?' Marline asked.

'Not hate it, no, but I was supposed to wear this to the Magnolia Ball. My uncle had arranged for me to dance with Prince Teodor.' Then she explained further. *'He has a dance sheet, only a small number of girls are asked to dance with him, but my uncle got me a slot. And well, now... We don't even know if he's alive. The ball might not be cancelled, but either way, it's not going to be the same.'*

'Well, the Dome Elite have been recalled now. If he's in the Dome they'll find him.'

'It was the Dome Elite who captured him in the first place.'

'No, it wasn't.' Marline's thoughts were loud and angry. *'Nobody from the Dome Elite was involved in this. I know all those guys, they come here drinking in the evening, so we girls know what they're saying, and they're all saying the same thing.'* Marline was emphatic. *'The Dome Elite did not do this. But they will find him, I can promise you. I bet you right now some soldier or troop is just about to find him. He'll be home by tea time, and the ball tomorrow night, well, it will go ahead as planned.'*

'Well,' Nell replied a little tearfully, *'I guess I have to have a dress then.'*

'Yes, you do, princess.'

'Should this not be full length?'

'No princess, you're not looking for marriage, are you?'

'No, I'm too young.'

'You're too young and Prince Teodor is too young. So you wear a short dress.'

'I won't be marrying Prince Teodor.' Nell said hastily, *'I don't even want to.'*

'Well,' Marline laughed inside her head. *'You must be the only girl on the planet who thinks like that.'*

Nell laughed. The two girls were smiling at each other a little shyly, but inside their heads they were full of joy.

'Do you think this dress suits me?'

'Yes, but the fit is not perfect. Can I introduce you to Janie, she's the lady who made this dress?'

'This dress is handmade?'

'Handcrafted princess, all these dresses are unique creations of craftsmanship. Also, if I was you, I would not use those blue accessories, too much matching. If it was me I would be looking at this coral coloured bag and shoes, and you need shimmering tights as well. We don't want people to look at your legs, but we have these new tights which are spun with threads of pure crystal. I just love them, they look and feel like pixie dust.'

As Marline waved forward the seamstress, and walked around the shop picking out accessories, she started to feel more confident. She really wanted to help this young princess, and she felt sure she was the best person in Domeside to do it.

Chapter 19. The Dome Debate

The army craft descended into the back courtyard of Magnolia Palace. During the two minute flight Sayginn had recovered from her faint. Yet, the brave face she had displayed on the podium, a mere façade for the press and her people, was gone. She strained and gasped as her entire body quivered in pain. The landing was smooth. Even as they touched down, the Regency Defence gently lifted her down onto a stretcher. Doctors ran forward, crouching under the rotating blades, and then jogging beside the stretcher, across the landing area and into the palace.

The medical area was on the first floor, so the stretcher hovered vertically up the well of the stairs and over the first floor bannister, while medics and Regency Guards ran up the stairs. Finally, Sayginn reached the white-tiled sterile medical centre, where medics cut away the soft wool riding-pants and cleaned the surrounding skin. The wound was deep. The bone had been scratched. Still, no expense would be spared to heal the Regent. The medics were now fitting a healing droid to her leg. Over the next hour this sophisticated machine would accelerate the growth and regeneration of the flesh by using chemicals and proteins. Even as the droid clamped shut around her thigh, the pain fell away like a heavy cloak; Sayginn glanced over impatiently to where nurses were preparing a bed.

"No," she growled, "I will not rest. Get me a change of clothes. The pain is gone."

"Your highness, for the leg to heal…" The doctor was concerned but not surprised.

"I have no time for rest, doctor," she replied. "The Dome Debate."

"Then at least use a hover chair, until the droid is finished. And Sayginn, you must not walk."

Instantly she saw the sense in the doctor's words and nodded briefly: "Prepare a chair!"

Patrick McGuire had arrived. He looked relieved to see that Sayginn was conscious.

"Patrick. Still no news?"

"No, but we have more help now. Why don't you come and see?"

Sayginn gingerly steered the hover chair to the top of the stairs, hesitated, then said:

"Here goes nothing."

She tipped the chair down the stairs and, with a gasp, realised that it was fine. The chair hovered elegantly down to the floor below. As she turned into the ballroom, she realised something had changed. At the centre of the desks was a huge three-dimensional representation of the Dome; it was drawn in gold, red and blue lines of light, a mesmerising apparition. As Sayginn watched the graphic span and expanded, focusing on the cap of the Dome. There, amidst the outlines of space, Sayginn saw green avatars moving around the area. Sayginn steered her hover chair around the display and in doing so, saw Nikato and Nell at a small table. Nikato was controlling the graphics.

"Regent Sayginn," he said, rising to his feet. "Those green shapes represent Karl Valvanchi and his men. They have found evidence of Teodor, as you suspected, in Chart Segat's bathroom. And they have been successful in their access to the computers."

"And this?"

"This graphic is drawn from the Dome's own files. For the first time, we have a full map of the black areas. We can track Karl Valvanchi and his men, and through this terminal we are receiving all their reports and data."

"And Teodor?"

Nikato shook his head.

"Karl can't get a fix yet. He may be drugged or unconscious."

Sayginn stared at Nikato. The Zaracan was talking about telepathy. She should know, she had given Karl all the codes and details he had asked for. They were counting on finding Teodor through mind to mind contact. Only, seemingly it did not work, if you were asleep. Asleep or unconscious? Oh, what have they done to you, my Teodor? Nell stepped over and took Sayginn's hand:

"Uncle Karl will find him and get him out. I know he will. We'll be able to watch their escape on this graphic. It will be like we are really there."

"Five thirty," Patrick repeated, without expression.

"I have to leave now, Sayginn said quietly. "The Dome Debate."

Patrick nodded once.

"We will go together."

"Good luck, Regent," Nikato said.

"I have the votes," Sayginn replied and smiled as she left.

"Yes, but they have your son," Nikato said softly as the door closed behind her.

**

As Patrick climbed into the car behind her, he said: "Don't be influenced by Nikato."

"I…" Sayginn hesitated. "He has threatened sanctions."

"They would not dare," Patrick replied. "Teodor is gone, we can appeal to the United Races."

"Can we?" Sayginn asked, helplessly. "How long will that take?"

Ashes she thought, all lies in ashes. Teodor had been kidnapped. Her duties remained unavoidable. All Sayginn wanted to do was to lock herself in the palace with a screen and communicator. She wanted to pore over the footage from outside Chart Segat's offices. She wanted to check the known prisons of the Dome and the military establishment. Of course, she had men doing this and everything else she asked for. She had more men, cyborgs and robots considering every possible option and following it up; meanwhile, she had to do her duty. Her duty involved turning up at all the pre-planned events, to show herself undefeated and unbowed by this most terrible of attacks. Sayginn was just not sure she could do this anymore.

Patrick looked at her strained face and patted her hand.

243

A short while later, Patrick and Sayginn entered together into the huge competition gym. In the light and shadows of the Dome, the conference table had been set up at the centre of a circle of blades mats. As the delegates arrived, they passed pairs of Dome Elite engaged in highly decorative, highly complex display fights, while Dome Elite soldiers in shining uniforms lined every pathway and stood to attention along each wall. Now, for the Dome Debate itself. It was with mechanical sadness that she entered the competition gym. It dawned on Sayginn that when Chart Segat had said he would recall the Dome Elite, he was probably going to do so anyway. She looked along the line of the sharply dressed young men. There was no denying this was a fine fighting force.

Behind the wall of Dome Elite, there were ropes to hold back the crowds, and large screens and amplification so everyone could watch. The Dome Debate was planned as a spectacle as exciting as the Magnolia Stakes. It was expected that the different parties would fight their corner as ferociously as the gorans had raced their race. In the car Sayginn had looked over the notes of her speech and remembered the brave phrases she had agreed weeks before. Her heart had failed her: she'd abandoned the papers on the seat of the car, and walked on empty handed.

Arriving last, Sayginn took her place at the head of the table. When she looked down the line of delegates, to the right were her supporters; they were quiet, subdued, uneasy. Everyone had expected this debate to be cancelled. Sayginn realised now it might have been preferable because it was unclear what the current charade might achieve. In the end Sayginn had insisted the debate go ahead because she felt in her heart that this was the key to Teodor's survival. Across from them, on the left, were Chart Segat's supporters; their eyes were full of glee that they tried hard to conceal. Sayginn looked down the lines. She no longer saw the individuals, but the Baronies they represented. The houses that owed their wealth to Frederon were backing Chart Segat. The houses that owed their wealth to Serge would vote for her.

"The Emperor still believes in Chart Segat," Sayginn thought.

Chart Segat spoke first. Sayginn and her supporters listened, as still and grim as cemetery statues. Across from them even their opponents were subdued, as if shamed into silence. Chart Segat joked, exclaimed, shouted and gestured, but his audience was unmoved. When he finished with a blistering attack on the Regency, there was no response, either applause or rebuke. He sat in silence with no-one offering any further comment or discussion.

Patrick McGuire stood up, bowed to Sayginn, and said simply:

244

"We still have no news of Prince Teodor. It is now thirty-one hours since he was kidnapped. We do, however, have these pictures from this morning."

Patrick showed the film of the Battle Borgs on the flying disk and the close up shot of Teodor's face where he was upside down inside the black rucksack.

There were shouts and exclamations from around the table. All turned to look at Chart Segat.

"Well, Chart," Patrick said patiently. "Do you recognise these borgs?"

"Are you accusing me?" Chart replied.

"No," Patrick replied. "I only asked whether you recognised these borgs, since the disk is travelling between the cap of the Dome and military units within the Dome. Both of which you know well."

"All I will say, is that if you re-elect me to the post of Dome Administrator, I will do all in my power to find these borgs and free the prince."

"Ok, I would just like to point out to the committee that we shared this intelligence with Chart Segat's office this morning, and they have already had five hours to trace these borgs," said Patrick.

This time Chart Segat said nothing.

"Let's vote, Regent?"

Sayginn realised she was stroking her thigh where the claw wound was aching. Suddenly she felt a little woozy. She found she could do nothing but stare at Chart Segat.

"Give me back my son," Sayginn said quietly. If Chart Segat heard her, he did not acknowledge her.

Sayginn then moved to the podium and spoke:

"Since the death of King Serge, we have seen the Dome Elite managed by Chart Segat. At first, yes, this was very helpful, but now what do we have? Reports of piracy! Reports of theft. Reports of scientists slaughtered as they undertook important research. And these fine young men who trust their futures to the Dome Elite, should they really be put under the power of this man? This man who continuously jokes about how he will 'throw badly behaved boys to the borgs.' Rumours continue that boys have been forced to fight those monsters with blunted blades. Maybe we don't have any proof, the truth is, we don't know. Maybe it is just a Domeside legend. But not my son.

This morning we saw evidence of my son being held against his will by Battle Borgs. My son is not just any boy. He is not just the only heir to King Serge. He is not just the only Heir to Emperor Frederon. He's a clever talented boy who has worked tirelessly for years to master the education and skills he needs to lead these great institutions.

And if this is how Chart Segat treats my Teodor, the finest of his generation, what hope then for the boys of Domeside that they will be treated fairly? If I were to have control of the Dome, I would treat each of these fighters as if he were my own son. Their wellbeing, education and the full development of their talents, so they may go on to make useful contributions to our great empire, would be my primary concern. For a fairer, gentler Dome, put me at the helm. Put me at the helm and help me find my son."

As she sat down, Chart Segat said nothing. He waited instead until the cameras turned towards him, then snorted in disdain.

"Give me the Dome," he replied. "Your son will survive."

It was out and out blackmail. Sayginn blanched and her supporters looked equally appalled. No-one dared make eye contact with either Sayginn or Patrick, and certainly none dared look at Chart Segat.

Each of the fifteen delegates had a black switch in front of them and two light-bulbs on their desk, red and green. A green light was a vote for Chart Segat to continue as Dome Administrator. A red light was a vote for Sayginn to deselect Chart Segat and take over.

On the screen above their heads, a countdown started, and each of the delegates reached for their dial. As the countdown reached zero, the delegates voted. Sayginn had closed her eyes. When she opened them, it was easy to count the votes. Down the left side of the council table where her supporters, there was a line of seven red lights. On the right side of the council table, where the supporters of Frederon and Chart Segat sat, there was a line of seven green lights.

As was her prerogative, Sayginn had the deciding vote. She now had sixty seconds to vote and decide the issue.

It was the moment, she thought. Please God, just free Teodor and I will vote the way you want.

She looked around the vast gym, the doors of the gym were maybe one hundred meters away, there was an entrance where her son could make a smiling appearance. For some reason, she imagined him in the suit and shoes he had worn the day before, appearing at her shoulder and kissing her on the cheek. Then she corrected herself and tried to imagine him in the angel's costume with his hair carefully curled, running towards her with a shout of delight: "I'm alright, mum!"

She kept looking, but there was no movement in the crowds surrounding the council table, and all of the doors remained firmly shut. A single tear ran down her face, but she kept looking, hoping beyond hope. In her mind's eye now she saw Teodor in ripped clothes with dirtied face and scared eyes, dumped before her, crawling out of a narrow black kitbag. She blinked and looked around her. On her side of the table, all of her supporters were staring at her. Patrick McGuire offered her a handkerchief. On the right side of the table, her opponents, none of them were making eye contact.

Chart Segat coughed.

"Regent Sayginn, I do recognise one of those borgs, and, therefore, I will go so far as to guarantee Prince Teodor will be sleeping in his bed in Magnolia Palace tonight, if I am re-elected."

It took a few moments for what Chart Segat had said to sink in. So he repeated himself:

"If I am re-elected, Teodor will walk free tonight."

"Sayginn, you must vote…" Patrick pointed to the clock, there were less than fifteen seconds left. All at once, Sayginn started to cry. At first, it was two quiet tears running down her face. Then her breath starting coming out in gasps, and between the gasps she was sobbing. Sayginn reached up to her face, as if not quite believing what was happening, when suddenly her body convulsed into loud howls. Too long had she kept this grief pent up. Not only for Teodor, but for Serge and Deodran as well.

"Give me back my son!" she cried, her voice broken with anguish, then again: "Give me back my son!" This time it was a howl. All at once she had lost all awareness of where she was.

"Where is my husband?" she wailed. "I want Serge."

Patrick stood up, looking ashen.

"Sayginn! Please, Sayginn."

"No, no. Teo! Teo! Give me back my Teo!"

Sayginn was no longer herself, sobbing and wailing. The clock had run its full sixty seconds, Sayginn had not voted. Now the vote would have to be rerun. Sayginn was sat at the top of the table sobbing into a handkerchief, as Patrick and two of her companions tried to comfort her. Chart Segat stood up to address the council. He looked shaken.

"Yes," he said. "We all still grieve for Serge. Serge was my friend too. He put me in charge here. He trusted me. He would trust me to do the best for his son and for the empire." He paused, then said forcefully:

"Vote for me and Teodor will be free tonight."

The lights all went out, ready for the vote to begin again. This time the outcome was clear.

There were fourteen green votes in favour of Chart Segat and one red vote in favour of Sayginn. The Dome Debate had been lost. Sayginn was the only one who had voted for herself to take power in the Dome, all fourteen other members had voted for Chart Segat to continue as Administrator of the Dome.

Chart Segat stood up in a posture of triumph and around the gym the assembled men roared.

Sayginn glanced back once at the result displayed on every screen. She was still shaking and weeping:

"My son. Give me back my son."

Book 6.
Day 2. Evening

Chapter 20. The Wine Cellar

When Teodor awoke it was dark. This time they had left him with his hands tied, but his legs free. He was cold. The floor was freezing. The air was cool. His vision cleared and he saw a brass plaque. He recognised the name, and looking round he saw his prison clearly. It was not a cell, but the wine cellar. He looked at the badge again. This was not just any wine cellar. This had been built by the finest master craftsmen on the planet; experts in their craft, they had also installed the wine cellars at Magnolia Palace. Teodor remembered being shown round by his proud father. The wine cellar perpetually maintained the wine at the ideal temperature, while protecting it from fire and explosions, rats and even insect infestations.

"I will deploy ten thousand cy-roaches to find you," his father had said.

Cy-rats and cy-roaches, they won't make it inside here, Father. Teodor thought. Then he saw something that made him smile, and he started to crawl across the floor towards the wine rack, then twisted and squirmed until he managed to grab hold of an abandoned bottle opener. It was a spiral corkscrew with a sharp point. It took a while, but after a long struggle, Teodor cut through his ties and found himself free again.

With a sigh, he shook out his limbs, then rolled, crawled and finally, stood up. He walked to where a leather armchair stood next to a tasting table. Teodor relaxed back and rolled his shoulders against the padded chair back. A short while later he stood up, went to a rack and picked out several bottles of wine before choosing one and using the corkscrew to open it. Next, he ransacked a low sideboard and found a glass. He danced a little jig when he found some packets of nuts. He placed all the items on the table, and then decided to check for his captors.

The only light in the wine cellar came from a high window. It was a dappled light reflecting off water, and it fell in a small triangle high in one corner of the cellar. Teodor knew this was deliberate to protect the wines, it also meant that most of the cellar was in darkness. Silently, Teodor now crept into the darkness, looking. There was only one entrance, and it was shut. He walked up to the door, pressed his ear to it and listened. Dare he try the handle? If he did they would know he was standing behind the door, then what should he expect, more drugs, more ties, more blows? Silently, he retreated to the armchair and table, poured himself a glass of wine and settled down to eat the nuts. Not for long though, as within minutes he was on his feet and climbing up the wine rack. He had spotted a high grill on one wall. This might be his way out.

Chapter 21. Preparations for a Party

Juke dropped Guy off outside House Jewel and held off giving him his money until the doorman came down to the car.

"Now you hand this in, and be sure they mark the amount correctly against your name. You worked hard today."

As Guy went to climb out, Juke reached and grabbed him by the arm, briefly pulling him back into the van:

"So, Chartsie's said he'll get you a place in the Dome Elite?"

"Yes, yes he has."

"He'll want something in return, you know that?"

"Yes, yes, he wants me to fight."

"Do you know who?"

"It won't be borgs," Guy joked. "He said he won't throw me to the Battle Borgs."

"And you believe him?"

Guy hesitated, did he believe Chart Segat?

"Look, Guy," Juke continued and nodded towards House Jewel: "They've offered you a job here, no?"

"Yes, they have said I could model."

"So? It's not factory work – you'll be well paid. You might even get some travel if you play your cards right."

"Yeah, but... you know they call the girls courtesans?"

"Yes, I know that."

"Do you know what they call the boys?"

"Don't listen to the tittle-tattle. Those fashion girls and boys, they have a choice. Ok, yes, some of them get ahead a lot faster with the right patron, but not always. Now, you're a good-looking kid, and you're clever too. Just look at Sebastian. No-one tells him what to do."

"Sebastian always wanted to be a model. He actually likes the clothes, the fabrics, the design, all that stuff."

"Sounds like you know the lingo too."

"I want to join the Dome Elite. I only ever wanted to join the Dome Elite."

"Ok Guy, I get it. And I've heard it all before. Chartsie… Well, you've made a pact with the devil there. And don't shake your head at me."

"I think Chart Segat might be my father."

"Really? Well, I suppose Chart Segat and Lloulou go way back, but just listen. When it comes to it, you think for yourself. Not the Dome Elite. Not House Jewel. Definitely not Chartsie. You think of only one person: Guy Erma. You hear me? That way you might just make it."

Guy nodded, speechless, his heart was thudding in his chest. There was really nothing he could say. Juke patted his arm:

"Go on, get going."

The doorman had seen the roll of money in Guy's hand and, with a genial smile, accompanied him to the front desk where they let him in behind the counter and into a small back office.

"What have you got for me, Guy?"

Ten minutes later Guy was heading out again. Just ten pounds in his pocket but close to a thousand marked up against his name. He checked the time then reached into his pack for his running blades, locked them onto his feet and sprinted off towards the Dome.

***

Lloulou turned and smiled as Guy came out of the bathroom wrapped in a thick warm towel. She pulled him towards her in a hug, and then helped dry him. Both ignored the mêlée of the changing rooms; a large room was full of glamorous young people preparing for a night in the Dome. Sly comparative appraisal, nervous gossip, the inevitable tragedy of the stained gown characterised this unique gathering of professionals, commonly known as Chartsie's court.

"Look," said Lloulou, pointing to the perfume 'Dagger'. It was a gift Guy had given Lloulou on her birthday. "Smells nice, huh?" She arched her long neck, and he sniffed appreciatively with a smile. "Now we've got to get you ready. You've got a new outfit for tonight, look."

Guy looked over apprehensively. The clothes were covered in cellophane but what he could see involved rather a lot of white and blue sequins.

"Do I have to wear that?"

"Chart Segat sent the instructions himself. Anyway, you will look very striking. Remember, the Riffaut have Teodor's contract this year but who says they will have it next year. Everyone noticed you last night and I want to make sure they keep noticing you."

"Like Chart Segat notices you?" Guy asked quietly.

"Hush now, he's a good man. Let Dana dry your hair and we'll do your make-up."

"Make-up?"

"Erederon, Guy, think Prince Erederon."

As the girl dried and fussed over his hair, Guy was thinking of a bright morning.

***

Two weeks before, Guy had gone down to the kitchen and persuaded the staff to let him take up Lloulou's tray. At the time, he had still been canvassing Lloulou, persuading her to talk to Chart Segat about the Dome Elite. So he had cajoled and charmed the kitchen staff to lay on some breakfast extras, and added a few flowers he had picked from the attic window box.

Guy had entered her bedroom as the sun came up, and while the doctor was still in attendance. Lloulou had barely glanced at him as he came through

255

the door, and simply pointed to a small table. She was, therefore, startled when he climbed onto the bed to kiss her good morning.

"Guy!"

The doctor coughed, somewhat impatiently. Guy saw he was holding a small piece of skin-coloured cloth. No, that wasn't cloth, it was artificial skin. Guy turned to take a proper look at Lloulou and saw that the right side of her face from the hairline to the chin was a mess of small cuts and black bruising.

"Lloulou!" Guy was upset.

"Oh, don't you worry," she had said, "the doc will have it repaired in no time. Did you bring me that beautiful breakfast?"

"Yes, I made it myself."

"My beautiful boy!"

"Hold still." It was the doctor, and the small tool in his hand hissed. Leaning with his head against Lloulou's neck Guy felt every twitch even as Lloulou did, he knew the tool was like a pricking needle. It would repair the skin well, but it was painful nonetheless. But not once did Lloulou flinch or draw away. Guy knew he should say something.

"I wish I was… you know…"

"Wish what?"

"I wish I was your boy."

"You are… (gasp!)" She grabbed Guy's hand and squeezed it in sudden pain. Guy saw the doctor was working close to the outline of her eye. "Oh, I've said it now!" Lloulou said, breathing hard. "I should have told you long ago. I am your mother."

"My mother?" All at once Guy was kissing every part of her, her ears, her neck and her hands.

"Hold still, Guy," Lloulou scolded,

"But you are my mother?"

"Do you think I'd take a chance with Chartsie's temper for anyone else?"

"Chartsie did that to you?"

"I should not have told him. Or I should have told him a long time ago. I don't know why I lied to him," she sighed. Guy was appalled. Who dared lie

256

to Chart Segat, and why? Lloulou saw his expression: "You were such a beautiful baby. You were my beautiful boy. I just wanted to protect you. I... Oh, why did I force her?"

Lloulou fell silent. She tried to look away, but the doctor put a hand to her chin and turned her face firmly back in place. Guy saw him applying jelly to a bruise that was already a touch yellow above her eyebrow.

"Force who?"

"Oh, I've told Chartsie now, so you might as well know. I swapped you. At birth. I swapped you with Marline. I forced her mother to take you. I said I needed a girl. I said it would not make any difference. I said I would swap you back. I said so many things, but I was lying... All I wanted was to keep you alive."

Guy watched the tears running down Lloulou's beautiful face, even a drop of yellow snot dripped from her nose. The Doctor had paused in his work. He handed her a damp cloth. She wiped her face gratefully, and took a moment to breathe. The doctor set to work again. He was working on the last three cuts that Guy now saw looked like scratches from nails.

"Marline is older than me..." Guy said doubtfully.

"No, no she isn't. That was another lie. But it was to protect you. He could not know there was a boy. He would have killed you. He would have killed Marline, but Chartsie... Chartsie talked him out of it. Oh, he was so good that night! Whatever anyone tells you. Chart Segat he's a good man."

Guy's head was spinning.

"Who would want to kill Marline?" he said at last.

"No, no, no." Lloulou was shaking her head. "Sssh. Chart Segat, he knows now. He'll take care of it. Chart Segat always takes care of his boys."

"What? Did he say I could join the Elite?"

Lloulou laughed a little sadly, then hugged him to her neck once more and whispered: "I only wanted to protect you, Guy." Guy did not know what she meant and could not think what else to ask.

As the doctor finished, Lloulou thanked him. She rose from her bed and washed her face, then went to sit in the window seat, taking the tray of food with her. Then she waved Guy to her side, before pulling him into her lap and kissing him.

257

"Hmmm, let's see this breakfast. Will you share it with me?"

So, Guy had sat with his mother on that bright morning, sharing buttered croissants and hot tea, while she told him of his birth and showed him a few photos of his baby years. For thirty sun-filled minutes, he had thought he was the happiest boy alive.

"Of course, this will have to remain our secret. With my career, I cannot have an illegitimate son, what would my customers say?" Guy nodded; of course, he knew this – it was the same for all the children born of models, their very existence was always denied.

"I don't mind that. And I will tell no-one."

"It doesn't matter whether you do. You are not registered so no-one has to believe you."

"Will you register me now?"

"I don't know, Guy. I'll do what Chart Segat tells me." Guy said nothing. Everyone said Lloulou had Chart Segat wrapped around her little finger. No-one knew what Guy knew. Chart Segat beat Lloulou, he took out his anger with his fists on her face and her body. She had tipped Guy's chin up to look into his eyes one more time:

"And you should do the same. Whatever Chart Segat asks, you must obey him. If not, he'll throw you to the borgs."

Guy laughed a little. Lloulou was deadly serious:

"Whatever Chartsie says, Guy, do you hear me?"

***

They had finished drying his hair, and the girl was now fussing with the shape and layering of his curls. Guy glanced at Lloulou as she stood with the hairdresser, who produced some hair spray and a small pair of scissors. Guy paused a moment. He found himself looking up at her face, searching for some trace of the cuts and bruises he remembered so clearly. There was perhaps a small imperfection close to her hairline, but the artificial skin had done its job, there was no sign, no scars at all, except... It struck him suddenly that the scars were all inside. Beyond the perfect skin, the perfumed hair, the painted lips, beyond that was a scarred, battered and frightened woman, and this was his mother.

"Lloulou?"

258

Lloulou bent down, for he had spoken in barely more than a whisper.

"Is Chart Segat my father?" Guy said quietly.

"Guy, what are you talking about? Is that what he told you?"

Guy hesitated, as he tried to remember, then said: "He said I was to be tested aboard the Emperor's yacht, so I thought…"

Lloulou smiled and interrupted him:

"Tomorrow, right? Well, you'll know tomorrow. So no more guessing. As for Chart Segat, whatever Chart Segat tells you to do, you have to do it." Guy hoped the sudden fear he felt did not show. "And make sure you win," she added.

"…or else he'll throw you to his borgs."

"No, he won't do that."

"Just make sure you win."

She smiled a brief, tight smile and bent to kiss him. He lifted his face to kiss her back. The kiss was over in an instant, but Guy held her gaze a moment longer.

"I've always loved you."

"You're going to be late."

"Goodbye, then."

Guy paused to look back a moment at the doorway to see Lloulou watching him leave. She had been his mother for less than a month, and already Guy knew it was over.

It was a short walk from the changing rooms to the top of the Dome. A short, steep climb up a metal stairwell that hung high in the rafters of the Dome. As he reached the last short flight there was a platform; Guy paused to look down at the busy centre below. It was the most complete view down inside the Dome. Unlike Chart Segat's room you could hear the crowds here. The wind blew up, bringing with it all the smells and flavours of the crowds and restaurants below.

Guy looked down at the clothes they had given him. He was wearing a brand new protection suit, and over it a blue chiffon blades uniform. They had kept the sequins to a minimum. Just a blue gem at his neck and a constellation of sparkles across the shoulders and along the tunic hemline, but otherwise it was a blades uniform. Well, Chart Segat had said it was a fight. A Demonstration fight, Des had said.

He remembered the white chiffon and gold they had used to make the angel costume Prince Teodor had worn. Did he look like a prince now? At this height, thought Guy, it was easy to imagine you were an angel. Standing on the narrow stairwell, high above the Dome looking down on all creation, he was that lone guardian angel, strong, silent, but above all, alone. All at once Guy was afraid. He gripped so hard onto the metal rail his knuckles shone white through his skin.

"I don't want to go!" he said, but nobody heard him. There must have been half a million people in the busy Dome that Saturday evening, but no-one to hear him.

"I don't want to," he whispered. This time he heard something. He looked back the way he had come and saw Marline coming after him. She was wearing heels but she ran none the less, albeit a little unsteadily. As she came up to him, she hugged him hard.

"Oh Guy, oh Guy," she said breathlessly. "You're going to get into the Dome Elite, I know you are."

Guy nodded just once. He certainly hoped so. She looked him up and down, then said:

"Are you fighting tonight? Is it a display fight?"

"Yes, well I don't think they have given me these clothes to throw me to the borgs," Guy said grimly, glad to say out loud what he had been thinking.

"No, no. They only throw losers to the borgs."

"Chartsie said he would not be throwing me to the borgs. He said so."

"Well, if Chartsie says so," Marline said uncertainly. "You have to do whatever Chartsie says, you know that?" Guy nodded. "Do you get paid?"

"What do you mean?"

"Well, I was at a party last night, and they were paying me four thousand five hundred."

Guy looked at her, astonished.

"Marline," he said. "Why do you want this money? I mean really?"

260

"I want to be free," she said abruptly. "I want to be free of all this. And to do that you have to have money. I've started making my own clothes. They are House Jewel fashion now, but one day there will be a House Marline. That sounds good, doesn't it? House Marline. I will have tonnes of money and I will be free to do whatever I want."

Guy thought of Lloulou, the best paid model in Domeside. Was she free, he wondered? Was she happy?

"House Marline," Guy repeated, thoughtfully. It sounded highly unlikely, but still he replied: "That's a great idea, Marline."

"And you're so good-looking. I'll want you as my first model."

"Now come on, Marline. You know I'm joining the Dome Elite."

"Why can't you do both? Guy Erma, fashion model and blades fighter. Hey, why not?"

Guy stood speechless for a moment.

"The guys would kill me, that's why. The other guys of the Dome Elite would actually kill me. They hate the fashion models."

"Yeah yeah, they're just jealous about the money."

Guy just shook his head:

"Yes, well. I'm not interested in money."

Marline nodded, she looked a little sad. She reached up to push his hair back over his ear. He clung harder onto the rail, as he felt his entire body sway, as if hit by a wave. He looked up at her. She was taller than him, but maybe only because of the heels. With her make-up done and dressed in finest House Jewel fashion, she was the most stunning new girl of Old Mill Lane. And she had been his friend for such a long time.

Guy felt awkward now, because he knew he was supposed to kiss her. She was only a short distance away, but he just did not know what to do next. He reached to take her hand, and eased a fraction closer. He looked up at her and unless he was mistaken, she was nervous too. This was much harder than he had thought it would be. Remember she is Marline, he told himself.

With this thought, he felt the warmth spreading through him. He rose onto his toes and ever so carefully, he kissed her. Pressing his lips to hers, but concentrating hard, so their teeth did not clash, their tongues did not touch. The sensation was overwhelming, waves of heat followed by walls of cold.

The softness of her lips lit an inferno in his heart. As they parted, he was breathless:

"I love you," he said quietly, and he meant it. She stood a moment looking down at him. She blinked just once, and while she did not speak, her eyes told him her reply. Then she batted her lashes, and stamped her foot, reclaiming her normal pose of sophistication. With a spin that set her skirts flying one way and her curls another, she set to leave:

"Bye then, Guy!" she said, blowing him a kiss. "Make sure you win!"

Guy just smiled and climbed the last four steps to his destination.

Chapter 22. The Gilded Cage

In the cap of the Dome, the event planners had finished their work. Karl looked round with interest now that the décor was fully in place. It was gruesome in parts but now they were bringing in numerous goran skins, small sofas and large reclining bags. The finishing was all gold, silver, magenta and red velvets. This was a night of amazing entertainment in preparation.

It looked like the night would start with blade fighting. A large gilded circular cage had been installed at the centre of the space. Karl saw that one of the disk-jets rose directly up into the blades space. A special blades mat had been manufactured in two concentric pieces: a circular rug to fit neatly on the disk and a rug in the shape of a ring to fit around the disk and complete the blades mat. As Karl watched, the decorators were checking the fit of the two rugs. The central rug was not correctly aligned, so as the disk rose up it jammed. As Karl watched, two technicians stretched out on the floor and tugged at the rug until it fitted correctly. With shouts and rapid withdrawal of hands, he watched as the disk smoothly moved up into the floor. The join between the disk rug and the circle rug fitted so perfectly the join all but disappeared. Karl was curious; the production team were excited about this detail and as Karl watched, one of the team leaders jumped onto the disk and shouted instructions:

"Let me try it. Let me try it."

As Karl watched, the engineer lowered then raised the disk, while the director posed and turned as if he were a blades fighter. Suddenly Karl had an inkling that at some point tonight fighters would rise on the disk and then cross blades within the gilded cage.

"It's going to be an epic night," a waitress said, seeing Karl staring. "The cages fold away after the fight and the party carries on."

263

"Only one fight?" Karl asked.

"Well, the running order is Victory Dinner downstairs and then a private party up here which starts with a fight." Karl paused. His communicator beeped. He glanced down and frowned. The Dome Debate had been lost. Chart Segat had been voted into power for five more years.

Nikato was calling him on his communicator: 'Pack up your stuff, you're coming home.'

'Nikki?'

'You have done a great job with the Dome computers, but you can analyse the data back at the embassy.'

'No, Nikki. I have to find the prince.'

'She betrayed us, Karl. Chart Segat has been voted back into power.'

'No, she didn't,' Karl replied quietly. 'She had to save her son.' He changed the subject abruptly. 'Nell! Are you there?'

'Yes, uncle.'

'Teodor – does he fight with blades?'

'Yes, yes of course.'

'Is he any good?'

'I guess… Why do you ask?'

'I know where he will be tonight.'

Nikki interrupted him: 'You must come home.'

Karl took on a mocking tone:

'Oh please, Dad, just a few more hours!'

***

"Patrick, we have a call from the Dome."

Patrick McGuire walked to the large screen. Regent Sayginn had retired to her suite. The doctors had recommended a sedative to help her sleep. Patrick was alone in the ballroom, with the rescue operation to oversee.

"We have to bring that boy home," he told his men. "That is our only mission now. We have to get him home."

He walked over to look at the large screen. There was static, and then Chart Segat appeared.

"Patrick!" Chart Segat looked surprised. "How is the Regent?"

"She is resting," Patrick said curtly.

"Well, we will get your boy back. I promise you, now I have power, we will get him back."

"If it had been up to me, you would not be in power now."

"Well Patrick, the Dome Debate decided otherwise, and since I am an administrator of the Dome, I wish to lodge an official complaint. We in the Dome have been subjected to an unfair attack. Yesterday we provided you full access to all of the facilities. Today we recalled the entire Dome Elite to search for the prince. So why, then, did you send in an attack team in secret today? Three of my prison staff have been attacked."

"I have no knowledge of such an attack," Patrick said briefly, but he knew Chart Segat was talking about Karl Valvanchi. He had already seen the tapes, including a brief interview with the boy lookalike.

"Patrick, I pledge myself and the Dome Elite to find and secure your boy. I want him on the throne of Freyne just as his father was. I also want to restore his reputation as one of the finest of our young people."

"How will you do that, Chart Segat?"

"Well, Patrick. I do not wish to spoil the surprise. But consider it a gift to you and the Regent. The boy will be free. He will be alive. But if my men have to deal with unprovoked attacks, who knows who might get hurt in the crossfire?"

"I will not withdraw my troops until he is found," Patrick said. "That is a completely unreasonable request."

"Of course, but think about my request, Patrick. You should be worried about your boy's security," and he laughed salaciously, "particularly as the night is growing dark, and here in the Dome the parties are starting. Who knows where the little prince may end up? What fun he might be having, or about to have?" It was a clear threat and Chart Segat was no longer laughing: "If you want him back then you should first withdraw your troops."

265

Patrick switched off the communication, then he turned and gave the order.

"Withdraw all the Regency Defence from the Dome. They are in danger."

"What about the prince?"

"The Dome Elite and Chart Segat are looking for him now."

'God help us all,' thought Patrick. He looked out the windows at the Dome now starting to light up for the evening's entertainment. *'Teodor is on his own now. On his own and at the mercy of Chart Segat and the Dome Elite.'*

Chapter 23. Monkey Masks Must be Worn

"Get dressed."

It was a blades uniform of fine red silk. Even the emblem on the front was familiar.

"After all," Teodor said to himself, "I always wear House... the Riffaut."

The monkey mask, a full head mask of red silk with only three holes for his eyes and mouth, was less welcome. He looked up at the Battle Borg and said resolutely:

"I'm not wearing that." He crossed his hands across his chest.

The borg did not reply. With a simple gesture, it grabbed and pushed Teodor's arms down. There was no resisting the brute force he used. Despite himself, Teodor had to let his arms fall to his side, the borg did not even notice the look of anger on his face. Instead, it reached him with blades protruding from his index finger and thumb. With an economy of strokes, the borg cut Teodor's clothes from his body. At the very last, he sliced through Teodor's shirt with a fast cut just a fraction too deep and left a long, thin, red line down his torso.

"I can't fight injured," Teodor gasped.

The borg looked at him and turned away. When he returned, he had a medical spray in his hand. He sprayed down the length of Teodor's body. The wound started to close. He sprayed again. Teodor winced, but fought to stay silent. The treatment stung, like a line of fire running up the length of his body. Had the borg noticed, wondered Teodor? Would a borg recognise bravery?

"Get dressed."

This time Teodor complied, resisting these machines was clearly futile. He nevertheless looked for any cameras, and then remembered the borgs could broadcast anything they saw, so maybe someone was watching. So, when the borg then presented him with fighting boots and jumping blades, together with cuffs and calf greaves, Teodor said aloud:

"I protest at this treatment, I am a prince of Freyne."

The borg had turned away. He had not, Teodor noticed, given him any hand blades.

***

"There you are Guy, and very fine you look. Come and sit by me."

Chart Segat had been standing welcoming his guests. Now he drew Guy Erma to a low sofa tucked away in a narrow corner. As they sat down together, Chart tugged on a rope and a curtain fell closed. Guy was alone with the Mayor of Domeside and the man was quiet. Guy could see the pores of his skin, and the small scar close to his ear. Was that the mark of repair surgery? He wondered. Guy could smell stale beer on his breath.

"What have they done to your face?" Chart Segat said.

"I think they wanted me to look more like Prince Erederon."

Chart Segat pulled out a handkerchief, licked one corner, and reached up to clean the eyeliner from Guy's cheeks.

"Eyeliner was something of an affectation Erederon adopted in his twenties. You don't need eyeliner to look like him. Why should you? Tomorrow we'll get you tested on the Emperor's yacht and then you'll be on your way."

"You are talking about the ID tests, aren't you?" Guy spoke at last. He had had time to think about what tests Chart Segat might mean. He had concluded that the only tests that were truly illegal were the ID blood, bone and DNA tests. "And my mother is Lloulou?"

"That's right," Chart Segat replied cheerily.

"And are you my father?"

Chart Segat looked surprised, then laughed. "Is that what you think? Is it not obvious to you? Obvious who your father is? It's been obvious for a while, even without the tests. Oh, you'll find out soon enough."

Guy froze. Find out what? Find out the identity of both his mother and father? Who were they? What did he mean? Was Chart Segat his father or not? Lloulou was admired by so many famous men. Barons, businessmen, celebrities… Chart Segat said he looked like his father. Guy wanted to look in the mirror. Chart Segat had said: it's been obvious for a while now. Who did he look like?

He suddenly remembered a conversation from the day before. Dana the hairdresser had said:

"He could pass as a young Erederon?"

And Lloulou had said:

"Do you want the Riffaut to take all the Imperial glory?"

Erederon? The dead prince, the only son of Emperor Frederon, Guy had been a baby when he had died. But his name was legend. For despite eight marriages, the Emperor had only had one son.

"Prince Erederon?" Guy stammered in disbelief.

Chart Segat burst out laughing.

"But I thought you were my father." Guy frowned.

"I'm not saying anything. I've said enough for now. Now you must focus on the fight tonight, I am expecting you to win."

If Guy was a bit deflated by this reply, he quickly adapted to the new topic:

"Of course," Guy grinned, then after a hesitation: "Who am I fighting?"

Chart Segat laughed again for a few moments.

"You will him beat him easily, I'm sure. And if not, I'll throw you to my borgs." The threat was made as a joke. Guy grinned easily back.

"I could beat a borg, too," Guy said recklessly.

"Could you, now?" Chart Segat looked at him curiously. "Well, don't worry, I won't do that to you."

"I will do anything you ask Chartsie. Anything."

Guy thought Chart Segat would laugh at him. Instead he looked at him steadily for several long minutes:

"Listen Guy, if you want to do something for me, then tell them I did not kill the King or that baby, Prince Deodran. Tell them that. Make them understand I am not their enemy."

Guy just stared at him, what did he mean? Chart Segat sighed.

"Go on, time for you to go." He shouted: "Des, are you there?"

Des came through the curtain. He looked both anxious and embarrassed. Guy saw Des look him up and down, and he seemed relieved at what he saw.

"You know what to do?" Chart Segat asked.

Des saluted his fist to his heart and waved to Guy to accompany him.

"Oh, Guy?" Chart Segat called as they left. "If you do lose badly, I might still throw you to my borgs, do you hear me?"

***

Whatever else, the Battle Borg was meticulous in his preparation, Teodor thought. He watched the man check his calves, his cuffs, and perfectly adjust his boots and foot blades. The equipment was nice quality too. Now that he was ready, Teodor longed to feel the weight of the daggers in his hands. Another borg arrived, with a short message:

"They are ready."

They handed him the monkey mask; Teodor hesitated. It will be hot, he thought. It will block my peripheral vision and dampen my hearing.

"Put it on," the borg said. Teodor glanced up. The machine would or could force him if he did not comply. He sighed and pulled the silk into place.

The borgs had extended their running blades, and they ran on each side of Teodor holding him by the elbow. It was a tight, secure grip from which Teodor knew he could not escape. They passed from the wine cellar out of the maintenance tunnel across the Dome's main atrium. There were crowds milling around and going to and from restaurants and entertainments, watching on large screens. They laughed and applauded to see the two borgs and a blade fighter dressed for the Riffaut. Teodor wanted to make himself

270

known. Only he was wearing the full face mask and they were running fast. They passed through the atrium in a few instants. Then they were standing on a disk and rising up through the Dome on a jet of fire. Teodor found himself looking over to see Magnolia Palace in the distance. Calling to his mother in his head:

Mummy, can you hear me?

My prince, I hear you.

Mother?

No, my name is Karl Valvanchi, and your mother sent me to rescue you.

Chapter 24. With Blades in Both Hands...

Guy was standing on the edge of a fighting mat, waiting. He looked around the cap of the Dome. For once the views both out over the city and down below into the Dome were obscured. The crowd was three deep with Dome Elite. There were very few women present, and no children, just a host of fighting men stood around the gilded fighting cage.

Guy walked confidently to the stool prepared for him. He looked across at his opponent's place, but it was still empty. So he took up his steel and set about sharpening his blades one last time.

It would be the first time he fought with unblunted blades. He polished the spine of the dagger with the ball of his thumb. He had received scratches and nips from training blades before, but this was different. These blades were sharp. What would it feel like to be cut during combat? Des came up and offered him a clean cloth to polish his blades. Guy said:

"I'm fighting to represent House Jewel. Why?"

"Well, it's a bit of a gimmick, I suppose."

"And who am I fighting?"

"You take a guess."

"I'm too nervous to guess."

Guy picked up his hand blades and spun them with his fingers on the palm of his hand.

"And if I win do I get to join the Dome Elite?"

Des did not reply. All at once they heard a fanfare and the lights dimmed. Guy looked up and watched the crowd disappear into the shadows as the lighting changed. A spot illuminated the blades mat, it was a silver circle of light at the centre of the cage. To Guy's astonishment and shouts from the crowd, the floor opened up, and a disk floated into place. At the centre were two tall Dome Elite Battle Borgs, and held firmly between them was a boy dressed in silks, emblazoned with the emblem of the Riffaut.

Guy saw the borgs discretely release the boy as they floated up through the floor, but most of the crowd saw nothing, for the cyborgs quickly concealed the chains within their armour plating. They handed the boy his blades and marched sharply away. So the small figure was left standing blinking in the light, peering beyond the gilded cage to the shadowy figures beyond, uneasily lifting his leaping blades from the theatrical mist that rolled across the floor.

At least he is a boy, thought Guy. He had had a moment of doubt when he thought he might have to raise his blades to fight a man or even a Battle Borg, but no, his opponent was a boy. But who could it be? Guy had already fought and beaten every boy his age in Domeside. The boy was wearing red silks. They bore a familiar emblem.

"See?" said Des. "The Riffaut. You're fighting a boy from the Riffaut. The gimmick is that some say you look like a young Erederon, and the Riffaut are all modelled to look like Teodor. So it's Prince Erederon vs. Prince Teodor, that's the gimmick."

Guy could not think what else to say.

"But…"

"Don't you want to fight?"

"No, of course I'll fight. I mean, it has to be a fair fight, right? I just can't think of any boy from the Riffaut who takes his blades that seriously. None who could stand against me, in any case. Sebastian gave up months ago."

"In that case," Des replied bluntly, "you should have no trouble winning. Because guess who the loser has to fight?"

He nodded where one of the two borgs had walked around to stand by the score board.

"There's going to be two fights?" Guy asked nervously.

"No more questions," Des said. "Just concentrate on this fight."

Des was already looking across the room. He seemed anxious, Guy thought. Why? And if this boy was a model, then why was he guarded by borgs?

After a moment or two, the boy wearing red silk saw Guy. Guy saw him looking, then drew himself up a little straighter. Their eyes met and for one small instant Guy thought he saw fear. The look changed; resolve replaced fear. The boy pushed his shoulders back. He nodded just once. Without further hesitation, he took the last two steps and sat on the stool prepared for him. He was ready. The fight could begin. Des put a hand on Guy's shoulder, and Guy handed back his steel.

Guy looked curiously across at his opponent once more. He was wearing a mask. A full face mask of red silk.

"What, does he not have a second?" asked Guy.

"There," Des said quietly, and they both watched as Tilson stepped up beside the boy.

***

"Tilson." Teodor smiled at the familiar face.

"Calm, Teodor, control."

"May I use your communicator? I need to call my mother."

Tilson looked a little taken aback and did not meet Teodor's eye. He replied curtly.

"No time for that, my prince. You must prepare yourself for a fight."

"I will not fight," Teodor said resolutely. "They cannot force me."

"They can force you. If you don't fight the boy, they'll give you another opponent." Tilson nodded grimly to the borg standing close by.

Teodor shook his head, a brief shake of disbelief.

"I won't fight."

"Fine. Don't fight." Tilson seemed to agree, but then he nodded to the crowd. "Don't fight and they will call you chicken, and this time they will have seen it with their own eyes. Are you chicken?"

"I am not."

"Well then, prepare yourself, that young man is quite a champion."

"Is it Guy Erma?"

"You know him?"

"Everyone knows Guy Erma," Teodor replied with a smile. Out of nowhere hope sparked inside of him. "At last!"

"At last?" Tilson replied.

In that instant, Teodor was exhilarated. Maybe this was not as bad as it could have been. A blades fight he could control. A blades fight, he might win.

"I am glad to finally meet him with blades in my hands."

"That's the spirit," Tilson replied. "Now go."

As the numbers started to count down on the fight clock, Teodor stood up. He was ready for a fight. Across from him, Guy Erma took his place. Teodor looked over at his opponent. As they had said, he was slim and perhaps a little taller than Teodor. They also said he was fast, thought Teodor; time to find out. He watched the numbers on the clock decreasing, and as the countdown continued, questions ran through his mind.

Five

Was he doing the right thing?

Four

Maybe he should just refuse to fight, would that be the right thing to do?

Three

So, this boy span like the wind and bit like a goran? Did he?

Two

And what if Teodor lost this fight? What then?

One

There was only one solution, he must win! Yes!

***

Guy bounded forward. The other fighter looked strong, confident even. Who could it be? There was no-one from the Riffaut who could raise a blade to him. Guy could tell it was not any of the boys he had fought in the Dome blades championship or any other fighter he knew. The build was not familiar, and the eyes were so clear and blue. So few people had blue eyes in Domeside, who could it be? Guy bent into a defensive posture. He decided to try a few passes just to test him, and then he would attack.

***

Teodor span three times in a fast progression of pirouettes, closing the gap between himself and his opponent. In doing so, he gained momentum and knocked aside the blade Guy offered by way of defence, and spinning in close, brought his closed fist and the handle of his blade down hard to strike Guy in the rib cage, just under the arm.

Teodor would have hit him firmly above the heart, a semi-mortal blow, but at the last moment Guy turned aside. Not fast enough to avoid the hit entirely, but enough to reduce the impact.

Under Teodor's hand, Guy shook and sidestepped a fraction before bringing his blade up. But it was a feeble defence, Teodor caught and pinched his wrist and twisted his arm up and behind his back. Teodor forced him off balance into a painful fall forward off his leaping blades and onto his knees. Carefully now, Teodor placed the point of his blade to the back of his opponent's neck.

"Do you yield?"

Above them on the score board the result flashed green under the Riffaut icons. Teodor had won the first round.

***

"I told you not to let him hit you!" Des was exasperated.

"I don't know who he is!" Guy gasped. "God that hurt."

"Of course it hurt, we looked at that this morning."

"This morning? But we were looking at Prince Teodor this morning," Guy said shakily. "Ouch!" Des was smearing jelly on the red marks on Guy's ribcage. He scanned it quickly, as well.

"It's not broken, but your ribs have been badly bruised. It will hurt in the morning. Right now, you have to fight."

"Ok. I'll fight. I'm not afraid. But why we are wearing masks?"

"Look, Chart Segat is over there. Just concentrate on the fight."

"Des, something is not right here."

"Will you stop thinking and just fight?"

***

Karl Valvanchi was standing in the shadow of Chart Segat's throne. Carefully, he reached inside the man's mind. He dropped in on a whispered conversation Chart Segat was having into an embedded microphone.

"'So help me God' does not mean anything. I need that promise in writing. I want guaranteed ongoing management of the Dome. A contract to provide specialist support to the Imperial Army and a free hand in everything else. And you get the Regent to drop all charges against me in connection with Serge's death."

Karl could only hear one side of the conversation.

"Well yes, if you want him tonight. If not, well, my borgs have been very restless recently. I might have to throw them a titbit, maybe two titbits. Yes, both of them. Your nephew and the one you have not tested yet."

"Well, persuade her to bring the marriage forward to tonight. I will only be convinced once you have made her your wife."

Karl Valvanchi pulled his mind probe back. He could not bear to hear any more. He knew he should listen to the remainder of the conversation, but whoever Chart Segat was talking to it did not sound good for Teodor, or, for that matter, for Sayginn. He had to get the boy out. But how?

The Dome Elite were so numerous. He was alone. If his disguise should slip... Still, it was a carnival atmosphere. The men were mostly laughing,

277

drinking and betting. Did the Dome Elite realise they were watching their prince?

Karl took time to reach out and shake the bars of the gilded cage. He used a sensor to test its materials. There was neither entrance nor exit to the cage. Either you were locked inside, or you were outside. He examined the hinges where the walls of the cage were joined together.

One way out was through the disk transport. Karl thought. In fact, it was possibly the only way out and the only way in.

***

Teodor let Tilson tighten his greaves, as the left one had come loose. He was watching the medication being applied to his opponent. The special fight remedies always worked immediately but were not without pain, either immediately or the next day. Teodor remembered how satisfying it had been to land his handle punch so successfully on the boy's torso.

"I hit him," Teodor told Tilson, elated. "Did you see how I hit him?"

"Crack a rib or two, why don't you?" Tilson said in jest, but his tone was fierce. Teodor knew he was proud of what he had seen.

"I thought he was fast."

"Calm, Teodor, control. He is fast. You caught him by surprise. Don't expect to get past him so easily next time."

"If I win will they let me go?"

"I don't know, my prince."

"But you can get me out of here?"

Tilson hesitated again.

"I am Dome Elite. I have to follow my orders."

"But who gives you your orders, am I not your prince? Your King?" Teodor paused as he considered who might have higher authority.

"Look over there, my prince."

Teodor could see nothing through the shadows, except the cameras spinning through the mist.

"I can't see," Teodor realised there were actual cameras. "Is this fight being broadcast? Is everyone watching this?"

278

"Not everyone, only a select audience."

"But who?"

Tilson shook his head and changed the subject.

"Get your blades out, my prince, the countdown has started."

Teodor saw the numbers flashing. He picked up his blades resolutely.

"If I win I get to go home, right?"

"Just fight, my prince, just fight."

"Best out of three or best out of five?" Teodor asked, without turning.

"Five," replied Tilson. "Now go."

Teodor paused just outside the circle. He knew exactly what he was going to do. He had to win three points out of five to win outright. As the count reduced to one, he stepped into the circle. As the zero appeared on the screen, Teodor ran two steps and leapt high in a tight somersault, so he landed almost on top of Guy Erma. Just in time, Guy stepped back, rocking as he fought to stay within the circle.

Now Teodor drew himself up to his full height with his blades high above his head, points directed down, towards his opponent. He let out a yell of defiance and realised at the same instant he had waited too long. Below him Guy Erma was moving, bringing a blade up towards Teodor's belly. Teodor swung his right blade down in a circle of fury. He knocked Guy's blade aside and caught the top of Guy's thigh with the point of his own blade. For a minute, it caught.

"Inside the join of his protection suit," Teodor pondered. As he pulled his blade free, orange and blue lights were flashing around the arena. Guy Erma twisted free from Teodor and Teodor wisely span the other way. Taking a defensive pose, he circled the mat opposite Guy Erma, trying to make sense of the flashing light. FIRST BLOOD the screen read.

Teodor looked at his blade. It was red. He had cut his opponent. More than that, Teodor realised Guy Erma was wearing a protective suit, where Teodor had none, just silks against his skin. He looked at the small amount of blood on his knife and immediately had a terrible foreboding. If his opponent should attack him back, then he would be in trouble.

"Then finish it," he heard the voice within his head. His father goading him as ever, to higher levels of perfection. "Finish it."

Teodor raced across the mat once more and was pleased to see a startled look of disbelief on his opponent's face. He attacked with three heavy blows, one from top right, one up and under from bottom left, right hand round again in a horizontal slice and finally, a swinging kick from the left. It was textbook black star except for the last kick. In a display, the kick always came from the right, since you would be off balance and a kick from the right was the more difficult. In this fight, Teodor brought his left to bear. He had the satisfaction of watching his jumping blades catch and jam into Guy's blades. Now the other boy was falling and at the very last he reached up to grab Teodor and pull him down after him but his fingers could not find purchase on Teodor's silks or his sweat-drenched arms.

In an instant, Teodor knew Guy was trying to grab the shielding he should be wearing on his arms, and not just the naked flesh. If Teodor had been wearing any protection then what might the outcome have been? Instead, Teodor let himself fall back onto his bottom into the blade ring, while Guy was propelled across the mat and out beyond the black line into the gilded fence beyond. Guy had landed outside the ring. He had lost another point.

"Two," thought Teodor, satisfied. He had his second point. His jumping blades were still caught up with Guy's so, as the light lit up to announce his victory, Teodor leant forward to disentangle his foot blade. In doing so, he reached to pull Guy Erma up into a sitting position.

"You all right?" he asked amicably. Guy Erma had been winded by the fall and was gasping to catch his breath.

"Take it easy," Teodor urged.

All at once Teodor felt a little sorry for the boy. He could hear the crowd booing and jeering. While it meant nothing to him, he guessed these men must know Guy. Didn't everyone know Guy Erma?

"Guy Erma, I'm glad to meet you."

The boy looked up at him, trying to read his face behind the mask.

"You know my name?"

"They said you were a great blades champion," Teodor said a little sadly. Had he even believed a boy from Domeside could beat a prince who had had hundreds of hours of tuition with the best tutors on the planet? He saw the boy glance with angry eyes at the score, as they both rose up on their fighting blades. Guy turned and spat angry words in Teodor's face.

"It's not over yet."

Teodor watched his opponent stalk back to his stool. Now he knew he should be worried.

***

"C'mon Guy, what is your problem?" Des shouted. "That was a classic move. You left yourself wide open, and he took you down. Where is your head?"

Guy pulled off the monkey mask and ran his hands through his hair.

"I can't concentrate with this thing on," Des handed him a towel. Guy gratefully wiped his face. He pushed his fingers into the bridge of his nose and massaged the soft flesh there.

"I have to win one point. I have to win at least one point."

"You have to win the next point," Des reminded him darkly. "C'mon, everything he has done so far has been text book. Now you know how strong he is. Go in there with some true Domeside flair. Try a reverse spiral, or the over and under. But expect him to have studied all the famous moves. So, he will have a response. Just be careful."

"Not if I take him at speed. He'll be lucky if he sees me coming."

"That's the spirit. Now go in there and get him."

Guy stood watching the numbers counting down to the start of the fight. Around him the crowd was quietening. The score was ominous: Two—Zero. Either Guy would win the next point or the fight would be over. No-one in the room was ready for the fight to end just yet.

"Go on, Guy!" he heard a voice yell.

"Get him, Guy!"

The shouts warmed Guy. At least some of the men still believed in him, even though it had been a pretty poor fight so far. Some of them still thought he could win. He was fighting for House Jewel and the Dome. He had to win. He kept moving on his blades, maintaining the warmth in his muscles. He looked over at his opponent; he looked relaxed. And why not? He was ahead on points.

The lights flashed to zero and both boys moved. Guy saw the other boy was trying to move away around the perimeter of the mat, clearly anticipating a direct attack, and assuming a defensive pose. Not quickly enough. Guy was on him and inside his defences before the boy had his blades up. Guy had his opponent trapped, one blade pushed up under his chin. At any moment, he could stab up into his face. His opponent had frozen. It was enough to win but Guy was not satisfied yet.

Guy drew his other blade back. He intended to slice away the silk tunic from the left side of his body, just above his heart. It was a winning blow. Non-lethal since he expected the other to be wearing a protective body, but an undisputed winning blow. He signalled his move with a minute flutter of the blade, which had the men around the cage on their feet and roaring. Louder than all the others, one well-known voice. Chart Segat shouted:

"Kill him, Guy! Just kill him!"

Guy smiled. Too late. In playing to the crowd, Guy had waited too long. He saw true terror in the other's eyes. All at once, Guy saw blood on the point of the blade under his opponent's chin. Guy knew he had not cut him. No, his opponent had pressed his chin down onto the blade knowing the sight of blood would distract him. Why? All at once, Guy saw the clumsy kick. A desperate knee rising up to his groin. Guy twisted aside. So the knee impacted his hip. As Guy moved, his opponent reached to push the blade away from his chin and then turned away. Guy brought his other blade up, slicing out. He felt something soft against his blade's cutting edge. Softness, he was not familiar with.

He had little time to check, for the boy was still spinning. He was trying to put some distance between them. Guy reached out casually with one foot, tripped his opponent and watched amazed as his opponent fought to keep his balance. He tumbled into an awkward forward roll, still desperate to get away. Guy saw his moment when the boy failed to rise immediately from the floor. Guy flew through the air and landed square across his opponent's chest. Then Guy had both blades crossed across his neck:

"Do you yield?"

The lights flashed the score above them. Two—One. One screen was flashing Second Blood. The crowd around the gilded fence were, finally, going mad. A voice cried again:

"Kill him, Guy!"

Guy smiled grimly; it had been a quick win. He wondered why his opponent had fought so hard right to the end. At the same time, he was aware that the body underneath him felt different. He removed his blades from the other's neck and took them both in one hand. It was a traditional sign of peace. With his spare hand, he gently patted the other's chest.

"Take it easy," he said with a smile. Then he patted him a second time. Either this boy was wearing ultra-thin protection, or he was naked under the silk. Guy started to stand, taking a moment to look down the other's body to where the boy should have been wearing synthetic leg mail. There was a long narrow cut from his groin to his knee. Guy remembered how he had planned to slice at his opponent's torso expecting the body protector to deflect the cutting edge. If this boy was wearing only light protection, would he have been spared? Guy stood up and reached to help the other up. But the boy in red just ignored his outstretched hand, neatly sprang to his feet, and with the smallest of limps, went back to his place.

As Guy returned to Des, he heard his opponent gasp. Tilson would be applying the skin healing spray, Guy knew well how much that burnt – doubly so, close to one's groin.

Good, he thought, his opponent would be weaker for it. He still had two points to win.

"Well done," Des said mildly. "A bit untidy, you should be careful about playing to the gallery. This is not a display match, but you nailed him in the end."

"I think he's only wearing light mail."

Des hesitated, glanced across the fighting mat to the opponent, then replied quickly.

"That's his choice, and not something for you to worry about."

Right, thought Guy, pulling off the monkey mask. He sat looking across at his opponent. He had to plan his next move carefully. He should expect the boy in red to come out fighting fast, wanting to win the point and end the match. He saw the other had taken his monkey mask off as well. He was towelling his cheeks and eyes, and then pushed his hair back with one hand. The move was familiar, as was the face. For a moment Guy was confused, could this really be a boy from the Riffaut? As Guy watched, a huge Battle Borg came up behind the other boy and there was a brief altercation. The cyborg went to force the monkey mask back on him. In the end, the boy pulled the mask back on himself. He looked truly miserable. Guy looked at the blue mask in his hand and sighed, then pulled it on. At least they both agreed on one thing: the masks were a pain.

The countdown started. Guy stepped up to the edge of the mat. He looked at the score and reminded himself: he had to win this point, otherwise he was out. He saw how the other boy moved his right leg a fraction slower than his left. Guy decided on his attack. As he spun in on the boy's right side, he realised the limp had been a trap. The boy in red silks had both blades up, and he was arching down on Guy. Guy was momentarily impressed, and then he cursed himself not to have anticipated such a simple ploy. They engaged in a fast blades fight that saw Guy back up a couple of steps before, with elegant ease, he increased the tempo and saw his opponent tensing in concentration as he replied.

'Aha, so my speed is causing you a problem,' Guy thought. 'I will remember that.'

He eased off, throwing up one last arching blow that sent the other leaping aside, now Guy had the space for another attack. Kicking his jumping blades over his head he span in with his blades low to reach and cut his opponent's legs. The other saw him coming and responded by twisting back in a hand spring. For an instant, they were in mid-air, heads down. They slashed at each other and their blades met, then they both span away. Guy was quicker to find his feet and pirouetted forward, blades outstretched. This time there was a quite satisfying tearing noise, as he split the red silk from the left shoulder blade down across his opponent's back to level with his kidney.

Guy paused as the crowd's cheers hit him like a wave. Blood was pearling up through the silk, where he had sliced into bare skin. So, the boy was wearing no protection at all! Why then was he fighting with unblunted blades? Guy was now on the defensive, because the cut, while impressive, was not a win, and across from him his opponent charged back.

Their blades clashed. Guy was hard pressed as the other boy rained down hard accurate blows. Each one was heavier than the next. All threatened to unbalance him. The edge of the mat was very close. Guy checked over his shoulder to see where his foot blades were in relation to the black line, a necessary but dangerous move. Guy saw the punch and felt the wind of it passing close to his cheek bone. He had spun ahead of it in a tight spiral, bringing his hand blades up with determined accuracy. In an instant, he had one point pressed to his opponent's heart, while he brought his second blade level with his eyes.

284

Had he stepped outside of the mat as he span round? He was so close to the edge. He saw the other boy looking down at his feet, he was inside… just. He might have put a blade outside as he turned. In fact, he was sure he had. Eye to eye, both boys were panting as they waited for the referee. Either Guy was disqualified, or he had won.

As the lights lit up Two—Two, Guy saw frustration flash in his opponent's eyes, followed by anger. Guy stepped back quickly. This time there were no words to say. Guy quickly backed to his stool.

"This is not a fair fight," Guy told Des. "He's not wearing any protection at all."

"Not your problem," Des replied shortly.

"I stepped off the blades mat."

"Did you? I didn't see it. You were bloody fast, that's all."

"They can't repair that cut across his back with skin spray."

"Again, not your problem."

"So he has to go into the next round injured and without protection?"

"I'm sorry Guy, but you have to win."

"Sorry for what?"

"Sorry for him."

Des nodded to the other boy leaning against the stool and panting with pain. Guy looked over and winced in sympathy. Both looked to where an extension had been flashed up; it would be three minutes until the next round. Des picked up Guy's gym jacket and helped him pull it on, closing the zip to his neck. Pausing to place his hand on Guy's shoulder, he said:

"Stay warm and conserve your strength, you have to win."

Chapter 25. "...the time of his life"

"Regent Sayginn, I have hacked a secret comms channel. It's beaming video from the cap of the Dome," Patrick said.

"On screen."

All around the ballroom the screens flashed black a few instants, then one by one the same scene appeared on each, and on the largest display the multiple images amalgamated to create an enormous 3D film. In the cap of the Dome, in Chart Segat's private space, a gilded fight cage had been erected. Men stood three or four deep yelling, as on the blades mat two small fighters, one wearing blue, one wearing red, were engaged in a blades fight.

"What?" said Sayginn. "Who is that?"

As they watched, the boy in red was cut with a sharp blade. He screamed. On a nearby screen, an analyst was running an ID check against a still of the screaming face.

"Iris scan. One hundred per cent match. It is the prince!"

"I don't understand!" cried Sayginn. "Chart Segat promised to free him. Now he has him fighting like a caged animal. We have to get him out of there. We have to go now. They can't stop us accessing the Dome now. Patrick, send your men. Go."

"Regent, wait, there's something else."

"What? Tell me quickly."

"The images, the reason I was able to hack them. They are being broadcast into this palace. They are being received and played on a screen on the first floor in the west wing."

"Frederon!" Sayginn said with a snarl. "Frederon is watching this match."

Sayginn did not wait, just accelerated the hover chair up the stairs and along the corridor. Patrick and the others raced to keep up. She burst into the salon without invitation and kept going until she found herself staring at the Emperor, who was resting on a sofa watching the blades match on a large screen. He was laughing with his entourage as she arrived.

"Do you think this is amusing?"

"House Jewel vs. House Riffaut," Frederon said. "Of course it's amusing."

"That's not…" Sayginn could not find the words, because she could see on his face that the Emperor knew what she was going to say.

"You should never have cancelled the fight, Sayginn. Look at your boy, he's having the time of his life."

"They are going to kill him. He's fighting without protection! And against a boy who everyone agrees is a far better fighter than him."

"Well, you should have more confidence. He seems to be holding his own rather well."

"How did you get this feed? Why didn't you tell me, if you knew?"

"Chart Segat," Frederon replied crisply. "Some of us still believe in him." He stood up. "Don't get peevish, Sayginn. I said to him that a good fight might do Teodor good. Although I had expected him to return him first."

"Frederon, how could you? Chart Segat killed Serge and murdered Deodran, how could you?"

"No, he didn't. Why would Chart Segat and the Elite plant those bombs, Sayginn? Look, this conversation is getting boring. We know where Teodor is. We have always known where he was. I presume you are sending your men over to retrieve him. I'll go with them. Chart Segat will not deny me. I will bring him home."

Chapter 26. Of Droids and of Disks

Karl Valvanchi looked guiltily over his shoulder as he heard the crowd of men roar their blood lust. He was no longer in the cap of the Dome. He had made his way to the disk transport control area at the back. He had not wanted to let Prince Teodor out of his sight, but with the prince locked inside a gilded cage, Karl could think of only one plan to get him out.

Guy Erma had won another point. The match was going to five points. Good, he had more time. There was a three-minute extension, too. Good, even more time. He paused as he saw the close-up of the deep, long cut across Teodor's back.

"I have to get that boy out," he muttered tersely. "But first I have to disperse those Dome Elite."

He walked to where Zeb was standing at the controls of the disk transport system. Three disks were standing in a rack alongside a circular door that opened out onto the Dome.

"After this, you head back to the embassy, Zeb. I can handle the rest of this myself."

Karl walked up to the control panel. Within seconds the keyboard lit up to his touch. Unexpectedly, a number of cupboards opened at his back. Inside there were neatly racked weapons and a stack of what looked like coiled steel ropes: snake droids.

"But Karl, what are you going to do?"

Karl picked up a snake droid and examined it with a grim smile.

"Just a small diversion."

***

288

Teodor stood holding onto his stool, but not sitting on it yet. He knew to climb onto the stool would rip his back further.

"Let me have a look, see if I can do anything," Tilson said gently.

Teodor walked a few steps around the stool. He stood while Tilson looked and carefully probed his back. Even the remnant of his silk vest as it brushed up against the scar was excruciatingly painful. After a few moments, Tilson said:

"I can give you morphine." He hesitated as both knew the drug would slow his responses.

"Against him?" Teodor asked. He could not think of anything worse than being even a fraction slower when faced with such an opponent.

"Well, it's not ideal. Can you fight with the pain?"

"Do I have any choice?"

"It's only one point, Teodor. You still have the strength to floor him. Take your time, find the opportunity. I've asked for an extension. Come and sit, rest a few moments. Take some aspirin. It will take the edge off it." He handed Teodor a glass of water specked with white. It was gassy water too. All the quicker to absorb the medicine into his blood stream. Gratefully now, he sat on a stool. He pulled off his monkey mask to drink.

"I'm just taking my medicine," he said as the Battle Borg stepped up alongside him. The borg had already picked up the monkey mask and was pushing it into Teodor's face. Teodor brushed him aside. The machine insisted. Teodor emptied the glass in one gulp. And only just, for the borg knocked the glass from his hand. He tried to force the monkey mask onto his face.

Teodor looked down at the shattered pieces below his stool. How Tilson had quickly stepped aside to avoid its fall. Then, picking up his blades, Teodor grabbed the facemask from the borg's hands. In a whirl of blades, he sliced the silk to narrow shreds, which twisted and span as they floated to the floor. The borg looked at him in disbelief, processing the action and looking for a solution. Teodor leapt down from the stool and out of the reach of the machine. The borg stepped after him. Teodor guessed that he might be safe on the blades mat, and indeed as he leapt within the black circle, the borg stopped and seemed to lose its direction.

Teodor now turned his face into the light and with deliberate intent, brushed his hair back from his face. Let them have a look at me, he thought. Let them see who I am. Then, as the silks brushed against his back again, he had an inspiration. He reached across his body and sliced the red silk with the Riffaut logo from his body. So he was standing wearing only black shorts, black boots, calf greaves and cuffs. Now there was no disguising how unprotected he was. Nor, indeed, who he was. With a blade in each hand, he was their prince and their King. Unprotected, unbowed, he was ready for the fight. Would anyone believe, seeing him standing there, that he was Sebastian or any of the other eight models?

Closing his hands around his blades, he pushed one fist into his hip and let the other hand fall straight by his side. He squared his shoulders and looked beyond the gilded cage. See me, he thought. See me and recognise my father, who always stood like this when he took hard decisions. As he lifted his chin in pride, he heard the crowd fall silent.

Look at me and be afraid, because I am not afraid. I am a prince.

***

"That is really Prince Teodor?" Guy said, looking across with his mouth open.

"Of course," Des said quietly. "Who did you expect it to be?"

Guy looked down at the blades in his hands and across at the prince. It was what he had dreamed of. Only he was wearing armour. He was as yet uninjured. And he was still wearing the stupid monkey mask.

"I can't do this," Guy said quietly. "It's not a fair fight."

Des gnashed his teeth together in exasperation:

"Do you want to face a Battle Borg with just a blunted blade in your hand?"

"Sorry?" Guy said astonished.

"The borgs are just there. What do you think is going to happen when this fight ends?"

"Chart Segat said he would not do that to me."

"If you get into the Dome Elite, the guys and I might be able to protect you. But if you lose this you should expect Chart Segat to throw you to his borgs tonight. Chartsie and his men will be baying for blood later tonight. Your blood. You have to win."

Guy stepped away from Des. The blood had drained from his face and his hands were freezing. He squeezed his blades once and then twice trying to restore the circulation.

"He won't do that to me," Guy said quickly.

"Oh, won't he?"

Guy glanced over his shoulder. From here he could clearly see Chart Segat in the vast armchair that he had as his throne. Around the fence the men were silent, uncertain. What should he do? What should any of them do? He looked up at Des one more time.

"There's nothing more Lloulou or I can do. You have to win."

Don't think of Chart Segat. Don't think of House Jewel. Don't think of the Dome Elite. Think of only one person, Guy Erma, and you might survive. Guy heard Juno's advice clearly. *Think of yourself.*

"I know. I will. I will win."

"Go get him, Guy."

Guy stepped up to the edge of the mat. He looked across at the prince and felt sorry for him. Prince Teodor could not know how much he needed to win. In any case, he was a prince, he was bound to be ransomed, rescued and delivered. He would be safe tonight.

Whereas Guy Erma was an unregistered Domeside orphan. Who would protect him?

"This is still not a fair fight," Guy said to himself, looking down at his armour and over at the questionable referee. "I have to win yes, but at least let it be a fair fight." All at once the numbers started to count down, and Guy knew what he must do.

Nine.

Reaching up to his ears, with his right hand he pulled the mask off and sliced it in two on the edge of his blade.

Eight.

With his left, he cut the tunic from his body, not even looking as the blue silk fell to the floor.

291

Seven.

He unclipped the buckle at this neck.

Six.

He tugged free the buckle at the centre of his chest.

Five.

He reached across to the buckle on his hip.

Four.

With a smooth move, he threw his protection vest aside and stood across from the prince. Yes, he was still wearing chain mail shorts that stretched down his thighs but there was nothing he could do about that now.

Three.

He ran both hands up over his face, pushing his black hair back. His Dome medallion glinted at the centre of his chest.

Two.

He span both blades across the palms of his hands.

One.

He stepped up to the fight and, with new resolution, faced his opponent. The crowd at his back was screaming their approval. Now, thought Guy, we are equal. He looked to see if the prince had noticed. Teodor gave a shy smile of approval and a respectful small bow. Guy nodded in return, and leapt forward to engage him. With new enthusiasm, they leapt into the fight and met in a clash of blades that was fast and accurate. Guy forced the pace, and realised that Teodor did not seem to have slowed noticeably. He probably had not taken morphine, Guy knew it was the last thing he would do at this stage.

The flying blades were very decorative. They were equally matched in height, strength, speed and accuracy, as they span across the mat keeping in close contact. Guy enjoyed the challenge. He had rarely faced such an equal opponent so close to him in age, but as he dodged a punch Teodor had added at the end of the last parry, he remembered this was not some demonstration.

Guy dived to the floor. Disappearing out of Teodor's reach and causing him to topple a little, Guy was already swinging his leg across the floor and slicing Teodor's jumping blades from underneath him.

Teodor fell forward, trying to throw himself bodily on top of Guy, but Guy had anticipated this and reached up to Teodor's shoulders. He rolled him over and pushed him down onto the floor and onto his back. Teodor screamed. In an instant Guy knew he would win and he went to leap on top of the prince, only the prince brought his leg up. Guy's momentum propelled him onto the prince's knee. Guy cried out as the knee punched into his belly, and it was all he could do to roll away. He lay panting on his stomach, glancing around to check as the prince was unsteadily getting to his feet.

'I have to get up,' thought Guy. At that moment the floor on which he lay fell away.

Guy fell. He realised, astonished, that the disk transport was in motion. A circular door in the floor was opening. Guy scrambled to his feet. The metal floor on which Guy stood was sliding away, opening up an abyss into the Dome below. Instinctively, Guy moved away from the drop. But the disk was closing itself away and very soon the floor would disappear from under his feet and he would fall! He looked up. Above him, the prince was staring over the edge looking down at him.

To Guy's unending wonder, the prince immediately reached down to grab his hand. Guy reached but failed to make contact, rocking on the edge of the large circular opening. At once the prince wrapped an arm around his waist and steadied him.

The Prince hauled Guy up onto the fighting mat. Guy glanced down and immediately felt sick. He had nearly fallen down there, all the way down into the Dome. It did not bear thinking about. He turned his back on the opening.

The prince was not moving, he seemed mesmerised by the hole that had opened in their fighting arena. Why had the door opened? Glancing round the gilded cage, Guy could hear the men shouting. "What now? Was this supposed to happen?" He looked at the scoreboard: two—two.

Now Teodor was also backing up. The prince had grabbed Guy by the arm, he was drawing him away from the opening. Guy threw a glance over his shoulder: another disk was coming up from below. There was nothing on it – well, no people anyway. Was that a piece of rope?

'What about the fight?' The clock was still ticking. He glanced across to Des, to see what he was doing. Then, out of the corner of his eye, he saw something move.

'The prince?'

The prince leapt on top of him. Guy knew such a body tackle was not strictly legal, but clearly the prince wanted to win. Guy fought to bring his blades up, but the prince wrestled him to the ground.

"Stop it!" the prince shouted.

Guy wriggled, desperate to free himself. He was not going to yield. He was not going to lose!

"Stop it!" the prince cried. "Look!"

The prince had yanked his head, pulling his hair back and forcing him to look, and now Guy saw it:

A snake droid. Above their heads bullets were spiralling out into the cap of the Dome. The shouts from beyond the golden cage had turned to screams. There was noise, smoke confusion. Someone was attacking them!

"Stay down," Teodor insisted.

"We need to get under it," Guy said.

"Yes, I know," the prince said angrily. "Go!"

On elbows and knees, they crawled onto the newly arrived disk platform and underneath the snake droid. Cowing in its shadow, for the moment at least they were safe.

"What in God's name is happening?" Guy muttered.

All around them the metal of the gilded cage was rocking and exploding. One panel was hit at the join and started to topple. A second followed suit. In a matter of seconds, the entire structure had collapsed inwards.

"I think someone is trying to rescue me," the prince said quietly.

Guy was barely listening. He looked for Des. Des was flat on the floor, was he injured? He looked for Tilson, it looked like Tilson might have escaped when the cage was destroyed. The Battle Borgs were both down. One was still twitching, but the other clearly dead.

"Rescue?" Guy repeated weakly.

The lights had gone out. Guy could see that the crush of men who had been pressed up against the gilded cage had dispersed. Chart Segat had disappeared from his vast throne. Some had fallen. Some looked injured. Some were crouching between these bodies, either hiding or trying to escape. Some men tried to shelter in the bathroom, but a long volley of fire saw the windows and mirrors shattered. The men threw themselves to the floor. And still the snake droid was shooting.

"Some rescue," Guy snapped.

"Yes, well, beggars can't be choosers," Teodor replied shortly.

Guy glanced at him and could not hold back a cough-like laugh:

"You're not a beggar… Sir."

The prince looked at him. Almost at once, his anxiety melted away. He smiled briefly. Guy felt him relaxing, and first checking for his blades the prince reached over and said into his ear:

"I suppose not. But you can call me Teo, Guy Erma."

"You know my name?"

"Everyone knows Guy Erma," Teodor smiled just once. He went back to peering out at the room, and then added seriously:

"I have to get out."

Guy nodded. Then he saw something and said:

"We both have to get out." The prince looked at him. Guy pointed up at the digits glowing on the underside of the snake's head: "That's a five-second fuse."

Teodor nodded and pointed to the bathroom.

"That's an iron clad jacuzzi. Can you run?

"It's shooting everything that moves."

Teodor pointed to the now much reduced tail of the snake. It would soon be out of bullets.

"Ten, nine, eight…" He was quickly counting down the last bullets. "Ready?"

Guy nodded.

"Five, four, three, two, one." The last bullet had been shot. They rose up on their blades and sprinted across the space. Around them, the other men were moving too, heading to the exit or throwing themselves flat on the floor behind couches. Guy and Teodor jumped as one into the Jacuzzi bath and stayed under the water. Above their heads, they saw the light flash gold, then back to black. Then they resurfaced, coughing and spluttering.

"I don't know why you think this is a rescue, that thing almost killed us," Guy protested.

As they watched, the disk transport started moving again, and what remained of the snake droid disappeared. Something else was coming.

"I need to get out fast. Is that the door?" Teodor said. Suddenly he grabbed Guy by the shoulder and put a blade to his neck. "Decide now: will you help me?" He pointed at the door.

"The Dome Elite went that way," Guy said a little sulkily. He reached up to push the blade away and looked to see where Chart Segat was. He had retreated into the next chamber, but now he was coming back with Dome Elite on all sides. All at once the double door slammed shut into Chart Segat's face. The locks slid closed. Who was controlling the doors? Still, all around, the Dome Elite were starting to stand up and dust themselves off. No-one was looking at them, yet. Teodor was looking somewhat fearfully at the uniformed men.

"Will you help me?" Teodor insisted, pushing the blade back under Guy's chin.

Guy reached up to the blade. The edge was sharp when he tried to push Teodor's hand away. The prince did not yield.

'Could he mean this?' Guy thought wearily. 'After everything else, now he was going to be killed by his prince.'

"I have to escape," Teodor insisted.

Guy tried to think, what were the odds of them getting out of the Dome from here? It had to be possible, didn't it? But if he helped the prince escape, how much more trouble would he be in?

"Whatever Chartsie says, you obey him." He remembered Lloulou's flat warning. He did not need to hear what Chart Segat was shouting from the other side of the door to know what he wanted. He saw Teodor looking nervously in the same direction.

'I am on my own,' Guy thought grimly. 'I have to decide.'

Guy looked straight at Teodor and said.

"There is another way out, but it will be dangerous, us being so wet."

"You swear to help me get out?"

He looked appraisingly at Teodor:

"Will there be a reward?"

The prince looked a little surprised but recovered quickly.

"What kind of reward?"

"I want to go with you to Magnolia Palace."

"Oh," Teodor sounded relieved.

Both turned to the sound of shots. They saw the double-door holding back Chart Segat, and his men was being shot apart.

"Tonight," Guy insisted.

Chapter 27. Flight from the Dome

In the cap of the Dome, another disk jet had appeared. As it rose up through the floor, all around small groups of Dome Elite were crouched, blades in hands, watching. They relaxed when they saw the disk was not bearing another snake droid but a single Dome Elite warrior, with blades in both hands.

Shape-shifted into a Dome Elite soldier, Karl scanned the cap of the Dome. He realised at once that the prince was gone. After a few minutes more he realised that his plan had worked. Zak's clever programming of the snake had succeeded. None of the Dome Elite had been injured, but all the Borgs were dead.

What had happened to Prince Teodor? He scanned for DNA traces, and a trail of blood droplets flashed bright orange in front of his eyes. He quickly followed their footsteps to the great bath. There he paused a moment, looking at the blades greaves and calf-protection abandoned at the side of the iron structure, in puddles of water. Glancing over his shoulder, he heard Chart Segat giving loud instructions, rallying the Dome Elite. Karl paused a moment, picked up the abandoned blades equipment and hid it his pack.

'No need to leave any clues for Chart Segat,' he thought grimly.

From the bathroom the trail was easier to follow. Clearly Prince Teodor was not alone. Karl made his way along the dark space between the bathroom wall and the outer pane of the Dome looking out onto the city, and found the open panel into the infrastructure of the Dome itself. Quickly now, Karl reattached the grille and tightened the screws. As he came out of the darkness, he bumped into a young Dome Elite guard:

"Did you see them?" the young man asked. "Did they get out through the verticals?"

Karl paused and theatrically looked over his shoulder. He could see the solder was dying to get into the space himself.

"They're not there," he replied.

"Do you mind?"

Karl stepped aside, he was thinking there was something very familiar about the young man. Before he had time to think about it, he heard a voice.

"Des, are they there? Can you see them?"

It was Chart Segat coming up close. Karl slipped away. From the shadows, he watched. Des was shaking his head as he reappeared.

"The grille was locked tight. If they had gotten out that way they would have left it open behind them. Besides which, they cannot climb with blade protection on."

"Prince Teodor could never climb like Guy does," Chart Segat said dismissively. "They must be hiding somewhere. Fifty to the man that finds them. C'mon Des, they can't be far."

Karl Valvanchi smiled as he listened. So the prince had got away, and the Dome Elite had no idea where he was. But Karl knew how to find him. He sent out a loud thought message:

'Where are you, my prince?'

***

Teodor realised he was climbing down the very structure of the Dome. Inside the verticals that supported the vast hexagons that made up the Dome, there was an intricate trellis of connected triangles. It was not wide. It was easy enough to find hand and foot holds. Only it was best not to look down. The drop beneath them, the sloping abyss right down the side of one of the highest pentagons of the Dome, was frightful. Beyond the next junction was a vertical descent. As Teodor thought of a long straight drop, his foot slipped and he found himself hanging by one hand. He must have yelled out because below him, Guy looked up.

Teodor peered down at him, realising how far he had fallen behind. He reached up above his head with his other hand. He wanted to catch hold with both hands but found he could not reach. He tried to lift one of his feet up to a strut, but the distance was too far. He tried his other leg. The pain in his fingers was excruciating, but he could not let go. Then he felt Guy underneath him. He looked down. Guy was pushing his shoulder up between his legs like a seat and propelling Teodor upwards. Teodor reached up again. His second hand caught. Now his right hand found a strut as well. He was pulling himself up and off Guy. Guy kept climbing up until they were alongside each other in the confined space. Guy reached up and stroked Teodor's hair.

"You haven't got the hang of it. Have you?"

"I can climb," Teodor said. "I'm not afraid." But he knew that he sounded afraid, very afraid. Guy nodded thoughtfully.

"Do you know the song 'goran rider'?"

"Goran rider?"

Guy started singing: "He was a no-good goran rider. What more can I say?"

Teodor joined in: "He made me laugh, he made me sigh and then he rode away!"

Guy laughed.

"Ok, so watch! *He was*... right hand... *a no good*... left foot... *goran rider* (pause).

What more... left hand... *can I*... right foot... *say*? Now breathe." Then Guy changed his voice to mimicry: "It very important to breathe."

Teodor laughed. He was thinking of the choir master in the cathedral, how he was always scolding him: "It's very important to breathe, Prince Teodor."

"Did he say that to you too?" he asked Guy.

"He said it more often to me. I was your understudy. He always made it clear I was nowhere near good enough."

"I'm sorry about that."

"Anyway... *He made me laugh* (right foot), *he made me cry* (left foot) *and then* (left hand) *he rode* (right hand) *away*."

"Breathe!" they both said together.

"Ok. So try it."

Teodor hesitated, and then started singing:

"*He was a no good goran...*"

"You need to sing louder..."

"Won't someone hear us?"

"No, can't you feel how cold it is? We're climbing down the outside of the Dome. No-one can hear us."

"... *goran rider*. What more can I say? *He made me laugh*. It works..." Teodor said excitedly, then started singing again. "*He made me sigh*, whoops wrong hand."

"Once you get started you can't stop until you reach the bottom. And sing a bit louder. It helps. The song blocks out everything else."

"You mean the fear?"

Guy smiled. "Well, if you were afraid, I expect it would. Do you want me to shimmy past, so I am below you if you need me again? We'll stop at the join?"

They were down in less time than Teodor would have thought possible, just two verses of the song Goran Riders. They sat perched at the intersection, peering down the long vertical.

"It's a long way down."

"Don't worry about it. We are not going all the way to the bottom, but you can see how dangerous this is going to be."

"No mistakes, huh?"

"Are you ok with that?"

"I can do it. I have to do it. And the song helps."

"Yes, it does, doesn't it?" Guy said. "It's not as far as it looks. We need to keep going, because it won't take them long to realise where we are."

"Oh?"

"We don't want them waiting for us at the bottom."

"Right. Let's get moving."

"Don't look down. I know I don't."

Teodor took a breath and started to sing again.

"Louder," called Guy, joining in. They continued, quickly moving hands and feet in turn until Guy led them out of the trellis into a more conventional air-conditioning tunnel.

Now Guy shot along, sliding on his hands and knees like a supersonic slug along the polished metal surface. Teodor threw himself after him. He caught up with him only to hear him counting.

"Five, or is that six?" Teodor saw him shaking the grille, but it did not budge.

"Go back," he whispered to Teodor. "It's the fifth exit. I think I miscounted." Teodor nodded and backed up as quickly as he had come. It was not far. Guy squeezed past to the grille. He reached to shake it, and then it came away in his hand.

"Phew!" Guy said. He let the grille drop below him. Teodor sighed with relief. He sat back and banged his head. He turned and saw a strange sight. Screwed to the inside of the air conditioning tunnel was a glass brick. Inside the brick, he could see soil and plants, and movement. There were insects inside the brick. He peered closer. It was an entire miniature world inside what looked like an industrial glass brick. He looked again. There was a metal device mounted to the side and then he noticed the screws. The screws attaching the glass brick to the wall were shiny and brand new.

Then he heard the voice inside his head:

Where are you, my prince?

Teodor looked at the miniature world across from him.

Here, he thought, *then looked down into the changing room. Here.*

What's that? Oh, now I see you. I will be there shortly, my prince.

***

"I thought this might happen," Guy told Teodor. He strode over to a nearby locker and threw it open. "I thought I might need to make a quick getaway." He laughed without humour. He saw Teodor glancing at him quickly. "But I only have one set of spare clothes," Guy's hands were shaking as he reached up to take down the trousers.

"You wear the sweatshirt and pants. I'll wear the t-shirt and jacket. I've got these," he pointed to his leggings. "It will look like I've been training."

"Are those my shoes?" said Teodor, walking over to the locker. "Did you bring them from the cathedral? For me? I saw you at the cathedral, do you remember?"

Teodor looked over gratefully at Guy. Guy turned away quickly, pulling on a shirt as he did, to hide his face. Suddenly he was red with shame.

"Can you wear your running blades with those?" Guy asked bluntly.

"Yes," Teodor turned them over. "They have the grooves here. Do you remember the cathedral?"

"Yes, I remember. We're going to need the running blades to get out."

"What, we need to be fast?"

"That. And I never walk anywhere. None of the Elite do. We don't want to draw attention to ourselves."

Teodor had sat down. Inexplicably, he was cradling his shoes. He looked like he longed to put them on. Guy saw he was running one index along the fine leather. He stretched out and touched him lightly of on his arm:

"Wear them if you like," Teodor looked so pleased and relieved that immediately Guy felt guilty.

Guy remembered standing watching the prince in his angel costume with the press. How he had bent and taken the shoes. How he had been afraid a teacher might see him. He could see Teodor was thinking too. He knew he had to say something. Guy walked up to Teodor a bit awkwardly.

"I did not bring those shoes here for you. How could I? I did not know this was going to happen."

***

Teodor was examining the sweatshirt, Guy had given him. With a curious eye he assessed the wear and tear, had these clothes ever been new? Now he looked closely at Guy. He saw his leanness was perhaps not just his natural build. The shadows under of eyes told a tale of anxiety and perhaps long hours of work. He looked up as Guy said:

"I did not bring those shoes here for you. How could I? I did not know this was going to happen."

Teodor nodded and said quietly:

"No, I know that. You stole them from the cathedral, didn't you? I noticed they were missing almost straight away. Before, well, before..." Teodor

303

sighed. This was not Guy's fault. Despite everything my father tried to do, real poverty still existed in Domeside. Teodor was looking at it right now. "It really doesn't matter now." He tied the laces and attached his running blades. "We should get going."

Guy had stolen his shoes. Somehow Teodor did not mind that, but he could sense there was another lie that Guy was hiding from him. It went beyond the fact that he had taken his shoes. There was a bigger, darker lie. Something important he had not yet told him. Or else why would he, a Dome Elite boy, need to make a 'quick getaway'? What was he so desperate to run away from that he risked his life in the verticals of the Dome?

Suddenly Teodor had a terrible foreboding. What did he know of this dark haired boy with his Dome medallion? He looked directly at him and asked:

"Will they be waiting outside?"

There was shock in the blue eyes, and Teodor saw honesty in amongst the confusion. He relaxed a fraction.

"Who? No. Well, yes," Guy said indecisively. "There are cameras outside. They will see us, of course. There are cameras everywhere," he said, pointing. "But if we are quick, we should stay ahead of them."

"Could I use your communicator? I need to call my mother."

"It's on the Dome network. They will identify your voice and be on us in minutes."

"Then we must move, and fast."

Guy had already moved to the door. Quickly now, Teodor followed.

"It's clear. Now let's go."

Only it wasn't. It wasn't clear.

From the double door, a troop of Dome Elite were charging round the curved perimeter. Guy tugged Teodor and they raced away from them. They were a good distance ahead, when Teodor glanced back:

"Battle Borgs!"

Guy looked over his shoulder and saw the borgs pushing through the line of Dome Elite. Then the shooting started. Guy was behind Teodor. He reached forward to press his head forward and down. As he did a shot rang out. It hit Guy's communicator, just centimetres from Teodor's back. Guy saw Teodor glance at the mangled metal on Guy's wrist, but neither stopped. They just pushed on faster, stretching their legs to lengthen their leaps.

"Faster," hissed Guy. "We have to go faster."

They passed another double door. Out of the corner of his eye Teodor saw movement. For a moment he despaired, not more Dome Elite. The door burst open behind them. It was a single Dome Elite soldier. He did not follow Guy and Teodor, instead he knelt and faced their pursuers. He pulled out his blades and now prepared to face down the oncoming Dome Elite.

Who is he? thought Teodor. He checked to see if Guy had seen, but the other boy just kept on running. Guy sprinted forward, only stopping as he reached the far end of the circular corridor and a final, vast double door. He stopped, holding the door open. Teodor came up alongside him. They both looked behind them. The Dome Elite men were slowing up, hesitating to see one of their own standing guard. Through their lines, the Battle Borgs were coming. As Teodor watched, the single guard metamorphosed.

No longer a Dome Elite guard, he was a tall man with white cropped hair who stood up and drew himself up to face the huge Battle Borgs alone. He reached an empty hand out towards them, and the borgs stopped. It took them a few steps to lose their momentum. It was a few instants before their weapons lowered, but as Teodor watched, the light dimmed in their eyes. The Battle Borgs came to a complete standstill just a metre ahead of where the man stood.

"Who was that?" Guy whispered, turning accusingly towards Teodor.

"I think my mother sent him to rescue me."

"Do we stop now then?"

'*Just run.*' The voice in Teodor's head was an order. '*Just run and don't look back.*'

"He's busy," Teodor said resolutely. "I need to escape, or at least find the Regency Defence."

"He's not Regency?"

"I don't know what he is."

***

He's lying, thought Guy. That's Killer Valvanski. He knows it and I know it. So the Regent sent Killer Valvanski into the heart of the Dome. The Elite would just hate that. The Elite would never forgive her.

For a moment Guy had a doubt. So, who am I fighting for? He thought he was helping his prince. But if his ally was Killer Valvanski, did that make him a traitor? He looked at the sweat pearling around the edge of Teodor's face. He saw the fear-filled way Teodor impatiently swept his hair from his face.

It's not his fault, Guy thought slowly. He's just a boy trying to get home. 'Ultimately I'm not yet a member of the Dome Elite either, I have to think of myself.' Suddenly, Guy was overtaken with urgent fear:

"Let's get out of here. Can you do this?"

Teodor looked around. Guy had leapt down an entire flight of eight steps down to an interim landing on the square staircase. Teodor nodded a little nervously and threw himself after Guy, accurately landing just beside him, but grateful when Guy reached to grab his arm and steady him on landing.

"Let's go," Guy said quietly and led the way. They made their way down the stairs in massive bounds that took them down flight after flight of steps. So, in a matter of minutes, they made their way down eight or ten stories. Guy pushed open the doors and they stepped out into the competition blades arena. He pulled Teodor after him as the prince looked up in wonder at the huge panes of the Dome. He looked around the vast arena which was the competition gym. Guy sighed. There were two Dome Elite guards standing inside the doors. Now they looked up and recognised him:

"Ah, Guy boy!" said the one Guy knew as Benjy. He was as round as he was tall, and Guy knew he was one of the very first Dome Elite. Since he rarely put in any time at the gym, for several years now he had been rewarded with duties of the guard posts at the car park or the back entrances of the stadiums. Now he stepped forward with a clipboard.

"I have a note here to return you to the cap of the Dome if I see you."

"Oh no," Guy replied dismayed and ignored Teodor's shocked gasp. The fat soldier glanced at Teodor then turned to look at Guy:

"What did you do this time? The call came from Chart Segat's office itself."

Guy shrugged and tried to smile.

"Hey Benjy, you know me. A bit of this, a bit of that. Ain't nothing illegal, mind. You know that."

"I know you." Benjy reached to sweep the hair back from Guy's eyes, pushing his head back a little to look in his face.

"And I know Chart Segat, or rather I know things about Chart Segat I wish I didn't." He bent down and whispered in Guy's ear: "So just you get out of here, and don't come back tonight, do you hear me?"

As Teodor leant in to hear the whisper, Benjy noticed him again. He looked at him for a minute then screwed up his eyes in concentration:

"And I know you," he clicked his fingers as if trying to remember. Guy was thinking furiously. He had to find a way to get Teodor out too. To his surprise, he heard Teodor say:

"Sebastian, my name is Sebastian. I'm from Ho… the Riffaut."

"That's right, one of them lookalikes," the other guard said. Guy groaned inwardly. This would never work, as seemed to be confirmed by what Benjy said next: "You should be at the party upstairs, no?"

"No," Teodor said quickly, and then to Guy's unending horror and delight, the prince said: "I have a client back at the House. A good client…" Guy checked. Yes, Teodor had Benjy's full attention now, but did he know what he was doing?

"I can give you a cut if you let me get there on time," Teodor said.

Now Guy was struggling not to laugh, he wondered if the cameras had picked up this exchange. He thought no-one would ever believe this. Finally, he could hear Sebastian roaring with laughter inside his head.

"You Riffaut boys get paid on Monday, right?" Benjy said quickly. "Well, make sure you come and see me, or the next time I see you you'll wish you had."

Guy felt embarrassed for Benjy and his obvious greed. Teodor suddenly looked a little pale. Guy watched as slowly Teodor nodded once, then twice, then finally said:

"I will come back on Monday."

Benjy just nodded, ambled back to his chair by the door, then picked up his newspaper once more.

"Quick thinking, kiddo," Guy whispered, then with a laugh. "I can't believe you said that." Teodor blushed.

"Don't you dare tell anyone," Teodor said crossly. "I'm not a fashion model. I'll never be a fashion model."

"Oh, I agree," Guy said, "I'm not a fashion model either. I'll never be a fashion model. Ever."

"Let's go," said Guy, as the paper went up in front of the guard's face. Guy knew Benjy was doing his best not to see where they went. "We should run."

Guy led Teodor in a sprint along the full length of the back wall, all around the vast competition gym. Then they were out the far side and out onto a broad curving avenue that led down to the atrium. As the door closed behind them, Guy paused to take a breath and started down at a more leisurely pace. The avenue was crowded. The atrium below them more so. It was time to mingle with the throng.

"You realise how much money you just promised to Benjy back there?" Guy asked slyly, as they walked in measured leaps, careful not to draw attention to themselves. When Teodor did not reply, he added: "You know how much Sebastian is earning this weekend?"

"Of course, you and Sebastian are friends?"

"Oh yeah, we go way back," Guy said. "Even from before he had the surgery."

"Well, he did mention the money. He suggested that if I pretended to be him, I should offer the Dome Elite a five per cent cut, about five hundred, which is a lot for a Dome Elite."

Guy paused. He quickly did the calculation and the resulting number was a shock:

"Really, ten thousand? I did not know it was that much."

He did not speak for a long while, instead concentrated on weaving his way through a large crowd in the atrium. There was a crowd of people fifty deep trying to leave the Dome.

"The Dome is in lock down," Guy said grimly. He was looking at how all the entrances had been closed, and long lines of people were queuing. Guy saw that it was the boys who were being closely searched, and not too kindly either. The men and women were being ignored. He looked over to see if

Teodor had seen it too. The prince looked dazed and weary – so close to freedom, yet so far.

"They are checking everyone on exit," Guy said.

Teodor nodded. Guy could see he did not understand. "They're not all like Benjy."

"We need to get out," Teodor said, his voice pitched high in panic. "If we stand here much longer they will find us. They will take us."

"I know that," Guy said, taking his hand and squeezing it. "I know how we can get out too. It's just that the person I know who will get us out is not on duty yet."

"We can't stay here," Teodor repeated.

"No," Guy sighed and looked around. "We need to hide." Across from them, the crowds, lights and music of Bistro Jewel seemed to beckon.

"Are you hungry?"

"Starving," Teodor admitted. "But if we can get back to…"

"Just now we need to hide, come with me."

Guy and Teodor had been trying to pass through the busy Bistro Jewel unnoticed. Guy had had a word with the head waiter as he came in, and he had been pointed towards the staff door. There was a dance act performing on the staircase stage. Most eyes were on the girls in their skimpy costumes. Guy and Teodor just kept their heads low and made for the kitchen. They didn't count on…

"Hi Guy! Have you finished for tonight?" It was Marline.

"Hmm… hmm," replied Guy without commitment, then: "You look nice!" She had changed into a short red tutu, with a black corset, and a striped over-skirt ruched up to reveal her legs and underclothes.

"They charged me fifteen hundred for this dress. Can you imagine? The first time I've had to pay. Still, I'll get four thousand two hundred for the party. I had to pay for the shoes too," she sighed. "I hope he notices me."

"Who?" Guy asked.

She preened a moment, then added: "I was at Chartsie's table for dinner, and I have been invited to Simon Ssochen's Magnolia Party. It's themed as Space Pirates." She pushed out her hip to show a fake sword.

"Guy," Teodor hissed, urgently miming the need for speed.

"Simon's saying he'll invite some of us girls to his island. You know, Paradise Bay?" She nodded seriously. "It's well paid, because it will be a whole week away. Anyway, I'm hoping he'll pick me."

"Guy," Teodor insisted in a whisper, but Marline noticed him and she was annoyed to be interrupted:

"Aren't you two supposed to be upstairs? Didn't Chartsie ask you to work?" She was talking to Guy, but looking at Teodor.

Oh no, thought Guy. Because he could think of nothing else, he reached up, turned her face towards him and away from Teodor. However, Marline was not easily distracted. She turned again to look at Teodor. Guy could see she was assessing him with a professional eye. Guy decided he would have to take the risk.

"I too want to be free, Marlene," he whispered firmly. She took a last look at Teodor. When she turned back to Guy her face was grim and still.

"They are looking for…" she hesitated, "for all the Riffaut models."

"I have to free him," Guy said anxiously.

"And he's going to pay you?" Marline said sharply, "How much?"

"More money," Guy searched for an answer to impress her. "More money than you could earn in a year."

Marline nodded approvingly.

"Well, Des is on duty from seven in the bistro tunnel. He always lets us girls sneak home for a snack or change of clothes. He'll let you through."

"Yes, I know"

"You'll need to hide until then."

"Yes, I know," said Guy. He shook Teodor, who was staring at Marline. "Let's go!"

"Good luck, Guy," Marline called after them.

"Was she your girlfriend?" Teodor whispered to Guy.

"Yes," Guy replied confidently.

"How old is she?"

"Fourteen."

Teodor frowned.

"But Simon Ssochen is about a hundred years old."

"I know, but Marline wants to be very rich. And Simon Ssochen is rich, you know?"

"She knew Chart Segat."

"Everyone in the Dome knows Chartsie," Guy replied with a sigh. "Don't worry, she won't tell. She's also my best friend."

The chef was coming towards them: "Now hush, let me do the talking."

Chapter 28. Soap Suds

The borgs had stopped. Zak had done it again, he had isolated the code that Karl needed to stop the borgs. Only now Karl faced two dozen Dome Elite guards. As he stood before them in his natural state, he could tell that they recognised him. Their only confusion was finding him at the heart of their Dome.

That won't last long, thought Karl. As he watched he saw one, then another of the Elite reaching for their blades.

Time to go. Karl dived through the doors and down the stairwell where he had seen Teodor escape and sprinted in pursuit. He shape-shifted back to a Freyne Dome Elite as he ran, but he was aware this might no longer protect him. Still at the entrance to the gym, the two door guards barely looked at Karl's ID. Karl headed across the gym and out to the atrium. The scene that greeted him was chaotic.

The last games had just finished and crowds were making for the exit. At the same time the Dome had gone into lockdown. All the doors out of the atrium were shut or heavily manned and Dome Elite were demanding the IDs of everyone. There would be no escaping through those doors.

'Where was the prince?'

***

Teodor found himself wearing a hat as well as an apron, and he was washing dishes. He had a little brush for scrubbing and a deep bowl of hot water and suds.

"The deal is," Guy explained, "we wash dishes until Joe arrives at seven, then we get supper for free. It's only fifteen minutes."

Teodor looked around the busy kitchen.

"Hiding in plain view. Are you sure we can't use a communicator?"

"No, they are all on the Dome network. They would recognise our voices straightaway, and then they would have us. Look, there are three exits here. They think we're trying to get out, they won't be looking for us here."

They worked in silence for a few moments. Teodor was uneasy. Surely the simplest thing now was to call his mother? He glanced around the kitchen, there were three doors he could see, but could he trust Guy? Teodor saw the burnt communicator on his wrist. The boy had saved his life, not just once, but in the climb down as well. They had got this far, just meters from the exit. He watched as Guy's Dome medallion slipped out from behind his apron. Guy caught it before it dipped into the soap suds.

"Why are you helping me?" Teodor nodded purposefully at Guy's medallion, still in his hand. "You're one of them, aren't you? You're Dome Elite Junior. Aren't you?"

"Not yet," Guy replied firmly.

Teodor wanted to believe him, so he said nothing, just waited.

"I want to join the Dome Elite. I want to join it very much. I'm the best blades fighter of my age in the Dome, and…"

"You're good at maths," Teodor finished thoughtfully. He spoke slowly now. He had to discover the truth. "So why would you not get a place?"

"Because I'm not registered, but Chart Segat said if I…"

Guy hesitated.

"If you what? What did Chart Segat want?"

"It was not a fair fight tonight," Guy said. "You being without protection. Both of us fighting with live blades."

"Yes, that was Chart Segat, he organised it that way," Teodor agreed. He added in a conciliatory way: "You didn't know."

"No, I didn't know until I cut you. Look, I'm sorry…"

"Don't change the subject. Tell me about Chart Segat." Teodor could see that Guy might have turned and walked or even run away, but they were chained to that spot by the duty they had to do the dishes. Teodor took a pan and rinsed it to give him time to breathe.

313

"I think they hoped… I think they thought I might kill you. When I went to knife your heart, I thought you were wearing protection. If I had cut you…"

"I pushed you aside though," Teodor remembered. "Just," he admitted with a sigh.

"I didn't want to kill you. I honestly thought… I have never fought anyone without protection before. I mean, it's basic Dome procedure. You fight blades – you wear protection. Not even the champions fight…" Guy faltered: "well, you hear stories of blades fights to the death, but I thought they were just that: stories."

"Guy, this is not about the blades fight. You were forced just as much as I was, I can see that. But even when you knew I was unprotected, even when you saw I was your prince, you were desperate to beat me. You must have known there would be consequences if you hurt me."

Guy did not speak for a few moments. He was shaking his head in denial, but not saying anything. Teodor waited. He was starting to wonder whether he should have trusted Guy at all.

"They told me I had to do what Chart Segat said. Whatever he said," Guy said shakily. "And if I did not…"

"What?" Teodor insisted, a little harshly. "What would make you consider killing your prince?"

"He would have…"

"What?" Teodor insisted.

"He said he would throw me to his borgs. He meant to…" Teodor stared at him, willing him to tell the truth. Something he could believe. Guy flinched under his gaze, then continued with new conviction:

"He would have locked me in that cage with two, maybe four, cyborgs. I would only have a blunted blade. He would have watched as they tormented, then killed me."

When Teodor spoke, it was if he was in a dream:

"He would throw you to his borgs. The only question, then, is how long before you died? An hour, six hours, a day?"

Guy swallowed nervously, so Teodor concluded:

"I didn't think he actually meant it."

314

"I didn't think he would do it either," Guy agreed. "Not to me. But there's this boy, Des. He's a friend of mine. He won the Dome Junior championship and the Emperor's medal. That was three years ago. He was just fourteen. Chart Segat sent him to fight the Battle Borgs."

He looked at Teodor. Now the prince had to know too. He said quietly: "Des was wearing his victor's gold, and some basic protective gear, I think. They let him have his own hand blades but still they made him fight for his life. Fight for his life for nearly three hours." Teodor reached out to steady Guy, holding his arm firmly as Guy swayed and blinked back tears.

"Des Parks? I know him," repeated Teodor. "I have his poster..."

Guy nodded slowly, but then he stopped. Teodor was pointing.

"Des Parks," he repeated. Guy turned to see Des standing looking at them.

"Marline told me I'd find you here."

Teodor and Guy exchanged glances. They were caught.

Des nodded to Teodor: "What's he still doing here?"

Guy replied calmly:

"The Dome is in lockdown. We can't get out. We needed something to eat."

He waved at the dishes they had cleaned. Teodor was glad that, for once, Guy was straightforward.

"I have duty in the bistro tunnel," Des said quietly.

"I know," Guy replied. "I was thinking, hoping, you might help?"

"Chartsie wants both of you back upstairs."

"Please Des. I did not win the fight."

"No, you didn't." He shot a glance of admiration at Teodor. "But you didn't lose either. I guess you both have to get out. I guess I'll have to close my eyes a moment while on duty?"

Des sounded fierce, but he winked at Teodor.

"Get your supper to go, and come with me. Where are you going to go?"

Teodor saw Guy hesitate, so he replied instead:

"Magnolia Palace."

315

Des shook his head regretfully: "All the bridges are closed."

"We'll have to use the south tunnel then," Guy said with a wince.

"You'll only get in by West Street," Des said. "And only if you get there quick."

Teodor wished he knew what they were talking about. West Street was a long avenue through Domeside. Was that the shortest way out?

"Go up to the attic now and eat your supper. You'll think of something. If you're quick, and if the tunnel goes all the way under the river as they say…"

"You're talking about the old network," Teodor interrupted eagerly, at last having something to say. "Yes, it comes out near the stables. My father told me."

Des lifted his hand, and pressing his index finger to his thumb, mimed for Teodor to be silent. Teodor stepped towards him, and in a whisper, he said:

"Why are you helping us? You were with Chart Segat at breakfast."

"And I told Chartsie what he was doing was not right."

"Yes, I know."

"But that's not the main reason, you heard what Guy just told you." Teodor looked at him closely. He wanted to believe him.

"They did it to me, they'll do it to him." Des pointed at Guy. "He's got no mother and no father. Just like me. Just get him out of here and don't send him back. You have to protect Guy. Promise me?"

Teodor hesitated, should he give his word?

"You have to promise, Prince Teodor. Otherwise, he'll be next. Chart Segat will throw Guy to the borgs, only this time he'll throw away the key as well. So give me your word, prince. Protect Guy."

Teodor was pale, as he finally understood. They were both speaking the truth. Des had used his title twice. Teodor knew exactly what he wanted. They needed his protection as their prince. He had to help them.

"As your prince, and Imperial Prince of all Freyne, I swear I will protect you, Guy Erma. So help me God."

It was an oath. Both Guy and Des saluted him, fists firm against their hearts. He nodded once. He could not fail now. In his head he heard a voice:

Now run, Teodor. Run.

***

Karl was sitting drinking coffee. He reached out with his telepathy. All at once his hands felt wet and soapy.

'Washing up?' he thought, bemused. 'But where?'

Not far away, he thought.

Karl had been able to hear the prince quite clearly ever since he walked into the House Jewel bistro. He had taken a table while he tried to fix on the exact location. The waiting staff had been quick to bring him drinks. He sipped the refreshment without tasting it, all the time listening to the prince.

Where were the kitchens?

Teodor clearly did not trust Guy Erma just yet, and Karl was thankful for that. He listened in on the conversation and sighed. Chart Segat had to go.

Karl saw the young Dome Elite at the same time as Teodor did. The prince was caught. Karl stood up, his drink spilling over the table. Then he saw them. The kitchen was open plan. Now he had turned he could see straight in, past the rows of cookers, past the prep tables to the far wall. He could see the young guard and the water pipes on the wall. He could not see the sink or the basin, but Prince Teodor and Guy Erma must be just there. It was all the equipment buzzing in the kitchen that made the connection seem distant.

The back tunnel, thought Karl. He checked his maps and he understood:

Now run, Teodor. Run.

***

"Frederon – where is my son?"

Sayginn knew she sounded like a banshee, but then why not? Hers was the desperate scream of a despairing mother. The Emperor had just arrived back from the Dome alone. He stood a moment, speechless, at the bottom of

317

the stairs. Sayginn sped across the ballroom on her hover chair. Now she was on the first step, barring his progress. Her grief knew no bounds.

"You promised me. If I agreed to marry you, you would give me my son."

"Sayginn, calm down. Let's step into the library, shall we?"

Inside the dark room where the lights of the Dome served as the only illumination, Sayginn manoeuvred herself forward on the chair, aiming punches at the Emperor while he ducked out of the way. She wanted to hit him. To kill him. This was all his fault. And she hated him. The Emperor stumbled back till perched against a table, he caught her fists and held them.

"You promised me, Frederon, you promised me."

As he continued to hold her arms, Sayginn sat, helplessly weeping. At last, Frederon went to pour himself a drink.

"Chart Segat does not know where he is. The Elite are looking for him. Looking for him for real now."

"Looking for him for real. You're saying Chart Segat and the Elite have had him all this time?"

Frederon nodded.

"Chart Segat used the Battle Borgs. Somehow he reprogrammed their base loyalty routines. They did whatever Chart Segat told them."

"And you knew?"

"Well, I did not know they would use Battle Borgs – the boy must have been terrified."

Sayginn could barely breathe for the waves of anger and despair that were running through her.

"My only son, Freddie. He was all I had left. My boy."

Sayginn could stand it no longer. She put her face in her hands and sobbed. After a while, Frederon sat down on a footstool nearby, drinking slowly.

"You were always so independent. That boy was your weak spot. I thought if I showed you. I thought you would see how you needed my protection."

"But why, Frederon? Why?"

318

"Chart Segat said there was an Imperial bastard. Not one of mine, a bastard who had been fathered by Erederon. I wanted to believe. I thought I could trust him. I wanted you to be my wife. I wanted my son's bastard to be my son…"

"And Teodor?"

"I never meant any harm to come to him. Chart Segat was supposed to take and hold him, hold him for twenty-four hours. I was right. In that time, you did agree to become my wife. I don't know if it started going wrong from the beginning, with the shooting in the cathedral. If I had known…"

"But what happened to him, Frederon? Where is Teodor now?"

"He escaped. There was an explosion, and he escaped."

"But how?"

"He had that boy with him. I don't know what Chart Segat did to either, or in fact both, of them, but they ran like scared rabbits. It looks like they made it out by climbing down the columns of the Dome. They have had some help. Whom did you send in there? Is it Killer Valvanski?"

Sayginn did not reply.

"He is slaughtering them. He detonated a snake droid in the cap of the Dome, and then he attacked the Dome Elite at a bottle neck at the top of some stairs. Who knows how many he has killed, how many he has injured?"

Sayginn said nothing. She picked up a picture of Prince Teodor from a table.

"Sayginn, he hacked the Dome computers. Chart told me they think he got everything, and then he set viruses that deleted everything else. It's complete chaos over there. And now we should assume he knows."

Sayginn reached to take a picture of Serge and Deodran.

"Now he knows about the small war Serge and Chart initiated, that you turned a blind eye to, on Sas Darona."

"Serge did not start any covert war. And I have not turned a blind eye to it. The Freyne recognise Zaracan sovereignty on Sas Darona," Sayginn said quietly.

"Yes, and I am sure the Valvanchi will believe you after this." Frederon said nothing. "Chart says he will use the Battle Borgs to bring the prince back, but you must call off Karl Valvanchi."

"Call off Karl Valvanchi? Of course."

Frederon wrapped his arms around her.

"Sayginn, darling, please. Just let me handle it. Chartsie trusts me." He held her there and then said, with new compassion and eagerness, "He can see. We're in this together now. I will find him. Then tonight we will celebrate, just you and me, man and woman, and tomorrow we will be married."

Sayginn placed the photo of Serge and Deodran face down on the table, perhaps hoping they had not heard what the Emperor had said. She was left holding the photo of Teodor, holding it tightly in two hands. The door burst open behind her.

"Regent Sayginn. We've found him. It's a definite match. Three cy-roaches and cy-rats! They have beamed in his exact location. I think we can get him out."

Sayginn looked up. She briefly kissed Teodor's photo, then turned to Frederon.

"Marry you? You still think I am going to marry you after all this? I would not marry you if you were the last man left alive."

***

With a small pack of food stowed in Guy's backpack, Teodor and Guy sprinted along the maintenance tunnel that connected the bistro to Old Mill Lane and up the eight flights of stairs to the top. All the doors into the main house were closed, and as they raced through the attic workshops, the rooms were dark with only moonlight shining down on the tidied tables. At last they found themselves in the small attic bedroom, and they picked their way through the sleeping children to a high window and climbed up and out onto a high widow's peak balcony. It was barely wide enough for two people to stand comfortably, being just an ornament at the highest point of House Jewel. There was an unparalleled view, with the Dome looming behind, Domeside with its bright avenues laid out below them, the black stretch of river, and beyond (Teodor thought more hopefully) the lights of Magnolia Palace. It still looked a long way away.

"I still can't quite believe we were up inside that thing. We climbed down from the top." Teodor nodded towards the Dome. "How on earth did you ever find such an exit? You must have been petrified."

"Not really, I have to climb it with ropes twice a year during the Spring Sweep; most of the boys know how to do it. Obviously most don't use it to escape from Chart Segat."

"Ah, the spring sweep. I was going to that one year, but my mother decided it was too dangerous. I think my father wanted me to have a go. It's to do with cleaning the inside of the Dome, isn't it?"

"Yes, they have to send droids up to do the actual cleaning, but the droids can get lost or keep going around in circles, so they send us kids up to lay down the ropes."

"But is that strictly necessary? Could they not just programme some super droid? And why do they need new ropes?"

"The ropes have to be replaced each year because the cleaning deteriorates them so badly they can break. As for the droids, they're expensive. Kids are cheap and quick. I can climb to the top of the Dome is less than thirty minutes. So it's cheap kids and ropes versus expensive cleaning fluids and droids. If a droid goes round in circles, or gets lost, it not only wastes time, it also costs more in terms of battery power and cleaning fluid. I think they did a study to show that by laying the ropes, kids can cut the overall cost by about forty per cent." Guy hesitated. "Besides, it's great fun. It's become one of the great Domeside traditions. They always lay on a fantastic lunch afterwards."

"You don't get paid?"

Guy shook his head.

"There's a big fuss if you make the fastest time. But, of course, going fast is dangerous."

Resolutely, they both turned with their backs to the Dome. There were no chairs, so they sat cross-legged on the floor. Guy shared out the food with careful precision. For several moments they just ate. The food was only partially warm, but they were ravenous. Teodor wiped his face on the paper wrapping. Guy was wiping his hands on his shirt and peering down.

"Des was right. They have locked the bridges."

Teodor was looking back to the entrance to the Dome. The security was tight – everyone, whether they were coming in or going out, was being searched. Where was the Regency Defence? He searched but could not see any red and silver uniforms at all. Why had his mother not sent them to find him?

"Shouldn't we be moving?"

"Eat first, we're going to need to be fast. So eat first."

Teodor saw something move. It was a glittering beetle. He reached to pick it up. A cy-roach. He let it nibble on a cut on his finger and then all at once he snapped it between his finger and thumb, and the cy-roach curled up into a small, blinking metallic ball. Teodor slipped the blinking ball into his pocket and did the same a second time. This time he put the blinking roach into Guy's pocket.

"What's that?"

"It's a beacon. They will see it and know you are one of the good guys."

"And that?" A large rat had raced over the roof. Teodor picked it up and let it nuzzle the cut on his neck.

"This rat is telling the Regency Defence exactly where I am."

"Great," Guy said, unconvinced. He pointed at a double line of Dome Elite jogging purposefully out of the Dome. About forty in all, he thought. They were coming down Old Mill Lane, it was not far. With their helmets reflecting the moonlight they looked like deadly beetles. Guy pointed:

"They know where we are."

"Des?" asked Teodor.

Guy's face darkened. "I hope he just told them straight out. You know he would not have had much choice."

"Would they have beaten him?"

"Even if they did, he would only have told them the minimum. He will have wanted to buy us some time. Even as they search the house we'll have time, but we must get moving."

"But how?" The line of Dome Elite had split into three; they were entering by several places. "They're coming in on all sides."

322

"It's dangerous," Teodor nodded grimly. He was still holding and stroking the cy-rat. Now, with regret, he placed it down on the ground. So Guy said: "Follow me."

"Look!" cried Teodor and pointed. Across the river, three hover cars were taking off from Magnolia Palace. Guy shook his head briefly.

"They won't get here in time. We have to go."

"They know where we are," Teodor said. "They know we're alive."

"C'mon, we need to stay that way."

Guy leapt over the high railing and landed lightly on the roof. Bending low, so his hands touched the floor, he ran along the ridge to the first chimney. He shimmied around and over it and then waved Teodor forward. Teodor was already over the railing, and he followed as quickly he dared, using his hands to balance as well as his feet. They climbed around the chimney stack. There was another ridge. Feet facing forward they slid and gripped their way down a last ridge to the roof's edge. There they paused. Guy was standing on the outer edge, looking down and then over to the next building. The roof overhung the road, but there was still a gap onto the next building. Guy checked briefly with Teodor. He ran a few steps up the tiles before turning, running, and leaping. He had landed firmly on the next house.

"It's not bad," he called. "Just take a run at it."

Teodor did exactly as Guy had done and threw himself through the air. He was relieved to feel Guy's hand grabbing and pulling him in, and then the shooting started. From a window in House Jewel several floors below, a Dome Elite Battle Borg leant out and shot up at them.

"C'mon," said Guy, and taking Teodor by the hand he climbed up the ridge and over the top. The shots followed them, with tiles exploding close by and fragments rushing by their hands and feet. They leapt over the far side, only it was slippery. Guy used his feet to brake his descent down the far side. Not so Teodor, he was unbalanced by a blast under his feet and fell over the edge, landing on his behind. The tiles were as sleek as a child's slide. Guy reached to catch him as he slipped past, but lost his foot-hold, and fell on top of Teodor, and the two rolled fast, across and down to where the two steep roofs met at right angles. Teodor caught a foot in each of the two gutters and braced his back into the corner. He pulled Guy over towards him, even as the boy flailed on the very edge.

Teodor was firmly wedged in the corner of the sloped roofs. Guy screamed, as he looked into the emptiness, seemingly unaware of the two arms hugging and rolling him onto the next roof. Teodor's feet were jamming and kicking Guy trainers into the gutters. The fall stopped as soon as it had started. Teodor reached out to touch Guy, as he shuddered and wailed in fear beside him.

"C'mon, get up!" Teodor cried.

Guy shook in a negative, shuddering reply.

"Calm, Guy. Control!" shouted Teodor. "Say it! Calm, Guy, control!" The shudder slowed to a quiver, and Guy stared towards him.

"Calllmmm..."

"Calm, Guy! Control!" Teodor was up now, bending over the other boy. Guy nodded and swallowed. Sitting upright, he shouted: "Calm, Guy! Control!" His voice was clear and strong.

"C'mon!" yelled Teodor. "Let's go." Guy now followed Teodor as they quickly ran along, then up the last pointed roof. The two boys were quick because they had to be quick. Bullets ricocheted as they came over the rim and slid down the far side. Cy-rats were running alongside them. Teodor saw one rat leap high in the air, in the path of a bullet. It fell down dead. That bullet might have hit him, he realised. Unexpectedly, a Dome Battle Borg stood on the flat window top; but as they were approaching there was a blur of fur at his ankles, he went to kick away the rats, and suddenly he was falling. Guy snatched the rifle from his opening hands. The leap was not as small as either boy would have liked, but then they didn't have enough time to worry. They had made it to the roof of the Riffaut.

All around them, crisscrossing bullets multiplied. Hiding in the shadow of the small box window, Teodor realised it would be impossible to escape over to the flat roof whilst they were so hemmed in by lethal exploding munitions. He looked round. Just three Battle Borgs on House Jewel, two more had appeared on the far side of Old Mill Lane.

'Is that all?' thought Teodor. 'Where are the Dome Elite?' Guy was firing at all of them at random. Teodor saw he was actually firing over the heads of their attackers.

"It's all right Guy. Those aren't Dome Elite, they are borgs?"

"Borgs?" Guy peered out. "They have reprogrammed the borgs."

"I think so. Come on."

Teodor knew it was time to take the initiative when a head appeared above them and to the right, next to the Riffaut's chimney.

"Give me that!" He grabbed the rifle and leapt onto the flat window box. First, he downed the borg by the chimney, even as it dived into the road. Teodor sent a volley of shots to the right. One borg was hit and the two other on House Jewel's roof dived for cover. Finally, Teodor aimed an arching blast across Old Mill Lane. Satisfied, Teodor grabbed Guy by the hand. Both ran up and over, and down onto a flat roof.

Another borg.

With the rifle under his arm and pointed ahead, Teodor fired with cruel accuracy. Beside him Guy flinched, as what had been a man fell under foot. Teodor grabbed Guy by the hand and together they leapt over the prostrate form. Guy curled his ankles and knees high as the destroyed borg reached up to grab his legs. Cy-rats bore down on him. Teodor did not even look. He was firing again. Guy squinted at the hard-set youthful features. Was not Prince Teodor reputed to be delicate and gentle? He was known for his charity works and his shy singing in the cathedral. Teodor glanced towards him. Guy was shocked by the fierce flame in his blue eyes.

Left, right, left, the race was not over. They leapt onto the far, steep roof, a box window, then onto to the Pleasure Palace, across another roof, another leap. The two boys now risked all to escape. Climb, slip, brake down, leap, then run. Panting Teodor led the way, tightly holding Guy's hand. Always sprinting, steep upwards incline, toes digging desperately into the slope, his heart pounding lest his well-worn boots should slip! Over the top, gauging the landing even as they fell. Knees bent for maximum deceleration if it was sloped, landing in a desperate sprint if it was flat.

A voice called out inside Teodor's head:

Go Teo, go! Don't look back! Don't slow down. Go! Now your only hope is in speed.

He looked to where Guy ran beside him, exactly level with him, matching him pace for pace, leap for leap. He wondered that they should be so equally matched in strength and determination. In the wind of their acceleration, he thought he could hear the words of a song Guy was murmuring.

'It's better than spending a life without riding the Whirlwind, Domeside Whirlwind.'

The race stopped as abruptly as it started. Teodor and Guy found themselves looking out into the emptiness of four large avenues: Beacon Place, Domeside Avenue ahead, Old Mill Lane to the right and West Street to the left. Teodor was angry as he looked down into the emptiness; there would be no escape from this building, either down onto the road or back the way they had come! He had taken a wrong leap! Hiding behind a metallic air-conditioning system, he looked back to see that their pursuers were in some disarray, seemingly fighting amongst themselves. Guy tugged on his sleeve, and pulled him to the top of a metallic fire-ladder:

"Look! West Street, and it's still unguarded. He did it. Des kept his mouth shut. We must run."

Guy was skidding down a last line of tiles and leaping onto a metal fire escape. Then he was powering down the metal stair. Teodor, spurred on by his words, chased him hard, so they landed almost on top of each other at the bottom. Guy led them back into the darkness of the narrowing alleyway.

"Help me with this." He had a hand on a sewer cap. They heaved it open and below was a ladder. Teodor hesitated, thinking grimly of his earlier experience in the sewers, but Guy just said impatiently:

"Just go down a bit. I'll need your help to pull this cap back." Teodor did what he was told. He climbed down a few rungs, but stayed up the top of the ladder. Guy slipped down beside him and together they pulled the cap back over their heads. Guy sighed with relief as they finally got it to fall flat into position.

"That should buy us a bit more time. Closing the entrance, they won't be sure where we've gone."

"Cy-wolves could smell us?" said Teodor.

"No, the Dome Elite don't have those, but they will guess soon enough. Time to get our blades back on. Switch on your torch."

"How far is it?"

"I don't know."

"How do we find our way?"

"We keep going down until we get to the lowest level and then we look for the tunnel."

"Is that it?"

326

"There are these," said Guy, shining his torch up at a strange, ancient gargoyle. It looked out of place, as if it had been moved and cemented upon the modern wall as decoration. "There are more of them as you go lower. We are looking for one that is shaped like a fish. The tunnel we need is itself very damp. Some say it's flooded further down. I don't rightly know. Anyway, it's our only chance."

"The floor is uneven."

"I know but I don't want to take my blades off yet. We'd be too easy to catch."

"We'll stick together…"

***

"They're in the sewers," Nell said unnecessarily. Nell and Sayginn were standing side by side in front of the laser representation of the Dome and its surrounding areas. Teodor and Guy were now represented by two red avatars with red beacons beating at their hearts. It was the signal coming from the cyroaches in their pockets. Karl Valvanchi had his own green avatars, and he was closing in from a different direction on the same point. Dome Elite and cyborgs were represented by a host of grey shapes milling in-between.

"If they can make it to this tunnel, they might go all the way under the river."

"No, we need to get them out before that," said Sayginn. "That tunnel is ancient and not in good repair. Also, look how complicated the route is. How would they find their way in the dark?"

"They're going so fast," said Nell.

"They're running on blades," replied Sayginn. "It's not very safe. It's not easy even on flat and straight ground, through narrow corridors, round blind bends and with irregular flooring."

As they watched, the two avatars seemed to tumble over each other, there was a pause, and then they set off again.

"Oh!" Nell said. "Oh no."

"What?" said Sayginn?

"They've taken a wrong turn. Oh, look at those Dome Elite, Battle Borgs too."

Sayginn peered at the map graphic, and the trajectory of her son.

"Oh no…"

Nell reached a microphone.

"Uncle Karl, can you see this? You've got to hurry up. You've got to get there first."

"I'm on my way." Karl's voice was warm and calm. Sayginn heard it and felt it spread through her mind and body.

***

Using small, efficient, accurate leaps they made their way along the maintenance tunnel, then Guy opened another grille and they lowered themselves into an older tunnel beneath. They heard footsteps even as they dropped through the hole. Guy scampered back up the ladder to close the grille and Teodor quickly climbed up to help. They were both crouched in the darkness as heavy boots passed overhead. Guy kept taking the lowest path. The tunnels kept getting darker, smaller and lower. They heard gunshots behind and above them, and the echoes of running feet.

The gargoyles did start to multiply. Now they started to look like they belonged, sticking out just above head height from the crumbling walls. Here, the tunnels were cleaner. There were fire exit signs, colourful posters advertising Magnolia specials and bright yellow lights.

"This is the touristy bit," muttered Guy. As they turned a corner they found themselves face-to-face with two Dome Elite Battle Borgs coming down from above. Guy threw himself backwards, stretching his body across Teodor's and pressing him back into the darkness of the wall.

The borgs kept coming. Guy was fumbling at his neck for his Dome medallion.

"Don't!" Teodor warned. "You're wanted too."

Teodor looked back along the corridor. It was narrow and straight, and even if they ran they would be easy targets. He turned back when he heard a thump. At the borgs' back, there was a man with white hair, he had leapt

328

down the stairwell. Now he raised his hand. The borgs stopped. The man turned towards Guy and Teodor. Teodor put up his hand to shield his vision from the bright lights shining like lasers from the man's eyes. The man looked at them both, then back up the stairs. More boots, more soldiers or borgs, were coming. All at once, he pointed at a black door marked 'private' across the corridor. As he pointed, the lock sprang and the door opened. Teodor quickly pointed his torch down the tunnel and found a fish gargoyle beyond.

"Go!" Teodor urged Guy, pushing him forward.

Keeping as much distance as they could between themselves and the alien, they leapt neatly down the indicated tunnel and looked back relieved as it slammed and locked behind them. As gunfire started again, they turned and sprinted down into darkness.

"That was too close," Guy said.

Teodor reflected that Guy might be talking about the Zaracan soldier, as much as he was of the Dome Elite.

"I think – no, I don't think, I know – that was Karl Valvanchi."

"Great, that's supposed to reassure me?"

"Perhaps not, but we know which side he is against."

They raced on. The tunnel was running steeply down now and with every leap it was getting more damp. Teodor touched the wall with relief: at last, they were under the river.

***

Karl Valvanchi counted five frozen Dome Elite. All were borgs. This did not surprise him. The men of the Dome Elite were noticeable by their absence. Ever since he had left the Dome it had been the same. He saw them running purposefully to orders, but he also saw them hold their blades and not throw them.

Loyal to Empire

The Dome Elite now knew they were in pursuit of their prince. Karl had a feeling that most of them thought this was wrong. So they had stepped aside, turned away, let him slip through their ranks. Without their tacit complicity,

329

he would never have got to this tunnel, to this position, to face off the Battle Borgs.

But now he was trapped. There was only one way out and at the top were the Dome Elite. They had let him in, but would they let him escape?

He took one last look at the fallen Battle Borgs and headed off through the same door Teodor and Guy had gone. His fate would be the same as theirs. If the boys escaped, he would escape. If the boys failed, he would fail.

***

Guy stopped. The tunnel was old, narrow, slippery and slimy. Now they were running through water. Just when they thought they could go no longer, the tunnel dipped again. The passage was now full of water.

"We have to go on. There's still air," Teodor said.

"It's still going down," Guy replied, pointing.

Teodor took time to look at the slope in the tunnel. With the water at this level it would be fully submerged in just a few meters.

"Let's look."

They carried on until they were submerged to the neck, and still the tunnel descended. There was a sign on the wall. It read: Freyne River Tunnel Administration. Across these words, the line of the water was clear. From the second 'n' in Tunnel, the words disappeared in the water. Guy reached up to cling onto the edge of the metal sign. Thankfully, it did not move. He could feel his legs being dragged and pushed on a strong current, ebbing and flowing.

"I'll try to swim," Teodor said. He grabbed the torch between his teeth.

"Don't go far," Guy replied.

Teodor just shook his head and dived. Alone in the dark, Guy pulled his own torch up out of the water. It flickered. He gave it a shake. He was trying to reach the inscription on the side. Were these fully waterproof? He fiddled with the torch for a while, then started to wonder about the prince. How long had he been underwater?

Just then, Teodor re-emerged with a smile.

330

"It's not far, it's not far. C'mon."

Guy shook his head briefly.

"You can't swim, can you?"

"Not well," Guy replied.

"Hang on to my waist and kick with your legs. Like a battlement kick we do in training, can you do that?" Guy nodded. "Oh and hold your breath. It's not far."

Under the water, still wearing their blades, they were stretched out like a long eel. Guy held firm onto Teodor's hips, and then realised he was in the way of Teodor's legs. Guy drew himself up, so his head rested on Teodor's backside. As Teodor's legs kicked the water beneath, he thrashed with his legs, wishing this was over.

The tidal movement was stronger under water, and they were rolled up against the wall. Guy lost his grip on Teodor and desperately reached to grab his waist band, only to feel Teodor reach down beside him and hook his hand into his belt, and then they were swimming again. When the wave came again, Guy held on tight, feeling them turn and twist in its curve, hugging hard onto Teodor and kicking as hard as he could. They spun once, then twice and finally righted themselves again. At least, Guy thought, they were the right way up. Guy found himself fighting to hold his lips tight together but his nostrils flared in fear. He felt at any moment he might burst if he did not breathe, then he felt something different.

Teodor had his feet on the floor. Guy reached his blades down to touch down as well. Next they were both powering along, legs pumping, arms wrapped around each other. The floor curved upwards. They were stumbling out of the water, Guy slipping at the very last so they tumbled to the ground, Guy's head falling onto Teodor's chest. They lay a few moments in the shallows, breathing hard and looking at how light from their torches reflected on the water and radiated around the new tunnel. Neither boy noticed that the beacon lights had gone out of the cy-roaches in their pockets.

***

Karl burst up out of the water and gasped for breath. Behind him was a sign, it read: Freyne River Tunnel Administration; from the second 'n' in Tunnel, the words disappeared into the water.

"Damn."

He reached down to his feet and pulled out the borg. It was not breathing. It was not moving. All its systems were waterlogged. In effect, it had drowned. Karl dived into the water again. He came back up a second time, dragging the second borg after him. It too had drowned.

He stood looking down where the tunnel disappeared under water. Both borgs had followed him. Then both had dived into the tunnel after the boys. Both had drowned. He paused. He checked his records. He scanned the maps inside his mind, looking. He connected with the graphics in Magnolia Palace.

For a moment, he touched Sayginn's mind as she paced alongside the vast three-dimensional image. The Cy-roach beacons had gone out. The two small red avatars had come to a standstill here.

He would have to dive again. This time he would have to look for bodies.

He sat down in the water. His head in his hands, he despaired.

Had they drowned? Were there bodies just a few feet away in these dark waters?

Karl was careful to shield his thoughts from Sayginn, but he knew Nikato was listening. Karl could see him too. Nikato was sitting quietly at a terminal, staring at an unchanging screen, not daring to look at either the Regent or his niece, both pacing impatiently around the large graphical display.

Karl heard something, and looked around. A patrol of six Dome Elite had arrived in the tunnel. They were men, not borgs. They stopped, taking it all in. The tunnel sloped away into the water. The two drowned borgs. Karl Valvanchi sitting with his head in his hands. He looked at them. He took a breath. He could not think of anything to say. Standing up, he took three deep breaths. He set aside any weapon, tool or gadget he did not need, placing them on dry ground at the feet of the Dome Elite as he dived once again into the water.

***

Guy coughed and spluttered while Teodor coughed, laughed and stroked his hair.

"Oh, that was good," said Teodor.

"I thought you said it was not far."

"I didn't think you would go."

"It felt like we were in a washing machine."

"Yes, but could you not feel the waves were propelling us upwards? It was harder swimming back to get you."

"I see," Guy said doubtfully. "I'm happy to believe you."

Teodor pushed Guy off him, then helped him to his feet. They both stood shaking, and tried to wipe the water from their limbs. Guy shivered.

"We can't stop here," said Teodor, pointing his torch up. The tunnel rose steeply now. "Let's run."

It was exciting to know they were coming out. This spurred them to run faster than their ebbing strength should have allowed. The tunnel on this side of the river was different. The fish gargoyles were less frequent or had been removed. Frequently at junctions they found the tunnels had been blocked by new building. After a while, emergency lighting came on, and it was clear the tunnel was used on occasion for maintenance. Finally, they stood at the junction of three tunnels. They pointed their torches up at the roof, looking for signs. The only fish gargoyle they could find was back the way they had come. The three tunnels were otherwise identical.

"There!" said Teodor at last. He pointed his torch at a small painted tile some way down the tunnel on the left. "The symbol of my house, these will lead us to the palace."

They followed the tiles along a narrow corridor. From the occasional lone tile, it became a line of tiles, and then a mosaic. There were ladders leading up from the tunnels as well. Each ladder looked new and was marked with numbers. Teodor climbed up one, but leapt back, disappointed:

"Locked. The covers are locked. Oh, where are the cameras?"

They continued on, two more ladders. Teodor climbed up to try the covers. The same result, the covers were locked, how would they get out of the tunnel? They had reached the end wall. Teodor looked back the way they had come, and climbed up the last ladder again. Guy found and opened a panel in the far wall. There was another tunnel, a crawl tunnel. It looked older, but it had older painted tiles as well.

"Ok," said Teodor. They pulled the panel shut behind them. They crawled along until they found a ladder. This time the top was bricked up: no exit.

"Keep trying," said Guy and they crawled on. The tunnel arched right, ever damper and older. They could see three lines of light from three separate openings. Teodor was meticulous. The first did not budge. So he climbed up to the second. Guy was amazed to hear the metal move. He looked up and saw Teodor haloed in faint moonlight.

"Thank God."

***

When Sayginn arrived in the tunnel, the Dome Elite were using their own divers. They had tied ropes to the divers and given them lamps attached to their heads and their hands. After the first team had come back empty-handed, they had sent back to the Dome for younger men. As Sayginn watched, two fifteen year old Dome Elite Juniors were being roped up to be sent into the tunnel.

"It's narrow, and the current will tumble you," the first diver was saying. "Try to stick together, but if you can't make it there's no shame in coming back. Try it once to get your bearings. If you feel ok, you can go back a second time…" The captain lowered his voice to a whisper "…to look for the bodies."

"They're wearing black," one boy said bleakly. The captain nodded.

"Is there a way through?" asked the other.

The captain shook his head, then, glancing up again at Sayginn:

"We don't know."

Karl Valvanchi, with a Dome towel draped over his shoulders, moved to stand closer to Sayginn. She glanced up at him but said nothing. The boys dived.

Sayginn stood leaning on a crutch and waiting, with the Dome Elite milling silently around. Dome Elite men had taken the drowned Battle Borgs away as she arrived. She had watched one group of divers enter the tunnel and reappear. Karl Valvanchi had explained in detail what he knew of the narrow turbulent waters.

"Teodor was a good swimmer," she repeated for the ninth time.

Karl nodded. Commander Tilson was standing a short distance away. Sayginn turned to him.

"Your boy, Guy Erma, could he swim?"

Tilson stood quietly without moving. He closed his eyes a moment.

"He could swim a bit. It's not part of the Elite curriculum. He's lived by the river all his life."

Sayginn moved uneasily. She could feel her concerns echoing through the Dome Elite men at her side. They too were waiting, waiting for the body of one of theirs to be retrieved from the depths.

The first boy returned. He was the slimmer, taller one. He stood a moment, gasping for breath. He shook his head.

"I couldn't see them."

Nobody moved. The captain spoke quietly to the boy.

"Yes, I'll go again. I'll just wait on Tony."

He looked back towards the entrance of the tunnel. They all looked back. The second teenage diver had not returned. The captain looked at his watch. He waded through the water to where another of his men was holding the end of Tony's rope. It was still spilling out. It was shaking. The Captain peered down at the water. The other boy quickly understood.

"Do you want me to go and look for him?"

The captain nodded.

"Don't take any unnecessary risks." The boy had already dived back into the tunnel. The captain grabbed his trailing rope as he went. There was silence in the tunnel, as they watched the one rope still moving, the other spilling out.

The ropes went slack. The captain started to pull. He gave orders to the other man to do the same. Now the ropes were coming back quickly, rising through the water, and then they saw the lights.

First one boy and then the other reappeared.

335

"We made it through," Tony said excitedly. "I got to the other side. The tunnel is not completely blocked."

"Yes," agreed the other. "I followed his rope. You can swim all the way through."

"And we looked on the way back. There are no bodies. I am sure there are no bodies. They must have made it."

"And there are footprints on the other side. You can see where somebody came out of the water. I was sure I saw two sets of footprints." The boy looked excited. "They made it," he said. "They escaped."

Both boys turned to look up at Sayginn. Tears were running down her face.

"Teodor is a good swimmer."

Beside her, the Dome Elite were cheering.

"Ok," said the captain. "That's sounds very good. Now we need to get a fixed rope in place, and then we can go and have a proper look. So this time Tony, I need you to…"

"I must get back to the palace," said Sayginn hurriedly. Karl nodded.

"You don't want to wait until they make all the checks?"

"No, I know he made it through. He'll be home now; I want to be there to greet him. Come with me."

Karl nodded.

"Let's go."

Chapter 29. Blue Barbrina at Rest

"Thank God."

Guy smiled as he watched Teodor disappear through the hatch. Guy followed as agile and as quick as his fast-ebbing strength would allow. Eagerly, he looked up and through, and as he did he immediately echoed Teodor's words, though not his sentiments.

"Oh God."

The hatch had opened up into the stall of a giant goran. Seemingly at its leisure, it was sprawled majestically across its bed of artificial straw. Yet the ice-white snow goran had its head and ears up and was watching them with keen interest. As Guy appeared, he bared his fangs and growled.

"Barbrina, Barbie baby," Teodor was soothing the giant cat. "He's my friend," then over his shoulder, "Secure the hatch, Guy; I'll just keep her calm."

"Ok." Guy pulled the lid back in place. He felt immensely safer now the tunnels were closed behind him. "I can't lock it."

"I'll do that," Teodor said. Looking and talking to the goran, he backed towards the sewer cap and then tapped a shut code on the keypad lock.

"It's jammed now. No-one can get it."

"How do we get out?"

The snow goran had its long paws stretched out across the entrance.

"It's ok. I'll talk to her. She's exhausted anyhow after this afternoon's race." Guy realised Teodor was talking about the giant goran. Guy watched with amazement as the prince walked calmly up to let the beast sniff, then lick, his face and neck. "She'll want to get your scent, as well. C'mon."

Guy had no intention of going anywhere near the gigantic animal. He knew only too well what they were capable of, but Teodor was urgently beckoning to him. "She won't relax until she knows you're also her friend."

"But I'm not her friend," Guy muttered as he reluctantly edged forward.

"Give me your hand," urged Teodor. Guy reached ahead of him. Teodor offered his hand up to the great goran's muzzle. Guy was sweating hard as he imagined watching the beast biting down on his arm and spending the rest of his life handless. The giant sniffed the air, looked straight at Guy and roared! Guy fell back to the floor, and froze.

"She's not happy," Teodor said quietly. "Look, we'll just sit a while. She'll calm down and then we can go."

Not Happy? Guy wondered. Was Teodor joking? He groaned inwardly as Teodor sat down in the crook of the goran's elbow, tugging Guy down beside him. Guy watched in dismay as Teodor snuggled into the deep fur of the goran's chest, pausing only to check on Guy.

"Lean here against me. If she smells me on you, she won't touch you. We'll get you a telepathic link tomorrow."

"I'd rather keep my thoughts to myself," Guy muttered. Unimpressed by the thought of surgery to allow him to spend time with giant gorans, what good was that in the real world?

"And with those kind of thoughts, we want you to keep them too," Teodor replied with a smile. Guy wondered if he was also telepathic. "No, it's only a goran safety link, not full telepathy. It's to save you being mauled out of hand."

"Save me from being mauled?" Guy asked. "Could you not have thought of that before you brought us up here?"

"Sssh, don't upset her. Stay calm."

"But she wouldn't hurt you. It's ok for you."

"She might if I did something particularly stupid."

"Like what?"

"Like bringing an ignorant Domesider into her stall. Now just relax, will you?"

338

Guy snorted in disgust. Ignorant Domesider indeed. He looked up and saw the goran was staring at him. Her glare was not in the least friendly. So, gingerly, he let himself lie back against the goran, angling himself so his head rested on Teodor's shoulder. Teodor immediately put an arm around him and pulled him closer.

"I'm just going to close my eyes a moment, and then I must find a communicator. I need to call my mother."

As Teodor relaxed, Guy let himself breathe in the aroma of the snow cat. It was supposed to be sexy. He decided it smelt like a slightly damp dog, but it was comforting, and the fur was silky smooth. He smiled as the giant rested its head on its paws. The monster did look a lot more relaxed. He saw it looking at them both but more specifically Teodor and there seemed to be a twinkle in that gaze.

Guy glanced up at Teodor to see if he had noticed, then he stopped, appalled. Teodor was fast asleep. He looked at the goran who was still calmly watching or maybe guarding them and the distant door. There was no choice really. He lay back deeper into the fur, leaning his cheek against Teodor's shoulder and closed his eyes.

***

Sayginn paced around and around the giant graphic of the Dome. On the screens around the ballroom were maps of the tunnels under the palace and analysts were scanning footage from a hundred new camera placements as well as audio feeds.

Nell was sleeping on a low sofa. Karl and Nikato were in conversation with the Captain of the Divers in the river tunnel.

"No, we have been through this a dozen times, and the passage is now completely lit. Their bodies are not there. Both boys made it."

"I'll use nanites and cy-roaches," said Karl. Nikato sighed. Nanites were not a technology the Zaracans had shared before. Karl shrugged.

"Sayginn, can you get me down to the tunnel at the other end of the water. From this end?"

"Yes, yes, you're right. We should get some people down there."

On the news, Chart Segat was being interviewed. He was explaining at some length how all the entertainments for Magnolia Weekend had been stopped out of respect for the 'two lost boys'. The news had a picture of the drowned tunnel, and a graphic of the boys swimming and tumbling in uncharted currents.

"Our hearts are with our beloved Regent Sayginn," Chart Segat was saying. "It is a terrible time for her. But now that my mandate has been renewed, I pledge my full co-operation to her and her new husband the Emperor. Myself and the people of the Domeside will do everything to repair the damage of this dark night."

"So you think the prince is dead?" The newscaster insisted.

Chart Segat sighed. He gave every impression of knowing something tragic, but not being able or permitted to speak of it.

"Those poor two lost boys," he repeated.

The news then changed and another reporter summarised:

"In an interview tonight, Chart Segat pledged his full support to the Emperor to rebuild Freyne 2 after the death of the prince. A death that at this moment is still unconfirmed. The only thing certain is that Prince Teodor, heir to both the Kingdom of Freyne 2 and the empire of Freyne, was last seen entering a deadly tunnel under the river. Whether he drowned or not has not yet been confirmed. He was accompanied by the young blades champion and Dome Elite Junior Guy Erma, who is also feared drowned."

Frederon was standing on the balcony above, looking down on the ballroom. He slapped the balcony rail in frustration.

"Where are they?" he growled.

***

When Guy opened his eyes it was morning. A girl was crouched down beside them speaking quietly to Teodor. Guy started moving unsteadily. He realised the girl must be a servant, by her clothes she looked like she worked with the gorans. Both Teodor and the girl reached to help him.

"Don't rush now," urged the girl.

"Stay close to me," said Teodor.

All at once the communicator on the girl's wrist sounded an urgent alarm. They all tensed and the giant goran sat up quickly, clearly perturbed. For the first time, even Guy could see it looked grumpy.

"Yes?" the girl whispered nervously. She was watching the goran with fear, but at the same time she was practically standing to attention. Guy noticed Teodor looked annoyed.

"Is he there? Is the prince there?" Guy thought he recognised the voice.

"Mother!" protested Teodor, pulling the communicator towards him.

"Give me a visual," the voice insisted. "Are you hurt? Tell me what you see, girl?"

"No, my lady, he's fine. He's completely filthy." She was whispering. Behind them Blue Barbrina was starting to pace. Teodor reached to touch the girl's arm. She nodded. At last a communicator, he thought briefly, then spoke in a whisper.

"Mother, Barbie does not like communicators, so I am switching this off until we get out of her stall."

"Teodor, don't you dare!"

Teodor switched off the communicator, and reached out to steady Guy. As the giant goran wound back and forward rubbing up against them, licking its jowls and snorting. The stable girl looked frightened but determined. Holding firm onto each other, Teodor got them to edge first one, then several steps towards the door. At the entrance, two other girls had appeared. As soon as they saw Blue Barbrina on her feet, they stopped running and with a balletic grace started to glide towards her, each taking a different wall of the stall. The goran watched them both approach, its head turning from left to right. Guy found himself behind both Teodor and the two girls. He relaxed a fraction and watched as the tallest of them reached a hand to the goran's muzzle. Teodor and the second girl reached up their hands towards the great goran. As Guy watched, the snow cat snorted one more time, then sank back into the hay, and even rolled over on his back. The girls laughed in low gentle purrs and

341

leant forward to playfully scratch his chest. Teodor took Guy firmly by the hand and led him quickly outside.

"Was that telepathy?" Guy asked when they were finally outside.

"Low level goran mind control, not like…" Teodor hesitated, "not like we saw earlier …em… last night." The girls came out of the stall. As quiet and smooth as ghosts they closed and carefully locked the low door. They shuttered the top opening. As the last latch slipped into place, all three squealed.

Guy jumped. He saw the girls had been concealing their excitement because of Blue Barbrina. Now they went wild, hugging and kissing Teodor. Guy found himself laughing with the girls as Teodor took it in turn to kiss, hug and squeeze each one, blushing a shade pinker with each embrace.

For the first time, Guy thought, Teodor seemed perfectly relaxed, crowded around as he was by the slim stable girls. He exchanged nonsensical conversations with them. These seemed to revolve around three key facts: one, he was alive; two, he was back; three, he had slept in the stables with Blue Barbrina. As Guy listened, he realised that to these girls nothing was as dangerous as a night with the great snow goran. They were full of advice and warnings, should he ever decide to do this again. The principle advice seemed to be that he should never sleep alone.

Guy found himself biting his lips, he was trying so hard not to laugh. While Teodor was listening carefully to each of them, and generally encouraging their shy kisses and quick hugs.

"And this is Guy Erma. He's my friend. He helped me escape."

The girls looked at Guy, as if for the first time.

"At least you brought us a handsome one."

In a few moments each of the girls in turn had kissed and hugged Guy, causing him to turn bright red. They giggled and Guy found himself laughing nervously.

"And here's my mother," Teodor sighed, and the girls slipped away.

"So," whispered Guy. "Are those all your girlfriends, I mean, how many are there?"

"Yes, I mean no, well not exactly." The Regent was getting out of the car. "I'll tell you later."

There was no time for Guy to ask anything more, because Teodor walked towards his mother. Regent Sayginn gathered Teodor in her arms. She hugged him for a long time with her eyes closed. Her face had a look of relief, then she kissed him on his hair, his forehead and briefly his lips:

"You're alive!"

Sayginn glanced at Guy, then back at Teodor.

"That was a good blades fight, you did well."

Teodor nodded just once.

"I didn't win though," Teodor said modestly. "Mother, may I introduce Guy Erma? He helped me escape."

"Ah, yes!" Guy had the distinct feeling the Regent was not entirely delighted to see him. Guy remembered with a sinking feeling their last encounter in the interrogation room, in the basement of the Magnolia Stakes racecourse. She, too, recognised him. He had not exactly lied to her, but he had not told the truth either. Did she know that? Her welcome was still cordial:

"Welcome to Magnolia Palace, Guy Erma. Now let's get you both to the medical centre."

Book 7.
Day 3. Morning

Interlude. Diplomatic Exchange

From: Ambassador Nikato Valvanchi II, Freyne 2
To: Ex-Ambassador Nikato Valvanchi I, Zarac 1

Father,

I regret to inform you that at the Dome Debate, Chart Segat was confirmed for another five years in power. So yet again, and despite our efforts, the Freyne refused to listen to our guidance.

I am now proceeding to Phase 2, as agreed.

Nikki.

From: Ex-Ambassador Nikato Valvanchi I, Zarac
To: Ambassador Nikato Valvanchi II, Freyne 2

My son, you have done well under very difficult circumstances. I think this kidnapping has undermined Chart Segat more than anything else he could have done.

Under his leadership, I do not believe the Dome will pose any credible threat going forward. The Regent is bound to restrict him in any way possible.

We also have undeniable proof of their actions on Sas Darona. I have no doubt the Regent will put an end to Dome Elite activity as well. The Sas Darona problem will therefore be at an end. Be patient.

You will be rewarded for your work. I am proposing that you become Ambassador on Freyne 1. I hope the council will agree.

Do not proceed with Phase 2. I repeat. DO NOT PROCEED.

Your father.

From: Ambassador Nikato Valvanchi II, Freyne 2
To: Ex-Ambassador Nikato Valvanchi I, Zarac 1

URGENT

Father,

I regret to inform you, one device has been activated. The technical readouts say it was triggered by an excess of heat.

Therefore Phase 2 is now underway. Request permission to proceed at once to Freyne 1.

N

From: Ex-Ambassador Nikato Valvanchi I, Zarac
To: Ambassador Nikato Valvanchi II, Freyne 2

This is very distressing news. I have informed the Council. They are also saddened, but the Council has decreed Phase 2 should continue as planned.

The Council have confirmed also your new post as Ambassador on Freyne 1.

This is a promotion, well done my son.

Your proud father.

P.S. Does Karl know?

From: Ambassador Nikato Valvanchi II, Freyne 2
To: Ex-Ambassador Nikato Valvanchi I, Zarac 1

Father,

Please confirm I should include my brother Karl in the Council's plans. He is after all only a military commander.

N

From: Ex-Ambassador Nikato Valvanchi I, Zarac
To: Ambassador Nikato Valvanchi II, Freyne 2

Negative. Do not inform Karl.

He will be more use to us if he is innocent.

Your loving father.

Chapter 30. Home Sweet Home

"What's your favourite food?" Teodor asked Guy.

The doctors had finished with their examination, and they were heading upstairs to Teodor's suite. A butler was on hand to ask what they wanted for lunch.

"Eggs and peas."

"Not a big Domeside pie?" Teodor said. "My favourite is a nice plump steak."

"I had Domeside pie on my birthday. It was a special treat. I was twelve." Guy stopped himself. It had indeed been an amazing outing: Lloulou had taken him to lunch in the bistro and ordered for him the most expensive dish on the menu: King-size Domeside Pie. Guy had been so excited and so moved he could hardly eat. Teodor stood waiting as Guy focused again, then, taking his forearm, he said:

"How about if this morning you have the best breakfast Magnolia Palace can provide?" Then to the nearby servant: "Ok, we'll have brunch as soon as it is available. All the trimmings, and pudding too." The butler bowed and headed off.

The boys had stopped at the top of the stairwell above the ballroom. They were distracted by the glowing laser display of the Dome: "What's that?"

Below was the palace ballroom with its horseshoes of hurriedly assembled workstations, walls of screens, cables, men, more screens and men.

"I think these are the guys who were trying to find us; me," Teodor said a little sadly. From below they had been spotted. Applause broke out, as men called to the boys and cheered.

"I'd better go down and say a few thank yous."

"I thought we were going to shower, then eat."

"Duty calls. You go if you like."

"No, I'm ok. I'll come."

Guy walked beside Teodor and watched the boy change again. Here was a politician in the making, working his way around the room, remembering names, and asking questions, accepting congratulations and laughing at anecdotes. Guy thought he saw the Teodor he knew for a few moments when they were shown the cy-wolves. Teodor bent down to pat, talk and hug the giant creatures, but then he was back on his feet talking to their captain, asking about casualties and praising their bravery.

**

"This is terrible, you know?" Teodor was showing Guy a news article about his mother at the Dome Debate. "My mother breaking down like that. Screaming and weeping in front of her council," Teodor sighed, for Guy did not really understand. "She'll never be able to rule now. Not properly."

Teodor placed the screen aside, switching off its content. The far door had opened and their guest had been ushered in.

"Welcome princess, we meet again."

Nell had been brought up to Teodor's chambers after a tense exchange with Regent Sayginn. Teodor had wanted to spend the entire day with Guy, but his mother had rung him twice to insist he receive the princess. Something Teodor had only agreed to do once his mother relented, saying he did not have to get dressed to receive her.

"Well princess, may I introduce Guy Erma." Guy was on his feet at once and saluted the girl Dome Elite fashion, fist to his heart. Teodor paused when he saw this, then continued a little uncertainly: "Princess, I am afraid you will have to excuse my companion and me. We have had a tiring night, and we are still at our leisure." Teodor was talking about the track suits they both wore. "If you think our attire is unsuitable, I will call my butler at once."

"My prince, on the contrary, please do not make any change on my account. On my planet we sometimes spend time outdoors on the beach in

351

casual clothes, and it is very relaxing. I am grateful just to spend any time with you after such a terrible ordeal."

"Well thank you," Teodor had not wanted to change in any case. "But tell me, princess, is this your original self? I know your people have clever camouflage skills."

"You are hard to deceive, my prince." She snapped her fingers once. "This is my original form."

Guy sat up with a small yelp. Teodor reached to calm him. They both sat back and observed her. From a freckled blonde with a frizzy mane of untidy hair, her skin had become a white shade of grey. Her pink lips changed to purple-pink. Her brown eyes turned black with white lashes and brows. Her hair was now white at the roots. It fell down her back in complex curls that rippled with a rainbow of colours.

"You look beautiful," Guy said softly.

Teodor agreed: "Come and sit down princess. We were about to eat – will you join us?"

"My prince, nothing would give me greater pleasure."

Guy was wondering how much longer Teodor would continue talking like a walking encyclopaedia. He wondered how he was supposed to address her. He had never met a princess before, let alone a Virgin Valvanchi princess of the Zaracan Democratic Union.

"Guy was extremely brave today," Teodor said loyally and warmly.

"Yes, my uncle Karl told me."

"Killer Valvanski is your..." Guy stopped himself, for both Teodor and Nell were looking at him in shock. He took a breath and said: "I mean Karl Valvanchi is your uncle?" It seemed unbelievable that a powerful military man like Karl should have a family.

"Do you know him well?" Teodor added smoothly.

"He's my uncle, and I have visited him on Sas Darona."

"You've been to Sas Darona?" Guy was astonished. "I thought it was in lock down."

"Yes, but I am Valvanchi," Nell said a little archly, then added: "There is one secure shuttle, it's any unauthorised flights which are locked down. The United Races has put in place a secure perimeter."

There was a pause, as Guy and Teodor thought about what she might mean by unauthorised flights. Teodor could see Guy was about to say something so he jumped in:

"Is it as beautiful as they say?"

"I saw gorans at sunset."

"In the wild?" Teodor sounded envious.

"Oh yes, it was the most amazing evening. You would have loved it Teo, I have some images... if you would like?"

"Not now," Teodor said quickly.

"Why is Sas Darona in lockdown?" Guy asked.

"Oh it's because of Mezzatorra," Nell replied.

"Mezzatorra?"

"Yes, the SDLA raided the base and stole eight poison pills."

"Hold on..." Teodor said thoughtfully. "Poison pills. The glass bricks with plague insects inside?"

"Yes, you know about them?"

Teodor said, after a little hesitation:

"Well it's just that I saw something in the air conditioning tunnels of the Dome, I thought I saw a poison pill."

"That's not funny, Teodor – tell me exactly what you saw."

Teodor described their climb down the Dome architecture. How they had found the open grille and how he had banged his head and thought he had seen a glass brick.

"It was new – or newly installed. The air-conditioning was filthy but the screws on the poison pills were bright and clean. That's what I found so peculiar."

Nell said nothing. She helped herself to a slice of bread, buttered it generously and ate it quickly, barely pausing to chew.

"What?" Guy said.

"Princess?" asked Teodor.

"As I said, a batch of eight poison pills was stolen from a place called Mezzatorra on Sas Darona a few months back. It was an SDLA attack, but my uncle thought they were assisted by..." She glanced at Guy. "By the Dome Elite."

"That's not possible!" Teodor protested. "The Freyne Empire recognises..."

Guy held up a hand to stop Teodor.

"Des was on Sas Darona for six months last year and," he paused, "this year too. He just came back," he said in a low voice. "He said something about Mezza – Mezzatorra? Is that how you say it?" He was going to say something more, but Nell was staring.

"What did this Des say about Mezzatorra?"

Guy remembered the mime Des had made, urging him to silence. So he changed tack: "The Elite have four separate bases. I mean, the planet is within easy reach of our fleet."

Teodor sat looking at Guy thoughtfully. At last he said: "Did my father know?"

"I think so. I think he and Chart Segat set out to gain some extra supplies of monazite. Quietly, obviously, but the Zaracans are based in a small corner of one continent. There is masses of space. For us, as well. The Zaracans know that."

"Monazite?" Teodor muttered. "Would the United Races have known or cared? We are so far from the centre."

"It's still illegal," Nell said.

"The Zaracan ownership of Sas Darona is a mere technicality, an administrative folly by some United Race bureaucrat who knows nothing of real space," Teodor said. "By rights, it should be part of the Freyne Empire."

"But by United Races law, it is under the protection of Zarac," Nell replied pertly.

"It is in our space – geography dictates it should be ours."

Teodor insisted.

"Point is..." Guy said at last. "Point is – and despite everything – why would the Dome Elite place a poison pill within the Dome? The Dome is our home. I mean, does anyone know what the plague might do in a neighbourhood like Domeside? It does not make any sense."

"Chart Segat," Teodor replied grimly. "Who knows what he is capable of?"

"You're wrong, Teodor. He told me to tell you he did not kill your father or your brother. He told me he did not do it, and I believe him. And this poison pill business, it is just stupid."

"Maybe, Guy. *Your mother only has one son. I have to worry about ten thousand men and boys.* That's what Chart Segat told me. It was the one thing he said that rang true."

"Are you sure you saw a poison pill?" Nell asked. "Because if the Dome Elite assisted the SDLA in the theft, as my uncle thinks…" She paused and changed her mind. "But I agree with Guy. It still makes no sense, why would the Dome Elite place a poison pill in their own Dome?"

"Let's forget it. My mother says I spent seventeen of the last thirty-six hours out of my head, all drugged up. Maybe I just imagined it. Right, pudding anyone? I think we all need some chocolate. I am sorry if I spoke strong words, princess."

"My prince, you are passionate about your people and your empire. I admire that. But yes, cake sounds good."

Teodor cut the cake and passed around slices, spoons, and dished out extra cream and friseburys.

"I'm trying to feed Guy up," he confided in Nell. "You know what? Everyone told me before I met him he was skinny and fast. They said he spun like the wind and bit like a goran. So I figure if he were less skinny, he would be less fast. I might beat him."

"Not likely," replied Guy and they all laughed.

*   *   *

Two floors below, Sayginn sat on a low sofa with Karl Valvanchi, sipping a glass of white wine. His hair was wet from when he had used her bathroom, and he was dressed only in a towel.

355

"I have asked them to send you some more clothes," Sayginn said, sitting on the edge of the sofa a short distance from him. "They won't be too long."

Sayginn knew she should not stare, but Karl was almost naked and the smooth flesh of his shoulders and chest was just a tantalising short stretch of the arm away. She knew she should not think about it, so she said something at the front of her mind.

"I'm not sure about that Domeside boy."

"He's just a boy," Karl reassured her.

"I'm not sure he is a suitable friend for Teodor."

"He is a great little blade fighter."

"Yes, but if he lives here with us, there's bound to be speculation. He's just too handsome, just too alluring, in all the wrong ways."

"Sayginn, he's just a boy. You think he's good-looking; it's not his fault. Blame his father, or his mother."

"And who are they, I wonder? I should have him tested, discover the worst, I guess. Chart Segat has sent me three messages saying he wants him back. If that doesn't tell you something?"

"Don't send him back to the Dome."

"Why not? Why wait until he is comfortable? Will it be easier when he is used to the palace? For him, or for Teo? No, I will give the instruction." She changed her voice and touched her communicator: "Tell Teodor to send Guy back to the Dome after they have had lunch." She switched off her communicator and sighed: "Now I feel better, now I can relax."

"Good," said Karl. "Have some more wine."

"You make me feel like I'm overdressed."

"Well, you are."

"But Karl—"

"You invited me to your private rooms, to shower and wait for new clothing. How many bedrooms are there in this palace?"

"Well, with the Emperor here…"

"And you have nothing better to do? Like spending time with your son, for instance?

356

Sayginn flushed.

"He's resting."

Another steward came quietly into the room with a trolley of food. He started setting the dishes on a rotating table alongside the bed. The table was on a huge pivot so it could be rotated across the bed to allow for eating at your leisure.

"I asked them to prepare you an Imperial bed banquet. You eat it in bed with your fingers."

"I have heard of this." Karl paused and looked straight at her:

Well, we have time. Now that Teodor is safe, we have plenty of time.

Chapter 31. Return to the Dome

"My prince, a message from your mother. Guy's mother has asked for him to be returned home."

"Sorry?" Teodor looked up at the steward, a little shocked.

"Your mother says Guy must return to the Dome after lunch."

The steward left as quickly as it had arrived, and Teodor spent a few fruitless minutes tapping on his communicator.

"It's no use. Mother has switched her device to private. I can't contact her. I don't want to send Guy back to Domeside," he explained to Nell.

"Yes, but if his mother…"

"I don't have a mother," Guy growled.

"And I promised Des I would not send Guy back to the Dome. A sworn promise." Teodor hesitated, he felt the fear again. It chilled him, and he looked at Guy. "Do you think Des is all right?"

"We should check on him."

"And Sebastian, do you think?"

Guy shrugged.

"The guys from the Riffaut who were also Dome Elite would have watched out for him. There's Marline too."

Nell was looking confused.

"We're talking about all the people who helped us escape," Teodor explained. "Look Guy, I can't argue with my mother." Guy gave him a look of disbelief. Teodor paused. Dare he disobey his mother? He considered this when suddenly a solution presented itself: "Ok, I cannot disobey a direct order, but she does not have to have it all her own way. I'm going with you to the Dome. And we're not going alone. I want a word with Chart Segat. And I want the Dome Elite."

"What do you want with the Dome Elite?" Guy asked curiously.

"I want them, that's all. The Dome Elite belong to the King of Freyne, and in his absence, his Regent."

"What are you going to do?" Nell asked curiously.

Teodor stood a moment thinking.

"The Dome Debate was lost because of me, but I think I can change that. I want a word with Chart Segat, that's all." Then, looking at Nell, he apologised. "I am sorry Nell. We're going to desert you."

"Oh no you're not, because I'm coming too."

About fifteen minutes later they were sitting together on the back seat of a vast car. Teodor had decided they should dress for the occasion. So Nell had changed into a white dress with a rainbow belt and her hair flowed in rainbow colours. Guy had picked a black tailored suit and matched it to a blue shirt, which he wore with the neck open, and the collar turned up. With his hair gelled back in place, even Nell gave him a second look. Mostly, though, Nell was admiring Teodor who had changed into his dress uniform of red and silver together with a ceremonial cap. The two huge golden gorans had been persuaded into the car. They seemed content enough to curl up at their feet. Teodor never stopped touching and talking to them even as he chatted to both Guy and Nell.

"My father told me that the Dome Elite belong to Freyne 2. They protect our planets. They used to be our personal body guards. That's why the blades championships started. Each year, the Dome Elite would compete for the twelve places in our personal bodyguard."

"Yes, I remember," Guy said. "It was not just the men. There used to be a competition among us boys for two of us to be around you and Deodran. Well, before…"

"Before Deodran died," Teodor finished and squeezed his hand. "It was the Dome bomb under the car. My mother replaced the Dome Elite with the Regency Defence. But it was never as good. Not really. Anyway, my mother backed off from the organisation of the Dome Elite as well. And I understand, as for a while I too blamed the Black and Gold, but then it became clear there was another bomb."

"The second bomb was nothing to do with the Dome Elite," Guy said passionately.

"Well," Teodor hesitated. "We don't know who was responsible for the second bomb."

"The Dome Elite did not place the first bomb either," Guy interrupted. "Yes, it was a Dome device, but we didn't put it there."

Teodor took his hand and squeezed it.

"I want to believe you, Guy. I want to believe you. " Teodor hesitated. "In fact, I do believe you. And when I saw the Dome Elite last night. It was not them who were chasing me. It was not them who imprisoned me. No, every single human I met within the Dome, you, Des, the man in the tunnels, Sebastian, Marline. Everyone wanted to help me."

"Chart Segat told me to tell you he did not kill your father, he did not kill your brother. And when he says that, he means the Dome Elite did not do it."

"But Chart Segat did kidnap me. And he now controls the Dome Elite. No, I must control the Dome, or my mother must. I intend to convince Chart Segat to give up his powers. I just need to say a few words."

Teodor sat in silence, Both Guy and Nell looked at him with curiosity, but before they could ask anything more, Teodor said:

"Nell, can you connect the three of us telepathically?" Teodor asked once they were in the car. The girl hesitated. "We don't know what awaits us in the Dome. If you would agree to boost my basic goran telepathy, well it might be useful."

"She has not got the powers to do that," Guy said with a sneer.

"Actually I have," Nell said a little waspishly. "And of course I will offer my power to you, my prince. I will provide any assistance you require."

"Thank you princess."

Nell smiled a little coyly, then moved to sit between Guy and Teodor. She then stretched out her arm and nodded to Teodor. He smiled and wound his arm around hers until the palm of his hand pressed against her hand. The both looked at Guy. He wrapped his arm around both their arms, and grabbed both their hands in his. For a moment they clung to one another.

"Close your eyes, Guy," Teodor said softly. "Look for the light."

Guy closed his eyes, and saw a line of white light. He bent to look into the light and suddenly he could hear them. He could hear Teodor's and Nell's thoughts.

'Can we use telepathy now?'

'Yes.'

'Can you hear us Guy?'

'YES!'

'I was thinking, if Guy shows us the changing room, I want to take a look to see if I was indeed imagining that poison pill. I know I saw something; maybe you could take a look.'

'Well,' Nell replied. *'we should get some pictures... But I mean, I honestly could not think of a worse place.'*

"Worse?" asked Guy and he had spoken aloud, he was so alarmed.

'Well the exponential rate of expansion of the cy-sect population. It would be vastly accelerated within the damp darkness of an air-conditioning tunnel.'

There was a pause, until finally, Teodor shared a final thought:

'Let's hope I was dreaming, then.'

Finally, Teodor spoke aloud for the first time: "Here we are. Guy, show us the way."

They were never going to pass unnoticed. Not with thirty-six Regency Defence men and cyborgs, eighteen cy-wolves, not to mention two huge gorans, accompanying them. Still, it was the three young people at the centre of this crowd that attracted the most attention. The crowds cheered and applauded as they passed. In the changing room, Teodor got one of the Regency Defence cyborgs to lift him first, then afterwards Nell. After she was placed on the ground, she stood for a few moments in complete silence. Finally, she said:

"I took some pictures of the serial number. I'll send them to my uncle. He may be able to identify the origin."

Teodor nodded. They were walking back out onto the main thoroughfare. Crowds were pausing to watch them.

"I guess we need to isolate it and make it safe."

"Yes. You should leave men here to guard it in case anyone interferes with it." Then, in a whisper, she added in thought speech: '*And Teodor, there may be more than one.*'

'*What makes you say that?*'

'*That raid on Sas Darona I told you about. Eight poison pills were stolen.*'

'*You say the shield went up, didn't it?*'

'*Yes, the shield went up, and everyone inside died.*'

'Teodor, what are you going to do?' Guy's thoughts were loud.

'Well, you told me yourself, next week is the Spring Sweep. They are already prepared for it. So we'll do that. Put up the ropes, send the droids through the Dome looking for poison pills, then isolate and neutralise them.'

'How easy are they to destroy, Nell?'

'Oh, there are several ways. Finding and isolating them is key.'

'*And if we have the Dome Elite to help us...*' Teodor said thoughtfully. '*I must have words with Chart Segat.*'

"Guy Erma! That is against Union rules." A loud voice called out to them. Teodor looked over, and standing on a table to get a view of them over the heads of the crowd was Sebastian. He leapt down from the table and pushed his way over to meet them. Teodor shook his hand energetically, but Sebastian still wanted to talk to Guy:

"You wearing the Riffaut is just unfair competition."

Guy burst out laughing and replied:

"What do you expect? I had to borrow some of Teodor's clothes."

Sebastian walked boldly up to Guy. Without asking, he buttoned Guy's jacket closed and adjusted his collar. He stepped back with a critical look.

"Better. Now you look fab in them. You'll put me out of a job."

"That's alright because I have another job for you," replied Teodor.

Guy nodded meaningfully. Sebastian turned around slowly.

"My prince?" Sebastian said with a bow.

"I want you to come and work in the palace as my personal valet. You know the clothes I like, so I want you to pick out my choices every day." Sebastian looked a bit stunned. Teodor lowered his voice, and continued: "You see, I was able to use the trick you told me, the one about pretending to be you. It helped me escape the Dome. So this would be my reward to you. If you want to accept it."

"Thank you. Oh yes, I would really like that."

"Sebastian," Guy interrupted. "Do you know where Des is? I mean, what happened to him?"

"Ah!" Sebastian's face fell. "He's not so good. He was also in the cells. He was still there this morning when they freed me. They had given him a good kicking. It depends how soon they let him go to a surgeon. As you know, the longer you leave an injury, the harder it is to heal."

Teodor nodded.

"Guy, take ten of the Regency Defence and go and release Des from his cell. I will go ahead. I want to speak with Chart Segat. Where is he, Sebastian?"

"He's in the competition gym."

"Ok, you go with Guy. Tell them you are working to my direct orders. Free Des and bring him to the gym also."

'Don't take any nonsense from anyone,' Teodor added in a firm thought voice.

'I won't,' replied Guy.

"Wait!" said Guy, just as Teodor turned to leave. "Sebastian, have you any idea where Marline is?"

"She left with Simon Ssochen last night. She's gone to his South Sea paradise. Lucky girl."

"Ah. Ok. Fine, I just wanted to see her," he said sadly.

'I will help her also, Guy.' Teodor said, using telepathy.

Guy nodded: *'I'll go and get Des.'* Already telepathic speech seemed natural and useful. Guy and Sebastian set off at a run.

***

The enormous competition gym was the scene of a vast demonstration of the Dome's best blades fighters. Only five blades mats were in use, but the hall had taken on a carnival atmosphere. There were stalls round the edges selling food. Seating had been raised around the five remaining blades mats; more seating was set up around the balcony that looked down onto the gym, but none of the seats were allocated. People seemed to be moving around freely, sometimes pausing in seats to watch a blades fight, more often just milling around.

The entire gym seemed to be in movement. Beyond the central areas, groups of men and boys were giving displays of blades throwing and gymnastics to the delight of crowds who had come in from across Domeside and indeed the entire capital. The beautiful models of Old Mill Lane wandered, surrounded by admirers, while small groups of off-world visitors clung close together taking photographs and cowering in front of the Battle Borgs.

Chart Segat had had his large chair moved down from the cap of the Dome and installed on the platform where, the day before, the Dome Debate committee had met. He was surrounded by a host of colourful guests, and of course Lloulou stood quietly in his shadow. Teodor walked straight towards him. He still had his two Gorans with him, plus a dozen Regency Defence and cy-wolves. But it was the gorans that caused the crowds to gasp and part. Only Chart Segat feigned not to notice his approach, and instead seemed intent on watching two men fight at blades.

"Chart Segat," Teodor called out. The blades fight stopped. Slowly around the gym, the men and boys, the onlookers and fashion-lovers turned to look at Prince Teodor who was standing in their midst in his full uniform with two huge gorans at his side.

"Chart Segat! You called and we came. You said you wanted Guy back."

Teodor saw Chart Segat look lazily at him. He seemed to count the Regency Defence, then relax a fraction before calling out in a bored voice:

"Prince Teodor, how good to see you. You are, as always, welcome in our Dome. Even an unannounced visit. But your cats must wait outside."

Teodor said nothing. He touched the minds of his giant gorans and they both roared. It was with some satisfaction that he saw the crowd – including Dome Elite – back off a little. Even Chart Segat looked perturbed. Conversations stopped, and Teodor realised that everyone was now turning to watch this encounter between himself and Chart Segat.

'*Good,*' he thought. '*I hope they all watch and take note.*'

"Chart Segat, the only reason I am here is to tell you that Guy Erma will not be returning to the Dome."

Chart Segat smiled. He stood up and drew himself up to his full height. He looked behind him and drew Lloulou forward alongside him.

"But Guy, he belongs here in Domeside." Chart Segat nodded at Lloulou, implying but not saying that she was his mother. What he did say was in fact a complete lie: "He is Dome Elite Junior, did he not tell you?"

"Don't lie to me Chart Segat. Guy told me the lists of Dome Elite Junior will not be published for another month. And I came here to tell you, you may have won the Dome Debate, but you will face trial for my kidnapping and for the murder of my father and brother."

"Thing is Teodor, you have to have proof for such an accusation."

"Oh, I am happy to bear witness against you," Teodor said carelessly.

Chart Segat had walked back and now towered over him. He is still trying to intimidate me, Teodor thought angrily. He used his telepathy to nudge one of the golden gorans. The yearling obediently leapt up and landed his two paws on the man's shoulders. The goran's weight was enough to knock the man over and pin him to the floor. On a sign from Teodor, the goran roared into Chart Segat's face. His jaws and lips brushed Chart Segat's features. The goran's breath blew Chart Segat's hair back from his face.

"Teodor!"

Teodor span around to where he saw Emperor Frederon standing up from another gilded chair alongside the blades mat. As he rose, the two young tiger goran cubs bounded along at his heels, then seeing Teodor's Golden gorans, they started to hiss and snarl. The Emperor reached down with his black varnished nails and pulled them back.

"Uncle!" Teodor was surprised at first. Both his gorans looked up, their faces showing the puzzlement and curiosity that Teodor managed to carefully mask. His mind was spinning. What was the Emperor doing here with Chart Segat?

"And who have we here?"

Nell, who had assumed her Freyne appearance for their trip to the Dome, now snapped her fingers:

"This is Nell, she is..." Teodor paused. Nell had changed. She no longer wore the white dress and rainbow hair. Her clothes had changed to a slim uniform in turquoise and white, her hair similarly had turned white with two thick stripes of turquoise running through it. These were the battle colours of the House Valvanchi. Nell knew well the antipathy that the Emperor had for her race and was hereby advertising her allegiance to the highest clan: the Valvanchi. In this garb, thought Teodor, she hardly needed any introduction.

"This is Princess Nell Valvanchi. She is the granddaughter of Nikato Valvanchi, the discoverer and unifier of the Freyne Empire."

This was the official title for Nell's grandfather. Frederon just snorted.

"Unifier indeed!" And one of his tiger gorans leapt towards Nell, claws out.

Teodor gave a nudge to one of his golden gorans, who smoothly curved his body around Nell, and lay across her feet. The tiger cub hissed at the larger beast, but retreated.

"My work counts for nothing," the Emperor continued. "I knew your grandfather. Other than postulate the possibility for a link between our planets he did nothing to forge the union. I created the empire, the Great Freyne Empire of the Thirteen!"

The Emperor, Teodor realised, was talking to the Dome Elite, not just to him. Some of the men even started to cheer, but as Teodor turned to look at them, they fell silent. Most now looked distinctly shame-faced. Teodor gazed up at his uncle. So Frederon wanted to control the Dome Elite as well. Teodor swallowed, wondering if he dare proceed. Simultaneously, both he and Teodor saw the flash of metal in Chart Segat's hand. Chart Segat was reaching up to knife the other golden goran.

"No," Teodor cried. It was a shouted imperative and the goran with its wild instincts moved faster than Teodor ever could and with a strength and deadly precision Teodor could barely imagine. The beast swiped at the blade and sent it spinning across the floor. Its claws passed close to Chart Segat's nose and cheeks.

"Let him go free!" the Emperor ordered. "You will need this man if you are to rule the Dome."

"My uncle, he took me captive. He beat me. He starved me. He would have killed me."

"Obey me, Teodor. Free him!"

Teodor hesitated, but Frederon was his Emperor.

Just then a shout came from behind. Guy, Des and Sebastian were charging through the far doors on blades. Guy was alongside Teodor in a couple of giant leaps. He bent to take off his blades, and bowed to the Emperor in one smooth move.

"My uncle, may I introduce Guy Erma. He helped me escape from the Dome."

The Emperor turned his hawkish gaze on Guy Erma. Teodor had not noticed, for he had turned to greet Des, and ask him briefly about his injuries:

"From this day forth you will be my personal bodyguard, if you accept…" He said in a whisper.

'*Help me, Teodor,*' Guy whispered.

Teodor turned to see that not only was the Emperor still staring at Guy but Chart Segat had stood up and had brushed himself off. The Emperor said curtly:

"This is the boy, is it not?"

"Yes, Guy is a good boy. Guy is one of us."

With this quip, Chart Segat had once again assumed his authority. The Emperor was smiling. Men were laughing. Chart Segat was already back in full power.

'*One of us?*' thought Teodor.

'*He's just trying to split us up.*' Guy replied quickly. '*Don't believe him!*'

Now Chart Segat placed a heavy hand on Guy's shoulder. Teodor saw Guy visibly pale. He seemed to shrink as well. More than that Teodor noticed the ring Chart Segat wore, with letters like teeth spelling out the words: Loyal to Empire, Fear only God. He looked around as Frederon and Chart Segat exchanged glances. Suddenly Teodor was chilled to his very soul. '*Chart Segat is loyal to empire,*' thought Teodor. '*He is loyal to my uncle Frederon, the Emperor of all Freyne. Why? Why did Chart Segat kidnap me on Frederon's orders?*'

Guy now replied:

'*Frederon was going to pardon him for King Serge's death, I heard him say so. Frederon said he would give him full control of the Dome Elite.*'

Suddenly Teodor understood.

'*So Chart Segat betrayed me. On Frederon's orders. If he stays in control of the Dome Elite, he will betray me again, my mother too. There will be more bombs under more cars, and we will not last long.*'

'*You need the Dome Elite. You need them, Teodor.*'

'*If they are loyal,*' Teodor replied.

Chart Segat still held Guy by the shoulder; now he bent to kiss him. Guy's thoughts turned into an anguished howl:

'*Please Teodor, you swore to protect me. You swore as a prince!*'

Both golden gorans roared. Remembering his promise, how with hands wet with soap-suds he had sworn to protect Guy Erma, Teodor realised the time had come. He had to face up to his promise.

"Chart Segat, let go of Guy Erma. He is not coming back to the Dome," Teodor said firmly.

Chart Segat laughed and shook his head, so Teodor continued:

"You will give up the Dome Elite, and then you will hand yourself in to the police. If you do not give yourself up, you will be arrested for my kidnapping later today."

Still Chart Segat had his hand on Guy's shoulder. Teodor stepped forward, took the hand, and lifted it away. "Give yourself up now, Chart Segat. This is my last warning."

Chart Segat laughed at this. He glanced at the Emperor and winked. Teodor looked over, the Emperor was not laughing.

'*Now,*' said Teodor.

'*Kill him!*' urged Guy again.

'Don't kill him,' replied Teodor and closed his eyes.

'I close my eyes a moment while on duty,' Teodor thought. *'I will not watch what happens next.'*

Suddenly the two gorans leapt forward. Teodor pulled Guy aside, and the Emperor backed up fast. Not so Chart Segat, who did not see the attack. Within a moment, he was flat on the floor. One large golden goran had pinned him to the ground. The other roared. Chart Segat threw both his arms up to protect his face.

Teodor stood over him and said, so that everyone – all the Dome Elite and most particularly the Emperor – could hear.

"Chart Segat. You organised my kidnap using Battle Borgs. You detained me without food or communicator. You drugged me and beat me as often as you saw fit. You then threw me unprotected into a cage to fight for my life. You said you would throw me to your borgs."

"Yes, but Teo," Chart Segat was pleading from the floor. "May I call you Teo? I never…"

"You also threatened to throw Guy Erma here to the borgs."

"That was a joke," Chart Segat protested.

"Three years ago you threw Des to the borgs."

"But…" Chart Segat started.

"You will never throw anything or any boy to your borgs ever again, do you hear me?"

"My prince, I…."

'Now,' thought Teodor. *'Don't kill him!'*

With one swift bite, the goran took Chart Segat's arms in his mouth. His teeth cut cleanly through flesh and bone above the elbows on both arms. The goran spat out the hands and forearms, sending them spinning away from him. Then both gorans leapt daintily away as Chart Segat's arms fell wide, with blood gushing out on both sides. The Dome administrator lay flat on the floor, his two arms wide like the red arms of a cross.

As one, the Dome Elite stepped back, the crowd was silent. Teodor took a moment to look at them. Each and every soldier was armed. It would take only one blade thrown between the eyes of his goran. Teodor could feel their quiet anger, or was it desperation? The soldiers were looking from Teodor to

Chart Segat to Frederon. They seemed wary of pledging any allegiance until the fight between these three was played out.

"Never again will you hand a boy to your borgs for torture." Teodor spoke with grim satisfaction. He nodded to two medics, standing at the side of the blades ring.

'They will give him arms,' Guy said uncertainly.

"Take him away, and make him well. But not his arms. Tell them to give him cyborg arms. As a reminder," Teodor repeated. As he spoke, each of his gorans picked up Chart Segat's hands and forearms, and greedily started to chew the flesh from the bones.

The Emperor looked down at Teodor. Cold respect glinted in his eyes, but he said nothing. Frederon knew that these young gorans were entirely under Teodor's control. If Teodor wanted to rip Chart Segat apart, he could not have chosen a better weapon. Dome Elite men had run forward. Teodor nodded, and tourniquets were applied. A stretcher was zooming into place.

Teodor drew himself up to his full height:

"The Dome Elite belongs to the Regent," he told the gathered men.

"Really?" The Emperor reached to spin Teodor round. He looked angry, and Teodor was faced with the fury of his hawk-like eyes, he stepped back to avoid the black claws. Teodor thought the Emperor was on the point of grabbing Guy. He pushed the Domeside boy behind him, and they both stepped clear of his grasp.

'Hold your ground, Teodor,' Guy said.

Teodor stopped and looked straight at the Emperor.

'I don't know why he wants you,' Teodor thought quickly.

'I don't think he does. What he wants is the Dome Elite,' Guy replied.

'I want the Dome Elite,' Teodor replied.

'No, you need the Dome Elite,' Guy reminded him.

With this thought firmly at the front of his mind, Teodor stepped forward to confront the Emperor.

"The Dome Elite belong to Freyne 2, and Freyne 2 is ruled by the Regent, my mother."

"Your mother was going to be my wife. Only now I think she will shortly be tried for treason herself," the Emperor replied slyly.

"I beg your pardon?"

"Look…"

The Emperor pointed his communicator at the screen, and there was the Regent. She was wrapped in the embrace of a man, and that man was Zaracan. Sayginn was kissing Karl Valvanchi.

"Oh my," Teodor heard himself say, glancing around at the many men who were looking up at the screen with interest. He caught sight of Nell putting a hand to her face in fear. He did not know what to think. His mother caught on camera kissing Karl Valvanchi. As they fell apart she looked flushed and breathless.

'She's kissing killer Valvanski…' Teodor heard Guy's thought clearly, and knew all the Dome Elite thought the same.

Mostly she was completely unaware of the crowd of people now watching. Already men around him were starting to whistle and shout foul words at the screen.

'She does not know we're watching,' Teodor replied and spoke angrily to the Emperor:

"How did you get these pictures? My mother's room is a black room. There should be no photography."

"What does it matter? Your mother and Killer Valvanski. And all Freyne is watching. I would not be surprised if she does not have to resign her position permanently. More importantly, how could the Dome Elite ever respect her now?"

"The Dome Elite have sworn…" started Teodor. Then, distracted by something on the screen, he said. "Oh, for goodness' sake, switch that off." But the images played on.

Helplessly, Teodor sent a message to Nell:

'Can you help with that screen?'

"The Dome Elite has sworn allegiance to the empire," the Emperor concluded smoothly. As always, every time he spoke, the crowd was attentive, they listened. "So maybe I…"

"NO," Teodor yelled. Impressively, all the screens turned black. The largest screen exploded off his hinges, before falling slowly down the wall to the floor. Just slow enough for the crowd to scatter ahead of it. For a moment, it rocked, and looked like it might fall forward, but in the end it settled at an angle with a single wire still connected above to the network.

They all looked at Teodor. Even the Emperor was silent.

'The Regent will never control the Dome Elite, not now,' Guy said quickly.

'Maybe, but they cannot belong to Frederon.' Teodor replied, then he spoke aloud:

"No, you will not take the Dome Elite." As Teodor spoke, the two gorans leapt to his side and roared in the Emperor's face. And then it happened. Only Teodor saw it. Only he and the Emperor were aware of it when it happened. The Emperor stepped back. Just one step back, but the Emperor had yielded ground when faced with Teodor's anger. Just one step, then three more. Teodor looked up at the Emperor in triumph. He nodded once and his golden gorans leapt forward and ripped the throats from the two tiger goran cubs, leaving them broken at the Emperor's feet. The Emperor did not even seem to notice. He was waiting. Teodor said:

"The Dome Elite belong to Freyne 2. They belong to the King."

'Teodor, don't do this,' Guy suddenly realised what Teodor was going to do.

'I have to do this,' Teodor replied. *'If I don't do this, I cannot protect you. I cannot protect any of us...'*

Teodor spoke in a loud, clear voice, as he said with conviction:

"The Dome Elite belong to the King of Freyne 2."

'And I swore to protect you.'

Putting one fist against his hip, Teodor drew himself up to his full height:

"I, Teodor, son of Serge…"

The Emperor frowned. Teodor swallowed and started again.

"I, Teodor, son of Serge… do claim this planet and its dependencies.

To rule as is my right,

to the benefit of my people,

as guided by our democratic institutions,

and proscribed by our laws.

So help me God."

The silence continued long after Teodor had spoken the oath. Frederon said nothing. Teodor saw he was looking around the gym, trying to sense the mood of the crowd.

'*Say it again*,' urged Guy.

With more forcefulness, and putting greater emphasis on each word Teodor spoke the oath a second time, gazing calmly up at his uncle, the Emperor:

"I, Teodor, son of Serge… do claim this planet and its dependencies.

To rule as is my right,

to the benefit of my people,

as guided by our democratic institutions,

and proscribed by our laws.

So help me God."

'*Now kneel!*' Teodor thought fiercely, looking round the assembled men.

'*Of course,*' replied Guy softly, and before Teodor could stop him, Guy knelt before Teodor and, taking his hand, pressed it to his forehead:

"Hail Teodor, King of Freyne."

Nell went down on one knee and said in a loud voice.

"Hail Teodor, King of Freyne," she said.

It had less of an impact than it should. In fact, a ripple of anger ran through the Dome Elite at the sight of the Valvanchi girl kneeling at his feet.

'*What about the Elite, why don't they kneel?*' Teodor thought impatiently.

'*Give them a minute, Teodor. They are just getting used to the idea. What about the borgs?*' Guy directed his thought to Nell: '*Give our powers a boost princess. We need to control the Battle Borgs.*'

Nell complied and throughout the gym the giant metal men went down on one knee:

"Hail Teodor, King of Freyne!"

'They're still not kneeling, Guy.'

'One more minute, Teodor...'

The Emperor was no longer smiling now. The Dome Elite looked nervous. Guy glanced back at Sebastian and Des. Quickly now, they both bent to one knee:

"Hail Teodor, King of Freyne!"

At this, the Battle Borgs, still kneeling, bent their heads and repeated:

"Hail Teodor, King of Freyne!"

'Now see,' Guy said.

As Teodor watched, first one by one, then in groups, men and women, in family groups or among their friends, went down on one or two knees. On the podium behind them, Lloulou had knelt, and with her a large crowd of models. Then all the young girls were kneeling, and with them their companions and children. Now it was the turn of the Dome Elite. First soldiers, then lieutenants, when a captain knelt his men knelt with him. When Tilson knelt, half the room shadowed him. Finally, the entire room of Dome Elite knelt and proclaimed:

"Hail Teodor, King of Freyne!"

When they had finally fallen silent, at the very last, Emperor Frederon bowed a small, slightly mocking, bow:

"Hail Teodor, King of Freyne."

There was silence around the gym. Frederon glanced around at the vast crowd of Dome Elite and Domeside people, and said with more force:

"Hail Teodor, King of Freyne. Hail Teodor, Head of the Dome Elite."

All at once the crowd was released. The crowd roared and screamed their approval, as with one voice they started to chant:

"Hail Teodor, King of Freyne. Hail Teodor, Head of the Dome Elite."

Teodor glanced one more time at Frederon. The Emperor was looking relaxed and was quietly applauding him. For once Teodor felt the Emperor was perhaps entirely on his side. He pulled himself up to his full height and waved at the crowds. All through the gym, the Dome Elite were falling into rows under the command of their captains. The civilians fell back until the

Dome Elite, fully five thousand strong, stood in neat rows across the gym, and in great circles all around the high watching balconies, and even out into the atrium beyond.

Teodor looked at them. For a moment, it felt like he held his breath. As one, the Dome Elite saluted, closed fist to the heart. Then they raised their voices:

"Loyal to Empire, fear only God."

The sheer force of their greeting was overwhelming. For one terrible moment, Teodor felt himself to be four-years-old again. His body rocked backwards. Then he felt a strong hand at the small of his back. Guy Erma, standing at his side, had reached behind him to steady him. And he had done so without anyone noticing.

'Guy!' Teodor thought gratefully.

'Just do your job!' Guy replied grimly.

Without further hesitation, Teodor saluted his troops, and they replied:

"Hail Teodor, King of Freyne."

The Emperor said:

"So, King Teodor, you have your command, what are your orders?"

The first part was easy, thought Teodor. He needed to replace Chart Segat, and he could think of one person who would be ideal for the job.

"Tilson, Commander Tilson."

His instructor stepped forward, and knelt to kiss his hand.

"Please can you head up the Dome Council?"

"Of course, my prince, but what are your commands?"

Teodor was quick to reply.

"I want to reinstate the Dome Elite as my personal guard. I want both Des and Guy to be part of that guard. I want the Battle Borgs returned to their barracks and their programming fully checked for interference and..." he stood a moment, considering.

He wanted Dome Elite places to go to Domeside boys. He wanted it to be illegal to work as a fashion model before the age of eighteen, or better still, twenty-one. He wanted the Dome to be a fairer, gentler place, but how?

'Don't forget the poison pills,' Nell sent him a thought reminder.

The Emperor saw his hesitation and was quick to step forward. He went to place a hand on Teodor's shoulder. Only the nearest goran growled and the Emperor hesitated, but still said:

"Of course, strictly speaking, you cannot be King without the agreement of the Barons. I will confer with them, on your behalf, over the next few days; they may decide that because of your youth…"

Teodor immediately understood the implied threat. The Emperor had more influence with the Barons than Teodor did. He would dictate their opinion. He would deprive Teodor of his crown and his power. Teodor felt his anger rising. At his side both his gorans were growling and hissing now. With confidence, Teodor replied:

"I am sorry, my uncle, but there will be no time for that. You see, this planet is under threat of extinction. And you are in extreme danger. As my Emperor, my lord and my uncle, I urge you to leave this planet as soon as you can."

"I'm sorry, Teo?"

"Yesterday, when I escaped from the Dome, I found this in the air conditioning tunnels of the Dome. Nell, please show us the pictures and explain."

Nell pointed her communicator at the screen.

"This is a poison pill found in the air conditioning tunnel above changing room…" She hesitated.

"Changing room on the seventeenth," confirmed Guy.

"I have information from my uncle, Karl Valvanchi. He has confirmed this is one of eight poison pills that were stolen from a place called Mezzatorra on Sas Darona."

"Thank you," said Teodor. "What we have to do now is check the infrastructure of the Dome and locate and isolate this and any other poison pill. Guy, please explain."

"Twice a year, the Dome has a Spring Sweep, when droids are sent through the tunnels to clear any blockage and disinfect all surfaces. Boys lay the ropes for the droids to follow. The next clean is due next week."

"So," concluded Teodor, "I must ask that this Spring Sweep be scheduled as soon as possible this afternoon. I will lead a team of boys in setting the ropes to guide the droids. It is imperative that we work together to find the poison pills, deadly planet killers that they are, and then isolate and neutralise them. So, you see, my Emperor. In this, our hour of danger, for your own protection you must go."

Emperor Frederon looked at the glass brick buzzing on screen, then back to Teodor.

"The Dome Elite did not do this," he said firmly, and then he glanced where Chart Segat had gone. "Did he?"

Teodor hesitated, before replying smoothly.

"That is not the point, my uncle. However, I will provide you with a Dome Elite escort to speed you to safety."

Frederon was still looking at the screen.

"Tilson," Teodor gave the command. "Your best men to escort the Emperor."

Frederon bent one last time to speak quietly to Teodor on leaving. He nodded briefly towards Nell as he spoke, but what he said, only Teodor heard:

"Valvanski have betrayed you, Teo."

Chapter 32. A Dome of Fire and Light

So it was that later that afternoon. Teodor was climbing out of the cap of the Dome to stand alongside Guy and Nell looking out over his city. The sky was bright, it was turning silver. The sun was larger than Teodor ever remembered. It was low in the sky, and soon there would be a rainbow of colours above them and the sun would set. The sky was full of noise and movement. Shuttles from the Dome were taking off and rerunning in quick succession, the Dome Elite was being evacuated, and from other parts of the city, hover cars were taking off, forming multi-layered queues, like a cloud of locusts waiting to pass the security posts.

Below in the street people were filing out of the houses, carrying possessions and children. They were joining long queues snaking out to the exits of Domeside. Teodor could see it was still good humoured and orderly; Dome Elite were manning the security posts, and the people trusted it would be safe.

Using Dome Elite as security for the evacuation had been the first and best decision of the day. The second decision, to announce a problem with the Dome's power plant, was more controversial. The population were more bemused than afraid by the order to evacuate and the exodus had the feeling of a cheerful carnival.

Teodor did not have long to reflect on what he saw. Guy showed him how to attach the rope to the top of the Dome, and then they both climbed down a short ladder. More boys and girls were arriving at the top every minute, and there was only a limited amount of space on top of the cap of the Dome.

***

378

On the fourth level of the Dome, a team of Zaracans worked with Dome Elite deploying robots throughout the air-conditioning system. Karl Valvanchi was in command. He had set a table against the wall and then stacked screens alongside it. Each screen relayed images from small robots that now travelled through the air-conditioning system. Around the small room a dozen different air-conditioning grilles were propped against the wall. As Karl watched, two technicians primed a small sphere-like machine with a large camera eye on the front and back. Using the remote control, the men made the camera rotate a full circle, and then hover left and right. They directed the robot into another air-conditioning tube. These machines were proving to be robust and fault-free; all the better, for the job would be completed more quickly.

Without warning, Karl broke into a chill sweat as he remembered Mezzatorra. Again and again the faces of his colleagues appeared before him, and he remembered the row of corpses laid out under the tall tree. How high would they stack the corpses if Sas Darona plague broke out in the heart of this vast Freyne City? He leant in towards the screens. At any moment, the monitors might show another pill, but this time it might be broken. Would there be any hope then, even in fast and furious flight?

Karl wished he was blissfully ignorant of the poison pill threat and possible subsequent plague. Those around him only worked with such calm efficiency because of their fearless innocence of what might come, whereas Karl himself felt true fear. How could he stop his hands shaking as he manipulated the robot? Why could he not bring himself to examine the signals?

I am Karl Valvanchi, Captain of the Zaracan army. I will not tremble like a fearful child.

He took a breath and focused on Sayginn and her son. They depended on him to find and neutralise these poison pills, so he had no choice. With renewed vigour, he scanned the information being relayed from the robots. He remembered the conversation he had had on his way there with Sayginn:

"You must come with me to Zarac 1. You need to escape this terror."

"But what about my people?"

"Make up an excuse, say you were invited to the fifth birthday of my son; we consider the fifth an important milestone."

"If I go, Teodor will have to stay. The people must have a leader."

"Then Teodor must go."

"Teodor and Guy…"

"Teodor, Guy, his entire little gang." They laughed. Sayginn had been watching with growing alarm as Teodor bestowed ranks and honours on those who had helped him.

Suddenly Karl stood up and went down on one knee at her feet. He kissed her hand. "Let me stay with you, Sayginn. I will stay, and we will fight this evil together."

"But how?" Sayginn asked. "How can you stay?"

***

In the light and shadows of the Dome, in the giant competition gym all had changed. No longer a competition space, the blades mats had been hastily rolled up. Instead, the space had been opened up to allow the offices of the far side to spill out into the space. In the light and shadow of the Dome, desks and screens had multiplied, as had Dome analysts as they monitored the feeds from the droids searching through the structure of the Dome. Two Dome Elite had found Guy emptying his locker and asked him to follow them. Guy was led to a small meeting room. Des was already there, and Guy knew something was different but not yet what. He looked around apprehensively.

"Ah Guy, why so worried?" Tilson said with a smile. "Here, this is for you. You've earned it."

Across the table, Tilson pushed a black jacket trimmed with yellow gold; the breast pocket embellished with the outline of the geodesic Dome and embroidered with the words: DOME ELITE JUNIOR. He then handed him a leather bound manual and, wrapped around the heavy book, a brand new Dome medallion.

Guy reached to touch the inscription with trepidation and looked up at Tilson:

"For me?"

"You've earned it. And I have had them prepare your entire battle travel kit as well." He pointed to a large black backpack with his name. Attached to which was a standard pack containing shiny new blades. Alongside was another larger pack, inscribed: CAPTAIN DES PARKS, DOME ELITE.

"Captain?" asked Guy; that was two grades higher than Des' previous rank.

"Well, it's only fitting for the prince's bodyguard," Tilson said. Des just grinned. Tilson continued: "Ok, we don't have much time. They will be lighting the firewall soon; then you'll be evacuated, and then they'll be in quarantine."

"You were explaining about the evacuation," Des said. "You said Freyne 1 will be dangerous."

"Yes, the Imperial Court is deadly to Prince – no, King – Teodor. The Imperial princesses are forever conspiring to replace him with their boyfriends and husbands, or – god help us – their sons."

"I did not think the princesses had any sons yet?"

"No, but that does not stop them conspiring to replace Teodor with prospective future sons, where they can."

"But Teodor has supporters too?" said Guy.

"Yes, he does, and they will become more vocal and more obvious as he grows older. He will have to marry at sixteen, because he also needs sons. Don't ever forget that. The more boys Teodor has in the Imperial nursery, the safer he'll be. But he knows that too. He has been well trained."

"There are Dome Elite at the Imperial Court – they are assigned mostly to transport and more are being evacuated there. I have given them orders about Teodor's safety, so trust them, and only them."

"What about the Imperial Guard?" asked Des.

"Not to be trusted," Tilson replied curtly. "Frederon had a hand in Teodor's kidnapping – he was trying to force the Regent to marry him. Chartsie was wrong to help the Emperor. But Sayginn was wrong to threaten to close the Dome and prosecute Chart Segat for King Serge's murder. The Dome Elite did not kill their King. But the plain fact is the Dome Elite did fail that day. Both our King and that baby prince were murdered; ten of our own also died. Those murders weakened the empire. Only Teodor can restore it now. He must quickly step into his father's shoes. I know he's young, but he might just be ready. He will need your help. You must always be loyal to him. Only him."

"As for these poison pills," Tilson sighed. "Treachery from the Valvanski, I think, though I am not sure how. Des here was at Mezzatorra. Des, you must be sure to tell them. Not today, obviously, but Guy and Teodor must learn what you know."

Des nodded grimly. Tilson looked at his watch. Guy's communicator buzzed.

"It's time," Tilson said quietly. "Now go." He walked them to the door, and at last he said. "I am Loyal to Empire, I fear only God."

"So help me God," Guy and Des replied together.

With a last nod, they set off running on blades.

***

There was a message from his mother, so Teodor headed out of the Dome and down Old Mill Lane. He held Nell by the arm as they went. She was still a bit wobbly on the blades he had given her, but she was smiling bravely and seemed to be holding on – just.

At his call, Des and Guy raced out of the Dome military quarters with light packs on their backs. Sebastian joined them from the Riffaut, jauntily jogging down the steps. He held a piece of parchment in his hands.

"Turns out I am one of Riffaut's very own bastards," he said, showing Teodor his birth certificate. "There were always rumours, but I did not know until today."

"You hang on to that," Teodor whispered back. "That paper, that inheritance, is worth a fortune."

"Don't I just know it?"

Sebastian laughed a little bitter, a little relieved.

"Do you still want to work for me?" Teodor asked cautiously. House Riffaut looked in turmoil. Models and staff were already leaving, lugging great suitcases and bags stuffed with clothes. "Maybe your future is here now?"

"No way, Teodor. I'm coming with you. I can always come back here."

They had arrived at the vacuum tunnels. Teodor casually stripped off his outer clothes and then they passed through the heat x-ray while he walked with the others in their underpants, through the vacuum tunnel and out onto the square. As Teodor pulled his clothes back on, he looked at the long line of people waiting to be checked and evacuated through the tunnel. Ahead of him, Karl Valvanchi was checking a small firewall device.

"We need more evacuation tunnels," he told his mother.

"They are coming."

"And the shield is going up."

"The shield has to go up."

Unnecessarily, Teodor waved his friends back, and then gave the signal. At Teodor's feet, a line of white fire shot high into the sky. It was followed at two-metre intervals in a circle around the Dome. From the crowds and inside the city, there were shouts and some screams. Teodor and the others looked up and watched how the fire curved in high above the Dome, searching and weaving until at last it connected. One by one the lines of fire found their destination and connected in one huge star of fire, high in the sky. Their trails of light were like the frame of an old umbrella. Then the fire buzzed, hummed and spat out sparkle. Finally, starting from the top, it spread. White hot lines of light were starting to spread and multiply. Starting from the top it was a vast spider's web, its arms and arches multiplying and interconnecting in an exponential fashion until the base was encased in a dome of white pulsing light.

"Teodor, they are moving the gorans tonight. I asked them to bring it forward. Just in case." Teodor looked up gratefully at his mother, why had he not thought of that?

"They have asked if you or I could lend a hand."

Teodor knew this was a ploy to get him out of Domeside, but this time he did not resist.

"I will go. Please call ahead to tell them."

He led his small group of friends to a waiting hover car: "Guy, I'll give instructions to my staff, but I'm counting on you to help Des and Sebastian settle in."

Chapter 33. The Fireplace in House Jewel

Karl Valvanchi stood at the front of the lecture theatre giving the talk about Sas Darona plague. It was the same talk they had given him when he had arrived on Sas Darona all those years before. He was even using the same slides.

The first slide was an image of an insect biting into human flesh. He explained what they were to a crowded room of Dome Elite, Police and Regency Defence. All listened in silence and without moving.

He showed the image of the larva and the cocoon.

You could not even hear the men breathing, they were so still.

"Crystallescence," Karl said. He opened his mouth to try and explain. Then stopped to show them a slide with the diagram of the hollowed out cocoon, and the minute insect inside.

He stood for a moment looking at the men across from him, and many cameras were beaming his talk throughout the city. His throat was dry. His hands were cold. His mind was blank. There were no words. He thought no words at all.

"Look, I'll show you."

He stood a few moments dialling up some information on his communicator, then he pointed it at the screen and at the cameras;

There she was again. Sonia, as seen by himself, as filmed by his helmet camera, still in the long grass behind the shimmering shield of fire.

"I saved one," Sonia showed him. A brick made of industrial glass and within it a mini-world of plants, soil, water and five or six insects, all mounted on the side a small explosive.

"Cy-sects?" he'd asked unnecessarily.

"This is Mezzatorra," Karl told the crowd. He fast forwarded the tape to double and then quadruple speed.

At first Sonia had moved a little restlessly, but she had been moving; towards the end she was still, as still as a statue. Finally, she seemed to doze, her body and face almost unrecognisable, just the shape of Sonia, not Sonia herself. In the setting sun her body shone, reflecting the light from a thousand different facets of the cy-sect cocoons: the crystallescence.

The beauty of it, Karl thought. Did he think it was beautiful? He glanced around the room, the men seemed indifferent. They did not know Sonia. The fast forward video did not capture her humanity. Karl saw the changing light, and knew what came next. He slowed the video to real time.

As the sun set, the cocoons split. For one moment, she was a quivering mass. Then her body dissolved into a cloud of plague flies. They rose up from her corpse in a cyclone. Nothing was left. The cy-sects seemed to smell Karl and a large group swerved, span and charged at the camera.

Around the lecture room, men leapt to their feet, shouting. There were screams around the building where people were watching in different rooms. Then silence. Karl looked around and over the crowded men.

Finally, he thought, they have understood.

Later, Karl wondered whether the Freyne had really understood. The population at large had been told it was a power surge drill. And they had to evacuate Domeside as a precautionary necessity. Karl walked along the wall looking through the shimmering wall of fire into Domeside and beyond. The lines of citizens queuing to exit through the vacuum tunnels were slow moving, but good tempered. Some had refused to evacuate. Most did so at their own pace. The population had been told to leave all but the essentials behind. It was peculiar what some people thought was essential. A mirror, perhaps if you were a model? A rocking chair, ok, maybe it was antique? But a collection of porcelain dogs? The evacuation of the Dome, on the other hand, seemed to be proceeding with military precision. Karl watched as the shuttles flew back and forth with determined speed.

"Where are the Dome Elite going?"

He asked Patrick McGuire at his side.

"To Space Station 1, and then spreading out to Stations 2 and 3, they have some large transports, but…"

"Tell them they can go to their bases on Sas Darona, I will sort out blanket refugee permissions for them," Karl said bluntly.

Patrick nodded, speechless but grateful.

"I will pass it on."

They had arrived at the control centre.

"I want to check the traps," Karl said.

"My men have them under surveillance."

"Nevertheless, before I leave."

"Seven poison pills have been found and neutralised, are you sure there were eight?"

"Do you want to take that chance?" Karl snapped back.

Karl and Patrick arrived at a desk with four screens, each showing a number of smaller images. Karl peered from image to image. All at once, one of the images turned red, and started to flash.

"Where is that?" Karl said at once.

"It's House Jewel," the analyst said after a moment. "It could be our last poison pill. It could be a false alarm."

"Send in a cyborg." Karl turned to Patrick: "For God's sake, get them to hurry up the evacuation."

"The Dome is all clear," the analyst said uncertainly.

"Just get me a cyborg to this location."

"That's House Jewel. There's a cyborg outside now. But the house has over seventy-five rooms, where do you want to start?"

Karl thought a moment.

"Have there been any repairs or decorating done quite recently, say in the last month?"

The analyst frowned.

"There's the new salon." A Dome Elite guard had come up behind Karl. He had the long black curls so characteristic of Domeside. He looked worried.

"They had engineers in to look at the chimney," the Dome Elite man said. "It was smoking the other night. It needed looking at."

"Send the cyborg to look at the new fireplace. Are you House Jewel?" Karl asked, knowing what the answer would be.

"Yes, I was," the Dome Elite replied. "A long time ago, mind, before Chart Segat. Is it true we can evacuate to Sas Darona?"

"Yes," Karl said quickly. "Yes, you can all go."

The man nodded, but he hung back, waiting and watching the cyborg on the screen.

"The cyborg is there," the analyst said. "What do you want him to do?"

On the screen, the cyborg was looking at the fireplace. It was methodical. It checked the front, and then one side and the other. There was a black grill to the right of the fireplace. But nothing moved. There was nothing to see.

"Get him to bang it," Karl said impatiently.

The cyborg went to touch the black grill. As he did, it dissolved into a cloud of minute black flies. The grill was not black at all. It was silver.

All at once there was silence in the control room, and in the silence, they could hear the low hum of the insects over the audio, and then something else. Coming from House Jewel. Girls' voices.

"Get those girls out of there!" someone shouted.

Karl said nothing. The swarm was moving, and the cyborg turned to watch it. In the office, Karl and the men watched as the cyborg watched. The flies were drawn to the smell of warm living blood. The girls did not even see them. They dropped their bags. They batted them away, still laughing. The swarm moved on, up the staircase and out through the door.

The girls looked at each other uncertainly, shrugging as they picked up their bags again. The tallest was very familiar, and she was elegant, as if walking the catwalk.

"Lloulou," the Dome Elite man said quietly.

On the audio tape they heard her say:

"Ow, I've been bitten." Lloulou was pulling back her sleeves. "Ow, those blighters really sting."

Book 8.
Day 3. Evening.

Chapter 34. Sunset on Freyne 2

"Everyone knows Guy Erma."

On a screen in the corner of the bedroom, Prince Teodor was on the news. They had given him a microphone and installed a podium at the far end of the Magnolia Palace ballroom for a hastily convened press conference. Teodor had been speaking for three or four minutes on his captivity and escape from the Dome.

"I knew of Guy Erma, by reputation of course. I had been told there was a superb thirteen-year-old blades fighter in Domeside, I had just never met him. What I had not expected was that everyone else in Domeside also knew Guy Erma. I was, however, glad to meet him on a blades mat. It felt right to meet him for the first time with blades in both hands."

"So you chose to fight Guy Erma in the cap of the Dome?"

Footage of the fight had been released by Chart Segat's press office, as evidence that the Dome Elite had 'found' Prince Teodor. Teodor hesitated, then finally replied:

"In retrospect, it was a great opportunity. As a direct result I gained my freedom, for it was Guy Erma who showed me the way out of the Dome. So yes, I was very glad to meet Guy Erma, he helped me escape and now I must urge all the people of Domeside: you, too, must make your escape. Leave your homes and your belongings, take your children, and yes, your pets, and get out of Domeside as quickly as you can."

"Can we interview Guy Erma?" asked one of the journalists, ignoring Teodor's last remarks. Teodor shook his head, and went to apologise. The Regency press team had said categorically that Guy Erma was too unprepared to face the press. Now that he was at the end of his session, Teodor could only agree. It had been a gruelling ten minutes. There was a long list of things he could not say, and it was only through creative phrasing of his replies that he managed to reply to some of the questions at all. However, just as Teodor was about to speak, Guy stepped up to the microphone:

"I will say what Teodor said. Leave Domeside now. It's dangerous…"

Sebastian switched off the screen:

"Brilliant Guy, not very subtle but to the point."

Guy shrugged, he was standing at the window ignoring the news as he looked out over the palace gardens.

"Look at the gorans, I had heard they raced them in the gardens, but I did not realise it was so close to the house."

Guy walked out onto the balcony. The palace staff had installed Sebastian and Des in rooms on either side of the room Teodor and Guy shared. The three had discovered the balcony as the quickest and most unobtrusive way to get from one room to another. After the initial euphoria – the running backwards and forwards comparing everything from bathroom fittings to communications hubs – they had settled down to watch the gorans in the garden.

"That's Teodor," said Guy and pointed. "He is riding Blue Barbrina." The enormous ice goran was charging up the avenue of trees at a quite eye-watering speed. As she came upon the house, it seemed to take all of Teodor's strength and all four of her great paws braking to twist into the sharp bend before racing along the front of the house. There was a thunder of paws under their window. She turned in three huge leaps about a giant chestnut, and then she was running again, gaining speed along the front of the house, before leaping onto the avenue and disappearing in a gust of shaken branches and leaves. Des and Guy cheered.

"Des?" Guy had had the question in his head for over an hour, looking for a chance to slip it into the conversation. "Des?"

"Yes, Guy."

He looked relaxed and indulgent; Guy decided it was worth a try:

"Do you know who my father is?"

"Guy, I was only a kid when you were born. I'm only three years older than you, so… You jealous of Sebastian?"

"No, not really, it was something Chartsie said, that's all. He said Lloulou was my mother. He definitely said that."

"Lloulou? She must have been pretty young. But there was some scandal, I don't know, but sometimes you would read about her having been a wild tearaway as a teenager. What did Chartsie say, exactly?"

"He said my life was going to change."

Des shrugged.

"Well, he was right there, your life has changed. Anyhow, I should head down there."

"Yeah, right."

"Look Guy, Teodor said there was a library and a collection of news stories. You know, the year of your birth. I'm sure there was some scandal way back, it might have been then, it might have been afterwards. But there might be something in the news."

"You think I should look?"

"There's a screen just there…" Des nodded to the small state-of-the-art comms platform Teodor had in the corner of his bedroom.

Guy nodded. Des headed off, leaving him alone with his thoughts. When he was out of earshot Guy said aloud to the night:

"Life's not fair. My life is not fair."

***

This was how Teodor found him, with three screens illuminated with photos and headlines, all dating back fourteen years. Teodor had come back from the stables and taken a shower and emerged with a towel at his waist. He shook his wet hair over Guy and laughed.

"You should get dressed," Guy said curtly.

"I can't find my shorts."

"What? Seb left your clothes on the bed." Guy pointed to where there were clothes laid out ready.

"Yes, but no shorts. It's ok, I told him."

"You told Seb to go and find your shorts?" Guy asked, incredulous.

"Well, yes…" Teodor hesitated.

"You don't know where they put your shorts?"

"No," Teodor said indifferently. The two looked at each other for a few moments, then finally Teodor said: "What? I've always had servants. Why would I know where my shorts are?" Teodor nodded at the screens and said:

"So, what's this?"

The main screen showed an old news story featuring two pregnant young women. One of them looked very familiar.

"Well, it's Lloulou, she got pregnant at fifteen. Only I thought she was my mum but here it says she gave birth to a daughter in April of the year I was born. So, well, I think it must be Marline, I mean I think Marline is her daughter."

"So, Marline's your sister?"

"No, no, how could she be? Marline was born in April, I was born in July…"

"You might have been born the year after?"

"So, that would mean I'm only, like, eleven years old. No…"

Sebastian came in, with a handful of underwear:

"Shorts and vest," he said to Teodor.

"Thanks."

"Say sorry to Seb, he's not your slave."

Teodor looked a little startled but said nothing, just retreated to his bedside to get changed. Sebastian spoke instead:

"No, it's alright Guy. His wardrobe is unbelievable, it's almost as big as one of the showrooms at the Riffaut."

"Why do you need so many clothes?" Guy asked nastily of Teodor, who was hesitating over two choices of shirt on the bed. Teodor looked up, stung by Guy's comments, and pulled on the shirt in his hand.

"If you're going to wear that shirt, you need the other trousers," Sebastian said.

"See…" Teodor waved at Sebastian, then said to Guy: "Do you think I like this stuff? I don't want to be a fashion model, but they force me. They say like a million jobs in Domeside depend on me wearing fashion. So I have to…"

"Look, don't wear that shirt," Sebastian was saying. Teodor sighed and threw off the offending item, and picked up the other one.

"Do you think I care?" He said angrily to Guy. "You, him, Lloulou, you all depend on me wearing fashion."

"Not me," said Guy spitefully. "I'm Dome Elite"

"Hey Guy," Sebastian interrupted. "Without Sayginn and Teodor, House Jewel would not have a roof on it."

Teodor and Guy fell silent, eyeing each other up, they looked ready for a fight. Sebastian tried to distract them by pointing at the screens.

"That was a sad story," Sebastian said. "They were both so young. Both teenagers, both models, both got 'caught out' – you know what I mean – during Magnolia Stakes weekend. They were both underage. Neither should have been working. They both got pregnant."

"How do you know?" Guy asked curiously.

"Well, it's a bit of Domeside folklore. The one on the right is Lloulou, when she was fifteen, she was dating Erederon. That's when she got pregnant."

"What? Prince Erederon?" Teodor asked sharply.

"Yep." Sebastian smiled at Teodor and added with emphasis: "And the baby was born in April."

"Wow!" Teodor whispered quietly.

"Yes, that's why Lloulou has always been so famous," Sebastian explained. "She bore Erederon's bastard child, even though in the end, her child was a baby girl."

"So what?" Guy asked. "Why 'wow!' Teodor?"

"My birthday is in June, if Lloulou had given birth to Erederon's son in April he would have been the Imperial bastard," Teodor said, then he explained further. "He would have been the next Emperor, well, provided... Well, anyway..." He frowned as he considered the implications, then shaking his head he changed the subject: "Why did you say it was a sad story, Sebastian?"

"The other girl, now that was sad. She committed suicide. She killed herself shortly after the birth of her baby."

Guy had not looked at the other girl. Now he saw another dark Domeside girl. Her face was very pretty, with a small upturned nose and a cheeky smile. She looked like someone he might have liked.

...Why did I force her? I promised her we would swap back. I made so many promises, but I lied. Guy remembered Lloulou's tears.

"What happened to her baby?"

"I don't know. Maybe he died. Maybe that's why she killed herself. Who knows?"

"He?" Teodor said.

"Yes, another a fatherless bastard boy born on Old Mill Lane, what of him?" Sebastian sounded bitter. Guy seemed to slump.

"You ok, Guy?" Teodor asked quietly, then: "Thanks Sebastian."

Sebastian took one look at Guy's face, nodded a little sadly and headed off.

"I'll call you when the food arrives, ok?"

"Thanks, Sebastian."

As Sebastian left, now fully dressed in coordinated fashion Teodor sat down next to Guy and took his hand.

"What is it, Guy?"

"It's just that I wanted to believe Lloulou was my mother. But if Marline was born in April, and Lloulou is Marline's mother, then how could I have been born in July?"

Teodor said nothing, just squeezed Guy's shoulder.

...That was another lie. We lied to protect you... Lloulou had said.

Guy was confused now, his research seemed to indicate that Lloulou was not his mother. If not her, then who was his father?

"We could get you tested," Teodor said.

"No!" Guy said, a little too quickly.

"It's only a pinprick, Guy!"

"No, if Lloulou's not my mother, well, I don't care who my father is... I really don't."

Teodor shook his head:

"Yes, you do. Otherwise why are you so upset?"

Guy looked at Teodor: *'And what if Chart Segat is my father?'*

'What? I didn't hear that, what did you say?'

Guy spoke aloud: "No, I'm upset because this means I'm not Lloulou's son, and I thought... I really thought... And I don't want to be tested. I mean, my father has never done nothing for me. I'm here now with you, and if I had a father he'd probably want money or fame or something. No, it was Lloulou I wanted."

"But Lloulou told you she was your mother, didn't she?"

Guy nodded despondently.

"Well then, she's your mother. And I don't care who your father is either," Teodor said. "You're my friend, and you're staying here for now."

"Really?"

"Well, I know you're Dome Elite, so I've said that you will train with me every day. I have Dome Elite trainers, you know? I said you had to come with them every morning to train with me."

"Oh!" Guy looked surprised, he had not realised that such plans were already being made. "Ok, that's good."

"And when you have holidays or half-days or weekends, you're to come here, too. In fact are you starting now, or in the new term?" Teodor asked.

"I don't know. If I start now, all the others will have had six months training already."

"Hmm, I thought so," Teodor said thoughtfully. "Thing is Guy, everyone says you're clever. Tilson gave me a long lecture when you climbed up through the Dome that second time. He told me you were the smartest, brightest boy ever to come out of Domeside, and I would be a fool if I did not have you living with me, learning with me, training with me. He said you could teach me more than I would ever learn with my tutors alone."

Guy said nothing, he was stunned at this praise, had Tilson really said all that? Teodor was still talking:

"And I sometimes have companions who come and stay with me. Bonnie Walesbury came last summer for six weeks."

"Bonnie Walesbury?"

"Oh, he's one of the Walesburys. Third son actually, but he's the same age as me. They were my father's strongest allies. It was sort of an experiment, and I mean Bonnie was fine, but he goes to school all year, so he thought he was coming here on holiday. So he was a bit naughty with some of my tutors. And he can't fight blades. His father never wanted him to learn. And of course he could not ride our gorans because he does not have the right implant. All he wanted to do was play racquets. So we were out playing racquets three times a day. I tell you, I was so bored by the end, I could have screamed. But he's a nice guy."

"Right," Guy was thinking. *'Gorans? Blades? Tutors?'* "Rich, is he?"

"I suppose... But you'll like him and it's not about money, Guy. Honestly..."

"Well, I don't care about money," Guy said carelessly.

"No, I know you don't. I don't either. Thing is, what about it? Tutors, blades, gorans and stuff? Would you like to stay here with me? At least until you start with the Dome Elite..."

"Well..."

"Listen, Guy, I like you. You helped me escape and you helped me today. With the Emperor." Then Teodor added: *'This telepathy thing Nell gave us is very useful.'*

'The Emperor said the Valvanski had betrayed you.'

"You heard that?"

"I think Nell heard him too." Teodor frowned, but said nothing, Guy continued. "Don't know what he meant though."

"No, nor do I. My mother trusts Karl Valvanchi. I like Nell."

"Yes, but they're aliens, Teodor. They're not Freyne."

"Sorry, Tilson told me you were clever? I'm wondering now if he was talking about you."

Guy punched Teodor and for a few moments they wrestled, Guy tumbling Teodor to the floor, until finally Teodor gave up:

"Ok, ok you win…"

"One thing I do like about being here with you is," Guy admitted, pulling Teodor up to his feet. "it gives me choices."

"Choices?"

"Ok, well when I was over there," Guy pointed through the window, "I had two choices. One, to join the Dome Elite. Two, to be a fashion model. And don't you go thinking, all fashion models are like Sebastian. He always had it easy, and now we know why. His father always knew who he was. No, it would not have been like that for me."

"But you would have gone to school?"

"You have to pay for school after twelve. And working comes first. That's how it starts, they tell you, you have to do this thing to cover the cost of school. Then you have to do this other thing. Then all at once you're doing everything they tell you, and still it's not enough."

Teodor said: " I will try and make some changes…"

Guy held up his hand:

"Yes, we need to do that. But for me now. I have a choice. I can be Dome Elite, but I can also study with you. I can study for the qualifications I need to join the Dome officer training programme. Then I really might become a pilot."

"Really, officer training? Is that what you want to do?"

"Yeah, I only wanted Dome Elite when that seemed like the best option. But if I can stay here, as your companion… I mean, are you sure your mum won't mind?"

"Guy, I'm the King now. They have to do what I say."

"Really?"

"Well, some of the time…" Teodor smiled. "I'll get you a title."

Sebastian called: "Food's ready."

"What?"

"You'll need a title, Prince Erma of something or other. I'll fix it."

"Prince Erma, really? Like Erederon?"

"Erederon the Great, not Prince Erederon – Best not get them mixed up, but why not? My Great-Grand-Uncle Erederon the Great was brought up in Domeside, he would be your namesake. C'mon, I'm starving."

As they sat down to eat, Des said to Teodor:

"Your mother sent a message, you're to go and see her after you've eaten."

***

Regent Sayginn was in her room and alone. Unusually she was sitting on a fireside goran rug, using the giant head as a backrest; she was looking through some correspondence. Teodor knew Karl Valvanchi had left only a short while before and he thought he had not seen her so peaceful since his father died.

"Teo!" She called him to her and drew him down on the rug. She set aside her screen. She wrapped her arms around him and hugged him up against her, before giving him a sip from her glass. All at once Teodor thought he was back to being her baby son. As the heat spread across his face and the drink warmed his neck and chest, he rubbed up close, putting his head on her shoulder.

She stroked his hair for a few moments, then said:

"There was an emergency council meeting tonight."

"You should have called me."

"Well, I didn't. I'm going to tell you now. They have found the first victims. They have secured the first seven poison pills, and we were beginning to hope the eighth did not exist, but then they discovered a number

400

of models, all from the same house. They had the distinctive crater-like bites on their arms, and their blood tests showed up positive."

"So the plague is loose?" Teodor asked, appalled.

"For the moment, they think there is probably only one nest. They have fully fired its location. They have sealed off House Jewel, and quarantined all those with bites. They are talking of setting a limited fire in House Jewel itself. They have to check for secondary nests, and also for animals, rats, cats and dogs who might also have been bitten. Even pigeons, all can be infected. And since the Dome has been checked from top to bottom, they are now starting to check all the houses down Old Mill Lane. The victims, well they were models and fashion house staff... And, well, there's no easy way to say it. They were all from House Jewel."

"I should have been at the council."

"It was a late emergency call – you were at your leisure."

"Yes, but..."

"Teo, you need some time to be a boy if you can. Tilson, Patrick, Karl and I have done all that was necessary."

Teodor said nothing, he took the tumbler from her hand and sipped the golden liqueur.

"Lloulou?"

Sayginn nodded. "She's in quarantine now. She'll stay there until... until... well, they will end her suffering and incinerate the body."

"Incinerate?"

"It has to be done, Teodor, before the crystallescence."

"Have you told Guy?"

"I'm trying to arrange for him to speak with her. It's too dangerous for any of you to go down to the quarantine station, but they are setting up a camera and microphone. Lloulou is not the first, and she is unlikely to be the last. She should not have to die alone, or at least die without saying goodbye."

Teodor reached up to take the glass in his mother's hand again. She hesitated, then held the glass to his mouth, but stopped him from drinking more than just a sip.

"Karl said earlier today that if there was an outbreak, they will probably all die."

"They fired the nest Teo. They sealed the house. The victims have been quarantined. The people of Domeside are evacuating or under curfew in their homes. Fire starters with hoses are looking for animal victims. There is still hope, Teo. Ok, the plague is loose, but there is hope that it can be contained."

"We are setting up a second and third firewall as well. The Valvanchis have suggested we set up multiple firewalls like the rings of an onion. Eventually, they say, one will hold. The city and the planet might be spared. However, one thing has been agreed. And I have had notes from all the members of the council, and the Emperors, and all of the Barons. They have all agreed. Now the plague has started, it is too dangerous for you to remain here. You and your friends are to be evacuated tonight."

"What?"

"Tonight. Before midnight."

"Am I to go to court?"

"I wish there was another solution. It's even more dangerous than you might think. The Emperor told me today there was another Imperial bastard. A son of Erederon somewhere in Domeside, Chart Segat knew who he was."

"The Emperor has proof of this?"

"I don't know, maybe it was just one of those rumours."

"Chart Segat was working for Frederon when he kidnapped me. But I still don't understand why the Emperor had Chart Segat do his dirty work, to then replace me with what? Some unknown Domeside boy?"

"It's hard to believe, I know. He was also trying to force my hand when it came to marriage."

"That's definitely off now?"

"Yes, he said he could not contemplate a woman who had sullied herself with a Valvanchi."

They both sat for moment thinking, and then Teodor started laughing:

"Did he really say that, sullied by a Valvanchi?"

"Yes," Sayginn was laughing too, he started to mimic the Emperor's tone and posture: "Sullied by a Valvanski... the thought of filthy alien hands..."

They laughed a few minutes longer and took two more sips from the glass.

A steward interrupted with a discrete cough. Teodor realised his mother had switched off all communications:

"Ma'am, the Valvanchis are here."

"Thank you, we're on our way."

Teodor said:

"You know Nell invited me to the fifth birthday of Karl Valvanchi's son on Zarac 1."

Sayginn smiled in agreement: "I remember."

"It sounded like fun, and it is only seventy-five days away."

Sayginn laughed.

"It would be seventy – no, one hundred and fifty days I did not have to spend at court?"

"Yes, at least one hundred and fifty days, which is why I said yes on your behalf. And Des, Sebastian and Guy are going with you."

"Mother!" Teodor hugged her with huge enthusiasm.

"And Teo, it's likely the United Races will impose a planet-wide quarantine."

"What does that mean?"

"It means, when you go, you cannot come back until the quarantine is lifted."

"But how long will that be?"

Chapter 35. A Political Union

"Karl, tell me that you are not going to do this."

"Just sign it, Nikato. I want it to be legal." Nikato sighed but signed.

"Karl, Mezzatorra was not your fault. This thing going on inside the Dome: it's not your fault." Nikato and Karl were sitting on the back seat of their hover car with all the windows and doors shut. It was perfectly private, while Nell had already gone up into the palace.

"We brought them in, Nikki. There had been no other traffic since the start of the outbreak. They must have been concealed in the crates of Sand Lizards. You know, that famous Sas Darona delicacy."

"Karl, everyone knows how thorough you are. How committed to containing the Sas Darona plague. I thought you would have checked the crates… "

"The crates of Sand Lizards arrived sealed. Sealed by the hunters who captured them that morning."

"These hunters were Sas Darona tribesmen? And you still did not check inside the crates then?"

"It was not a hostile tribe, they always supplied our cases, so…"

Nikato shrugged, he seemed a little sad.

"That's how they brought them in, as you said. You trusted them, and why not? And why not if they had been your long-term suppliers?"

"Yes, but Nikki, on Saturday, when I entered the Dome, I was travelling in the van of an air-conditioning engineer."

"You know, we always own the companies who provide our services, where we can."

"The poison pills were only recently installed in the maintenance and air-conditioning tunnels. The one in House Jewel was only installed yesterday."

Karl felt sick when he thought of Andor, the man he had seen working on the air-conditioning systems. Had they been planting the poison pills, even as he had tried to rescue Prince Teodor? He had known there was something odd about Andor, but poison pills?

"You say that, but eventually the Freyne will be looking for those kinds of connections, they will get to us eventually."

"Only if you suggest it as a line of enquiry," snapped Nikato. "And in any case, who would believe it? I mean, why? What motive do we have? Tell me that?"

"You tell me, you're the one who attends the Symposium for Development and Expansion. You know what they discuss in closed sessions of the Zaracan Council. How the Freyne are too primitive? How the Freyne are too aggressive?"

"And now you have seen their politics, the poverty, and the sheer depravity of their lives."

"And I agreed with you. The Dome must close, but the empire must fall? Nikato, I ask you: really? We should be doing more to help them, not... We had a responsibility to keep them safe from the dangers of poison pills."

"Are you saying we had a hand in the actions of the SDLA?"

"Well, somebody provided the explosives that blew open the vault. Explosives that do not exist within the Freyne Empire."

"But the Freyne trade with others, we know that. The Dome Elite trade with many alien races. And you provided proof that the Dome Elite was backing the SDLA."

"We are responsible for this mess, Nikato. I am sorry, but we are. The monazite rationing. The SDLA. The poison pills. Chart Segat kidnapping Teodor to stop the Dome Debate. It was we who wanted that debate. Not Sayginn. The Freyne was happy with the Dome as it was."

"Oh, with troops of vicious Battle Borgs, toying with and then killing boys for fun?"

Karl said nothing. He was thinking how they should put an extra wall of fire around Magnolia Palace to try and keep it safe. At least they knew the south tunnel from Domeside was blocked by water. The rats, cats, dogs, people, might make it through that whirlpool. Cy-sects could not.

"Did you do this thing, Nikato? Did you?"

"Karl," Nikato was adamant. "The Freyne brought this on themselves. If the prince had not been kidnapped... If the Dome Debate had gone ahead..." Nikato paused and said, with emphasis: "Perhaps if you had managed to free Prince Teodor before the Dome Debate."

"Nikki, that's not fair. I did everything I possibly could..."

Nikato held up a hand:

"You do not have to worry whether you bought in the poison pills, whether you failed to rescue the prince. The fact is, the council decreed that the Dome must be closed. The Dome had to close, Karl."

Karl reran his words a couple of times. It was neither a denial nor an agreement. A diplomatic reply if ever he had heard one. What did that mean?

"And you're leaving now? In their hour of need?"

"I have a new posting on Freyne 1, as Ambassador to the Emperor."

Karl did not say anything. He thought how in some circles Nikato's time on Freyne 2 would be deemed a success. The Dome had been closed. The Dome Elite dispersed. So now it was time for a promotion, promotion to the Freyne 1 and the Imperial Court. *God help the Freyne Emperor*, he thought bleakly, then remembering it was the Emperor who had organised the kidnapping of his own nephew: *God help Nikato. Maybe they deserve each other.*

"But I will say this. If you decide to do this thing, if you decide to stay here, I won't let you die. I will make sure they send you everything you need."

"Not just for me Nikato, I want to save the people. I will need resources to keep the firewalls burning, if nothing else. There may be famine and other illnesses."

"Anything. Anything you need. You will get it. I will see to it that you have everything you need to save and restore this planet. After all, it is the only working democracy in the Freyne Empire. I think that's why we thought it was weak. And yes, I will support you, this marriage, and these planets."

"We have no choice. After all, we did this, and we killed her husband too, it seems."

"Karl, you don't know that. Listen to me. I will protect the prince. He will attend one of our schools. The Council will support that. And he will return."

"Well, that's something. He will do well in one of our schools, I think," Karl said smoothly, trying but failing to hold his sarcasm in check.

Nikato nodded: "He will be a great Emperor and an ally."

"Well, that's good," Karl did not conceal his anger. "Shall we go in?"

Chapter 36. A Death in the Family

"Hurry Guy, there's not much time."

Guy was coming down the stairs with Teodor. Des and Sebastian were just behind, with the bags. Four kit bags only and a trip of a lifetime. Sayginn called to Guy:

"Boys, you must hurry. There is not much time left."

She led them into an office. On a large screen above the desk there was a window, a window into what looked like a hospital room, only the glass was grey and opaque, it was hard to peer through it. There was someone beyond the glass. Guy recognised her first:

"Lloulou."

Guy stared at the screen and quickly his eyes adjusted. He could see she was standing, but only just. Half leaning against a bed, she looked a little flushed and was breathing heavily.

"She's in the quarantine centre in Domeside," Sayginn explained. "I am sorry Guy, but they have confirmed it is plague."

Guy was barely listening. Finally, he asked:

"Was she bitten?"

On the screen, Lloulou was rolling up her sleeve to show him. Guy stepped closer to the screen. The closer he got, the more it felt like he was, in fact, looking through a window, not at the screen. For a moment he thought Lloulou was just there, on the other of the glass. He went to touch the screen; only the focus changed and the doctor stepped into view.

"She has a dozen bites on her neck and shoulders."

"What's going to happen to her?"

"She said she wanted to see you, to speak with you, and then we will end her suffering." Teodor stepped up and took Guy's hand, as the doctor continued: "We will need to end her suffering before the crystallescence."

Guy pushed Teodor aside and waved the doctor away. The focus on the screen changed again. Again Guy was standing at the window. He raised his hand to place it on the glass. Across the city in the quarantine centre, Lloulou also raised her hand. Their two hands matched themselves one to another. It was like they touched one last time.

"How long?" asked Teodor.

"Five minutes, ten minutes max. Her bloods… Well, you need to say your goodbyes, and then let me do my job."

"Say something," whispered Teodor. Guy nodded, but what should he say?

"I don't want you to go," Guy said looking at Lloulou.

"I don't want to go either," Lloulou's voice was croaky. "And I'm sorry I couldn't protect you from Chart Segat. I'm so sorry."

"It doesn't matter anymore. Teodor and I, well, we took his arms. He will never hurt anyone ever again. Not me, not you, not Des, not anyone."

Lloulou was sobbing now. Guy could not tell if it was grief or relief.

"Mother, please," he whispered.

"Oh, my son…"

"But I'm not your son. Marline. The papers said Marline was your daughter."

"No, I told you. You are my son, but I swapped you. Marline for you, you were swapped just after you were born."

"But Marline is older than me."

"No, no… Oh, Guy." Lloulou was shaking her head. She looked beyond him: "You have a new mother now, Guy, and a brother. You must forget about me. Forget all about the things I told you. Just forget everything. You have a whole new life. Just take that. Accept it. Forget the rest."

Guy knew at the very last she was trying to protect him. He glanced back at Teodor. Teodor, King of Freyne, Son of Empire, the next Emperor of Freyne, unless Emperor Frederon had a son. Unless the Emperor had a grandson, a bastard grandson who would replace Teodor as the Emperor of all Freyne. For a moment, Guy thought his heart would stop. Through the screen Lloulou was still whispering: "Don't take the tests. Please don't take the tests. Honestly, you don't want to know. You have a new life now. A new life. A new life."

Guy looked at Teodor once more. Honest, trustworthy and brave. He turned back to Lloulou:

"You're right mother, you're right. I don't want any of that. I don't want any of that. I will refuse the tests. I am a Domeside orphan and I was born in July."

Lloulou smiled then, and her tears melted away.

"Doctor, I'm ready," she said.

"No, please," Guy begged.

"If I go now, I will save you all." She looked from one to another. "Possibly the best thing I could do. Please, doctor."

A white cyborg was sent into the vacuum chamber. He pressed a patch to Lloulou's arm, and she almost immediately collapsed. Monitors on the screen overhead showed her vital signs drop away even as she fell, and the cyborg carried her to a metal bed that was, in fact, a large tray lying on rollers. With one swift move, the cyborg pushed the body into the incinerator, and the door slammed shut.

Overhead the screen showed Lloulou dead in the incinerator tunnel. The cyborg froze its hand on the burn button, and then in the red and gold light of the incinerator, her body seemed to shine and reflect light from all angles. Then the light started to shimmer. It was the reflection of several thousand wings shaking as they dried. For a moment she looked like a shining multi-faceted diamond, or perhaps a crafted crystal.

It was why it was called crystallescence. The last moment of humanity of a Sas Darona plague victim. The last moment before the body exploded into a cloud of cy-sects spinning outwards in all directions, taking flight, looking for an exit and then… Bang… The surgeon had pressed the override button and the tube filled with light and flames.

Teodor held Guy firmly by one arm, Sebastian by the other. Des was at his back. Guy did not move, nor say a word, but tears streamed down his frozen face.

"Now you know why you must leave," Sayginn told Teodor, wiping his face. Only then did Teodor realise he was also weeping.

"But mother – you will be all alone."

"No Teodor, she won't. I am staying with her." It was Karl Valvanchi. "Your mother has agreed to marry me."

Relief flooded over Teodor. Now Karl Valvanchi had spoken the words, he knew it was true. He knew he was released. He nodded.

"What time are we leaving?"

"They are waiting for you now."

In the hall, Des and Teodor waited. Sebastian had gone with a tear-stained Guy to freshen up.

"What happened to Chart Segat, did you hear?" asked Teodor quietly.

"They evacuated him with the Dome hospital and clinic teams," Des replied.

"Where did he go?"

"Some are going to Freyne 1, some to Sas Darona. You heard that Karl Valvanchi has given a blanket evacuation visa for the Dome Elite to go to Sas Darona?"

"Do you know how many Elite got out?"

"Almost eight thousand, four evacuated to the southern continent. Two thousand were on shuttles or the space stations when the shield went up. Three thousand, mostly the men with families still trapped in Domeside and, of course, the Borgs, they have all stayed behind to fight the plague."

"Will all the Elite be evacuated to Sas Darona eventually?"

"Well, thanks to your father, they have excellent facilities there."

"I wish my father had told me more about his plans for Sas Darona."

"It could be a trap obviously, but I think Tilson intends to disperse them on touch down. They have a good fleet now, and enough contacts not to be completely stranded, if push comes to shove," Des finished grimly.

411

"But the Zaracans don't know where the bases are?" Des shook his head once. "Then why would Karl do that?"

"Your Mum? He loves her, and he knows she needs the Elite. You too, Teodor – you need the Elite. And if they are evacuated to Sas Darona with no beers and bars, no girls wearing fashion… All they have to do is train. At the end of the Quarantine – well watch out! Karl's dressing it up as a temporary crisis visa because the space stations were overloaded with evacuees, but he's done you a real favour. The Dome Elite has been saved, they will come out stronger in the end, stronger than ever before. Chartsie should never have thrown his lot in with the Emperor. You are our King, Teodor. You are the rightful ruler of Freyne 2, and of the empire I hope."

"One day," Teodor replied. "Having the Elite should help me get the empire."

"Dead right," Des replied with a smile.

"I hate being in debt to the Valvanchis though. And it's about to get worse."

"What else can you do? You need to buy yourself some time. You need four years. Four years and then you will be a man."

Guy had reappeared. He looked pale but resolute. Guy, Teodor, Des and Sebastian took the last staircase down to the entrance hall.

Inside the front door of the palace, the Regency cleric performed a brief marriage ceremony. All of the participants except two wore travelling clothes and the couple were hemmed in by travelling cases around their feet,

"Sayginn and Karl, I hereby join you together as man and wife. Please repeat your vows with me."

"Do you promise to love, cherish and nurture each other now, through sickness and health, through riches and poverty?"

'*I don't understand this,*' Guy said, moving close to Teodor. '*Did not the Emperor warn us against the Valvanski?*'

'*How can a husband betray his wife?*' Teodor replied. '*No, if there was a betrayal, this marriage should protect us in the future.*'

"Until death us do part," Karl said.

"Until death us do part," Sayginn repeated.

'*Should?*' Guy repeated.

'Karl Valvanchi has pledged to stay and protect my mother and this planet against the plague. That's good enough for me. He did not have to do that.'

Karl slipped a signet ring bearing the insignia of the Valvanchi house from his hand to hers and they said as one:

"So help me God."

The ceremony was over. They kissed briefly. Nell and Teodor threw handfuls of rose petals, plucked from a nearby bouquet. Sayginn examined the ring and showed it to her son. The symbolism was clear to all. Regent Sayginn and with her, her planets and her son, now all came under the protection of the Valvanchis.

They started to say their goodbyes.

Sayginn hugged Teodor.

"I think we said our goodbyes earlier, you know how much I love you."

"Yes mother, I do."

"And Guy, take good care of my son, he loves you and so do I. Des, Sebastian, good luck."

"Goodbye Uncle Karl. I will miss you."

"It's just another battle. I promise I will be victorious."

"You must go," Sayginn said to Teodor.

"Go," Karl echoed to Nell.

Chapter 37. The Dome is Closed

"Sayginn, you need to speak to the people."

Patrick McGuire had stood and waited throughout the wedding ceremony and the goodbyes, but now he was clearly impatient. "Sayginn, you need to tell the people what to expect and how to fight it. In Domeside those who have been bitten are now dying. The people have to know what to expect and how to protect themselves."

"Some will survive, surely?" She turned to Karl.

"Yes, more will survive than will die, but still, too many will die. You need to talk to the people."

"What about the Dome Elite?"

"They are helping now; they have taken on Fire Starter duties, and now I have given instructions about identifying the plague victims, ending their misery, they have set up a processing centre. They have incinerators and they are also using their flame throwers. But the people need to see you, know that you are involved. You also need to tell them the King and his companions have been evacuated, it will give them hope. Hope that some, at least, will survive."

"It's sounds horrific. Is there anything more we can do? Karl?"

Karl shook his head.

"It's going to be a long night."

"We are ready to fire the Dome," Patrick said again.

Sayginn and Karl followed Patrick back to the ballroom.

"We suspect the nests may have spread. Even though the Dome was given the 'all clear' six hours ago, that is long enough for the cy-sects to build a hundred nests. In fact, cy-roaches have found and reported between four and ten nests in the infrastructure; some are quite small but some are almost ready to swarm."

"Why four to ten, don't we know for sure?"

"Well, we need verification of a nest, i.e. two reports, but the cy-sects are attacking the cy-roaches, so even if one roach finds a nest, the second is nearly always destroyed."

"The cy-sects are learning insects," Karl said.

"So we are right to fire bomb the Dome."

"I'm not sure about right," Patrick sounded gloomy.

"Have you evacuated?" Asked Karl.

"Yes, we sounded the evacuation about thirty minutes ago; we have been sounding them every five minutes so there is no-one in the structure who cannot know something is happening."

"Regent, we have alarms sounding at the vacuum port of the Dome Wall."

"On screen!"

Now the screens showed the main square of the Dome. As they watched, a line of heavily armoured Dome Elite infantry was charging down towards the Dome Wall. As Sayginn watched, guns appeared through the windows and walls from two neighbouring buildings, and suddenly the Regency Guard on the Dome Wall were under heavy artillery attack from a cannon that had been installed on the second floor workrooms of the Fashion Houses. The people of Domeside were trying to escape.

"They have to hold!" yelled Karl.

"I'll call up the reserves," Patrick added. "All men currently resting must report for duty. Fully armed."

"Have we got enough men?" Sayginn asked, as she watched Dome Elite placing ladders and small pieces of scaffolding to scale the wall.

"Can men pass through the wall of fire?"

"With severe burns, yes of course; but if they are infected, the plague will come through too. The plague flies will be unharmed."

"Send in aerial support," Sayginn ordered. "This has to stop."

The missile screamed towards the square. There was warning of a few instants. The Dome Elite seemed to disperse. There was an explosion. As the visibility on the main cameras was clouded by smoke, other cameras showed the Dome Elite in full retreat. In fact, the attack on the Domeside wall seemed all but over. When the debris and smoke cleared, Dome Elite and civilian casualties carpeted the square. One cannon emplacement had toppled out of the building; the other still fired, but intermittently.

Sayginn stared at the scene that was detailed over the screens before her.

"What are we doing? Massacring our own people?"

"They're not dead," said Patrick. As they watched, Sayginn saw many of the infantry had survived the blast, the armour they wore having protected them. Others were regrouping all around the side roads and alleyways.

"Call in reinforcements. The wall has to hold."

"Put me on loudspeaker, broadcast this everywhere."

"We do not wish to destroy the Dome," Sayginn said, as if in reply. "That is not our plan, we have evacuated the Dome and we are only injecting liquid fire into the beams, not the wider structure. We have to destroy those nests. We will now start the countdown to the ignition of the liquid fire."

"Ten." Patrick McGuire started the countdown.

"People of Domeside." Sayginn spoke in a clear, determined voice.

"Nine."

"We have to kill the cy-sects which are nesting in the structure…"

"Eight."

"of the Dome. The cy-sects are in the beams…"

"Seven."

"so, we will fire the beams."

"Six."

"If we can destroy the cy-sects…"

"Five."

"we may be able…"

416

"Four."

"to lift the quarantine…"

"Three."

"and free you people…"

"Two."

"You people of Domeside…"

Above them, the screens merged into one display, a vast image of the Dome against the darkening early evening sky. "One."

In an instant the Dome was alight, as the fire blazed down the vertical and horizontal beams of the geodesic structure, so the metal turned from silver to molten gold. So for an instant, the Dome shone from the inside like a luminescent golden shimmering apparition. At the apotheosis of the light, they heard a loud wave of deafening cracks, and from the crowds watching in Domeside, screams. The great glass panes had shattered and exploded outwards. A great rain of shimmering crystals fell down on Domeside, the structure passed from gold to red, and then black. Then there was silence.

The shining geodesic structure, the most famous landmark of Freyne 2, was a charred skeleton, naked of all its covering and black to its core.

"Well," said Sayginn quietly and she took Karl's hand. "We did what you asked for in the end. The Dome is closed."

Epilogue

Teodor dreamt of the camp in the snow, the dome-shaped cabins, the light, fast scooters, the yapping, powerful dogs, and the goran cub with ice-white fur and steel-blue eyes. He had known from first sight they would call it Blue.

"Blue Barbrina," his father had said. "In just two years' time she will race in the Magnolia Stakes."

Teodor remembered hugging the cub as it licked his hands and clawed at his shiny weatherproof jacket.

"She likes the reflection," his father explained. "She has seen nothing like that before." They sat in a half-open dome – the fire dome it was called – with a raging fire at the centre of a circular sofa. It was the central meeting point and focus of their camp, and a colossal extravagance. Most of the heat and all of the light was wasted across the vastness of the Sas Darona ice cap, and the fuel had to be flown in at great cost. The experience of sitting within its warm glow while looking out at the polar night was something they all relished, and Teodor felt sure it was a view he would never forget.

Chart Segat had been there, and he had said:

"That's a true champion – the alpha female of her pack. The mother was not pleased to see her go."

"She would be pleased if she knew the glory that awaits her," Teodor said, and then he looked over: "Ah, he's here."

The alien ambassador had arrived, just an hour ago. He had refused to join the Imperial party for the goran hunt the day before, and now he claimed his only purpose was to check that only one cub was being removed.

"Of course, we'll only take one cub," Teodor remembered his father muttering: "I gave my word, didn't I? And we left the mother and the litter unharmed."

They watched as the tall man with the long mane of hair made his way to the fire dome. Teodor watched him closely. He had only recently learnt that the Zaracans were telepaths. They rarely displayed their powers amongst the Freyne though. Could you tell if he was using telepathy, just by looking?

"Be careful Serge," Chart Segat said quickly. "I do not trust Nikki Valvanchi. So be careful what you say."

"I have to ask, Chart – there's so much room to spare on Sas Darona. It would be an excellent training ground for your Elite and I can't see how they would object to us mining for monazite. It's a resource they are not even exploiting. If they agree, think of the benefits, the benefits for our future?"

His father had kissed Teodor on the head and stood up. His father's bodyguards were the very best, carefully selected by repeated competitions amongst all ranks of the Dome Elite. They stood to attention as his father rose, and then shadowed him as he walked forward to greet Nikato Valvanchi. Teodor watched him go. His father was doing most of the talking. The ambassador just listened, but wasn't that true of all diplomats? Teodor was distracted by a Dome Elite Junior who winked at him as he piled some further logs on the fire. Other Dome men were setting a buffet table for lunch. Sayginn and Deodran were coming across the camp to join him.

"I love him so very much," Teodor confided to Segat. For a brief instant, Teodor saw the concern written across Segat's face where he had been watching Serge and Nikato: "Don't you?"

Teodor absentmindedly kissed the goran cub. Its warm softness was always comforting. Segat roughed the animal between the ears, but Teodor had meant his father and nodded meaningfully in the direction where he had gone.

"Yes," replied Segat. "Yes, I love him as much as you do."

Teodor smiled, and then they both stood up to greet Sayginn and Deodran. Deodran sat down quickly next to Teodor. He carefully placed the cub in his brother's lap, still holding it with one hand while Deodran kissed and stroked it.

"Thank you Teo," his mother said and kissed him on the forehead. She sat down next to Chart Segat. He reached to take her hand and kiss it, not once, but three times. She playfully pushed him away. They laughed at some secret joke but only for a moment. Now they rose to greet the other Barons and guests who were entering the Dome. Teodor saw Bonnie Walesbury approaching, he was already laughing, and then there was a buffet. It was going to be a great party. For one last moment, Teodor looked out over the snow. His father was now quite a distance away and he was still talking to the tall, enigmatic alien.

"We're screwed," he heard someone say.

The images of the snow camp disappeared, and suddenly Teodor was looking into Chart Segat's face. He could feel and smell his breath on his face. "My boys, I take care of them," Chart Segat said. Then he was falling hard onto his blades mat, his back splitting on impact. Then the lights went out, and out of the shadows men leapt towards him.

"Remember you are King," his mother said.

Then he was falling again, down between the buildings of Old Mill Lane, down the trellis inside the Dome's structure, rolling inside a cocktail table, falling and tumbling, falling and tumbling. It was all pain and darkness; he scuffed his knees, his skin turned black, split with deep cracks, and underneath, cybernetics were revealed.

"I think in this case, we just lie back and enjoy the ride." It was another voice.

"What's he doing here?" The same voice. Wet hands. Soap suds on a Dome medallion.

"My communicator is on the Dome network, they'll track you at once..." Guy was explaining.

"Do you want to be thrown to the Battle Borgs of Dome, to fight for your life?"

Teodor opened his eyes. He didn't know where he was. He was in an aircraft, no, a spacecraft. He was in an armchair. A goran rug had been tucked around him. Teodor focused and saw Sebastian and Des laughing quietly together. What were they doing here? They were seated on the edge of a large

420

window, looking out into space. He was on board the Valvanchi flyer. Karl Valvanchi's fifth birthday party. He was travelling to Zarac 1. He had been dreaming. The snow park, his father, Chart Segat.

Sebastian noticed him at once:

"Guy! Teo's awake now."

Teodor turned and saw Guy was talking with Nell just a short distance away. Guy walked over and sat beside him.

"Hi, are you ok?"

'Where are we? Are we safe?'

Teodor sent Guy an abrupt thought message, alongside the garbled images he remembered from his dream. Guy looked at him in astonishment and patted his hand.

'Yes, we're safe. You didn't fall. You escaped. We escaped together. And Des didn't say that thing about Battle Borgs to you, he said it to me. You're just mixed up. And Chart Segat, well, we chopped his arms off. You have to hang onto that.'

'But I felt it...'

'Careful, I think SHE can hear us when we talk with our minds.'

Guy was motioning to Nell who was standing a little way off, looking a little stunned.

Teodor looked at Nell. The nightmare was fading now. He swallowed once, then coughed as he spoke with his voice:

"How long was I asleep?"

"You crashed out just after we took off."

He pushed aside the goran fur someone had laid over him, and went to look out the window.

"Can we still see Freyne?"

"No," Des replied.

"This craft is going just a little bit faster than your average shuttle," laughed Sebastian.

"Is that what you meant when you said about enjoying the ride?"

"Sorry, I did not mean for you to hear that," Sebastian apologised.

"But if we only left an hour ago…" Teodor peered through the window. "Which direction is Freyne?" Both Des and Sebastian pointed. Teodor looked, but he could see nothing, just a distant star.

"That's not right," he muttered.

"No, it's not," Des agreed. "This is not a long distance craft. It's small, snug even, for such a long journey."

"Nell," Teodor called to the girl. "Where are we going?"

" Zarac 1, as discussed."

"And that's seventy-five days away, right?"

"No, not with this ship. As Des rightly said, this flyer is too small for such a journey. No, we will be landing on Zarac 1 tomorrow night."

"As I said," whispered Sebastian, just loud enough for Nell to hear, "enjoy the ride."

Teodor watched Nell blush then frown, fighting hard to conceal her emotions. She was still hiding something. He decided to try a direct question:

"So are we your prisoners?"

Nell looked quite shocked. At that moment Ambassador Nikato appeared at the open door. He gave Teodor a sharp look.

"You boys are our guests. You are not prisoners," Nikato said firmly. "None of you will be harmed. We will look after and educate you. We will care for you." He gave Teodor such a look, that he realised that it was perhaps not just Nell who had picked up the echoes of his nightmare. Nikato continued:

"And when the quarantine is lifted, you will return to your homes. I hope you will all be stronger and wiser."

'The Emperor said the Valvanchi would betray us,' Guy said quietly.

'Past tense, he said the Valvanski had betrayed us,' Teodor replied vaguely.

Their thoughts were cut across by a loud clear voice:

'I never have, never will, not now or ever betray you, my princes!' It was Nell, she was looking directly at them both. *'So help me God.'* And with this thought she pressed her hand to her heart.

Guy and Teodor fell apart, aware that they dare neither speak nor think in her presence. Des and Sebastian had closed in to stand at their side. All four were carefully looking first at Nikato and then at Nell.

Nikato bowed his head just once as if in greeting, but Nell smiled brightly and said:

"Think of it as an adventure?"

Appendix 1. Names and Places

Name	Meaning
B	
BARONS	There are twelve Barons in the empire of Freyne. They head up the twelve families, each of which has a seat at the high council of empire, advisors to the Emperor.
BATTLE BORG	Half-man, half-robot, Battle Borgs tend to be older cyborgs who have had multiple modifications made. They are more machine than human, and can be unsafe around women and children since they are unaware of their own strength and unable to control their impulses.
BISTRO JEWEL	This is a large restaurant-bar in the atrium of the Dome, run as a concession of the fashion house Jewel and as a showcase of their products.
BLADES	This is the fighting sport of choice of the young men of the Freyne Empire. In duels, two young men face each other within a fighting ring, wearing running/spring blades on their feet and using two daggers – a blade in each hand. They also wear calf greaves embedded with triple blades up the back of their legs and triple-bladed gauntlets on each arm. In total, the fighters face each other with 14 cutting blades. They fight three or five rounds. Importantly, if at any time a fighter steps outside of the fighting ring they are disqualified. The winner in any round is the fighter who gets close enough to his opponent to wield a mortal blow: either a stab to the heart or the head. The tradition then is to shout: Do you yield?
BLUE BARBRINA	Two metre high racing snow cat originally from Sas Darona. At the time of this story it is the Regent's best racer, and due to compete in

	the Magnolia Stakes.
C	
CHARTSIE / CHART SEGAT	Administrator of the Freyne Dome, Mayor of Domeside, former political ally of King Serge.
COMMUNICA TOR	Communication device which includes voice and video.
CREAM CAROLINA	Giant racing cat.
CRYSTALLES CENCE	Last stage of Sas Darona plague when the victim is converted into crystal-like cocoons, hosts to the plague flies.
CYBORG	Cybernetic man: half-man, half-robot – normal lifespan about two years. Appears to be 100% human.
CY-ROACHES	Cybernetic cockroach: half cockroach, half robot – used for surveillance.
CY-SECT	Cybernetic insect: enhanced Sas Darona plague fly – more deadly, faster to breed, quicker to evolve.
CY-WOLVES	Cybernetic wolves: half-robot, half-wolf.
D	
DEODRAN	Younger brother of Teodor, prince of Freyne. Died two years before this story, killed by a terrorist bomb.
DES PARKS	Dome Elite soldier and champion blades fighter.
DOME	The largest geodesic Dome in the Freyne Empire. Made up of 33 vast triangles and house entertainments, sports fields, casinos, hotels, an ancient village square and cathedral, a small port and a military training facility for

	10,000 men and boys.
DOME DEBATE	Debate of whether Chart Segat should continue as the administrator of the Dome.
DOME ELITE	Military unit drawing on the men and boys of the inner city wards of Domeside. Uniform is black and gold.
DOME MEDALLION	Identification tag worn by the Dome Elite. On one side is the name and ID, and the motto 'Loyal to Empire, Fear only God'.
DOMESIDE	Inner-city neighbourhood of the capital of Freyne 2.
DOMESIDE EVENING NEWS	Local newspaper of Domeside.
E	
EDDIE / **EREDERON**	Only son of Frederon, Emperor of Freyne. Died before this story begins.
ERSTAG HOUSE	Palace of Emperor Frederon on Freyne 1.
E.R.M.A.	Initials of the Imperial bastard, father to current Emperor, Frederon, historic and great Emperor of Freyne. ERMA stands for: Erederon Roderick Marco Andreus.

In Domeside, Erma is given as a surname for boys of unknown paternity. |
F	
FIGHTING BLADES	Hand-held weapons used in blades fighting.
FIREWALL	Slim wall of dense, intense fire that is used to contain forest fires and Sas Darona plague flies.
FREDDIE /	Emperor of the 13 planets of Freyne.

FREDERON	
FREYNE	Empire of 12 planets, asteroid mining, gas planets, out-posts and colonies. Freyne claims a 13th planet but is in disagreement with United Races as to ownership.
G	
GAUNTLETS	Leather arm protectors embedded with three curved blades, worn when fighting with blades.
GORAN	Giant racing cat.
GREAVES	Leather calf protectors embedded with three curved blades, worn when fighting with blades.
GOVE (& JON)	Twin brothers. Geneticists based at Mezzatorra, a centre of research into entomology on Sas Darona. Murdered in raid by SDLA.
GUY ERMA	13 year old boy born in House Jewel, good at maths and blades, applicant to the Dome Elite, unregistered, no known father or mother.
H	
HOUSE JEWEL	Fashion House, one of the eight houses at the heart of the Freyne fashion and tailoring Industry.
I	
IMPERIAL RINA	Giant racing goran, raised by Emperor Frederon.
IMPERIAL GUARD	Bodyguards of Emperor Frederon. Wear the magenta and gold of the Imperial house.
J	
JON (& GOVE)	Twin brothers. Geneticists based at Mezzatorra, a centre of research into

430

	entomology on Sas Darona. Murdered in raid by SDLA.
JUKE	Market Trader (Fruit & Veg) Domeside. Employs Guy Erma.
K	
KARL VALVANCHI	Name of the third son of Nikato Valvanchi. Does not appear in this story.
KARL VALVANCHI II	Commander of Zaracan Democratic Forces on Sas Darona, son of Karl Valvanchi.
KARL VALVANCHI III	Five-year-old son of Karl Valvanchi II, living on Zarac 1 in Valvanchi House.
KARL VALVANCHI CURSE	Though Karl Valvanchi the third is only five years old, there is an old prophecy that says Karl Valvanchi III will never survive to father a son of his own. Thus giving rise to the Karl-Valvanchi Curse.
L	
LLOULOU	Model of Fashion House Jewel, probable age 29.
LUCY	Stable girl in the goran stables at Magnolia Palace. Tends to Prince Teodor's gorans.
M	
MAGNOLIA PALACE	Palace of Regent Sayginn and Prince Teodor of Freyne 2.
MAGNOLIA WEEKEND	Festival of Flowers and Fashion. Takes place each spring on Freyne 2.
MARLINE	Newest Fashion Model of House Jewel, age 14.
MEZZATORRA	Research base on Sas Darona.

MONAZITE	Precious metal used to create space magnets. Extracted from Samarium. At the time of this story, it was in short supply.
N	
NELL / SIMONELLE VALVANCHI	Native of Zarac, telepath and shape-shifter, daughter of Simonelle Valvanchi, age 13.
NIKKI / NIKATO VALVANCHI	Zaracan Ambassador to Freyne 2.
O	
OLD MILL LANE	Avenue in Domeside where fashion houses Jewel and the Riffaut are located.
P	
PATRICK MCGUIRE	Prime Minister on Freyne 2, head of Regent Sayginn's ten-year-old Democratic Government.
POISON PILL	Glass brick containing miniature eco-system where plague flies can live, until released by small explosive mounted on the outside and remotely detonated.
R	
REGENCY DEFENCE	Personal guard to Regent Sayginn. Wear red and silver of Freyne 2.
RIFFAUT / THE RIFFAUT / HOUSE RIFFAUT	Fashion House, one of the eight houses at the heart of the Freyne fashion and tailoring industry.
RUNNING BLADES	Curved metal extensions that are worn on the sole of shoes during blades combat, but also commonly worn by the soldiers and trainees of the Dome Elite. Running blades help the wearer run faster and further, leap higher and

	turn tighter. Boys of Domeside such as Guy Erma are rarely seen without them.
S	
SAS DARONA	Planet on the outer rim of space, currently under licence for exploration to the Zaracan Democratic Union, also claimed by the Freyne Empire.
SAS DARONA PLAGUE	Plague native to Sas Darona, deadly to all animal and human species on Sas Darona.
SAS DARONA SAND LIZARDS	Large fat lizards of the Sas Darona Savannah known for their fine white flesh.
SAYGINN / REGENT SAYGINN	Queen of Freyne 2, Regent and ruler of six planets in the place of King Teodor who is only 13 years old. Probably age 32.
SDLA	Sas Darona Liberation Army, generic name given to tribes attacking the Zaracan bases on Sas Darona.
SEBASTIAN	Teenage model and impersonator of Prince Teodor, from the Riffaut fashion house, age 17.
SERGE / King SERGE	King of Freyne 2, husband to Sayginn, father of Teodor and Deodran. Established the Dome as a place of education and training for the men and boys of Domeside, the poorest quarter of his capital city. Died two years before this story begins.
SNAKE DROID	Weapon in the shape of a snake, a long line of connected bullets ending in an explosive.
SONIA	Young researcher working in Mezzatorra, research base on Sas Darona. Killed by Sas Darona Plague.
ST JOSEPH'S	Name of ancient cathedral and modern clinic,

	both located at the heart of the Dome.
T	
TEO / **PRINCE** **TEODOR**	13-year-old son of King Serge and Queen Sayginn, and great nephew and only surviving male descendent of Emperor Frederon. King of Freyne 2 and heir to the Imperial empire, goran rider, blades fighter, trained in all necessary skills required for leadership.
TILSON	Commander of the Dome Elite and senior instructor of the Dome blades programme.
U	
UNITED RACES	Government body of known space.
V	
VALVANCHI	Name of a great house of the Zaracan Democratic Union, specialists in diplomatic relations and great explorers.
VALVANCHI HOUSE	Home of the Valvanchis on Zarac 1.
W	
WALESBURY (LORD)	Baron of Freyne Empire, resident on Freyne 2. Loyal to King Serge, Regent Sayginn and Prince Teodor.
WEST STREET	Street in Domeside, off Old Mill Lane.
Z	
ZARAC	Capital planet of Zaracan Democratic Union.
ZARACAN DEMOCRATI C UNION	Great power of the United Races.

Amazon reviews are important!

If you have enjoyed this book, please add a review on Amazon. In that way other readers will also find and enjoy this book.

Check out our website:
http:///www.sally-ann-melia.com
for prizes for the best of the reviews.

Other versions of this book

This book is also available as a hardback from Amazon and many other retailers. For a signed copy paperback or hardback see
http:// www.sally-ann-melia.com

Why don't you treat yourself to the hardback,
to enjoy on your shelf?

Other books by Sally Ann Melia

"It wasn't like looking for a needle in a hay -stack, it was like feeling for a needle in a hay barn wearing gloves and a blindfold – that's what Chris told me. He was talking about the Search for Extra Terrestrial Life, an impossible pursuit until… two aliens, yes two, landed into Paris."

A short novella, 56pp Aliens in Paris available as an e-book, in paperback and hardback, from Amazon and many other retailers.

Coming 2015

Guy Erma and the Araneidae Dome

8573978R00257

Printed in Great Britain
by Amazon.co.uk, Ltd.,
Marston Gate.